RANDOM
HOUSE
LARGE
PRINT

★ DAUGHTER OF WAR ★

DAUGHTER
★ OF ★
WAR

★★★★★★★★

BRAD TAYLOR

A Pike Logan Thriller

Copyright © 2019 by Brad Taylor

All rights reserved.
Published in the United States of America by Random House Large Print in association with Dutton, an imprint of Penguin Random House LLC.

Cover design by Pete Garceau
Cover photographs: background © Julian Kaesler/
Getty Images; woman © Creative Family/Shutterstock

The Library of Congress has established a
Cataloging-in-Publication record for this title.

ISBN: 978-1-9848-2755-5

www.randomhouse.com/largeprint

FIRST LARGE PRINT EDITION

Printed in the United States of America

10 9 8 7 6 5 4 3 2 1

This Large Print edition published in accord with
the standards of the N.A.V.H.

For Jessica (Horvath) Renheim,
the editor with the name of a supervillian
but the skills of a superhero on the page.
Thank you for all you have done for Pike Logan.

Out of the night that covers me,
Black as the pit from pole to pole,
I thank whatever gods may be
For my unconquerable soul.

In the fell clutch of circumstance
I have not winced nor cried aloud.
Under the bludgeonings of chance
My head is bloody, but unbowed.

Beyond this place of wrath and tears
Looms but the Horror of the shade,
And yet the menace of the years
Finds and shall find me unafraid.

It matters not how strait the gate,
How charged with punishments the scroll,
I am the master of my fate,
I am the captain of my soul.

William Ernest Henley

1
★
★ ★

The man sat placidly in a utilitarian metal chair, staring straight ahead at a barren wall of cinder block. His arms were in his lap, but they showed no tension. No indication of what he knew was to come.

Positioned in the center of the room, he and his chair were the sole occupiers of the space. No desks, no bookshelves, and certainly no decorations on the rough concrete that surrounded him. Just him. The only break was a stainless steel pipe that hung above his head, with what looked like a shower nozzle on the end.

Behind a thick pane of glass on the left wall, three men stared at him intently, waiting on the inevitable.

Standing behind the two seated men, Dr. Chin Mae-jung watched the soul inside the room, and wondered, **What goes through a man's mind when death is near, and stalking?** That was imprecise, and not fitting of his scientific background. Not stalking. Coming in for the payment in full with the certitude of an avalanche. Not the death of a teenager in a car crash, or a soldier in a gunfight, where both felt invincible right up until the windshield shattered or the bullet tore through the body, ripping the soul free in the span of a heartbeat. No, a death where one **knew** it was coming. Staring you in the face. An inexorable slide to the abyss that one can't stop. What goes through a man's head? Did he think about his family? His life? A favorite memory? How could he sit there so patiently, knowing he was going to die?

The inside of the room was cold, with condensation seeping through the walls. The same cold Dr. Chin Mae-jung had dealt with his entire professional life, but he certainly hadn't expected to test his child on a living, breathing human being. He had enjoyed the scientific research he'd accomplished within these walls, but honestly, given a choice, he thought the manner of death he was about to impose as a result of his research to be grotesque.

But that might not matter in an hour, because he would be forced to prove he'd succeeded. And would most likely die just like the man in the chair. He wondered if he'd go out with the same placid expression on his face. The same calm.

The man in the chair wasn't chained to it. There was nothing keeping him in place. He was free to run around like a rat attempting to avoid a snake, shouting and yelling at the injustice, and yet he did not. The only thing keeping him in the chair was his own shame.

Once the chief scientist for North Korea's nuclear ambitions, he had overseen a test that had collapsed the mountain that contained it with the force of a magnitude seven earthquake, crushing hundreds, shattering years of developmental technology, and setting back Kim Jong-un's quest to be a nuclear power.

It wasn't his fault. He'd told the command the risks when they wanted to test a hydrogen bomb. But that mattered little now.

The world debated why North Korea had paused its nuclear tests. Was it sanctions, the threat of violence on behalf of the United States, or was North Korea playing some level of 3-D chess? The answer was more mundane: They simply couldn't. Which made the Supreme Leader angry, leading to the application of blame.

Leading to the man in the chair.

This execution served a dual purpose, as it was testing a new form of nerve agent, one that became inert after an hour of exposure to the atmosphere. Something Kim Jong-un wanted very badly.

Talking heads across the world theorized about North Korea's nuclear ambition, but they consistently missed the point of why Jong-un was working to achieve it. Nuclear weapons were a boogeyman only to the West, as there were plenty of ways to provide the same or greater deaths, and North Korea worked hard to achieve those goals as well. The world just didn't seem to care about that.

North Korea had upward of five thousand tons of chemical and biological munitions—enough to ensure more deaths than any number of nuclear bombs could accomplish—but their use came at a cost, as, once fired, they made the terrain uninhabitable, just like nuclear weapons. Kim Jong-un looked at the problem holistically, and wanted a solution. The nuclear program was designed to keep the United States from conducting a preemptive attack, something the chemical and biological weapons had inexplicably failed to do, but his end goal was a reunified Korean peninsula under his command. To do that, he needed to kill a great many people, breaking the back of the despised South Korean regime, but not in such a way that he couldn't occupy the terrain afterward.

Which is where Chin's research came in. He'd worked on the weapon for years, solely as a functionary of the North Korean state. He'd never thought about where it would be used, or, more precisely, whom it would kill.

Kim Jong-un had labeled every weapon he made with some outlandish title, but in this case, he'd kept it secret, calling it the same name as one of his ballistic missiles on the off chance it would end up in some intelligence chatter. Chin's weapon was called the Hwasong, like the Hwasong-12 missile, or the newly launched Hwasong-15, but unlike the missile systems, it wasn't given a number. It was given a color—red.

The faceless bureaucrat next to the lone telephone in the control room said, "What are you waiting for?"

Turning his eyes from the man in the chair, Chin wanted to say, "For you to get the hell out of my life." He couldn't, of course. The bureaucrat had the ear of the Supreme Leader, and as such, he held Chin's life in his hands.

Chin said, "The command."

"You have it."

Chin leaned over the desk and pressed an innocuous red button. One of many on the control panel. He rose slowly, knowing what he was going to see. What was unknown was what he would feel in an hour.

A gray mist sprang out of the stainless steel nozzle above the man's head, the only reaction from the man in the chair being his glancing up at the droplets spackling his skull. It spewed its odorless, colorless death for a fraction of a second, but it was enough.

The three men in the control room leaned forward, two unsure of what they would see. One not wanting to see it.

The man in the chair sat still for another second, dropping his head into his chest. Five seconds passed with no response. The bureaucrat looked at Chin, about to form a question, when the man's legs shot out.

The prisoner jumped up, staring at the panel of

glass, and shouted. Chin saw the effects taking hold. The man's face became necrotic, turning blue. He yelled something else, and then fell to the floor. His body began bucking up and down, his legs kicking the ground as if that would stop the climb of the neurotoxin, every muscle in his being receiving signals to contract. Including the lungs.

The man began frothing at the mouth, his entire body vibrating, his hands slapping the floor. Chin saw the dark stain of his bowels releasing forcefully, an embarrassing sight, and Chin wondered if these two functionaries would see the same thing when he entered the room.

Within thirty seconds, the man ceased movement. The bureaucrat said, "And now we wait."

An hour later, Chin was dressed in a chemical/biological suit and descending the stairs to the chamber. He put his hand on the door latch, wanting yet again to tell the men in the control room to initiate the vacuum protocol and follow-on decontamination of the room, but he knew that wasn't going to happen. The whole point was to see if his creation worked.

He turned the handle and swung the door open, hearing a slight exhale of air, as if the dead man in the room were sighing. He knew he'd now contaminated the entire hallway with the death in the room.

Or not.

He walked to the body, the breath from his mask rasping out, a labored effort to keep him alive. He

glanced up at the window and saw the two functionaries staring at him intently. Chin checked the
body and said, "He's dead," then realized nobody
could hear him. He glanced up again, and saw the
primary bureaucrat motion for him to remove his
mask. He didn't want to.

But he did.

He stood tense for a moment, waiting on the
symptoms. Waiting on what he didn't understand.
For all of his work on the weapon, he had no idea
what it would feel like to be killed by it. He took two
deep breaths, then began running, sprinting back
out of the room. He charged up the stairs, his forward motion designed to keep from him the awful
truth that he was dead. He barged into the control
room, breathing heavily and sweating.

The two men looked at him in horror, one leaping
out of his chair, wondering if he'd brought the death
with him. Chin saw the reaction and felt the anger
flow, reminding him he was alive.

He took two more breaths, looked at his hands,
and said, "You can calm down. The trial was a success. You can go into that room now as well. If you
want."

The bureaucrat sagged back in his chair, shaking
his head, a slow smile spreading on his face. He said,
"The Leader will be pleased."

Chin nodded, then realized he'd had no thoughts
before he'd removed the mask. No grand visions of
his life. No fond recollections before he faced his

eternal solution. He'd been simply paralyzed with the fear of death. He remembered the man in the chair, and the fact brought him shame. He was sure the man had thought more on his death than he had. Sure that man held more honor than he did.

The bureaucrat picked up the phone, telling Chin his work was done and waving him away. Chin staggered toward the door, still amazed he was alive, and heard the bureaucrat say into the phone, "It was a success. Tell the contact we will transfer it at his location. But tell him it will cost him much more than he expected."

Chin left the room, not thinking of the words the man had said into the phone. Not realizing there was profit to be made from what he'd designed, profit that would help alleviate the pain of the sanctions imposed on his country. He was only thinking that he was still alive. At least for a few more days in the Hermit Kingdom.

It would be later, when he saw the deaths, that he would realize he was but a pawn in a game of someone else's choosing.

2

★★

The throng began to grow in front of the palace, and Amena sensed that their fortunes were looking better. The changing of the guard at the Prince's Palace of Monaco was always a draw, and while this time it did not seem as crowded as usual, it was still large enough to provide a target.

Set high on a hill overlooking the famed harbor of Monte Carlo, the Prince's Palace was as grand as one would expect, with a courtyard surrounded by buildings constructed like a copy of Versailles. Once an actual fortress, today it was the official residence of the prince of Monaco, and a tourist destination not unlike a myriad of other European palaces.

Amena looked at her brother, Adnan, and smiled. Today was going to be a good day. If they were lucky, they would get enough loot to last them an entire week. Which would be nice, because if they returned to this ceremony too often—if the tourists complained a little too much about getting their pockets picked or their cameras stolen—they'd spoil the area like a fisherman overworking a pond. Because of it, she restricted their excursions here to once every other week, even though it was the richest environment in all of Monte Carlo. And counterintuitively, also the easiest.

When the ceremonial changing of the guard occurred, the tourist crowds packed into the square, all pressing forward against the ropes with cell phones and digital cameras focused on the parade, squeezed together until they were touching, not really paying any mind to the bodies rubbing against them left and right, their attention focused on the ceremony and not on their valuables.

On the outskirts of the courtyard, sitting on a park bench overlooking the Mediterranean Sea, Amena ignored the view, instead focusing on the tourists, still swelling five minutes before the start of the ceremony. She sent Adnan out to scout. He returned and said, "I found one. A fat guy with a selfie stick and baggy pants. His wallet is in his back pocket."

She said, "How deep?"

"He's wearing jeans. Not deep at all. Easy in— easy out."

"No, I mean how deep in the crowd?"

"He's in the second row. We'll have to work our way to him, but if you do it right, we'll get out clean."

"Nationality?"

Amena knew that the Americans were the easiest to steal from. They always felt themselves invincible.

The hardest were the Koreans. She imagined that country was full of pickpockets, because they were almost supernaturally aware.

"I don't know, but he speaks English."

"Good. Okay. Lead me to him."

"What's the play?"

"Let the parade start, then you do the cell phone plea. Just like last time."

Adnan said, "But our phone's camera doesn't work. Last time, it caused the target to question."

Amena snapped, "Just do it."

Adnan knew better than to disobey his older sister. Not after she'd gotten him through the barrel bombs in Aleppo, and then the crossing. At this point, she was more revered to him than their own father. An incurable optimist, she seemed to genuinely believe that better times were just around the corner, and he relied on her every day for his own sanity.

He held up an old iPhone 4S they'd stolen a few weeks earlier, and said, "Just get the wallet before I have to hand him this piece of crap."

Because it had no service, a cracked screen, and an inoperable camera, Amena had decided to keep it for decoy work instead of attempting to sell it.

Amena nodded, then stood, saying, "Lead the way."

They crossed the courtyard, a seemingly innocent thirteen-year-old girl following a doe-eyed eleven-year-old boy, their practiced mannerisms hiding the fact that they were much more worldly than their ages let on. They appeared just like any other gaggle of such children romping around, their parents clearly somewhere on the grounds.

They reached the back of the crowd, and Adnan pointed to an older guy two levels in, a selfie stick held in the air above the heads of those around him. Amena studied him, seeing a protruding gut ballooning out a tucked-in polo shirt over a pair of jeans, and a huge silver handlebar mustache. She noticed the mustache had crumbs in it, giving her confidence. The man had no attention to detail. And best yet, she could see the top of his wallet edging out of the patch pocket of his jeans.

The ceremony started with a shouted command, and the soldiers began marching in a practiced formation toward the palace, the tourists kept at bay by a pair of ropes. She motioned to Adnan, and they both began worming their way into the crowd, the drums from the marching soldiers beating the air. Adnan got in front of the man's gut and said in English, "Can you take a picture for me with your stick?"

The target ignored him, and Adnan pulled his sleeve. Irritated, the man said, "What?"

Adnan repeated the question, and held out his phone. Amena waited until the man was focused solely on Adnan, then snaked her hand to his pocket, shielding the move with her body. She snicked the wallet with two fingers in a practiced move, then turned to retreat. The wallet was ripped out of her hand. Astonished, she rotated back, and saw it dangling below the man's waist, a thin nylon cord attached to a corner and running back into the pocket of the jeans.

Before she could even assimilate that her "easy mark" was much more switched on than he portrayed, he whirled around, felt his dangling wallet strike his legs, and grabbed her arm, shouting for the police. Adnan sprang forward, using his smaller hands to rip the man's bigger one free, then both children squirmed through the crowd in a panic, the target behind them shouting for help. For someone to stop them.

Amena and Adnan wove through the people like snakes through grass, Amena hearing the target behind them simply bulling his way forward, the shouts of the crowd marking his passing. Within seconds, others were trying to stop her, but she was too quick, slapping some hands away and sliding through others like a greased pig at a county fair.

She broke free of the crowd, searching for Adnan, and saw the bear of a man coming for her, slamming two people to the pavement. Adnan sprang out from behind him, and they both began sprinting, Amena shouting in Arabic, "Toward the church!"

Outside of leaping over the cliffs into the sea, there were only two ways to escape the courtyard, and one would lead them deeper into the crowds. Which left Rue Colonel Bellando de Castro, the road to the

Monaco Cathedral, a claustrophobic lane lined with buildings.

They ran to the back of the parade square, their target's bellows fading behind them as he huffed, trying to catch up. Amena saw two policemen on the far side of the field orient on them, then begin to run to cut them off. It was a footrace now. She saw the arch over the top of Rue Colonel Bellando, only a hundred feet away, two more policemen loitering near it, oblivious to the drama playing out.

She heard her target still shouting behind her, falling farther and farther back, then the original policemen began blowing whistles, causing the two at the arch to snap their heads in confusion. The running cops shouted and pointed at the pair of scampering children.

She reached the arch and the two policemen finally realized she and her brother were the objects of the running cops. They tried to snatch her, and she slapped their hands away, ducking under their arms. She tripped on the cobblestones, slamming to the ground on her knees and rolling forward. Adnan used her diversion to dart behind their backs. They whirled to him, but he was already past. He jerked her to her feet, and they were through the cordon, sprinting down the street and dodging pedestrian tourists, Amena desperately searching for a place to hide.

She realized her call to run toward the Monaco Cathedral had been a bad choice, as Rue Colonel

Bellando was boxed in with buildings on both the left and the right, leaving them one choice—to run straight ahead. The pedestrian crowds would help, but she knew she couldn't outrun a radio, and when they broke out into the open at the cathedral, other police would be waiting.

The road took a bend, blocking the view from the parade ground, and she saw an alley to the left, a hamburger stand with tables scattered haphazardly about fifty meters in, the alley continuing past it. She grabbed Adnan's hand and shouted, "This way!"

They sprinted past the food stand and continued running deeper and deeper into the palace complex, hearing the bleating whistles of the cops fade as they continued straight down Rue Colonel Bellando. Eventually, Amena slowed, gasping for air, and she realized they were alone. She sagged against a wall, catching her breath.

Hands on his knees, sucking in oxygen, Adnan said, "What happened?"

"That idiot had a pickpocket wallet, but the cord was hidden."

Adnan laughed, and said, "At least we got away."

Amena grimaced, and began slowly walking back the way they had come, saying, "But we can't return here for a long time. If ever. And we got nothing."

They reached the hamburger stand and she saw the road ahead, afraid to take it just yet. Wanting to get a feel for the response. Most likely it would be nothing, as the cops wouldn't waste their time searching for a couple of kids, but it wouldn't do to give them an easy target. She said, "Let's wait here for a bit and see what happens."

She dug into her pocket, pulling out the last of her change. She said, "Get us a couple of Cokes to keep the guy at the register happy." The last thing they needed was to be shooed away as vagrants.

Adnan went to the counter, and she took a seat at a table with a view of the road, two tables away from a man talking on a cell phone.

She kept her eye on the street, patiently waiting to see if there was still police activity, then the man's voice on the phone penetrated. He was speaking Arabic. With an accent from Syria.

Adnan returned, and she said in English, "Any change?"

Adnan looked at her in confusion, and she flicked her eyes to the man. He heard the conversation, and understood. She didn't want the man to hear them speak Arabic—and possibly realize they were refugees. Illegal refugees.

Adnan sat down and handed her a can of Coke, saying, "It was actually more than you gave me, but he let it slide."

She said, "Keep an eye on the street," then discreetly turned to glance at the man. He was tall and lanky, wearing a tailored suit and tie, with a swarthy complexion, black hair, and a large black mustache, his eyes hidden by sunglasses.

She strained her ears, hearing snippets of the conversation, and understood he **was** from Syria, and he did something with the government. Unbidden, the realization sent a spasm of rage through her. She wanted to harm him. Wanted to give him just a small taste of the punishment her family had experienced at the hands of the despot Bashar al-Assad.

Then she noticed his phone. A brand-new iPhone X, worth at least five hundred US dollars on the streets of Monaco.

He finished his call and stood, picking up his trash and depositing it in a bin. He walked to Rue Colonel Bellando without a glance back.

Amena said, "Come on. Let's follow him."

Startled, Adnan said, "Why?"

She said, "A little payback."

3
★★★

The cab pulled up the circular drive and I saw a Ferrari Portofino and a Porsche 911 Cabriolet on either side of the hotel entrance. We were in a minivan, which pretty much summed up our status.

I said, "Looks like someone's gone a little overboard on this one, but I'm not complaining."

The cab stopped, and an unctuous bellman ripped the door open. To my left, my partner in crime, Jennifer, said, "This'll be the first time getting pulled from an actual project will be a step up."

Behind me, my 2IC, Knuckles, said, "Living with the Taskforce motto. Money is no object."

We exited the van in front of the Hermitage Hotel in Monte Carlo, me suitably impressed with the cars out front, wondering who would park a Ferrari at the curb like it was a VW. It wouldn't be until later that I learned it was all a charade, with the hotel renting the cars and rotating them daily to keep up a Hollywood image that just didn't exist.

Monte Carlo, in the principality of Monaco, had a reputation as a rich man's playground, and to some extent, it was deserved. Situated on the French Riviera just up the coast from Cannes and Nice, known for the Monaco Grand Prix, Princess Grace, and the famed Monte Carlo Casino, it had its fair share of celebrities sailing into the harbor on yachts that cost more than the income of most countries, but at its heart, it was just a city. With a density rivaling Hong Kong in persons living per square inch, it couldn't possibly live up to the hype it portrayed, because, while that same density ranked as the highest number of millionaires in the world, the majority of people living and working inside its borders were not lucky enough to be anointed citizenship, and scraped a living by catering to the wealthy.

We spilled out of the cab like a clown car, and the bellman asked if he could take our luggage. I would have said hell no, because that sort of thing just aggravated me, but Veep, the youngest person on our team, beat me to the punch, saying, "Yes, that would be great. We'll be in four separate rooms. Is that a problem?"

Of course the bellman said no, because it meant four separate tips for a load of luggage I could have carried myself.

We entered the opulent lobby, full of marble columns and impeccable granite floors, and Veep said, "I never stayed at a hotel like this on spring break."

I scoffed and said, "Oh, bullshit. The president's

son never stayed at a place like this? You seemed to know your way around outside with the bellman."

Nicholas Hannister had earned his callsign, Veep, when his father had been the vice president of the United States. Now his father was the most powerful man in the world, and I was still trying to get the son to forget his heritage and just become a member of the team. Four months ago, he would have shut up and taken the jab, afraid to say anything. Now he gave it back, which I considered a little bit of a breakthrough.

"I said on **spring break**. You know, when you get a break from college and have to pay your way to get the babes? Oh, wait. I forgot. You never went to college. But surely you've seen YouTube videos."

That would have been an incredible insult from any other man, but from my team, it meant nothing. I was Good Will Hunting and they all knew it. Especially in our chosen profession.

I saw Jennifer flash her eyes in anger, not liking what he'd said, actually taking offense at what was meant for me. She'd earned her college degree the hard way, six years after initially dropping out to marry an abusive husband, and had learned that a piece of paper didn't equal intelligence.

She blurted out, "He **has** a degree. He worked hard—" and I grabbed her hand, shutting her up. Yeah, I had a degree, but he was right. I'd never been a full-time student. But that was irrelevant, and Veep knew it, not the least because the first time we'd met was behind the barrel of a gun when I'd saved his life.

I said, "Touché, little millennial. Touché."

Jennifer relaxed, and Veep smiled, understanding the subliminal jab. I **had** the babe.

Round card score: Pike Logan.

We walked to the reception desk, and the final man on our team, Brett Thorpe, said, "No offense, Koko, but this beats the hell out of that hotel in Eze."

Jennifer ignored the use of her callsign, which she despised, instead looking around the lobby in a mock study. She arched an eyebrow and said, "Yeah, but there's no church here to work on," then saw an advertisement on a wall and grinned, saying, "But there is a spa. And like Knuckles said, money is no object to the Taskforce."

Jennifer and I were partners in a company called Grolier Recovery Services, which ostensibly facilitated archaeological work around the world. In reality, it was an elaborate cover organization used by the United States government to facilitate penetration of denied areas to put some threat into the ground. Knuckles, Veep, and Brett were all members of special operations or the CIA, but were acting as "employees" of the company, and as such, every once in a while, instead of getting into gunfights, we had to actually do some archaeological work.

With a degree in anthropology, and a true love for history, Jennifer really enjoyed these trips, but I always found them exceedingly boring. Even so, I understood why we did them. If you wanted to portray a real company, you had to have more than a web page. You had to have a history of doing what you professed you did, to include a network of contacts in that business world and a track record of success. Especially when trying to get through customs in a country that was less than hospitable to the United States.

And it didn't hurt to keep Jennifer happy. That kept **me** happy.

We'd been in the French town of Eze, a medieval village just outside of Monaco that had changed little since the Crusades. Well, the buildings hadn't changed, but the proprietors certainly had. Pedestrian only, built on a mountain with narrow stairwells that tested the hearts of the elderly tourists, Eze looked exactly like it had seven hundred years ago, except now it was full of art galleries and perfume shops.

Near the top of the mountain village was a church that was being renovated with the help of an American university. Called the Notre Dame de l'Assomption, it was younger than the surrounding area—having been built in the eighteenth century—and during the renovations, the university had found a graveyard. A much, much older graveyard than the church. Since the village had bounced between Italian and French provenance, a three-way fight had ensued as to who would get to excavate the find, with both France and Italy claiming the bodies, and the university claiming the discovery.

We had been contracted by the university to help with the dispute, as such things were a Grolier specialty. It would have been easy work, too, giving Jennifer a chance to really enjoy some old bones, but we'd only been in-country for four days when our commander, Kurt Hale, had called, telling me to get the team to Monte Carlo for a situation that had to be resolved **right now**.

With the United States government, everything was a damn crisis. We never seemed to be able to see past our own headlights, constantly surprised when something happened that had been brewing for years. This crisis was a little bit unique, though, because Kurt had brought in two different teams to deal with it—something that rarely happened.

Brett said, "Am I supposed to pay for my room, or is this taken care of?"

I said, "It's taken care of."

We walked as a group to the check-in desk, all of us taking in the marble surroundings and feeling a little underdressed. The reservations were under my company name, because there was no way that we could reserve a room as "Top Secret Commando Unit," even if the funds were coming from the Taskforce through multiple cutouts.

In short order, we went to our separate rooms, where I immediately hooked my laptop to a VPN to see exactly what the state of play was.

Jennifer moved her things around, getting settled, while I checked messages. I could tell she was a little antsy, but I assumed it was because of being pulled from our contract. I was wrong.

I closed the laptop and said, "Nothing new. Only handle we have on the guy is his reservation tonight at the restaurant, and then at the casino."

Jennifer came out of the bathroom and said, "That's it?"

I said, "Yep, but it can't be that hard. How many Koreans do you think are running around here? He'll stick out like Brett."

Brett was African American, another small population here in Monaco.

She said, "I'd like a little more than a name and nationality to go on. The target isn't a member of an FTO group, and why two teams? If it's just a simple Alpha mission? Something more is in play, and we're being kept in the dark."

While I didn't believe Kurt Hale would keep something from me, she **did** have a point. It was true our mission was only Alpha, but we'd already been given authority for Omega if we thought the guy was dirty, meaning it was my choice. My decision. Like the fact that two separate teams were operating in Monaco with two separate covers, it was unusual. As was the target.

The charter for the Taskforce was limited to designated substate groups on the State Department's Foreign Terrorist Organizations list, something that was updated continually. The Taskforce was a scalpel against such assholes, but our boundaries ended with them. We didn't do state organizations, even if they sponsored such groups. The United States had plenty of others who did that, like the CIA and the intelligence organs of the Department of Defense.

Which begged the question of why we were chasing a North Korean pretending to be a billionaire South Korean on the shores of the Côte d'Azur.

4
★★

Yasir al-Shami wandered past the Monaco Cathedral, seeing a line of people snaking inside, and decided to take the opportunity to check his backtrail. He'd picked the outdoor eatery to highlight anyone who might be interested in him, and all he'd seen were a couple of kids and two policemen blowing whistles, but he'd learned through a lifetime of clandestine operations that just because you didn't spot a tail didn't mean there wasn't one. It always paid to double-check.

He entered the line, then began to file past the tombs of previous rulers of Monaco. The line moved slowly, voices hushed, eventually circling at the front of the cathedral and heading back out on the far side, each person stopping for an extra beat at Princess Grace's final resting spot, allowing him to study anyone suspicious who might have entered after him. A single male, a couple that didn't fit, anyone acting like him and showing more interest in the line of people than the graves.

He saw nothing and exited back into the sunshine, sure he was clean.

He continued east, casually strolling and blending in with the other pedestrians. Eventually, he reached a long five-story building that seemed to be built into the side of the cliff, the southern facade slipping two floors below the land he was on, going all the way down to the ocean. A sign out front proclaimed MUSÉE OCÉANOGRAPHIQUE DE MONACO. The national aquarium of Monaco, the oldest continually operating aquarium in the world, and one made famous by Jacques Cousteau. Yasir cared not a whit about any of that, preferring to eat his fish on a plate with some lemon instead of watching them swim, but it **was** the designated meeting site.

He paid to enter, and ignored the multitude of tourists pressed against a giant Plexiglas wall, staring at the sea creatures beyond. He looked at a map hanging on a column, found an elevator, and rode it straight to the roof.

He exited, looking for the terrace restaurant, but finding instead a thirty-foot-tall metal sculpture of a shark held up by its tail, its mouth agape with gleaming metal teeth as if it had just been caught, tourists in front taking selfies. He turned around, and saw the restaurant on the western side, tables spread out and pay telescopes being used to gaze out along the coastline.

He scanned the crowd, not looking for a signal as he ordinarily would have done. No signal was needed. He was looking for an ethnicity. At a far table, he saw an Asian man in a suit, another standing behind him.

He walked over and pulled out a chair, saying, "Song Hae-gook, I presume?"

The man behind the seated Asian rapidly advanced, and the seated man held up a hand, saying, "Yes. Yasir al-Shami?"

Yasir nodded and said, "You picked a strange place to conduct business."

"I portray what a rich man would do. I'm not going to meet you in a dark alley like the slime you deal with in Syria. And I can control access here."

Another Asian security man exited the elevator and joined them, saying something in Korean. Song nodded and said, "You're clean."

Yasir realized Song had deployed countersurveillance, protecting the meeting. The fact allayed his concerns about the location, and the skills of the man across the table.

He nodded and said, "Glad to see the professionalism."

Song laughed and said, "If you remember, in the past it was my people who taught Assad's intelligence agencies how to operate. Which means we taught you."

A member of the elite Air Force Intelligence Directorate—which had very little to do with Air Force intelligence—Yasir had never been instructed by a North Korean, but he had no doubt that what Song said was true. That had been before his time. Before the civil war, and before North Korea's leader, Kim Jong-un, had used two females to kill his half brother with nerve gas in Malaysia. North Korea's intelligence agency had proved its ability to penetrate another sovereign country, plan an operation, and execute it successfully.

Yasir said, "My leadership appreciates what you have done for them in the past, and what you're willing to do now."

Song said, "Straight to business. I like that. Are you prepared to pay the agreed price?"

Surprised, Yasir said, "No. Not here. I was told I was but the conduit. You would pass me the information I needed to meet someone else. You understand, we have to check what you're giving us. Make sure it's real."

"And how are you going to do that? Breathe it in? No. You'll trust us. As you must."

"We can test it. That's not hard at all. I have the equipment."

Song leaned back and said, "You can test for the agent, but how will you test for the fact that it expires? Pour it on the ground and watch the pedestrians?"

Yasir said, "So it's real? You've created Red Mercury?"

Song laughed and said, "You Arabs. Always looking for a myth. No, it's not the fabled 'Red Mercury.'

It's just a nerve agent that kills without remorse, and then kills itself."

Yasir let the insult slide, the prehistoric part of his brain wanting to punish the man for the insult. He said, "That's what we want. So what's next?"

Song said, "Why? Why do you want that? My command wants to know."

"Not your business. We'll pay what you asked, but we don't need to tell you why." Yasir smiled and said, "You have a problem with the sanctions. They're crippling you. The money is all that matters."

Song said, "Yes, we're looking for separate income streams, but make no mistake, we're not willing to sell what you call 'Red Mercury' just because. If we were, there are a hundred terrorist groups who are willing. We chose you, and with that choice comes some forewarning. We need to know."

Yasir had been given clearance for the answer, but now grudgingly didn't want to provide it. But that wouldn't play well if he returned empty-handed. This conversation would be relayed, he was sure. He said, "We're giving it to the White Flags. You've heard of them?"

Song scoffed and said, "Yes. The rebirth of ISIS. The ones now fighting yet again in Iraq and Syria. What will that do? They're your enemy. Are you crazy?"

"Yes, we fight them, but we also talk to them. They are good for the regime. They make it so that **we** are the bastion fighting terrorism. Now that ISIS has been driven into the ground, they are becoming the main insurgent group, and if we can make them look like the terrorists they are, we solidify our credibility."

"You have contacts with them?"

"Yes. We always have. They're recruited from ISIS and the Nusra Front."

Song nodded, thinking through the ramifications. He said, "So you intend to use the weapon in Syria. And you don't want to taint the ground it's used upon because you intend to reclaim it. You only want to show the world how bad the White Flags are, using a weapon that can't be traced back to you. Am I reading that correctly?"

Yasir was startled at how quickly Song had ascertained their plot. Yasir himself had created the plan, and had thought it extremely clever.

He said, "Yes. That's what we're going to do. The White Flags will use it against a US Special Forces outpost, killing them, and then we'll side with the Americans, demanding to help eradicate the terrorists. The outcry in the United States will only be good for us. We are on the way to victory, but we need to get the United States to either join us or withdraw. Either way, this will work."

"And how will you control the weapon once it's transferred?"

"That's our problem, but make no mistake, the White Flags trust me. I've helped the man in charge in the past, when he was in the Nusra Front. They'll do what I say. The chance to kill a bunch of US Special Forces will be too good to pass up. Those bastards have been killing the Front for years."

"And the Americans? How will you control them?"

Yasir smiled and said, "I have contacts there as well."

Song arched an eyebrow and said, "What's that mean?"

Yasir said, "You only get so much intelligence. Have I passed the test?"

Song remained silent for a moment, and Yasir knew he was considering leveraging the weapon for more information. Yasir cut it short. "That's all I'm saying to you. Take it back to your people, or end this whole transaction. I came here to buy a weapon, and that's it."

Song sat for a few more seconds, then seemed to come to a decision. He said, "You have an iPhone Ten? Yes? Like it was directed?"

Yasir held up his cell and said, "Yes. Although I don't know why this phone matters."

"Give it to me."

He passed it across, and Song handed it to the man behind him. Yasir watched the security man manipulate the phone, going through menu after menu, then insert a device into the lightning port. Five seconds later, he handed it back.

Song said, "Turn on your AirPort."

Yasir did, looking at Song expectantly. His phone dinged, asking him if he wanted to open something with an extension he didn't recognize. It wasn't a picture or a document.

Song said, "Accept it. It's your next instructions, and it'll be embedded in your phone. Nobody can find it."

Yasir did, then said, "So now what?"

"Now you go to Switzerland. The weapon is held there. The passcode I just sent has your instructions for the next step. The men you'll meet will match your phone with theirs. And then, of course, you must be prepared to pay."

Yasir said, "Switzerland?"

"Yes. Don't question. Just follow the instructions. We'll leave here first. Remain in place for thirty minutes."

Yasir nodded, and Song stood, saying, "I believe you are what they said you'd be, but don't mess this up. The men in Switzerland are under deep cover. You compromise them, and we'll come find you like we did Kim Jong-nam. The only difference will be they won't have to decontaminate your death location."

Yasir set the phone on the table and smiled. "Stop with the threats. You aren't the only ones who know how to operate. I've lived in a cauldron for seven years with people trying to kill me. All you've done is eat potatoes trying to stave off a famine."

Song scowled at the slight, whirling around and leaving. The two men with him glared, and Yasir gave it right back.

5

⋆⋆

Jennifer came out of the bathroom dressed to the nines, and, man alive, she was a heartbreaker. Wearing a slinky black dress, a string of pearls, her blond hair somehow magically being up but still spilling around her neck, she looked like she did this for a living on the pages of a fashion magazine.

She bent over, putting on her heels and giving me a shot of her cleavage. I wasn't sure if that was intended, but I certainly appreciated it. It had taken me about half as long to get ready, because all I had to do was put on a black suit with a black tie. No bow tie. I'm not that damn pathetic.

She stood back up, looked at me, and said, "You sure we shouldn't repeat the Caymans? No offense, but you don't look like a debonair guy."

I glanced in the mirror of our room, wanting to see Daniel Craig or Sean Connery. While there were some hints of that, it remained only a hint. With my close-cropped brown hair and a jagged scar from a childhood accident threading its way across my brow and into my cheek, I looked more like a Serbian Mafia man. Or a pirate, which is what I preferred to think.

I said, "No way am I missing out on the casino. It's the heart of this whole city. No, it's me. Not lover boy. He's got his own mission tonight."

She was referring to Knuckles and a mission similar to this we'd once done in the Cayman Islands, when he'd been the one wearing the suit. Knuckles was a SEAL, with all that entailed, but he was one handsome man, standing at six foot two, with his shoulders stretching out about a foot on each side over his waist, a face that looked like some cologne model's, and a head of black hair like a hipster guitarist.

Then Jennifer got to the heart of it, because that was her specialty. "Is it because Carly is working with Johnny's team?"

Carly was a CIA case officer who Knuckles had once dated, which wouldn't be that big of a deal, but he'd gotten her a shot at selection—with my endorsement—as only the second woman to do so, Jennifer being the first. They were no longer dating, and she'd pulled out of selection. Her choice.

As much as I wanted to see the casino, Jennifer was correct on why I'd decided to take the role instead of giving it to Knuckles. I didn't want any old-flame crap to squirrel up our mission. Better to give Knuckles the breaking-and-entering portion, even if I had a scar on my face.

Even so, I fibbed a little. I said, "Johnny's team has a completely different cover than ours. We don't know each other. Carly working with them is irrelevant."

Jennifer said, "Why is she even here?"

I looked at her, wondering if **she** wasn't pissed that Carly had quit. Jennifer had put a lot of time into preparing Carly as the only female to pass Taskforce Assessment and Selection, but she had to know that selection was what it was. A cut line.

I said, "She's still an operations officer of the CIA Clandestine Service, assigned to the Taskforce. A case officer. She's the liaison for that CIA guy we have to meet after tonight. The one who said he'd only talk to one of his tribe. And anyway, this mission is right up her alley."

Jennifer said nothing, going back to the mirror. I said, "What's up?"

She fiddled with her earrings and said, "I can't believe she didn't pass. I just wonder."

"Wonder if the he-man woman-haters flushed her out?"

She turned around and said, "Yes. They tried to do it to me. I just wonder if she got on the Volkswagen bus because she wanted to."

Leaving selection of your own volition was called Voluntary Withdrawal, or VW. Which had been turned into slang as the Volkswagen bus. I said, "Don't turn this into a conspiracy. Don't put this on the guys. **You** didn't quit. Selection is there for a reason, and she saw she wasn't a good fit. She loves being a case officer, so let her do that."

She said, "This is going to be awkward."

Meaning, she'd spent so much time getting Carly ready that she was afraid to actually see her now. None of us had since she'd quit.

I said, "No it won't. We don't know them. You aren't even going to talk to her. They're on a separate cover, with a separate mission. Full stop. Just focus on our task. The end state is recovering the data from the breach."

In 2014, China had penetrated the United States Office of Personnel Management, stealing the records of upward of four million government workers. In that breach were the security check documents for our most sensitive members of the US government. Called the SF86 background check, each one was a detailed dossier of anyone who had achieved a security clearance, to include everything up to top secret, sensitive compartmented information. With that data, China could penetrate a host of agents operating in cover—literally just about anyone who had been given a clearance to work clandestinely. It was a disaster of epic proportions that had barely made the news. Since then, the Taskforce had started doing their own background checks, not trusting our very own government, but the damage was done.

What we'd been told by the Taskforce was that a North Korean posing as a South Korean business-man was attempting to sell the data to a Syrian.

Which was the fire we'd been sent to put out. We had sensitive assets operating in Syria, and there was no way we could allow the breach to spread.

They'd determined that the transfer was going to happen in Monaco, which left the usual assets of the US government in a quandary. Monaco had no CIA station to speak of, and the timeline was short. The director of the CIA—a member of the Oversight Council who controlled Taskforce activity—had actually punted, saying he couldn't get the mission done. And so we'd been called in.

My mission was to make contact with the Korean tonight and then follow him until he met the Syrian. Johnny's team would focus on the Syrian once we identified him. The end state was the prevention of the passing of the information. It could be a dark web address, a thumb drive, or hell, with North Korea, a five-and-a-quarter-inch floppy disk. Either way, we were going to stop it.

Knuckles and Veep were going to break into the Korean's room the minute we had eyes on him, ripping through whatever electronics he had and putting surveillance devices in place. Brett was a floater for whatever I decided. Jennifer and I were the primary surveillance of the target.

Jennifer adjusted her dress, dropping the conversation about Carly. She said, "You know that guy's been here for two days. Don't you wonder if we've already missed the contact?"

I said, "We can only do what we can do. We have

the anchor tonight. I'm not going crazy because the Taskforce decided this was an emergency."

She said, "Your name is on that list, isn't it?"

I fingered the Glock on the inside of my belt and said, "Yeah, it is. From my time in the Special Mission Unit. Makes it a little personal."

She smiled and said, "Then I guess I have to be on my best behavior."

I grinned at her all dolled up and looking like something out of a **Playboy** photo shoot before the clothes came off, and said, "There's no reason to get stupid."

She laughed and said, "Seriously, did you think about what I just said? We don't even know where this guy is, and he's been here for two days."

6

★
★ ★

Amena saw the man enter the Oceanographic Museum and paused. They didn't have the money to enter the museum, but there was another way.

Adnan saw her look and said, "No, we're not sneaking in."

She said, "Yes. We are. We're going to steal that man's phone."

Adnan threw up his hands and said, "Why does this guy's phone matter? We can find another one tomorrow."

Amena glared at him and said, "It matters."

Adnan said nothing for a heartbeat, then said, "This is not worth it."

"No, this **is** worth it. That man deserves it. I heard him talking."

Adnan played his final card, saying, "Father will be home soon, and it'll take us at least an hour to get back. He'll be there before we are, and he won't be pleased."

Amena said, "He'll be pleased with me. That man

works for the regime that sent us away. The man who killed Mother."

Adnan stomped about, completing a circle, then said, "We can't do this! You're asking too much."

Amena looked him in the eye and said, "This is for **Mother**."

And that was enough. Adnan had been the first to pull the rubble away from the body of their mother, and she knew it.

His voice barely above a whisper, he said, "Okay."

She gave him a grim smile and said, "Come on. We'll enter the same way I always do."

The museum was a favorite of Amena's. A place of solitude and reflection, where she could pretend she was someone else before she went back to stealing from people she'd never met. She knew what she was doing was wrong, and pined for an existence like Jacques Cousteau, a man allowed to pursue something he loved. And yet she also understood that Jacques Cousteau was but a myth for people like her. He had achieved a life at the pinnacle of the apex—pursuing a dream of self-actualization. She was still at the bottom of the pyramid, fighting for survival. And she understood why. Cousteau didn't grow up with barrel bombs destroying everything he knew, and the man inside the museum had helped to launch them.

She said, "Come on," and they circled back around the building the way they'd come, leaving the road and sliding down the wall toward the cliff. Amena reached the edge and looked over, seeing the water of the Mediterranean a hundred feet below, the museum itself built directly into the rock, running another two stories down until it stopped about thirty feet above the water.

Built in 1910, the structure had a modern-day veneer of security out front, with metal detectors and cameras, but a Victorian-age level of security in the back, the only protection being a simple window latch—if one could reach it.

Amena began sliding down the grass of the cliff, one hand on the building and the other on the rocks to her right. She reached the first window—the one she'd used many times before—and peeked inside. A workroom of the museum, outside of the exhibits, it housed mops and other cleaning supplies, with a stack of paintings against the wall. More of a store-room than an office, with a desk piled with books and dust, she'd never seen anyone inside of it. And she didn't see anyone now.

The window was decades old with multiple layers of paint, the panes of glass surrounded by ancient metal. She pried the bottom edge, and it came free. As it had the first time she'd found it. It opened enough for her to snake her hand in and reach the crank, and she started turning, the window opening wider and wider, but each inch it did made it harder to turn. Eventually, she stopped, seeing a gap of about a foot and a half. Enough.

She said, "You first."

Adnan slipped by her, his hands holding the window ledge and his eyes on the rocks below. He hoisted himself up, then slithered inside. She followed.

She moved immediately to the door and cracked it.

He said, "What now?"

She peeked out the door, saying, "Now we find him," and slipped through.

They were on the second level, the one dedicated to housing the aquarium's offices. She ran lightly to a stairwell, ignoring the signs saying the exit was only to be used in an emergency, knowing from past intrusions that it wasn't alarmed. She climbed down a floor, to the bottom level, and stopped, making sure Adnan was behind her. When she saw him, she opened the door and exited into the flow of people.

Amena skipped past the exhibits, not looking at any of them, then was held up by a cluster of visitors staring at the ocean thirty feet below them—a jagged hole in the floor showing an original research portal, covered by a rough-iron grate.

Amena bulled through the crowd, having seen the hole many times before, reentering the exhibit hall with a laser focus on finding the man with the phone. She passed a bench in front of a Plexiglas wall illuminated by a black light, behind it a swarm of jellyfish billowing and flowing.

Adnan said, "Wait, shouldn't we stop here?"

Amena scowled, not liking the joke. It was her favorite place in the aquarium. A spot where she could sit and watch for hours, wishing her life were different. She said nothing, charging onward.

Eventually, they had cleared all four floors of exhibits without a sighting, and Adnan said, "Let's just go home. This is getting stupid."

Amena went to the elevator and said, "We haven't seen the roof."

"The roof? It's just a restaurant."

The door opened, and Amena said, "Yes, it is. Come on."

Adnan dutifully followed her, muttering under his breath. The elevator went up to the top and Amena exited just as three Asian men entered.

She ignored them, saying to Adnan, "Just one lap, then we'll go home."

She saw one of the Asians look at her weirdly, and she realized it was because she was speaking Arabic. She hid her eyes and raced away.

She went around the giant metal shark, ignoring the people taking selfies, but didn't see the man with the phone. She was beginning to think she'd missed him somewhere inside, and that Adnan was correct. This **was** stupid. Then Adnan came running to her. He said, "I found him. In the restaurant."

He led her back to the elevator vestibule, went inside, then cracked open the door and pointed. She leaned over and saw the Syrian, sitting at a table all by himself, his phone in front of him on the glass tabletop.

She withdrew back inside and said, "Hold the door to the stairs open."

"What are you going to do?"

"Steal that phone. And I'll be coming back on the run. No sneaking here."

7

★
★★

Reluctant, Adnan said, "Amena . . . this is stupid."

"Just hold the door. It'll work out. We know this place like the back of our hand, and most of the hallways and exhibits are dark. We'll get away easily back through the window we used while he's still searching. He's a rich man, and that phone will feed us for a month."

Adnan said nothing else, turning from the elevator to the stairwell door. He tested it, finding it unlocked. Amena nodded, then said, "Can you lock it?"

He fiddled with the bar handle, seeing he could, in fact, lock it closed. He said, "Yes."

"Good. The key is to beat him down the first flight of stairs. If he's right behind us, it's trouble. I get through, and you slam the door closed. From there, we go straight to the office."

"What if he's on top of us?"

"I'll throw the phone at him. He'll be more worried about that."

Adnan nodded, but she could tell he was still unhappy. She took a deep breath, then left the vestibule. She quickly surveyed the restaurant, noting where waiters were loitering, where the kitchen exit was located, and how the tables were arranged. She didn't want to repeat running through a gauntlet of people trying to stop her. She wanted a clean line back to the vestibule.

She wasn't going to get it. The man's table was the second farthest away in the room, right next to the outdoor area. In between the vestibule and him were multiple tables, with two occupied by patrons. She had a choice of either running past the wait station or weaving between the two occupied tables. She decided on the tables, as the patrons were seated and focused on their conversations, while the waiters were standing and focused on the activity in the room. She decided the tables were a lesser threat.

She circled around as if she were going outside, to the deck, then began to shadow the wall until she was approaching the man's back, with her lane to the door directly in front of her, straight between the occupied tables. Her breath quickened, her pulse beginning to race. She glanced at the bartender and saw his back was turned. One waiter was helping a table behind her, on the deck, and another was at the wait station, filling glasses of water.

She came within arm's reach of her target, staring

at the back of his head, afraid to commit. She figured she would have a space of one second, maybe a second and a half, before he reacted, and she needed every bit of it to put distance between him and her. She wavered in her commitment. It wasn't enough time.

A memory of her mother floated out. A **good** memory. Not the one that forced her awake most nights, sweating and screaming—the one where her mother was severed in two—but a memory of gathering flowers, the warm summer day illuminating her mother's hair.

She took it as an omen, and surged forward, banishing her fear. She brushed past his shoulder, reached over his arm, and snatched the phone.

Before her hand had even left the table, he leapt up, surprising her with his reaction time. Scaring her. She felt her adrenaline surge and took off running, feeling his hand snatch the collar of her shirt. She jerked her head forward, feeling the collar tear and the hand drop free, but she knew he was on top of her.

She reached the gap between the two tables, seeing the patrons all startled at the commotion. One tourist stood, and she flung his chair behind her.

She heard a ferocious crash, and finally dared to look behind her, still running flat out. The Syrian was on the floor, having fallen over the chair, the other patrons now waving their arms and yelling.

She refocused on her escape, and the bartender

came over the wood of the bar, landing in front of her, blocking her way forward. She knew the phone would do nothing to stop him. Getting rid of it now meant little. He waved his arms, attempting to wrap her up, and she let him. He spoke to her in French, telling her to quit fighting. She struggled for a second, then stopped, appearing to give in.

She saw the Syrian rise, covered in some liquid that had fallen off the table, his sunglasses askew on his face, the rage emanating out. She felt the bartender's arms relax, and she shot her free hand to her rear, slid it up his groin, then squeezed his genitals with a strength born of fear. He shrieked, a high-pitched wail, and released her, falling back and holding his privates.

The Syrian began running toward her, and she darted the final feet to the vestibule. She ripped the door open and saw Adnan, eyes wide, holding the stairwell door. She shouted, "Run, run!" and went by him, hearing it slam shut behind her.

They took the steps two at a time, the rattling of the door above echoing through the stairwell. They reached the next landing and Adnan stopped. Amena said, "No. Keep going."

They skipped to the next floor, then the one beyond, and Amena paused, catching her breath. Adnan said, "What was all of that noise? The screaming?"

In between hitches of breath, she said, "He was much faster than I thought. They almost caught me."

Adnan cracked the door and said, "We're on the entrance floor. What do you want to do?"

She thought about it, bringing up the floor plan in her mind. They would have to go through the exhibits, threading their way past the tourists, but then they'd be in the main foyer. There was a ticket taker there, but he didn't have a radio, so it was unlikely he would know what had just occurred. They could run straight out the front door. Once they were on the street, they could disappear.

The original plan would lead them deeper into the aquarium, to the floor of offices, and the workers most certainly had telephones at their desks. For all she knew, one of the rooms was the security office itself, full of police.

She said, "We leave from here. Walk like guests until we get to the lobby. Then run out."

Adnan nodded, and Amena noticed his hand was shaking. She said, "Don't worry. We'll get out." She held up the phone and said, "This was worth it."

She opened the door, the exit gloomy to protect the exhibits, the light from inside the stairwell spilling out. She got her bearings, and said, "Left. We need to go left."

Across the hall, she heard a bell chime, and saw the elevator door open, exposing the Syrian and the bartender, the latter holding a small radio. The Syrian locked eyes with her and shouted. The bartender used the radio. She panicked, saying, "Go, go!"

They raced down the hallway, hearing the footsteps behind them, and Adnan jerked her to the left, deeper into the aquarium. She said, "What are you doing?"

He took off running again, saying, "He had a radio. We can't get out of the front."

She followed, saying, "We can't get out of the office either."

He said, "I know. There is another way."

Amena chased him past tanks full of coral and seahorses, then down a long escalator, going to the lowest level. She reached the bottom, hearing the pounding of feet above, and said, "What are you doing? This is going the wrong way."

He looked behind her, and she saw his eyes grow wide. He said, "They're coming!"

He ran around the corner and she saw the Syrian barreling down the escalator, the bartender not far behind, still shouting into his radio. She followed, not thinking clearly, now in a full panic. She turned the corner, and she saw the jellyfish again, this time with two small boys sitting on the bench in rapt attention at their dance. She kept her eyes on the back of her brother, racing by them without a glance. She saw the hole in the floor ahead, more tourists gathered around it. Behind her, she heard the Syrian yelling. To her front, down the hallway, she saw two security guards coming right at them.

This is it. We're done.

Adnan ran into the crowd of people around the hole, pushing through them and sliding toward the grate. Amena stopped, seeing the guards to the front and the Syrian to the rear. She shouted, "Adnan!"

He looked at her and she tossed him the phone, saying, "I'll lead them away. I'll get caught. You hide."

He said, "No, no! This is it!"

And she watched him slide into the hole and disappear. Her mouth fell open, the crowd around the grate gasping in shock. One man turned and saw the guards coming forward. He jogged to them and began shouting in French, waving his arms, engaging them. They stopped running.

She heard footsteps behind her and saw the Syrian was only twenty meters away, bellowing like a bull. She darted to the hole, squeezing between the startled tourists. She looked down at the sea thirty feet below, seeing her brother treading water and staring back at her. She turned around, saw the Syrian reaching for her, and slid into the hole, scraping past the iron grate that would block all but a child.

She hung by her arms, her hands clamped like a vise to the grate, her feet dangling below her, afraid to let go. The Syrian reached through the grate and grabbed her arm, violently trying to pull her up. She sank her teeth into his thumb, tearing the flesh. He screamed, and jerked his hand back like he'd been stung by a bee.

She took one more look at the frothing water below, and let go.

8

★★★

We crossed the parking lot from the restaurant toward the famed Monte Carlo Casino, about ten minutes behind our target. Out front, of course, was a line of cars that would make any gearhead drool, with Ferraris and Lamborghinis showcased behind a yellow cotton rope. It looked like a museum display, which is pretty much what it was. I'd been told the secret by our valet at the hotel, and now it just made me grin.

Jennifer saw my amusement and said, "It's not that bad. They're just keeping up an image. Same as you and me. I'm just surprised we're actually going to the casino. I'm waiting on you to spring something else on me, like maybe I have to climb a rope to the roof while you get to go inside."

I said, "Come on. I look good, you look good. Nothing else will go wrong."

She grinned and said, "Sure. If today is any indication, we're getting some high adventure before the night is over." Which made **me** smile, because we both loved a little high adventure.

Jennifer was on her third outfit of the day, because after she'd gotten all dolled up, we'd found out that we had to waste the remainder of our afternoon meeting the CIA guy for his "input" on the Syrian connection. The one where Carly was supposed to act as liaison, because apparently us DoD folks couldn't understand English. Jennifer, of course, was incensed, because getting ready for the night is sacrosanct for a female, and it doesn't work in reverse, but now she was supposed to do it. Not my fault that all I had to do was put on a tie.

Our plan had been to meet Knuckles and Veep in the exquisite cocktail bar on the first floor of the Hermitage, reviewing final mission planning for their cracking of the Korean's hotel room, but we were short-circuited with this new demand. The CIA meeting was supposed to happen tomorrow—**after** the mission—but Kurt gave the order, so off we went.

Because Monaco had no real CIA station to speak of, our guy had been pulled in from Turkey, where he was apparently hip-deep in a lot of Syrian intrigue. Some James Bond–type who had deep-cover penetration inside the Assad regime, and could vet any intel we brought him regarding Syrian threats. I thought it was bullshit to begin with, but when the director of the CIA had deferred to Taskforce control, he'd also stipulated that we coordinate with this asshole. Pardon me, I misspelled "asset."

Representing our team were Jennifer and me. From the other team, Carly and Axe. Which was potentially a bit of a problem, because I had no idea how Carly would react to seeing me after she'd quit selection. She knew I'd worked very hard to get her a shot, putting my name on the line, not to mention all the work Jennifer had done getting her ready, but now wasn't the time to have any emotion interfere with our mission. It was complicated enough.

Carly had been thrown into a mission with my team a few years ago, when she was still in the CIA. She was a little bit of a hothead, who executed what **she** thought was right, regardless of what anybody else said. Which is to say, we butted heads a lot, but I truly respected her. She had talent, but I knew her VW from selection might make her hostile or awkward when she saw me, possibly affecting our mission. She was just built that way, and I understood, because I probably would have reacted the same damn way.

I knew a guy who was one of the best in the world as a Ranger, having served for a decade in one battalion or another. He went Special Forces, and couldn't take the perceived lack of discipline. It just wasn't for him. He quit, but not because he wasn't worthy. Because it wasn't for him. I was sure Carly's situation was the same. She just didn't want to be Jennifer, and there was nothing wrong with that.

At the end of the day, she was the CIA case officer, and the natural choice to lead the meeting. As for

Axe, I knew him very well. He was Johnny's 2IC, and he'd asked for Carly on the team after he'd found out she was attempting selection, and when she had thrown in the towel, he'd asked for her to come anyway because of her CIA knowledge. Kurt had agreed because it placated the D/CIA's decision to defer to Taskforce control. Something he'd **never** done before.

We'd met the CIA guy on the wharf, right next to the harbor, at one of the ubiquitous outdoor eateries overlooking the expensive yachts, and my first impression wasn't good. He'd immediately asked if our "backtrail" was clean, and if I was an idiot for walking right to his table. Yeah, he was playing the tradecraft card like he was deep inside Moscow.

I said, "Backtrail is good. But I'm wondering about this location you've chosen. I didn't see any reason to duck and dodge when your table has a clear view from about four thousand different vantage points." I flicked my head toward the harbor and said, "You check all of those houses for telescopes, cameras, or directional microphones?"

He started to say something and I cut him off, "Stop the dick measuring. You're meeting us because I've **killed** more men on surveillance operations than you have just watching. It's why I'm here. I'm the chosen one, not you. And trust me, if I thought this meeting was compromised, you wouldn't have seen my face."

Jennifer grabbed my arm, seeing I was going into

asshole mode, but he deserved it. He started to stand, and I said, "Sit the fuck down, before I kill you as well."

I gave him my pirate stare, and he sat down. Because, when push came to shove, that damn scar on my face paid dividends.

He said, "I'm not talking until the CIA liaison arrives. As far as I'm concerned, you aren't cleared."

I pulled out a chair and said, "Fine by me." I stuck out my hand and said, "Pike Logan, and this is Jennifer Cahill."

He reluctantly took it, and I said, "Look, we're on the same team. I have my mission, and apparently you can help in that. I'm not trying to be an asshole."

Jennifer said, "He's really not. It just comes naturally."

I scowled, and he chuckled. He said, "I'm David Periwinkle, and I don't work here in Monaco." Which was his way of saying he was much more important than to be stationed at a backwater like Monaco.

I said, "I know. We're trying to stop the passing of the Chinese penetration of OPM. Hell, your name might be on that list."

He shook his head and said, "No way are the North Koreans selling OPM data to the Syrians."

His arrogance was insulting. How the hell would he know more than everyone else?

I said, "Maybe they are, maybe they aren't. That's why I'm here. To figure it out."

He nodded, then said, "I'm not talking until the liaison arrives."

Jennifer, whose sole purpose was to sit back and record what I missed—mannerisms, offhand comments, reactions while I was focused on the conversation, all things that I would use later—touched my arm, and I turned, seeing Carly and Axe walking up from the harbor. Carly was a short girl with a bob cut. Axe was about six foot four, with a bald head and a beard. She looked like a surfer. He looked like the character you'd choose on Call of Duty.

They turned in, and then Carly caught my eye. I saw the hesitation. A split second of shame. I stood up, wanting to get to her before the asshole at the table could overhear. I heard Jennifer's chair slide back as well. I went to them, fist-bumping Axe, and then turned to Carly. I wrapped her in a hug and then, when I was close to her ear, said, "I heard. Makes no difference to me. You're still Carly, and I've seen your skill. Your choice. Not mine. Yours."

She pulled back from me, and I saw the relief. She was doing what she wanted, and appreciated my approval. She turned to Jennifer, which was an approval much greater than mine, and got the same response. But unlike me, Jennifer treated her as a friend, without any stigma of selection. Just hugged her like she missed her. Which, given Jennifer, was probably the best thing she could have done.

Axe said, "What's the story with the spook?"

I said, "He's an asshole. He's waiting on Carly."

Carly turned to me, and I said, "Yeah, you heard that right. He wants to talk to you. Won't talk to me."

She smiled and said, "I can't imagine why."

Jennifer said, "I can. You should have seen the initial meeting."

Carly started walking, saying, "I don't have to. I've seen it before."

I poked her in the shoulder from behind and hissed, "No fucking around here. The guy is a class-A dick. Jason Bourne, as far as he's concerned."

She turned around and said, "I deal with class-A dicks all the time. Trust me."

Axe scowled, and she said, "Present company excluded. I was talking about Pike."

He laughed, I frowned, and Carly smiled. And I knew we were good. I said, "Just work your CIA magic."

We sat down at the table, and Mr. Pencildicker, or whatever his name was, began telling us what he knew. Which wasn't much. He apparently had a source inside the Syrian Air Force intelligence section who was highly placed, and who said that no such transfer was going to happen. As far as Pencildicker was concerned, it was a waste of time. But he did offer to stay and validate any photos we got of the Syrian. Passing it up the chain and figuring out who he was. Typical.

We'd left there, letting Axe and Carly go first,

then went back to the hotel room for Jennifer to do her presto-chango thing again. While I waited, Knuckles showed up. He banged on the door, I let him in, and he said, "So?"

I said, "So about what you would expect. Nothing. He's willing to help when we get something, but nothing proactive."

"So the B and E is still on?"

"Yeah. We get eyes on him, and you punch the room. Get anything you can."

Jennifer came out of the bathroom, looking yet again like a heartbreaker, and Knuckles said, "You know, you're much better at the breaking and entering than I am. And I'm much better-looking than you."

I grinned and said, "Nice try. I'm going to the casino."

Jennifer walked over to him and said, "Help me?"

He zipped up her dress and said, "You know I'm the man for this mission."

She glanced at me and said, "Last time we did this, you tried to drown me. I'll take my chances with the Neanderthal."

He laughed and said, "As long as you guys keep eyes on the target. I don't want to be surprised."

I said, "No issues there. We need to go. Asshole agent man made us late."

He turned serious and said, "No, really, Pike. Veep's good, but he's not you. Don't let that guy or his security get back to the room without telling me. The protocols for ripping through his laptops or whatever else is up there will take an hour."

I nodded. "Don't worry about that. You'll have plenty of warning."

9

★ ★ ★

We reached the entrance to the famed Monte Carlo Casino, and Jennifer took my hand, looking for all the world like a Bond girl. Actually, better than most Bond girls. I squeezed it, and we passed by a bunch of tourists wearing cutoff jeans and tacky T-shirts. Not what I expected to see outside this glitzy casino. I was about to learn that everything I'd seen in a Bond movie was a Hollywood charade.

We entered the casino, dressed to the nines, like we thought we needed to be, and I felt like a child learning Santa Claus wasn't real. We walked through the ornate doors, into the cavern of the casino, and the best way I can describe it was that it was shabby. Worn down from years of use, it was basically one large room with a sparse collection of gaming tables. Two roulette wheels, two blackjack tables, and two craps pits. Outside of a bar on the left, that was it.

People turned to look at us—because the place

was that damn small—and Jennifer said, "I think we overdressed."

And we had. The actual gaming space was like a basement casino someone was running in Detroit. Where the hell was James Bond?

Jennifer asked the maître d', "Is this it?"

He sniffed and said, "This isn't Las Vegas."

I thought, **You got that right.**

I said, "We're going to the private rooms. Where are they?"

He pointed toward a doorway in the back and said, "Keep walking," apparently insulted that we weren't in awe.

We left him, crossing the room and entering an alcove with a couple of slot machines and very few people putting in coins. Vegas in a microcosm, but no James Bond to be found. To the right was a guy in a tux standing in front of a velvet rope. That was more like it. I went to him and said, "We'd like to play."

I showed him our key card from the hotel—which gave us access, because, my Lord, that damn place was expensive—and he let us in.

He parted the rope, and we finally saw people dressed like we were. There were two active tables, one with the entourage of Koreans, an Arab guy, and a married couple filling out the seats, the other included Axe, Carly, some guy in a cowboy hat, and a fat man in a suit, leaving one empty spot.

Both tables were playing five-card draw. Another busted myth. I was expecting Texas Hold'em.

I tugged Jennifer's arm to get her to slow down and called Brett on my earpiece, him currently eating ice cream and bored out of his mind.

"Blood, we're in. Target acquired at the poker table."

Like Jennifer, he didn't allow anyone to use his callsign unless it was on the radio, because they both hated the ones they were given. All I got back was, "Roger that. I guess I'm in for a long night."

I smiled and said, "Depends on how quickly I can lose Taskforce money. Side bet on me beating Axe?"

"No way. That guy is the worst player I've ever seen."

I said, "Good call."

"I see some of Johnny's team out here, doing the same thing I'm doing."

Johnny had dispersed like I had, hoping to follow the Syrian to a bed-down and search his room.

I said, "Roger that. Break, break, Knuckles, I have eyes on. You're cleared to enter."

I got, "Roger all. Tell me if there's a change. We're moving to the room now."

I poked Jennifer in the hip, and we walked to Axe's table. I took the one available seat, sandwiched between the cowboy and the fat guy. Axe was on the right end, with Carly behind him. I settled in to play, wondering how this would work now that there were no more seats at the table. How would the

Syrian show up here? And then thought that maybe the Arab **was** the Syrian.

I flicked my eyes to Axe, then to the Arab, and he shook his head. He'd already thought the same thing, and had somehow ascertained that the Arab was not the droid we were looking for. Or maybe he was, and it was a Jedi mind trick. I trusted Axe's judgment, but it paid to keep all options open.

After introductions—with Axe telling me his name was Sam, and Carly saying her name was Regina—we began playing. I knew I was pushing it by remaining in the room with the Korean, potentially burning me for long-term operations, but it didn't really matter. According to our intel, he was meeting the Syrian within the next twenty-four hours, and so I had this one mission tonight. If it was a bust, the Taskforce would figure out what to do, and tomorrow I'd be back looking at old bones in Eze.

After thirty minutes, my earpiece came alive, Knuckles telling me they were in. They had found a laptop and an iPad, were in contact with the reach-back hacker cell, and were starting to drain both.

Up until this point, I'll admit the fat guy had been crushing me. Well, both the cowboy and me, because Axe folded his damn cards at any call. Now, though, I was holding a full house, and I was going to drive that pot to the roof.

The fat guy was a pretty good player. He'd slowly drained my stack of chips, but then again, he was probably cheating, because there was no way he was beating me on skill. As I was about to show.

I bet, and it went around the table, everyone matching but Axe. Of course, he folded. When asked if I wanted more cards, I said no, vainly trying to channel all of the bland faces I'd seen in the World Series of Poker. I wished I'd brought my sunglasses.

The fat guy was next. He put down two cards, and I saw one of the Korean security men at the other table look at his phone, then lean into the target's ear, whispering something. I saw the Korean's eyes squint, then whisper back. The security man nodded, flicked his head to his partner, and left the room. Which was not good. We had the Korean as a target, but I couldn't let his counterparts leave without keeping eyes on. For all I knew, they were the ones meeting the Syrian.

I caught Axe's eye, and saw he felt the same way. The fat guy bit on my poker ploy, and raised the bet a considerable sum. **Damn it.**

I saw the other security man disappear from the room and folded, spitting out, "Take it. I have to use the bathroom."

I pushed my chair back harder than I wanted, asked the dealer to watch my chips, and stomped off, Jennifer behind me. We entered the main hall and the Koreans were nowhere to be seen. I said, "I've got to go back in there. You take the security men. Keep on them and see what they're up to. If they contact the Syrian, call me on the net, and I'll break Axe free."

She said, "You want me to do this alone?"

I held up a finger and said onto the net, "Blood, Blood, this is Pike, the Korean team has split in half. I still have control of the target, but have lost contact with the security detail. Koko's going to search in here, and if it's clean, she's on the way out. Keep eyes on the front door."

He came back immediately, saying, "I've got them. One's looking at his phone, the other's lighting a cigarette."

Jennifer heard the call and nodded. On the net, but looking at her, I said, "She's on the way out. Keep me abreast of what's going on, but I'll be back at the table and can't answer."

Jennifer turned to leave and, off the net, I said, "Hey, they could be meeting the Syrian, but they could be going back to the hotel room. Keep Knuckles in the loop."

She said, "You think that's a possibility?"

"Yeah. The timing is strange. We got the call that Knuckles was in, then they looked at their phone. He could have tripped something they set up."

She said, "Which means they'll be looking for the boogeyman."

I smiled and said, "Very good, young Jedi. Keep on them, but like a ghost. I don't want to have to come save you."

She grinned and said, "More likely I'll be back here telling you how to play cards."

I smiled and watched her fast-walk out. When she was gone, I went back to the table, seeing Axe had folded again. I took my seat and winked at him, showing absolute confidence that I didn't feel.

10

⁂

Tagir Kurbanov saw the man outside the ring, and knew he wasn't a spectator. He was something else. Tagir tapped gloves with his opponent and the bell rang, the two tearing into each other like lions over a kill. Tagir heard the crowd shouting, all of them fighters like him, and redoubled his efforts. He was, after all, from Dagestan. A country proud of its fighters.

He snapped two jabs, threw a right cross that missed, then was wrapped up by his opponent around the waist. Hoisted off the ground, he was slammed into the canvas, his opponent trying to succeed through brute force. He broke the hands around his waist, lashed out with an elbow, and connected, stunning his opponent. Which ended up being enough.

He leapt on the man with a ferocity born from fights where the vanquished lost much more than a simple match, pounding his opponent's face in strikes that caused a mask of blood, batting through the feeble attempts to block his blows.

The referee slapped him in the back, waving his arms that the fight was over, but Tagir didn't quit. The man's face began to split apart, his body lying unconscious on the canvas, and Tagir kept pounding it, trying to break bones. The referee grabbed him around the waist and forcefully threw him back. Tagir leapt up, about to attack him as well, and then snapped out of it, his conscious mind returning to the gym.

He felt embarrassment. He'd slipped time and believed he was somewhere else. Not in a ring, but in a fight to the death. Something he knew about.

The referee screamed at him, jabbing a finger in his face and telling him he was disqualified. He staggered away, seeing the man outside the ring again, waiting by the door to the gym.

He ducked under the ropes, heading to the locker room and ignoring the shouting from the other fighters. They didn't know what he did. They didn't know what a fight was like outside of a ring with a referee. He went inside, toweled off the sweat, sat on a bench, and waited.

The man entered, saying, "So you still fight."

"Yes. It pays the bills. Unlike you assholes."

The man laughed and said, "I guess you know who I am."

"I don't know you, but I know you work for Wagner. I could smell that stench above the sweat."

The man nodded. He was pasty and flaccid, but he held the air of power, something Tagir understood from his past employment. Unlike him, Tagir was hard. With deep-set eyes, jet-black hair, a nose that had been broken more than once, and a fight record that was solidified in the arena moments ago, Tagir looked like the killer he was.

The man said, "Yes, I do work for Wagner. My name is Dmitri Pavlov, and I've been instructed to hire you for a specific mission. A delicate mission."

Tagir smiled and said, "Like the Donbass? Like Aleppo? They're all 'delicate.' Cut the bullshit. What you mean is you want a Russian solution without a Russian fingerprint."

Wagner was the largest private military contractor in Russia, a country that actually forbade private military companies as illegal. But like most of the reality in Russia, it was only forbidden when the company in question wasn't advancing Russian interests. Wagner had fought in the Donbass region of Ukraine, and continued in the cauldron of Syria, allowing the country to say there weren't any Russian "military members" in those conflicts. Tagir himself had been to both, barely surviving an engagement in Syria where Wagner had decided that taking an oil refinery would be a good decision for its own monetary gain.

In February of 2018, they'd crossed the Euphrates River, a demarcation line adjudicated between the United States and Russia. An agreement that meant nobody would encroach without repercussions, but Wagner believed that it was a chimera. The United States wouldn't stop them, and the company had been promised 25 percent of the proceeds from a refinery in US-supported control. They went on their own. They'd advanced with Russian T-72 tanks and a battalion constructed of a motley crew of Syrian fighters mixed with Russian mercenaries, driving toward a refinery in the hands of Kurdish fighters under the protection of the United States.

They'd swiftly taken the terrain, the Kurdish fighters leaving the battlefield against the onslaught, and they'd begun to believe that they were the most powerful force in the land, watching the hated Kurds flee under the armored attack.

And then they'd learned a lesson that had rarely reared its ugly head. The United States had shown time and time again that they would promise protection, only to let that promise wither on the vine. This time was different.

Led by US Special Forces members on the ground, the pathetic vacillation of the past vanished. The Kurds began to fight back. And they brought the entire destructive force of the United States with them. The artillery and airpower was relentless, decimating the armored advance.

The entire mission ended up a fiasco, with the battalion wiped out—to include upward of two hundred dead and wounded Russian contractors—but the Russian high command simply buried the fact that actual Russians had died in the assault. The press stories went back and forth, with some breathlessly talking about how the United States had taken on the Russian "army," leading to World War III, and others saying it was a big lie in the mystical cauldron of Syria, but Tagir had learned a hard truth: It was all about the money.

He'd been evacuated with a leg wound, and had been instructed that his silence would pay dividends. He'd gone home to Dagestan, and as a reward for remaining quiet, had been given a choice slot in Ramzan Kadyrov's mixed martial arts academy.

As the head of the Chechen Republic, Ramzan had built a formidable entertainment machine called Akhmat MMA, full of propaganda and hype, and many clamoring to earn admittance. The children of Dagestan and Chechnya were fighters, and this was an honor. Ramzan, a fierce fighter himself, wanted to build a fighting academy rivaling the vaunted UFC in the United States, centering his entire reign on the results, something that his master, Putin, enjoyed. Everyone in the North Caucasus was a fighter, and it was better for them to be fighting one another than the Russian state.

Tagir had felt at home, enjoying the challenge and believing that the Russian state would honor its promise, but when he'd seen the man outside the ring, he'd realized there had been no reward for his silence. Only the advancing of what the state wanted. Perfecting his killing skills.

Tagir watched Dmitri take a seat on a bench, and opened his locker, saying, "What do you want of me?"

Dmitri said, "We require someone who protects the state. Someone who cherishes Russia."

Annoyed, Tagir turned to him and advanced, peeling off the bloodied hand wraps. He said, "Cut the bullshit. What do you want?"

Dmitri picked at some lint on his pants and said, "We want you to find a device. A phone. We have a friend from Syria who's lost it. We want you to find it, and then kill anyone who's seen it."

Tagir kept unwrapping his wrists, turning back to his locker. The silence dragged on, neither man speaking. Finally, he said, "Why me?"

"Because you know the Côte d'Azur. Because you work for Wagner."

"I don't anymore."

"Yes, you do. Or you'll lose everything that we've given you for your sacrifices."

Tagir turned around and said, "My sacrifices, or my silence?"

Dmitri said, "Call it what you want, but we need this device back."

Tagir closed his locker and turned around, saying, "What's in the device? Why?"

Dmitri shook his head and said, "You don't question. You execute."

Tagir smiled and said, "If you want my skill, you'll answer my damn questions. I'm not running to the sounds of the guns because you ask. I did that once before, and it didn't end well."

Dmitri hesitated, then said, "Look, the GRU is helping a man from inside Syrian intelligence. I don't know what they're doing—honestly I don't— but he's lost a phone that has sensitive data on it. It was stolen by a child. A street urchin. And we need to get that phone back. That's all I know. The GRU is going crazy over it. They asked if Wagner could help, and your name came up."

"So I get the phone back? That's it?"

"Yes. Well, you'll have to kill anyone who's potentially seen it."

Tagir paused, then said, "Kill them." Not a question. A statement.

"Yes."

"What's on that phone? What could be so important?"

"I have no idea. I get the contract, and I execute."

Dmitri reached into his pocket and pulled out a thick envelope. "Here's your plane ticket. The GRU is tracking the phone. You fly tonight. The phone is in Monaco."

Tagir took the papers and said, "I'm alone on this?"

Dmitri said, "Not at all. A lot of the property in and around Monte Carlo is owned by one Russian or another. We have contacts, and they'll facilitate your travel."

Tagir knew that to be true from the time he'd spent in the area. There were so many Russians that instead of French/English menus in the restaurants, they were French/Russian. He turned back to his locker, looking in the mirror.

He said, "When I kill them, will I be acknowledged by the state?"

"What do you mean?"

"I mean, I've killed many men for you, and nobody cares. My men have died, my brothers have been slaughtered, and you don't give a good Goddamn. For once, I'd like to be acknowledged, instead of hidden."

Dmitri stammered, then said, "We of course understand what you're doing for the motherland. We believe that—"

Tagir cut him off, saying, "You fucking sicken me."

Dmitri stood up, incensed, saying, "You work for the state, and that should be enough. You work for me. Your apartment, your stipend, your ability to fight in the arena is because of me. Say no, and go back to living on the streets of Dagestan."

Unfortunately for Dmitri, even after seeing the fight, he failed to realize the death that was in the room.

Tagir slowly turned and said, "You think you own me? Seriously? Give me your hand."

Confused, Dmitri said, "What?"

"Give me your hand!"

Hesitant, Dmitri held out his hand. Tagir took it,

rotated it around, and then placed his thumb on the joint of the center finger, holding it loosely and looking Dmitri in the eye. He said, "Is this for the state, or for Wagner?"

Dmitri said, "I don't understand."

Tagir said, "It's a simple question. Is this for the motherland or for your profits?"

Confused, Dmitri began trying to worm his hand away. He said, "You'll get a lot of money!"

Tagir pressed his thumb forward, torquing the hand to the left, controlling the joint. He looked into the eyes of Dmitri, seeing the pain. In that moment, Dmitri realized that money meant nothing to Tagir.

He shouted, "This isn't for Wagner! It comes from the highest levels. It's not for profit."

Tagir twisted the joint a bit harder, eliciting a yelp from Dmitri and causing him to fall to his knees. Tagir held the joint lock for a breath, then let go of the hand. He said, "I'll do it. But not for the money. Remember that, because if I find out you're lying, I'll pretend you've seen the phone."

He exited the room, leaving the Russian on the floor holding his damaged wrist.

11

★★

Jennifer exited the building and saw the two Koreans in front of her. She went down the steps, studiously ignoring them and keying her radio, "Blood, Blood, I'm out. You have me?"

He said, "Yeah, Koko, I got you. So does everyone else near me. I think they believe you're someone famous. They're all looking. Exit fast, or the Koreans are going to notice."

She did so, going past them into the street, saying, "They're probably wondering why I'm the only one dressed up. That place wasn't what I envisioned."

He said, "I see you. Keep going straight. I'll link up. And by the way, since Pike can't say anything on the net, can we just skip the callsigns?"

She kept walking, saying, "You'll get no argument from me."

Jennifer walked toward the fountain in front of the casino—a large circular mirror on a pedestal showing the reflection of the pool below. She used it to keep eyes on the two Koreans, seeing them descend the stairs. She said, "They're on the move. Where are you?"

She felt someone tap her on the shoulder, and jumped a little. Brett appeared next to her and admired her in the mirror. He said, "You look like a heartbreaker. Gonna be hard to say I'm your date for this surveillance effort."

She turned to him and smiled, saying, "Not hard at all. You should have seen who I started the night with."

He returned to the Koreans in the mirror and said, "I'm not seeing how we make this work. We stick out like a sore thumb with you in that getup. Pike should have left you inside. We don't look like we match."

Jennifer said, "It's not that bad. I'm dressed for a night out, and you're sort of dressed for a night out."

Brett said, "Too late anyway. Here we go."

Jennifer looked in the mirror and saw the Koreans circling around the fountain to the right. Brett slid his hand into hers and started walking left, on the opposite side of the fountain. He said, "What indicators do we have?"

"None, really. One used his phone, whispered to the target, he gave them an order, and then they left."

"Did he talk on the phone?"

"Nope. Just looked at it. Pike thinks it could be an alert from the hotel room. Speaking of which . . ." She keyed her earpiece and said, "Knuckles, Knuckles, this is Koko."

She heard, "Go."

"You get the call about the team splitting?"

"Yeah. You're on them, right?"

"I am. I'm with Blood now, and we've got eyes on, but Pike wanted to relay that they could be headed back to you. They left right after your call saying you were in."

"Pike thinks I hit a trip wire in here? Something they set up?"

"He doesn't know. He just wanted me to keep you on your toes."

"While he plays poker?"

She smiled and said, "Pretty much."

The Koreans went around the fountain gardens and entered the shopping area to the north of the casino, Brett and Jennifer falling in behind them. One of the Koreans glanced back, and both Jennifer and Brett caught the look.

Brett said, "We need to let 'em go."

Jennifer said, "If they circle to the west, they'll end up at the back entrance to the hotel."

"Nothing we can do about that. If Knuckles **did** trip an alarm, they'll know it was a team, and they'll be looking for the bad man behind them. We're getting hot. Gotta let 'em go for a second."

He keyed the radio and said, "Knuckles, this is Blood, our heat state is elevated. We've got to let them wander a bit before we reengage, but they might be headed your way. They'll be unsighted for a couple of minutes."

Knuckles came back and said, "Can you keep tabs at all, or does unsighted mean you might lose them?"

"We might lose them."

"Well, that's just great. What's the time hack to our location?"

Jennifer pulled a map up on her phone and whispered, "Five minutes. Maybe less."

Brett relayed, and Knuckles said, "We've got at least fifteen left. We need eyes on, fuck the heat state. I'm either breaking out of here now, mission abort, or staying, and I can't stay without eyes on."

Jennifer saw the Koreans disappear. Literally, they were in view one second and gone the next. She keyed her earpiece and said, "Knuckles, unsighted, I say again, unsighted."

He said, "I'm breaking down."

Brett said, "No, no. We're on them. They went down a stairwell. Hang on."

He sprinted across the gardens and found a slash in the ground. An escalator leading below the surface of the gardens. Jennifer said, "I read about this. There are tunnels underneath the streets all over the place here."

Brett stepped on the escalator, an electronic eye springing it to life, the noise spreading out like a fog. He said, "Come on."

They went down the short escalator, reaching the bottom, and Jennifer saw a tunnel snaking out left and right, empty, the lighting harsh, with shadows that reminded her of a horror movie. She whispered, "Which way?"

Brett held up a hand, and she remained mute. Then she heard them. The clacking of heels echoing in the empty tunnel. He pointed left, toward the hotel, and she nodded. They began following, and their own shoes began making noise, overshadowing the Koreans'. Brett stopped and whispered, "Take off your heels."

He removed his shoes, and she did the same, now barefoot. He whispered, "We're going fast." She nodded, and he took off at a trot. Not really a run, but with enough speed to overtake the echoes they were hearing.

They went about a hundred meters, and Brett stopped, holding his hand in the air. Jennifer strained her ears, but heard nothing. She saw Brett's expression, and realized he thought they'd missed them. Or they'd stopped and were conducting the meeting with the Syrian.

He pointed forward, and rounded another corner, moving fast, and she saw his head snap back like it had a string attached to it. One of the Koreans appeared, leaping at him and grabbing an arm. She saw Brett flip in the air and slam into the ground. She caught something out of the corner of her eye, then what felt like a baseball bat slammed into her side, knocking her into the wall. She bounced off it, falling to her knees. She looked up, seeing the other Korean man in a fighting stance. Behind him, she saw Brett struggling to rise, the first Korean on him, thumping him in the head.

Her enemy snapped his hips, whirling his leg in a tae kwon do spinning kick with enough force to crack her skull. Without conscious thought, she did what she'd been trained to do, an instinctive reaction born from relentless sessions with Pike. She sprang to her feet, and in the span of a microsecond, the foot whipping around, she executed, slamming her eyes closed just before impact, waiting on the pain.

She succeeded in deflecting the kick, leaching off the energy of the blow as she rotated around, and trapped the enemy's leg.

It staggered her, slamming her into the wall again, but in no way cracked any bones. Like catching an impossible pass, amazed the ball was in her hands, she opened her eyes, and was as surprised as he was at the turn of events. She saw his eyes widen in shock, and thought, **Yeah, asshole. Girl fights back.**

He began to spin to get out of her grasp, and she worked against him, twisting his knee and locking up his ankle. She pushed forward, using her body weight to fold the joint, driving her elbow into his thigh for a fulcrum and dropping to the ground. She heard the gristle snap, and then his scream. She released his leg and grabbed a handle of hair in both hands, slamming his head into the marble of the wall. He dropped without another sound.

She whirled to the other fight, seeing Brett on his back, with his legs locked around the neck of his opponent in a triangle choke, his hands controlling the Korean's arms. He fought back furiously, but Brett was relentless. The man went limp, and Brett took a breath, then kicked him away.

Brett touched his nose, the blood running freely, and said, "Shit, that didn't work out."

He rolled over, seeing the man she'd taken down, and said, "Remind me never to make fun of you again."

She smiled and pulled him to his feet, saying, "What do we do now?"

He withdrew a micro beacon the size of a quarter, slit a seam at the base of the Korean's jacket, and dropped it into the hole. He said, "Search them. That's all we can do. We're done for any further operations against these targets."

12

✦ ★ ✦

The sun spilled its fading light across the Côte d'Azur, a spectacular view spread across some of the most expensive real estate in the world, but Amena was not impressed, having seen it every day for the past two months. Sitting on the roof of the old fort, she was more enthralled with her new iPhone X.

She had intended to go into town and sell it today, but she couldn't bring herself to do so, clinging to it like Gollum's ring. Amazingly, the phone had been unlocked, and her first order of business had been to change all the security parameters. After she had complete control, she'd used the data connection to access the Internet. Unlike most of the civilized world, she didn't often have the chance to visit the World Wide Web, and was reluctant to give up the phone. She knew eventually the Syrian would shut off the connection, but until he did, she could search the internet for news stories of her homeland, and watch YouTube videos of the United States. She knew Aleppo was lost to her, but someday, she was going to America, and she wanted to know how to act when she did.

She was fascinated by Kim Kardashian, endlessly watching clip after clip of her television show, convinced that the Kardashian family was stereotypical of the United States. Midway through the latest video, the phone died. She'd stolen a lightning port charger, but had forgotten to use it last night.

She sighed, put the phone in her jacket pocket, and let her legs dangle over the roof of the fort, not wanting to go back inside just yet. She finally noticed the view, seeing the village of Eze below her, the Moyenne Corniche snaking in front of the hill the town was built on.

Like the aquarium, Eze was one of her favorite places in her new land. She told Adnan that it was because it was full of tourists, and thus ripe for fleecing, but in reality, it reminded her of home. Of Aleppo. It was an ancient town not unlike her own destroyed city, complete with narrow cobblestone footpaths and stone structures built eons ago. She loved wandering its alleys pretending she was home. A bittersweet feeling, because she knew she was never going back to Aleppo. Not after her mother had been slaughtered.

Her father had realized that remaining in Syria would be a death sentence for the remainder of his family, regardless of whether it came from the rebels or the government. Using every bit of money he had, he'd bought the family a way to Europe through the notorious smuggling industry that had sprung to life after the civil war had turned into a bonfire. Once a respected pharmacist—a man of means—he'd been reduced to a rat on the run. He'd done what he could to save them, and now worked as a janitor in a hotel. She understood why they'd made the perilous journey, but still couldn't come to grips with the fact that she was an alien in a land that hated her, for no other reason than she'd fled a land that hated her. It was confusing.

She saw a flash of headlights on the road leading to the fort and pulled her legs up, away from view. Two men exited the car, and she immediately thought they were geocaching—a game where people placed items in caches around the countryside, and then posted them online for others to find with a GPS. The fort had a couple of caches, and she'd met the players in the past. Geocachers would be the only people who came to the park after it closed. It had happened before.

The driver of the vehicle studied what she thought was a GPS, the screen glowing on his face. She saw he was tall, and not a teenager—the usual types who did the searching. He was old. Maybe even thirty. And he was big. He looked like an athlete, even through the clothes. The other man was slender, with a large gold chain around his neck. He, too, was older than the usual cache hunters.

The driver turned to the gold chain and said, "It disappeared."

Amena was surprised he was speaking English, even more so because his accent was Russian.

Gold Chain said, "What do you want to do?"

"It's here. We just need to search for it. Someone turned it off. There was a light at the back of this place. We'll start there."

The driver stowed his device and stalked into the park. She knew where the cache was from previous attempts, and waited on him to start down the hill, toward the fence line at the base of the park. He did not. He circled directly underneath her, heading toward her new home.

They had been granted a small room at the back of an old French defensive fortification called Fort de la Revère, plopped in the center of a national park. An ancestor of the Maginot Line, ensconced in hectares of walking paths, the fort had been built in the nineteenth century because the terrain could control the coast. It was now a place where tourists came for the same reason—because it was the best place to obtain a view of the coast. It had last been used in World War II to house British pilots who had been captured, and her family now lived in what had once been a prison. And still was one, to a certain extent.

While their corner had intermittent power, allow-ing them to use a space heater and a small electric stove, the rooms were definitely austere, with noth-ing more in the way of modern conveniences, forcing them to walk down the hill to a construction site to use porta potties and fill water buckets from an outside faucet. She didn't complain, because she knew the risks the people who'd helped them were taking.

They had made the arduous crossing of the Mediterranean in a leaky dhow with fourteen other families. Just shy of the Italian shore, the boat had capsized, spilling all of them into the water. Bobbing among the waves, the refugees all fighting for a piece of flotsam to stay above the water, the Italian navy had arrived, saving their lives.

They'd been transported inland to a brutal refugee camp on the French-Italian border with the nickname the Jungle, where Amena had earned her first taste of the hatred and fear she brought with her.

After a month living like animals, her father had had enough. He'd begun seeking options, eventually meeting a kind old man who'd turned his retirement years into building an underground railroad. They'd been spirited across the border in the dead of night, then given the contact of a Frenchman who worked for a nongovernmental organization specializing in renewable energy. On the side, he helped refugees escape the squalor of the camps.

He'd facilitated their travel into France, and had set them up at Fort Revère, where he had a contract with the French government to build a plethora of sustainable energy projects, to include an education facility to showcase his efforts, which was key, because it meant the old fort had been provided power.

They had been at the fort for nearly two months, and she could tell her father was growing tired again, just as he had in the camp. He had been an important man with a college degree, and it grated on him to mop floors, especially since the majority of French people were unwelcoming toward refugees.

They needed to get deeper into Europe. To Germany, or even Norway, and her father had told her it would happen, but in her mind's eye the United States was the prize. If she could get there, the world would open up. Everyone hated her here, but she'd read the stories about the United States. They didn't care where you came from. There was no such thing as a French superiority complex or Nordic royalty in America. They only cared if you would work to achieve what you wanted. And she knew she could work. She doubted many in America had dodged barrel bombs just to get a bucket of water.

She watched the men circle the edge of the fort and continue on. She scurried across the roof to keep pace. They continued straight to the corner, where the light from her father's single lamp spilled out, and she became alarmed. She ran to a roof access, a bastion porthole to allow the reloading of guns that no longer existed, and one her father kept open to facilitate a breeze through their little corner of the old prison. She looked down, and saw her father quizzing Adnan about their activities the day before.

He had no idea his children had become common

pickpockets, and she had no desire to disabuse him of the notion that they were just scampering about, acting like kids the world over. She knew he hated leaving them alone, feeling he was failing them, but she understood it was the opposite. She was failing **him** by her actions, but in her mind it was necessary. He didn't want to confront how they existed. He didn't ever question how they had more milk than they should have, or had a meal when they should be eating dirt. His paltry earnings as a janitor in no way matched the money she made fleecing tourists. He chose to pretend. And now that mistake was coming home.

She leaned into the gap in the roof, caught Adnan's eye, and the men knocked on the door. She retreated from view.

Startled, her father looked at Adnan, then went hesitantly to the door. He cracked it, his face reflecting fear. He said, "Yes?"

The man said, "**As-Salaam-Alaikum.**" And Amena felt her own fear sink deep into her belly. Nobody who spoke English with a Russian accent would also speak Arabic. He was something special.

Confused, not knowing if he should slam the door closed or talk, her father gave the answer, "**Wa-Alaikum-Salaam.**"

In English, the man said, "My Arabic is a bit rusty. May I come in?"

Her father said, "Why? Who are you?"

The man smiled and said, "I'm your worst nightmare, or maybe your best friend. You have a cell phone that was stolen, and I've been tasked to get it back. I can pay in money, or pay in blood."

She saw the confusion on her father's face, and felt the heat of the phone in her pocket. He said, "I have no idea what you're talking about. How did you find us here?"

And the man quit the charade of civility. He slammed the door open, saw Adnan scampering to escape, and grabbed him by the throat. He said, "Tell me where the phone is, and I'll let him live. I don't have time to negotiate."

Her father stammered in shock, and Adnan said, "Amena has it! Amena has it!"

Stunned yet again, her father stood mute. The man said, "Where is Amena?"

Her father didn't answer, and the man looked down at Adnan and said, "Did you play with the phone?"

He said, "Yes, but just to look at the Internet. I'm sorry. We didn't do anything bad with it. It still works, and she has it. She'll give it to you."

He said, "Too late for that."

He placed one hand on her brother's skull, the other on his throat, bent his head back, and a snap reverberated through the old cell, like a dry stick broken over a knee. It was that quick. He let the body drop, and Amena felt her world collapse, a blighting of the sun, a retreat from humanity that she'd only felt once before, when they'd found her mother's body. An impotent rage consumed her, just as it had staring at her mother's broken corpse. The fragility of human existence was driven home yet again, only this time she was at fault.

She rolled over onto the roof, taking in great gasps of air, and heard the man talk again.

"Where is Amena? I need that phone."

Her father screamed, a feral, animal sound, and she rolled over to the hole. She saw her father attack the man, then saw the man stop the assault like he was batting a kitten away.

Gold Chain wrapped her father in his arms, and the driver put a blade to his neck, holding him still. He said, "Where is the phone?"

Her father struggled, babbling incoherently, and the driver said, "Is it in here?"

Her father lashed out with a foot, kicking the driver in his groin, causing him to double over. When the man rose, she saw the rage, and he drew the knife across her father's carotid arteries, the head falling back and exposing a gaping wound, the blood jetting over her father's shirt. Amena screamed. The driver let the body drop, and looked up. Amena saw the lifeless eyes staring right into hers.

He said, "Come down here, girl."

She fell back, and then began running to the front of the fort, hearing her steps echoing off the stone.

13

★★★

David Periwinkle looked at the grainy image in front of him and thought, **What the hell is he doing here?**

He'd been aggravated at getting jerked from Turkey to assist some ridiculous SOCOM gung ho military team, knowing they'd be a clown fest, but now they'd actually found something. Last night, they'd done their usual bull-in-a-china-shop routine and gotten into a fight with the North Korean agents, something he'd expected to happen because those jerks had no idea how espionage worked. But instead of pulling back, they'd forged ahead, swapping out teams. The only smart thing they'd done. The other team had picked up the follow, which had led to the man in the photograph.

A man Periwinkle recognized. They'd actually found a connection between North Korea and the upper echelon of the Assad regime. Unfortunately, they'd also found his most highly placed source in the wilderness of mirrors that was Syria. And now

Periwinkle had to make a choice—was this mission worth the price the United States would pay for losing access? If they took this guy down, Periwinkle—and the United States—would lose the ability to see inside the Syrian machine. Was the OPM hack worth that? The data was already out in the wild, and there was nothing the US could do about it. China could give it to anyone it wanted, and that country wasn't in Periwinkle's portfolio. His area of expertise was Syria, something he considered much more important to US national security.

He knew the team was going to take the Syrian down tonight in some misguided attempt at closing off an intelligence leak that had already happened, like closing the barn door after the horses had fled. When they did so, they'd close off all intelligence into the Assad regime.

He tapped his pencil on the table, trying to make a judgment. Trying to justify what he was about to do. He decided the intelligence coming out of the source was too sensitive to risk. What General Yasir al-Shami could provide the United States was much more important than a two-year-old hack, and Periwinkle was his sole contact.

Yasir had broken off all contact when the United States had begun backing the Kurds in the fight against the regime, and then, one month ago, he'd resurfaced, promising a final burst of intelligence before dropping off the net yet again. Surprisingly, just two days ago, he'd reinitiated contact through an intermediary in Turkey. Periwinkle hadn't even had time to shack up a cable reflecting the news because he'd been pulled into this Monaco fiasco, and now the general was here, about to be taken down.

He reached into a bag at the feet of the desk in the makeshift embassy office he'd been given and pulled out a flip phone. He dialed a number, knowing the Syrian would have a similar phone with him. Or at least he hoped the general did. For both of their sakes.

14

★
★ ★

Colonel Kurt Hale booted up his laptop, typing in the multiple passwords required to get past the NSA type-one encryption standards. He watched the members of the Oversight Council fill their seats while he waited. He saw Secretary of State Amanda Croft enter, then approach. **Uh-oh.** None of the council ever talked to him before he briefed. They didn't want to appear as if they supported what he was about to say, knowing they would have to vote on the outcome afterward. It was an unwritten rule, and one that he liked. All he wanted to do was brief and get out. He didn't come to these meetings to make friends.

George Wolffe, his deputy commander, stood up in an effort to intercept her, but it did no good. She ignored him as if he were a stray cat. At thirty-five, she was younger than most who'd held the post, but before getting tapped for the SECSTATE job, she'd been a fire-eater at a global energy company, and had worked all over the world spinning deals with every country on earth, be they despots destroying human rights or liberal democracies. Kurt was sure she was a ball-breaker, not the least because she was attractive, an attribute he knew had worked against her in the rarefied corporate air where she strived to be seen as intelligent.

She reached him, and he waited, unsure of what to say.

She said, "Before this gets started, I want you to know that I will not use emotion in my vote. I want you to understand that."

He nodded, confused.

She said, "And I'd appreciate discretion in this matter. It will have no effect when it comes to my vote, and there's no reason for the rest of the Council to start second-guessing my actions based on my personal life."

Now really confused, he said, "Yes, ma'am. I understand."

She took her seat, and Kurt caught George's eye. He just shrugged. He had no idea what the discussion was about either.

Kurt saw two Secret Service men enter, sweep the room, then one talked into a radio. Ten seconds later, the president of the United States, Philip Hannister, entered. A slender man with thinning gray hair, he looked more like the economist he was than the president, but Kurt knew from experience the bifocals he wore hid a spine of steel. A man who never wasted words, President Hannister took his seat and simply nodded.

Knowing that everything he said was going on the record, Kurt started with an introduction: "As requested by the Council, this is the update briefing on Operation Nickel Steel, the first joint CIA/ Taskforce operation."

He punched a button and a long-view picture of a group of men appeared on the screen behind him.

"As you know, through CIA assets, we had positive identification of a North Korean asset attempting to pass security information of US intelligence and DoD members gleaned through the Chinese OPM hack in 2015. Because the CIA had no capability to interdict, you granted me Alpha authority to explore, with follow-on Omega authority for a takedown if we confirmed a meeting with Syrian assets."

Kurt paused, knowing the next part was going to aggravate the many members of the Council who'd said that this mission was outside the Taskforce portfolio. Tasked with counterterrorism only, he couldn't argue that point. But he followed orders, and when directed, he had executed.

He flipped the slide, revealing a close-up photo of an Asian man with two security personnel. "This was our target, and we successfully breached his room, where we gathered significant intelligence, but—"

Amanda Croft interrupted, "What do you mean 'was' your target?"

Kurt took a breath and said, "We were forced to interact with the security detail in a manner that would preclude the team continuing surveillance."

Croft said, "What does that mean?"

"We believe the Korean team had established an electronic intrusion alarm in their room. A trip wire, basically, and when we breached the room, they were alerted. In order to finish the sweep of the room, we were forced to interdict them."

"Meaning you did what, exactly?"

He smiled and said, "We did what we do. We removed them from the equation in a nonlethal manner."

The national security advisor, Alexander Palmer, interjected, saying, "You had no authority for that."

Instinctively, Kurt smelled blood in the water, with skittish members of the Council looking for any reason to question this mission. He worked quickly to shut down the line of inquiry lest it derail the rest of the briefing, most notably, his request for future activities.

He said, "Sir, they initiated, not us. They attacked our team, and we removed the threat. They were not permanently harmed, and in so doing, we successfully extracted intelligence from electronic devices in the room. In addition, we placed a beacon on one of the security men, which led to this man."

Before he could get another question, he flipped the slide to a picture of a black-haired male with a thick mustache.

Kurt said, "This is the Syrian, still unidentified. Using the beacon we'd placed on the Korean, we located the meeting site, a restaurant on the waterfront of the harbor. Two Koreans met him there, and we saw him pass a cell phone across. The Koreans did something with the phone, and handed it back. That was the extent of the meeting, although the team did report that it wasn't a cordial affair. The Koreans looked decidedly aggravated, and the Syrian looked scared. We ran the picture by the CIA case officer provided by Kerry, and he had no idea who the man is."

Kurt turned to the D/CIA and said, "Kerry, anything to add?"

"Not really. The case officer we pulled from Turkey knows more about Syrian personalities than anyone on earth. In the past, he's run sources deep inside the Assad regime. If he couldn't get a positive ID, nobody can."

President Hannister said, "So they passed the data?"

Kurt said, "Maybe. We're not sure. Using a separate team, we followed him to his bed-down at a hotel in Monaco, and we were preparing to duplicate what we did with the Koreans, but just before walking in here I was informed that he'd disappeared."

Croft said, "What do you mean?"

"He checked out of the hotel and vanished. We couldn't keep eyes on him twenty-four/seven without compromising our team, and in a gap in coverage, he left."

Palmer said, "Which is why this should have been a CIA operation."

Kurt said, "Sir, manhunting is what we do. It's our specialty, and we're better at it than anyone else on earth, but we can't work miracles. This isn't some Hollywood movie. He had a reservation for two more days. The gap in coverage was prudent while we dedicated assets to researching and defeating the hotel security."

Palmer scowled, and looked at the D/CIA for support. Instead, Kerry nodded his head, saying, "Even if I'd had a team there, we couldn't do what you ask. We have to deal with the real world. It's not a Taskforce mistake. Every indicator was we had the time, and if you have the time, you use the time. You don't push the issue. It's like the Syrian's command called him away for some reason. It happens. You can't predict it."

Inwardly, Kurt smiled, because now was the time for the vaunted CIA to throw the Taskforce under the bus, and yet Kerry had not. Kurt was glad for the support. He kept his expression neutral, but nodded slightly when Kerry caught his eye.

Palmer turned away from the D/CIA and said, "So what now? Just let them have the data?"

"No, sir. The team that was compromised also gleaned significant data from the Korean's hotel room. From their communications pattern, we've located a node inside a server farm in Switzerland. The node shows the same fingerprints that were used on the

North Korean hack of Sony in 2014. It's a gateway, and possibly the repository of the OPM data."

President Hannister said, "But if he's already passed it to the Syrian, what's the point?"

Kerry held up a hand, saying, "May I?" Kurt nodded.

Kerry turned to the president and said, "The passing of the OPM data to the Syrian is not optimal by any stretch, but there is still intelligence to be gleaned by learning exactly **what** was passed. We **think** we know what China got from the hack, but it would be better to know positively, so we can mitigate it. If they've got a lead, I say let them go."

President Hannister took that in, then turned back to Kurt. "So, what, exactly, are you asking?"

Kurt took a breath and said, "Pike Logan's team was the one forced into compromise. I had to get them clean from Monaco, so I sent them to Switzerland. They're currently buying space on the same server farm. Give me the word, and I'll penetrate that farm and learn everything the Koreans are doing."

Palmer said, "You're already executing a mission?"

"No, sir, I'm just executing Alpha. All they're doing is taking a tour of the location and asking for pricing. You tell me to quit, and they'll be on the first thing smoking back to America."

Palmer shook his head, convinced Kurt was subverting the chain of command. He said, "Now's the time to put this back into the box. Let the CIA explore the server farm. I'm sure they can do it remotely. Get the Taskforce back on their charter. I understand why we used them for the initial mission, but this is traditional intelligence work, and we don't need to be expanding their portfolio."

Expecting this, Kurt said, "It's the Council's call, but understand that the Swiss farm was chosen for a reason. It's in an old cold war bunker built to withstand a nuclear blast, and has more digital security than the CIA itself. A remote penetration could take up to half a year. We want the information, then it's going to have to be physical, and Pike has already done the reconnaissance. The CIA could most certainly do the mission but"—he looked at Kerry Bostwick—"I don't think they could execute for at least a month, is that right?"

Kerry nodded and said, "We could do it with TAO, but I'd have to create a team, read on the chief of station in Bern, then conduct detailed planning. He's right. If Pike's already done the legwork, there's no reason to switch horses. We might lose the data, and I'm not looking for a turf war."

Kurt breathed a sigh of relief, then heard Alexander Palmer snort. He said, "This is getting out of control. The Taskforce mission is counterterrorism, and lately it's been anything but. Last time it was a coup in Lesotho, now it's this. We're breaking the damn charter for convenience."

Kurt said nothing, watching the president rub his eyes in contemplation, and then he received support from a least expected quarter.

Amanda Croft said, "Sir, I see the wisdom of what Kerry is saying. If the CIA doesn't have the assets, and we're concerned about national security, then why are we dancing around who does the mission? Is the Taskforce charter that sacred?"

She was fairly new to the Council, and to government, but that wasn't the shocking part to Kurt. Clearly, she didn't understand the ramifications of what she was proposing, but the true seismic shift was having a secretary of state actually advocate for a military operation. It was a first for Kurt, as all previous SECSTATEs had been one stick-in-the-mud after another, demanding diplomatic solutions and fighting anything he did.

He hid his surprise and waited. Hannister looked up and said, "Okay. Put it to a vote." Which was the same as saying, **I agree with the mission, will anyone tell me I'm wrong?** Technically, the Council could, but Kurt knew they wouldn't.

Five minutes later, it was over, execute authority granted. Kurt was policing up his laptop when President Hannister approached. Kurt stopped what he was doing, saying, "Sir?"

Hannister waved away the Secret Service member near him, then said, "Is Nick on this mission?"

Taken aback, Kurt paused, then said, "Yes, sir, he is. He's on Pike's team."

Hannister pulled his glasses off his face and pretended to clean them, saying, "Pike. Yes. We've had a few bits of high adventure with him."

Kurt said, "Yes, that's true. But every one has been in our favor. Don't forget that."

Hannister put his glasses back on, patted Kurt on the shoulder, and said, "Okay, Kurt. If you say so."

He walked out of the room, leaving Kurt to wonder about the exchange, and then Amanda Croft approached. He thought, **What the hell is going on**, and she said, "My vote wasn't swayed by anything other than national security. Remember that."

Confused again, he said, "Yes, ma'am. I know."

She said, "Is Knuckles in Switzerland with Pike?"

She'd met Knuckles on a previous Oversight Council presentation, and Kurt was surprised she'd remembered him. Unfortunately, the president asking about his son was one thing, but this was breaching protocol.

He said, "Ma'am, I can't tell you that. The Council controls overarching permission for operations, but I control the tactical execution. It's for both our protection."

A little miffed, she said, "I understand," and walked out of the room without another word.

Kurt finished packing up his equipment, the room now empty except for George Wolffe. Kurt said, "Let's get the hell out of here before someone else asks me a personal question."

George said, "What on earth was that with the SECSTATE?"

"I don't know, but I'm going to find out."

15

✦✦
✦✦

Panting in terror, Amena sprinted to the front of the fort, then flung herself over the roof, hanging on with her hands. She dropped to the ground and began running downhill, away from the building. Away from the horror it held. The image of her father's neck split in two was burned into her brain, her brother underneath his feet, his dead eyes staring at the ceiling. She couldn't think straight. Truth be told, she couldn't think at all, just like when the boat sank, and they had all fought for survival in the Mediterranean Sea, screaming and begging for someone to save them. Only this time, she knew it was just her. She was all that was left. There was no Italian navy. There were only two men who wanted to kill her for a phone she'd stolen.

She heard the footsteps of the killers rounding the corner, and a powerful flashlight splashed over her. She heard, "There!" and she took off down the side of the slope, running pell-mell through the brush.

She turned to look behind her and hit the chain-link fence at the base of the park head-on, slamming into it and bouncing back to the ground. She saw the flashlights coming toward her. She leapt up, scaled the fence, and fell to the other side.

She picked herself up and ran down the hill, the bushes slapping and cutting at her as she went. She hit a rock and tripped, falling forward and rolling, bouncing downhill until she slammed into a tree. Her breath knocked out, she remained still.

To her right was a ribbon of road lined with another chain-link fence, the first before she reached the main highway of the Moyenne Corniche. She saw the flickering lights of the expensive houses hidden in the woods and thought about running to them, but she knew the residents would probably just turn her over to the men chasing her. Everyone here in the land of the rich saw her as a threat. Everyone hated her.

She lay on the ground, catching her breath, a part of her wanting to quit. Wanting it all to end. She had nothing left, and was tired of running, both literally and figuratively.

Her mother swam into her vision, and she heard her voice, telling her a mantra she had chanted throughout the bombardment of their city, whenever the darkness fell and they'd fought for pure survival.

If it is to be, it is up to me.

The words grew louder in her head, a mantra giving her strength. **IF IT IS TO BE, IT IS UP TO ME.**

She saw her mother's visage, prodding her, telling

her to fight. The kind eyes, the loving touch. The iron will. She squeezed her eyes shut, focusing on her mother's face, then leapt up with renewed energy. **She** was the one in control here, not them. She knew where she was, having walked these woods every single day from the Eze train station. They could chase her, but only she knew where she was going.

She scrambled over the fence next to the ribbon of asphalt and crossed the road. She sprinted faster than she should have down the hill, heading toward the coast, and felt a drop of water on her arm. Rain? She kept going, then felt another. She stopped, holding her arm up in the dying twilight. She saw red, the same red that had gushed out of her father's neck. The memory slammed into her, and she sagged to the ground, dazed, wondering if it was his, staring at the blood on her arm in the fading light as if it held her father's life force.

She realized that couldn't be, and snapped out of her trance, frantically searching her body. She discovered a scalp wound leaking blood down her face and mixing with her sweat. She gingerly touched it, and found it was just a scratch. Something that had happened during her fall.

She pressed a hand against it and considered her options, now of sounder mind. She decided to get to the Eze train station and leave, creating as much distance as she could between the men hunting her and here. Get to Nice or Monaco.

She heard rocks spilling down the slope and

snapped her head upward. Only one light was coming down now, much more slowly than she had. She
couldn't believe it. One of them was still chasing her.

She began slipping down the slope at a speed that
would have been out of control, but she used the
trees to maintain her pace, slapping a hand against a
trunk or branch like a gymnast on the uneven bars.
Something she used to do with Adnan on their daily
trek to the train station. Before, it had been for fun.
Now it was saving her life.

She barreled down the hill, hearing the man shout
at her. What on earth did they want? Was the phone
that important to them?

She spilled onto the shoulder of the Moyenne
Corniche, the middle road between the famed
Grande Corniche at the top of the mountain chain
and the Basse Corniche along the coast, and the
same sad road Princess Grace Kelly had died on. She
saw a car approaching, and she jumped out to flag it
down. The car slammed on its brakes and she ran to
the driver's door. It opened, and a man stepped out,
wearing a gold chain.

One of the killers.

She stumbled back, and he shouted at her. She
sprinted across the blacktop, heading toward the
parking lot of the Eze mountain village, a primordial
survival instinct taking hold, all thought of the train
station gone.

She heard the door slam and the car spin its tires,
coming after her. She ran through the lot, dodging

between the scattered cars until she reached a tourist information hutch. It was closed. She looked behind her and saw the headlights of the car gunning toward her location, and a flashlight bouncing down the slope across the Corniche. They were still coming.

She ran up the cobblestone path that led into the heart of Eze. She passed a restaurant at the base, people staring at her from an outdoor eating area. She thought about running into the restaurant, but feared that in the confusion they'd just turn her over to the men. She had no doubt that her enemies would be able to talk their way through anything. Or just kill her outright. She needed to evade them, and that would mean evading everyone else.

She realized she was making a scene and slowed to a walk. The sun had finally set, leaving the path in a murky gloom that she hoped would hide the blood and her disheveled appearance.

She kept walking up the hill, into the town, going into an area she knew well, but it wasn't without risk. The village was pedestrian only, with a rat warren of alleys, cobblestone lanes, and shops every step of the way. The entire town had one entrance— which meant one exit. When she passed the stone arch into the town proper, she would have effectively locked herself in. But it was too late to change now. She certainly couldn't go back to the parking lot.

She passed through the arch, and saw another problem. A major tourist attraction, the mountain village had changed from a defensive fortification to one infested with cafés, eateries, art galleries, and hotels. Unfortunately, she'd spent so much time in Eze that she was known, and on her last trip, she'd found that the store owners had banded together, keeping an eye out for her and her brother. Like the parade ground, she didn't pickpocket here too often, but she'd visited much more, and they'd made the connection—or at least suspected. She and her brother had been chased out on their last visit with threats to call the police.

At this hour most of the art galleries and shops were still open, and if the owners saw her, they might alert her pursuers of her location. Or even help in the pursuit if the men chasing her proclaimed she had stolen a phone from them.

She sidled up the rough steps, avoiding the light from an art gallery built into the stone like a cave. One she used to enjoy visiting because of the paintings of the shoreline, fantasizing about hanging one over a fireplace in America. The shop owner had always been nice to her, but she couldn't trust that now.

A few steps farther was another shop on the opposite side of the alley. A cheap tourist store, with the dragon lady who had chased her and her brother out days earlier. She passed the first one on the stone wall to the right, and then began to slink past the other on the left, avoiding the feeble light. She saw the owner outside, talking to a tourist, and paused.

And then she heard the pounding footsteps behind

her. She turned, and saw Gold Chain coming up the stairs at a trot. He recognized her, and began sprinting. The store owner heard the commotion, and turned to look, locking eyes with Amena. She saw the woman scowl, and her world shrank.

She took off running past the store, hearing the owner shout at her about the police. She took the first staircase to the right, knowing it led to a little patio with the first fountain the village had ever seen. Built in 1930, it had once been a focal point for the entire town, as before then, from the village's creation in medieval times, every bit of water had to be brought up the mountain from the valley below on the backs of the people living there.

The history only mattered to her because she knew the small square had no shops for the owner to coordinate a response, only the residences of the historical families who had lived in Eze for generations.

She scrambled up the steps and entered an open area of about thirty feet, with doors and alleys leading off it. She darted behind the fountain, hiding in the dark. She heard Gold Chain run past her, continuing on, and breathed a sigh of relief. Then she heard another set of pounding feet.

She peeked around the fountain, and saw the man who'd killed her brother.

Unlike his partner, he was scanning left and right, exploring. He was within seconds of finding her. She panicked, breaking from her cover and running up the stairs, following the man with the gold chain.

She heard the footsteps behind her and knew she was now trapped. Her only hope was that Gold Chain had run past the next intersection, the one that led to the church.

Her lungs on fire, begging her to stop, she continued, the mantra in her head,

If it is to be, it is up to me.

She reached a turnoff to a steep rock path that led down into a winding garden near the church. Gold Chain had kept going. She'd lucked out.

She bounded down the rough stone, hearing the killer behind her follow. She reached the dirt path, a drop to her right falling a hundred feet down into the valley and a cliff to her left rising up to the top of the mountain, but she knew the garden was split with multiple paths. All she had to do was keep him from knowing which one she'd taken.

The path widened, and she entered the church's courtyard, her confidence faltering at the sight in front of her. The place was full of ropes and tape for some sort of excavation, all of it hindering her ability to maneuver. The only path open was to the right, and she took it, wanting to keep ahead of the man behind her.

She circled around the church, still running. She reached a split in the trail—a rough stone stairwell leading to the ancient remains of the citadel at the top of the mountain, and another one leading lower, circling around the mountain to a garden area with a view of the coast. She slowed, not wanting to give away her choice.

She heard the man behind her, his feet slapping the pavestones surrounding the church, and went up, now no longer running, but moving as silently as she could, hoping he would think she was trying to escape back down the mountain.

She reached the crest of the citadel, a stone structure that was now nothing more than a few pillars and a viewing deck, and paused, listening. The footsteps grew fainter. The trick had worked. She smiled, and then heard a scuffling in front of her.

She peeked over the edge and saw Gold Chain circling the perimeter of the flagstones, looking for her. He went to the edge that overlooked the lower path she'd avoided, staring at something. She heard a shout, and knew the killer of her brother was down there, looking up from seventy feet below. He would tell the man she hadn't come that way. He would get the man to search the other trail.

They would find her.

Gold Chain leaned over the railing, holding a hand to his ear, and she shot out from the stairwell, running right at him. He was so focused on the killer below that he didn't hear her coming until she was within ten feet. He whirled around, and she hit him just above the waist, using the low railing as leverage.

His mouth opened in shock, and he grabbed her

arm. She kept pushing, and he went over, screaming, ripping the sleeve of her shirt. She watched him fall in what seemed like slow motion, his mouth open, his legs flipping over and his arms flailing to stop the inevitable. He screamed all the way down, the sound cut short when he slammed into a concrete bench with his back, his head hitting a rock and exploding open like a watermelon.

She stared with an open mouth, not able to turn away from what she'd done. She'd taken a life. Killed just like they had.

The man who'd snapped her brother's neck ran to the body, and then looked up. She saw the lifeless eyes again, and realized he didn't even care what she'd done. All he wanted was her.

She saw him turn around and sprint back the way he'd come, and she knew she'd won. She had to beat him to the lower level, but he didn't know Eze like she did. Didn't realize that the paths wound around like spaghetti, and for every one entrance, there were two or three exits.

She ignored the way she'd come and ran to the citadel's primary entrance, skipping down the stone steps three at a time, knowing that he would have to circle the entire church facility, and she'd be able to slip by him.

She reached the lower level, the church entrance she'd taken before to her left, and heard a shout, sending a bolt of fear through her. Then she heard footsteps in front of her.

She had no idea who they were, but she certainly couldn't stop. She entered back into the maze of alleys, and ran headlong into two gendarmes coming up the stairs, followed by the evil dragon lady from the tourist store.

She tried to squirm past them, but they caught her, swinging her around. She struggled like a feral animal, and they became violent, shouting and shoving her to the ground facedown. She looked up, on her belly, and saw the killer. He was standing still, boring into her with his eyes. He stared, waiting to see if she escaped. Wanting her to.

She saw the death in his eyes and quit fighting, letting them take her.

16

✦✦✦

Knuckles said, "Are you kidding me? You didn't want me in the room at the casino because of Carly? That's just stupid, man. I told you the breakup was amicable. Shit, I was the first one she called when she VW'd. **Me. I** was the one she wanted to tell."

Incredulous, I ignored his statement about Carly, focusing on what he'd said previously. I said, "Are you kidding **me**? You're boinking the secretary of state? And you didn't say anything to me? What the hell. We never keep secrets from each other."

He said, "Oh, this from the guy who thought because I used to boink Carly I can't do the mission. I wonder why I didn't tell you."

Jennifer said, "Can this wait until the op is over? You guys are **both** killing me."

We were sitting inside a Gulfstream G650—what we called the Rock Star bird—on a private runway in the canton of Bern, deep in the Swiss Alps. We were about to attempt to crack an old cold war nuclear bunker with more than forty different levels of security in order to glean intelligence that was critical for the defense of the United States—but that could wait. Knuckles's revelation was just too much.

Earlier, after passing my SITREP on the current operation to our command, Kurt Hale had ended by asking to talk to Knuckles in private. I, of course, had agreed, but had spent the entire time since the call badgering him about what had been discussed. Turned out, Kurt had asked Knuckles some probing questions about his relationship with the SECSTATE, and, after waffling a bit, Knuckles had finally come clean. At least to Kurt. It had taken me thirty minutes of nagging to get him to say the same thing to me.

I held up a hand to Jennifer, cutting her off, and said, "Wait a minute, Knuckles. I just did what I thought was best for the mission. You can't hold that against me, and it doesn't compare to what you just said. I can't believe you're dating the damn secretary of state of the United States of America. Where the hell did that come from?"

Knuckles ignored my question, saying, "You didn't talk to me about Carly. You just made a decision, and you did it based on your relationship with Jennifer."

She snapped her head up, a questioning look on her face, but he was probably right. I might've let my support of Jennifer cloud my judgment. Jennifer was the first—and still only—female who had passed

Assessment and Selection, and I was extremely protective of her, which might have caused me to project what I would have felt onto Knuckles.

I said nothing for a moment, then nodded, saying, "Okay. I'll give you that. Maybe I screwed up."

He said, "Maybe, my ass. I told you this fraternization shit would never work. You can't keep on an even keel because you're boinking your business partner, and you're so damn protective of her, you put that on me."

Jennifer wound up to say something, but he put a hand on her arm and said, "I'm just kidding. You know I love you." He turned to me and said, "But there's a little truth there."

I said, "Okay, okay. I get you and Carly are good, and I'm glad to hear it. She doesn't need the baggage, but what the hell is up with the SECSTATE?"

He just shrugged and said, "Kurt took me to an Oversight Council meeting when you were running around Africa. I sold the mission based on my good looks and charm, and the next thing I knew, she looked me up. She's a little hammer, and she's wicked smart. It's nothing serious, really, and it's supposed to be a damn secret. I have no idea how Kurt found out."

From the back of the van, Veep said, "I'm loving hearing how you Gen-X guys get women, but I'm online with Creed. He's ready to go."

In the seat next to him, Brett said, "Thank God.

I'm sick of hearing this white-bread dating crap. Can we just go shoot someone?"

I laughed and said, "No. Not this time. We won't need to."

Jennifer started packing her kit, saying, "Don't blame me. I said to shut up ages ago."

Brett left his chair to help her, as they were going to be a team, saying, "I'm with you. I'm not sure I want to go inside with these snowflakes. You, I trust."

I caught Knuckles's eye and winked, then turned around in the seat, saying, "What's Creed got? How far could he get in?"

"He's confirmed the server map, but that's about it." Veep turned the laptop around and pointed at the screen, saying, "That's the box you want."

Knuckles leaned in, memorizing the icons that represented the server room. He said, "So it **is** level four."

"Yeah, Creed says you should have expected that. The North Koreans would want the tightest security possible."

Switzerland had maintained its neutrality since forever, but in World War II they hadn't relied on the promises of all of the belligerents around them to keep them that way. Having watched Germany steamroll all of Europe, they'd prepared to make such an invasion of their country much harder. They'd built more than twenty thousand military bunkers all over the country, burrowing into the mountains of the Swiss Alps and hiding them in plain sight, with entrances that looked like everything from a barn to a ski chalet. Once the cold war started, the Swiss went even further, passing a law in 1963 requiring a fallout shelter for every single citizen. The land was blistered with secret and not-so-secret bunkers dotting every canton.

After the fall of the Soviet Union, the fear had subsided somewhat, and the Swiss government began selling off the bunkers to corporations for repurposing. Some had been made into hotels, others into something as esoteric as a cheese-ripening facility, but the one idea that had really taken hold was that of a cloud data storage center. While companies such as Amazon could claim ironclad cybersecurity, they were still vulnerable to physical attack, and ingenious entrepreneurs in Switzerland had seized on the added benefit of an impenetrable facility. They'd turned the bunkers into data centers that were immune to physical attack.

The bunker we were targeting was one of the largest, with its own ecosystem in place for complete self-reliance. It had its own hydroelectric power grid, and was hardened against everything up to a nuclear attack, to include an electromagnetic pulse strike. Nothing could affect the data within its confines, a feature that was worth the price to many. Want to ensure that the secret recipe of Kentucky Fried

Chicken's eleven herbs and spices survived after the apocalypse? Switzerland was your ticket.

Besides data, entrepreneurs had used the bunkers to exploit one other niche: circumventing the new Swiss banking laws. Before 2013, the Swiss had been famous for its numbered bank accounts and absolute discretion, but the world community eventually grew tired of unscrupulous tax evaders and outright criminals using the accounts for illicit purposes. In 2013, the drumbeat against these infamous numbered accounts caused the Swiss to take an ax to their reputation for secrecy. No longer was your numbered account impervious to outside investigation.

Ever ingenious, Swiss entrepreneurs had started converting the bunkers to secure storage for anything one wanted to hide, effectively taking a bank account with a digital monetary amount and trading it for a bunker with a physical storage of monetary items. Gold, silver, artwork, stocks, bonds, you name it, was now housed in bunkers all over the country, and they offered absolute security, along with the famed Swiss discretion, as the bunker storage was outside the scope of Swiss banking laws.

Which was something we intended to use to penetrate the server farm.

17

★★

I turned to Veep and said, "Is Creed sure the HVAC hack is going to cause the disruption we need?"

He said, "Oh, yeah. All of those servers run up a tremendous heat base. They need to be almost icebox cold at all times to protect the data. If we shut off the HVAC to that server room, they're going to react, putting in temporary coolant devices until they can get it back online. They'll have to turn off the alarms to do so."

Our target bunker was a hybrid arrangement, and it was huge. Built four stories into the ground, it had been split in half, with one side used for the data storage, and the other used as individual room-size safe-deposit boxes. Using the Grolier Recovery Services cover, we'd rented a room on the safe-deposit side, ostensibly to store archaeological items we'd found in a war-torn country. We'd told the man that we were protecting them until we could determine provenance, which struck a chord with him, because Switzerland's banks had a seedy historical underbelly of trafficking in Jewish wealth during the Holocaust. He hadn't questioned our bona fides too intently, satisfied with the Grolier cover, and we now had a room ready to deposit our "items."

The bunker was impregnable from the outside, both virtually and physically, but the majority of the defenses were focused outward. Get inside the bunker, and we could peel it open. Not without some work, of course, but like Odysseus and the Trojan Horse, all we needed to do was get past the gates of Troy.

Jennifer began putting climbing gear into a crate—two sets of wall climbers, two descenders, and a hundred and fifty feet of black kernmantle rope. I said, "You still going to fit?"

She judged the box and nodded. "Plenty of room."

While she finished her load-out, Brett had swung open a section of the aircraft wall and was digging through what looked like a deep medicine cabinet, holding up pieces of tech gear for Veep to approve or disapprove.

The Rock Star bird was leased to my company through about forty-two thousand cutouts, and on the surface was just like every other Gulfstream, but like everything in the Taskforce, it was decidedly unique. Hidden inside of it were a myriad of different intelligence, surveillance, and reconnaissance capabilities, along with a complete small-arms arsenal packed in its walls.

Brett held up a pen-testing Wi-Fi probe that

looked like a cell phone on steroids, with two wires that terminated in alligator clips and a thick two-inch antenna. Veep said, "That's it. You'll have to cut to the bare metal on the terminal wires, but that'll give you access to the SCADA system running the HVAC. Give it to me, I need to have Creed load it."

Brett handed the device to Veep, and I said, "You got our stuff?"

He pulled out a tablet, held it up, and said, "Got the tools. This is all you need inside, right?"

"Yep."

He put it in his crate, looked at Jennifer, and said, "Why are we the only ones dressed like this? All we're missing is a car full of clowns."

Both of them were wearing black Under Armour compression pants, long-sleeve shirts, and tightly laced rock climbing shoes, making them look like circus performers.

She smiled and said, "Better to be the high-wire act. We can leave the clown car to these two."

Veep handed the pen-testing device back, saying, "Creed's loaded it with the HVAC manufacturer's software. Should be plug and play. You override the system, inject the malware, and it should just shut off. It'll probably take them forty-five minutes of software searching to find the error before they can get it back online."

It would have been nice if we'd been able to go

through the Swiss government to get the information we needed, but since the bunker was now in private hands, that would require a slew of warrants and other legal maneuverings, which made it out of the question. The best the Taskforce could do was procure a blueprint of what the company had turned the bunker into, complete with the various manufacturers of every industrial piece of equipment in the place—something we were about to exploit.

Brett placed his equipment in his crate and Jennifer looked at me, saying, "Tell 'em we're ready for pickup."

The company that owned the bunker managed the airstrip where we'd landed, and because of the exclusivity of the setup, they allowed access 24/7. We'd told them we were coming, and that we had sensitive items that needed to be secured immediately. After landing, we requested a vehicle to transport our items, but told them we were required to prepare them first.

I said, "Okay, remember, we've got about thirty minutes total. Creed says forty-five, but I don't want to push it. We can't get it done in that window, we withdraw. We can try again another day."

I got a nod from the crew. I said, "Veep, make the call." He dialed the phone, and I looked at Jennifer and Brett. "Time to become some precious cargo."

Jennifer smiled and began climbing into her crate, saying, "**Become** precious cargo?"

She curled up at the bottom of the crate and I slid the lid in place, leaving a crack of about an inch. I leaned forward and whispered, "Get this done and you'll get a prize tonight."

"Yeah, yeah. Promises, promises. My job is easy. **You're** the one with the potential to screw this up."

I said, "True," and slid the cover closed, fastening it on the far side with clamps. I looked at Knuckles, seeing he'd closed the other crate over Brett. I said, "Veep, make sure Creed is awake. That asshole has a habit of falling asleep on these things."

Bartholomew Creedwater was our reach-back hacker—and the one who would walk us through what we needed to do once inside. He was an expert at his trade, which was the reason I'd personally requested him for this mission, but he **did** have a habit of mentally wandering off sometimes.

I heard Veep's computer bleep, then Creed came through, sounding like a mechanical drone through the VPN. "Hey, that's not fair. I'm on it."

Veep smiled and I said, "I had no doubt."

Knuckles looked out the window, saying, "Our ride's here."

I lowered the door to the aircraft, seeing an SUV and what looked like an airport baggage tractor towing a trailer.

Knuckles and I picked up Jennifer and carted her outside, placing her on the trailer. I went to talk to the guy in the SUV, showing him my badge access for clearance while Veep and Knuckles loaded Brett's crate. In short order, we were driving toward the entrance to the bunker.

We were cleared through the outer security, a lone building surrounded by razor wire with about a half dozen guys inside, and then approached the entrance. It looked exactly like you'd think it would: a giant face of granite with two large doors in the front. Something Blofeld might have built.

We drove up a ramp, and the door to the left began sliding back, revealing a long, dimly lit tunnel, with another guard shack just inside. We exited the SUV and repeated the security procedures, only this time with both Knuckles and me having to go through a retinal scan, and then we were allowed to proceed.

We got on the back of the trailer and drove down the tunnel to a large freight elevator, then descended three floors, finding yet another security checkpoint. We passed that, now into the storage facility itself. We drove by multiple rooms that were originally built to house humans in the event of nuclear war, but were now turned into individual safes. We stopped at door 33-A, and the driver said, "Okay, sir, this is you."

I said, "Thank you. We have to build a small containment facility inside to house the items, so it'll be about an hour."

He nodded, the Swiss discretion coming to the

fore. "Sir, take the time you need. You know the button on the inside to press for my return, yes?"

"Yep. I'll let you know when we're done."

We unlocked our door with our badges, and hauled in Jennifer, then Brett. The door closed, and we were inside the gates of Troy.

18

✦
✦ ✦

Amena said not a word to the police, pretending that she didn't understand what they were asking, hoping they'd let her go like they had in the past.

She'd been manhandled quite roughly at the old village, the men treating her with just enough violence that she was sure it was an act to get her to never come back. It had given her hope that they'd only try to scare her, then release her. They'd marched her down the mountain in full view of the tourists, and she was convinced it was to prove that they were dedicated to preventing vermin like her from affecting the holidays of those who'd paid dearly to get to the Côte d'Azur.

On the way down, she'd seen the killer following at a distance, his dead eyes on her, hunting her like a shark swimming after a wounded seal.

They'd loaded her in a car, then driven to a Gendarmerie Nationale substation on Boulevard du Maréchal Leclerc. Across the Grande Corniche, and only about a mile from the mountain village, it wasn't as far as she'd hoped they'd go. She'd wanted them to take her as far as Nice, but they'd at least left the killer behind.

She'd been taken to a small interrogation room, and had been questioned over and over again, the main interrogator becoming aggravated at her head shaking, but she wasn't going to let them know she spoke both English and French. Eventually, they'd plugged in her phone, letting it charge. When it finally came to life, the interrogator began looking through it. She didn't care. He could have the damn thing. In fact, she wanted him to take it. It had killed her entire family.

She took a sip of water from a bottle they'd provided, and tried to look innocent while the man scrolled through the phone. He'd held it up, asking another question, and she just shook her head, beginning to relax for the first time. She was safe. The killer was long gone. They would eventually release her, and she'd fade into the background.

That future was shattered when a gendarme had entered jabbering about a dead man in the garden of Eze. Her interrogator had hardened at the news, now convinced he wasn't dealing with a simple pickpocket, but something much more sinister. He stood up, angry, and someone else knocked on the door. Another policeman entered, replacing the one with the news about the dead civilian. He said, "Sir, there's a man outside who says this girl is his daughter."

Her interrogator said, "What?"

"Yes, sir. Her father is here."

"He's in the building?"

"Yes."

There was a pop from the front of the police station. Faint, but distinct.

The policeman and the interrogator paused, turning toward the door, and she knew what it was. The fear flooded through her, a terror unlike any she'd ever felt. She spoke for the first time, in broken French.

"It's him. He's here."

She saw the gendarme's eyes go wide at her words. He said, "You speak French? What did you say?"

She stood up, frantic, grabbing his sleeve and saying, "It's him! We need to hide! We need to go!"

And then the shooting started just outside the door.

Tagir studied the front entrance to the gendarmerie station, seeing it wouldn't be much of an issue to attack. A sleepy backwater, he could only spot one man in the window, and he wasn't that attentive. The hard part would be getting over the chain-link fence that surrounded the place.

He'd watched the child get taken by the police, and followed at a polite distance, not wanting to highlight he even cared. They'd made a show of taking her through the town, parading her in front of all the shops in an effort to showcase their incredible skill at stopping petty crime, aggravating him because it effectively prevented an interdiction.

He never saw the phone, but he was sure she had it.

They'd reached the bottom of the town, and he'd watched her get dragged off to a police car, thrown in the back, and driven away. He had no way to follow them, as the keys to his car were in the pocket of a dead man in the garden. He could hot-wire it, but he didn't bother. It would take much too long before they disappeared.

He knew it was only a matter of time before the body was found, and the girl implicated in the investigation. It was getting messy.

Honestly, he didn't care one way or the other. He wasn't vested in the outcome, but he **did** have a mission. All he needed to prove was that he'd done his best. He called Dmitri Pavlov, relaying what had occurred. Dmitri had become irate.

"The **police** have the phone? Is that what you said?"

"No. That's not what I said. I said the police have the girl, and I believe she has the phone. I can't confirm either way."

Tagir heard nothing but breathing. He said, "Dmitri, are you there? What do you want me to do?"

Dmitri said, "Take Gregor and get the phone back. Whatever you need to do."

"Gregor's dead."

"**What?**"

"Gregor's dead. I don't have time to explain. He was stupid, and he paid for it."

Tagir could almost see the consequences spinning in Dmitri's head. The Kremlin's loss of confidence in Dmitri's ability, along with the loss of contracts for his company. And possibly the loss of his own life. The thought pleased Tagir.

Dmitri said, "Can you interdict now?"

"No. I have no idea where they took her."

"Can't you track the phone?"

"No. It's turned off."

He heard nothing again, then a stream of expletives, accusing him of idiocy and threatening him and his family. He interrupted the rant, speaking softly, "Dmitri . . . Dmitri . . . Dmitri . . ." Eventually, he got through. "Dmitri, do not claim what you cannot do. My family died in Grozny. I'm all that's left. If you want to threaten me, then do so, but be sure of what you say, because I'm not someone to be trifled with."

Dmitri remained quiet. Tagir said, "Do you want me to continue?"

Tagir heard nothing for a moment, then, "Yes, yes, but how?"

Tagir felt a vibration in his pocket. He pulled out the phone-tracking handset and said, "You are the luckiest man in the world. The phone is active."

"Where?"

"Stand by. I'll pull up the map."

Tagir manipulated the device, bringing up a

Google Maps image, and saw the location. He said, "It's in a police station about a mile from here. What do you want me to do?"

He heard more breathing, Dmitri working through what the effects would be, more specifically the effects against him. Tagir raised his voice, saying, "Dmitri, I have the phone now, I might not in twenty minutes. What do you want?"

"Kill them. Kill them all. Anyone who could have seen that phone."

Tagir said, "You sure?"

"Yes. Whoever has seen that phone must be eliminated. Do it."

Tagir hung up and ran to the car Gregor had parked. The door was unlocked, but it still took him twenty minutes to hot-wire the ignition. He eventually achieved success, only having to stop once for a couple walking past.

Thirty minutes after the girl had been taken, he sat in his car outside the fence of the station, intently studying the setup. Getting the phone was one thing, but getting himself in trouble was a bridge too far.

He saw the station had little in the way of active security. At this time of night, there were probably only two or four men inside. He had no idea if any of them had seen the phone, but he had to assume they had. They would all have to die.

He backed out, drove up the road, and parked in a roundabout on the hill above the station, then stalked to the fence. He peered through, seeing the single man now had another with him. He walked up the driveway, getting to the gate. He waved his hand at a camera, waiting on a voice. He heard "Can I help you?"

"Yes. I think you have my daughter in there. She was taken from Eze."

He heard a buzz, and the gate opened. He walked swiftly to the building, going to the man sitting behind a waist-high counter. The policeman said, "You know the girl we arrested from Eze?"

Tagir said, "Yes. She is my daughter."

The desk sergeant said a word to the other policeman, and he scurried away, trotting down a long hallway. The desk sergeant said, "Can I see some identification, please?"

Tagir reached into his back pocket as if he were retrieving a wallet. Instead, he pulled out a folding knife and pressed a button. The blade snicked into life, and the policeman's eyes shot open wide. He scrambled for a pistol on his belt, trying to scoot his chair back. Tagir snagged the man's sleeve, pulling him forward onto the desk, and stabbed him in the neck. The policeman gargled, falling out of the chair with his hands clamped on his carotid artery, the blood flowing between his fingers like a faucet had been opened.

Tagir jumped over the counter and snatched the pistol from the policeman's holster, ignoring the obscene noises he was making. He racked a round into the chamber, put the barrel against the policeman's head, and pulled the trigger, shattering the man's skull. The body ceased moving.

Tagir turned toward the hallway, walking down it with the pistol in a two-handed grip, scanning back and forth. A door to his right abruptly opened, a policeman sticking his head out at the noise. Tagir shot him just above his nose, the round flinging the body against a wall. A door opened farther down, a policeman behind it peering out. Tagir crouched, lined up his sights, and fired a double tap, seeing a blossom of red erupt on the man's chest. The body dropped to the ground, the door bumping into a lifeless head, and Tagir charged forward, kicking it open.

He saw the girl at the back of the room, then another policeman drawing a pistol. Surprised, Tagir jumped over the body in the doorway, put the front sight on the other man, and jerked the trigger twice. One round smashed through a window and the other hit the man in the bicep. The bullet caused the policeman to drop his weapon, but not his will to fight. He threw himself at Tagir, slapping both hands on Tagir's pistol in an attempt to control the barrel.

Tagir swept the man's feet out from under him, bringing him to the ground. Bringing him into Tagir's element. They wrestled for the pistol, and the girl leapt over them, snatching the cell phone off a bench, ripping out the cord plugged into a wall.

She disappeared through the door, and Tagir shouted in frustration. He released one hand from the pistol, punched the gaping wound in the policeman's arm, and heard the policeman scream. The wounded arm went limp, and the policeman desperately tried to continue fighting with only one good hand. Tagir rolled on top of the man and slowly forced the pistol toward his head, as if they were in an arm wrestling match. The barrel reached the policeman's face. He said, "No, no, no . . ."

Tagir pulled the trigger, exploding the room in noise and brain matter. He rolled off the man and raced to the front, searching for the girl. He ran into the lobby and saw a final policeman, this one with his weapon out and prepared.

Tagir saw the muzzle flash and hit the floor, rolling behind a desk.

The man fired repeatedly, spraying rounds in an uncontrolled spasmodic release of fear. Outside of two that punctured the steel next to Tagir's head, the rest of the shots went wide. Tagir heard the weapon lock open on an empty magazine and rose up, firing twice, then dropped again behind cover. He heard a thump, and hesitated, listening for movement.

The room was quiet, the smell of cordite heavy in the air. He slowly peered around the desk, his weapon out, and saw the legs of the final policeman, a pool of blood spreading out. He leapt up and raced through the front door, scanning left and right, seeing nothing but an empty parking lot.

The girl was gone. Again.

19

★★

I put my ear against the door, hearing the tractor disappearing down the hallway, then nodded at Knuckles. He began opening the crates as I dragged a rack of empty shelves away from the wall of our safe room.

Jennifer crawled out first, then Brett. Jennifer started laying out her climbing kit, and Brett turned to his crate, pulling out a device that looked like an old World War II hand radio, about the size of a loaf of bread. He tossed it to me, and Knuckles pushed the crates to the corner, everyone working in a practiced rhythm. He put one on top of the other, and I lightly jumped up, turning on the device.

A small screen in the back of the handset lit up, and I placed it against the ceiling. The device was a portable X-ray machine, allowing me to penetrate the concrete, looking for a seam.

The bunker was originally built for one reason only: to guarantee the survival of the people within it. As such, it had no inside security. It wasn't built as a fighting platform. Its entire purpose was survival. If the worst happened—if the nuclear holocaust appeared—and you made it within its confines, you were a friend, which left glaring vulnerabilities within it that the new owners had basically plastered over.

Using the blueprints, we'd found ventilation shafts threaded throughout the bunker designed to bring fresh air to the denizens who might be living inside it for months. Every dormitory room had a shaft that led to it, and those dormitories had now been turned into individual safes. It was a weakness we were going to exploit.

The new owners—rightly so—thought a three-foot-square ventilation shaft inside each safe room wouldn't project the image of security they wanted, and so they'd plastered them over, painting the surface to look just like the cement and rock next to it. But I knew the shaft was there. I just had to find it.

While I looked for the seam, Jennifer and Knuckles spread a sheet on the floor to catch the evidence of what we were about to do. I started in the corner, running the radar scope back out, and hit the leading edge of the shaft. From there, it was a simple matter to outline the edges of the hole. I marked them, then said, "Give me the quickie saw."

Knuckles handed me a cordless tool with a circular blade made of diamond-impregnated graphite, and I went to work, grinding through the facade they'd built, the noise much louder than I wanted. I stopped, saying, "Brett, check outside the door."

He did so and said, "It's clear."

I went as fast as I could, the masonry inevitably giving way to my saw, the residue falling onto the sheet below. I went past the second corner and said, "Knuckles."

He jumped up, knowing what I wanted, placing his hands in the center as I continued around the edges. Within five minutes, I was done, and Knuckles slowly lowered the centerpiece, handing it to Brett.

We both jumped down and I said, "Okay, here we go. Knuckles, get our kit ready. Jennifer, it's on you now."

Jennifer looked uncharacteristically hesitant and I said, "Hey, you good? Surely you're not worried about the climb?"

Jennifer was what I would classify as a freak when it came to climbing things. She'd once been a performer for Cirque du Soleil, and could slither up plate glass if you let her spit on her hands. This climb was routine, especially since she had assistance in the form of vacuum suction devices. She **did** have to go four stories to the top, but even if something failed, she could chimney in the shaft and fix the problem. It wasn't like she was free-climbing the North Face of Everest.

She smiled and said, "You know better than that. I just don't like the lack of communications. Once Brett and I get up, we'll have no idea of your status. No way to know if the hack worked."

The problem with working inside a bunker was

that no radio signals could penetrate the rock. Once she left, we'd lose the ability to talk, because we still had to follow the laws of physics. One of these days the Taskforce would figure out how Hollywood could do such a thing in the movies, but it hadn't happened yet.

I said, "Just stick with the plan. Get up there, drop the rope, hit the HVAC, and then get back. Your job will be done. If we penetrate, we penetrate. If we can't, we can't."

"What if you penetrate and **then** things go bad? I won't know, and can't react."

I grinned and said, "We'll deal with it. Unlike Wonder Woman, the fate of the free world actually doesn't rest on your shoulders. Get going."

I saw her relax at my words, turning to Brett for her wall climbers—two powered suction disks with a short rope ending in a loop for her feet. He said, "Ready, Wonder Woman?"

She rolled a coil of rope on her shoulders and jumped onto the crate. She glanced at Knuckles, then snuck a kiss on my lips. I returned it, because I'd learned it was just stupid trying to get her to hide her emotions. She worked better letting them out. I pulled back and Knuckles said, "You two sicken me."

I laughed and said, "Let's go."

Jennifer climbed on my shoulders and said, "Catch me if I fall?"

I winked. "As you wish."

Knuckles rolled his eyes and said, "Okay, my manhood is fleeing. Get going."

She slid her hands into the climbing devices and I hoisted her up, lifting her into the shaft. She stood on my shoulders with my hands on her butt and engaged the suction, twisting a rod in first one disk, then the other. She tested the hold, then put her feet in the loops dangling down, and began climbing, one hand after the other. It was a slow walk with her having to release the vacuum in one climber, slide it higher, reengage the suction, then repeat with the other one. When she was up high enough, I said, "Brett."

He jumped up and said, "I don't need you holding my butt."

I said, "Too bad."

He grinned, then followed Jennifer, crawling up my body while I pushed him higher. He seated his climbing disks against the shaft, and then he, too, snaked his way up.

When they were lost from sight, I dropped back down, setting the timer on my watch. Knuckles said, "I'm with Jennifer. I don't like this no commo thing."

Knuckles was always a stickler for prior planning, wanting everything nailed down tight before we executed, which was unique in the SEAL community, to say the least. I tended to deal with the curveballs as they came, because no plan survived first contact, but he had a point. Without communication, we were set on our path. You can't flex when you can't talk. We could only do what we'd agreed on beforehand, relying on Jennifer and Brett to do exactly what we'd planned regardless of something going wrong.

I said, "I don't like it either, but at least we aren't facing anything more than pepper spray here. Worse comes to worst, we'll just fight our way out."

We knew from research that the guards were forbidden from carrying weapons for fear of a shoot-out damaging the very servers they were there to protect. In essence, the company would rather them die than harm the valuable data.

Knuckles pulled out a climbing-seat harness from the crate and handed it to me, then withdrew his own. We cinched ourselves into the webbing, working silently. Fifteen minutes later a rope snaked out of the hole, followed by another. They'd made it to the top.

I tested the hold, then attached a prusik climbing device—a mechanical aid used by arborists to scale trees—and slid the free running end through my harness. I reached up and yanked on the rope, sliding it through the device and rising into the air. In short order, I was headed into the shaft. I went fifteen feet up, and saw an opening to my right. Our highway to the other side of the bunker.

I crawled inside it, released the rope through my carabiner, unhooked the prusik device, and said, "I'm in."

Knuckles said, "Drop it."

I held the prusik device over the hole and let it go. In five minutes I saw Knuckles appear. I snagged the rope, pulling him inside the horizontal shaft. He detangled himself, let the rope fall back into the shaft, and said, "That took longer than we planned."

I looked at my watch and saw he was right. The clock wouldn't start until Creed cut the HVAC, but we needed to be on top of the shaft when that happened. We would need every bit of that time.

I said, "We can make it up on the crawl."

I turned on my headlamp and we started moving on our hands and knees, going west into the heart of the bunker. We skipped over several holes, black chasms leading down to the dormitories that were now safes, the company having sealed them all like they had in our room.

Eventually, we reached a shaft that wasn't sealed, the light from below illuminating our tunnel, a bundle of Cat 7 cables running out. The first server room.

I paused, looked at my map, and whispered, "Four shafts to go."

Knuckles nodded, put a night vision monocular to his eye and looked down the hole. He said, "Still see the infrared. The alarms are still on."

The company had sealed up all of the shafts leading to the secure safe rooms, but had utilized those same shafts to run their cabling for the data side of the house. Because the shafts were still gapingly open, leading into the server rooms, the company had placed protection at their exits in the form of infrared lasers. If we broke the plane of the lights, an alarm would go off, alerting security.

I said, "I guess Creed's going to earn his money."

I crawled across the shaft and kept going. Knuckles followed, saying, "Or we are."

Five minutes later, I was looking down the shaft of our server room with my own night vision, seeing a crisscrossing of infrared lasers. Creed had not shut down the server-room HVAC systems, because the alarms were still on.

Knuckles said, "What now?"

I started to answer, and then felt the air pressure drop in the bunker. It was a small thing, but I sensed it in my ears. I saw that Knuckles felt it, too. I opened my jaw, popping my ears, and said, "O ye of little faith."

Knuckles looked into the shaft with his night vision and said, "You are one lucky son of a bitch."

Seven minutes later we heard the door break. Two men entered and started pushing in mobile air conditioners. They set four in place and then left, presumably going to the next room that Creed had affected.

I said, "We win. Let's go."

20

★★

Knuckles seated another climbing disk on the floor of the shaft we were in, twisting the knob and gaining suction. He ran a length of knotted rope through the handle, cinched it tight, then let the free end drop down through the ceiling. He said, "You first, Batman."

I grinned and lowered myself down. I got to the end of the rope and was still about fifteen feet above the ground. I let go, dropping lightly to the floor. Five seconds later my 2IC landed next to me.

We both paused for a moment, listening. Nothing seemed out of the ordinary. Knuckles said, "We're good. Let's get it done."

I nodded and surveyed the room. There were four rows of servers, with seven servers per stack. I looked at the map in my hand and began counting. **One, two, three.** I moved to that server row, thinking, **Right stack.** I stood in front of the machines and then went from bottom to top, counting again. **One, two, three, four.**

I pointed and said, "This is it."

Knuckles positioned himself behind it and said, "Ready, ready."

He put one hand on the Ethernet cable snaking out from the server, pinching the release pin. I swung my small rucksack to the ground and pulled out a tablet with a foot of Ethernet cable dangling out. I booted it up, looked at him, and nodded. He unplugged the server, jamming the cable into my device. I inserted my own Ethernet into the server. And we held our breath.

No matter what happened, there would be a disruption of service. It might only be a split second, but it was there for someone to find.

I looked at the screen, and it started providing words, like a ghost in the machine. But the words weren't what I wanted to read.

Creed sent: **This is not the box.**

I wanted to scream. I typed, **What the hell are you saying? This IS the box.**

I waited and saw, **It is NOT. Pike, go one higher.**

I looked at Knuckles and said, "Creed says it's the wrong box. Get ready to pull."

He grasped the Ethernet cable, looking at me for the count. I put my hand on the cable for the next server and gave him a rundown. He snapped our cable out, I did the same, and we plugged in again.

And waited.

The screen scrolled with typing, and I wanted to

punch the wall. What came out was **Wrong box. Nothing here.**

I typed, **Wrong box? Or wrong hacker? I'm about to rip your head off. Find something!**

He wrote, **Pike, it's the wrong box. Go one lower.**

Knuckles looked at me in amazement, and I knew what he was feeling. We both wanted to crush the damn computer nerds back at headquarters.

I said, "One more time. Lower server." Knuckles put his hand on the cable, and I did the same on the lower box. I said, "One, two, three, go!"

And we waited. Seven seconds in, the screen said, **This is it. You got it. Give me five minutes.**

I relaxed, saying, "Finally."

Leaning against the wall, Knuckles looked relieved. For about two seconds. He felt a change in air pressure and perked up, saying, "Your ears just pop?"

I looked at him and he said, "HVAC is going."

I heard the whine of the system, and Knuckles said, "We gotta go, right now. Before they turn the alarms on again."

We heard a click, and Knuckles ran to the center of the room, looking up with his night vision. He said, "Alarm's set. Only way out now is the front door."

Shit.

We heard the door open and ducked down behind the server tray. Knuckles whispered, "Take him?"

I said, "No. Not until he finds us."

"What happens when he finds the rope?"

I looked up and saw our lifeline snaking out of the shaft into the room, gently blowing in the breeze. I prayed it wouldn't make contact with one of the laser beams. I whispered, "Let it go."

He grinned and hissed, "Okay, but I'm not going down because your damn date couldn't shut off air-conditioning."

The man began removing the temporary coolant devices, walking all over the server room. We remained in a crouch, hiding behind the racks and circling away from him.

Eventually, he was done, none the wiser about the rope dangling from the shaft. When he was gone, Knuckles said, "So what now? We can't get out without tripping the alarm."

I said, "I know. But Jennifer knows that as well. Give her a chance."

"Jennifer? We can't even talk to her."

I said, "Yeah, but she knows we didn't get our thirty minutes."

No sooner had he said it than my ears popped again. I looked at him and said, "That's my girl."

He grinned and said, "Never had a doubt."

The man came in the room again, pushing the portable air conditioners and bitching, then left. I heard the door close and wasted no time. I typed, **You good? We need to bolt.**

The screen said, **Yes. I'm good.**

I unplugged our tablet, shoved it in my rucksack,

then looked up, seeing the lasers off, but knowing they wouldn't be for long. I jumped up, snagging the rope and free-climbing into the shaft. I pulled myself into the horizontal section, rolled over to the hole, and saw Knuckles coming up. He struggled to enter the shaft, and I said, "Come on. Get your legs up!"

I hoisted him higher, pulling him into the horizontal section, and the laser alarms initiated right below his feet, stabbing the darkness in a futile endeavor to catch us. He rolled over, took a breath, and said, "Whatever Jennifer did, I owe her a beer."

I chuckled and said, "Rum and Coke. She doesn't drink beer. Come on. We still have to get out."

We low-crawled back to our safe room, moving as fast as we could. We reached it and I saw the rope was gone. I lowered myself into the hole and slid down, using my hands and knees to slow the descent. I reached the ceiling of the room and dropped through, hitting the ground hard. Behind me, Knuckles did the same.

I saw Brett and said, "What the hell happened?"

He said, "We cut the HVAC, but it didn't take thirty minutes for them to fix it. It took like five. We were already in the shaft, coming back, when it initiated. We had to make a call. Sorry about the rope, but we couldn't waste time with a slow climb. Jennifer decided to go back up. She cut it again while I rigged our rope for a fast rappel."

"What if we'd been caught?"

"Hey, Jennifer said you'd figure it out, and I believed her, because she's damn near impossible to tell no. And she was right, so stop bitching. It was the best we could do, given the circumstances."

I smiled and said, "Well, your best was good enough. Where is she?"

He laughed and pointed, saying, "In her crate. Like we dictated in the plan."

While Knuckles and Brett cleaned up our mess, hiding the residue and our gear, I slid her crate open, seeing her curled up in a ball, eyes wide. I said, "You going to wish your way out of here? If I hadn't shown back up?"

Chagrined, she sat up, saying, "We had an issue. The HVAC kicked on much earlier than Creed said. I had to make a decision. We had to—"

I cut her off, saying, "I know. You saved the day, Wonder Woman."

She smiled and said, "So it worked?"

"As far as I know. Creed said he got what he needed."

Knuckles said, "We're done here."

I said, "Get back in the crate."

She said, "What about the hole?"

I said, "Taskforce problem. We're out of here."

Because of the exclusivity of the bunker, the only people allowed inside the room were the renters—us—so I didn't worry about the management finding our handiwork with the ceiling. The

Taskforce would send a separate team to rebuild it in a day or two, pretending to be removing the items from the safe.

Jennifer nodded and crouched back into her crate. I slid the top over her, saw Brett was hidden as well, and pushed the button next to the door, alerting the management team that we were done.

21

Yasir al-Shami stepped onto the small ferry, showing his hotel key card, wondering if the man would allow it as payment. He'd been told it would give him free passage, but he still wasn't sure.

The boat driver nodded, and he scurried to the back, taking a seat on the bench at the rear. The rest of the cabin filled up, and they left the dock on the east bank of Lake Geneva, the boat driver absolutely bored at his job. Back and forth, back and forth, back and forth, it was a monotonous, rote existence, leaving him jaded to the view that left the others on the small craft enthralled, including Yasir.

As a fixer for the Syrian regime, Yasir had traveled to many places outside of his war-torn country. In fact, after a tour as a commander of one of the secret prisons in Damascus, he preferred it, but most of those trips involved yet another Arab country. Iran, Qatar, one short trip to Egypt. He'd spent some time in Turkey, and while that country had more to offer than his own, it didn't measure to the splendor of Switzerland.

In all of those countries, while he'd been able to escape the prison and its stench of urine and the sound of men's souls being torn apart, the view was essentially the same. He'd enjoyed Monaco, but Switzerland was on another level completely.

Lake Geneva stretched out before them, the water flat as a pane of glass, the reflection hiding what was below, as if it held a secret. That was okay. He had secrets of his own to keep.

He could see the Swiss Alps in the distance—the tops still white from the passing winter—marveling at the sight. Someday . . . someday soon . . . he'd leave the cauldron of Syria for good. Leave the devastation of the only home he'd ever known—and gladly. Move somewhere like this or Monaco. He couldn't afford Monaco just yet, but he could afford Geneva. After this mission anyway.

Yasir wasn't an evil man, at least not in his eyes. He'd seen distasteful things—had commanded distasteful things—but he did what he had to do to survive. He was no different than a German guard at Auschwitz. While the West called such men evil, in his mind he understood. What was the guard to do? Commit suicide?

He'd ingratiated himself to the regime, rose through the ranks of Syrian Air Force intelligence—a modern-day Gestapo with all that entailed—doing what was necessary to succeed. It had cost the lives of many, many men, women, and children, but it wasn't at his own hand. All he'd done was follow orders. Round up a family here, capture the grandparents there—all on the orders of the regime. He didn't personally do any of the heinous things he'd seen. There were other men who could execute the dirty tasks. Men who enjoyed the work.

The distinction would be lost on him, but in truth he was the banality of evil. He was the German administrator who made the trains full of human cattle run on time. The German housewife who smelled the smokestacks but still delivered milk to the soldiers at the camps. Yasir was the inevitable weakness of the human condition.

And he would feel the pain of that weakness soon.

The ferry motored out from the dock of the quay, passing by a giant geyser of water sprouting from Lake Geneva. Called the Jet d'Eau, the fountain sprayed five hundred feet into the air, reminding Yasir of a gushing wound, the water tirelessly seeking the sky before inevitably falling back to earth. He reveled in the fact that it was only water, letting him forget about the horrors he'd seen done to the men in his prison. It was beautiful, and he took it as a sign of his chosen path.

The boat sliced through the lake, disrupting the calm on the surface and leaving a churn in its wake. Soon enough, they were docking at the Quai du Mont-Blanc on the western shore.

Yasir exited, walked past the food stands up to

street level. He checked a map, got his bearings, and then strode north about a hundred meters. He saw an archway and took it, walking into a courtyard that was once pristine, but now held a shabby, faded feel, the landscaping bordering on overgrown, with decrepit bicycles chained to the iron grates surrounding the individual trees. He looked around the businesses occupying the lower terrace of the yard, ignoring the travel agencies and tour companies flying Swiss flags, the storefronts bursting with brochures. He saw a single oak door with a brass plaque next to it reading GAUSTURE HOLDINGS.

He pulled out his phone, cycled through the apps on the surface, and found what he'd been given. He clicked on it, seeing a key appear. A bar code with a Bluetooth button. Waiting on him to initiate.

He stared at it, wondering if he was walking into a trap.

The instructions on his cell had been precise—to the point of being overbearing. There was to be no face-to-face meeting as he'd done in Monaco. Not that he wanted one. He'd met killers in his time—in fact, had commanded them in the cauldron of the secret prisons—but the North Koreans were untethered from even the low constraints in which he'd operated. Their second meeting—when he'd lied about dropping his phone in the toilet and thus destroying the data that had been given—hadn't been pleasant. The only ones who had shown up were the security men, and they'd let him know in no uncertain terms that his life was predicated on success. President Assad didn't tolerate slipshod performance, which is why Yasir was still alive, but the Koreans were on another level.

He'd arrived in Geneva knowing he was about to meet a team of killers. Men who—unlike him—were brainwashed into believing everything their "dear leader" directed them against. If they hadn't been, they would never have been allowed to leave the Hermit Kingdom.

Switzerland was one of the few countries on earth—outside of the usual Axis of Evil—that allowed the North Koreans to roam about freely. Known as a neutral country, and a member of the Neutral Nations Supervisory Commission, Switzerland had a history of dealing with rogue states, and that history lent itself to Switzerland being used by those same countries.

To be sure, the United States leveraged the hell out of that status, as it had served a good purpose since the end of World War II. When the US wanted to talk to North Vietnam, it was done through Switzerland. When the US embassy was seized in Iran, it was Switzerland that was the go-between—a role the country still carries out on the United States' behalf. When America wants to talk to North Korea, it's Switzerland that broaches the issue. As a result, Switzerland had become one of the sole European playgrounds for nations that had been eschewed on the world stage. Kim Jong-un himself had attended a university in Bern, and there were multiple other organizations that facilitated exchanges.

Besides being the founding location of the United Nations, Switzerland had a unique body called the Geneva Centre for Security Policy. Designed to foster security cooperation and peace throughout the world, it necessitated that those from countries that had—to put it mildly—less than stellar humanitarian reputations be allowed to attend.

A contingent of ten officers from North Korea had been attending the center since 2011. And those officers had not been vetted by anyone except North Korea. Yasir was sure the team he was meeting had been slotted in those positions within the last few weeks, and that he was meeting not a team of regular North Korean officers, but Kim Jong-un's private band of merry killers. The same ones who had been responsible for murdering Jong-un's half brother in Malaysia with nerve gas.

Besides that small detail, this meeting would allow Yasir to get free from the Assad regime. He'd been given a significant amount of money to pay for the Red Mercury, but the Koreans would only see about two-thirds of it. He'd already siphoned off his cut. That, along with his upcoming payment from the CIA, would be enough to set up his retirement. If he could live long enough to see it.

Earlier that day, he'd checked into his hotel on the outskirts of the old town, spending less than thirty minutes in the room. He pulled back the curtain for light, seeing a park fronting the eastern bank of the lake, walkers and bikers scurrying to and fro, none worrying about being killed just by being in the open.

I could live here.

He'd smiled at the thought, then refocused on his mission. He pulled out a map and traced a route to his designated meeting site, the Cathedral of St. Pierre.

The North Koreans had stipulated only one marker in between his hotel and the church, a street called Passage des Degrés-de-Poules. It was just south of the church, and only about a seven-minute walk from his hotel. He checked his watch, fidgeted in his room for twenty minutes, then left.

He'd nodded at the concierge and exited out the revolving door onto the main avenue fronting the park. He walked for a hundred meters, then hooked into an alley, moving fast through it until he reached the next road to the west. He saw an open area lined with coffee shops and scuttled to the first one, taking a seat and eyeing the alley. He didn't think the North Koreans knew where he was staying, but he certainly wasn't going to make it easy for them if they did.

After five minutes, Yasir felt a little foolish worrying about surveillance, and continued on his way. Eight minutes later he saw that the North Koreans were way ahead of him.

22

★★
★★

It turned out the North Koreans had no need to follow him, because Passage des Degrés-de-Poules wasn't a street. It was a narrow tunnel in the side of a building. A long dark stairwell that led up to the courtyard of the church. He grimaced, knowing that he'd walked right into their surveillance bubble. He was being watched, and the watchers would be looking to see if he was alone—either from his allies or enemies.

He entered the tunnel, seeing the light at the top of the stairwell, and realized it was a perfect kill zone. He hesitated, looking behind him. He saw nothing—but then again, he wouldn't expect to, if they were good. And he knew the North Koreans were good.

He took the stairs three at a time, running toward the daylight like a soul seeking heaven. He broke out into a courtyard, his lungs on fire, startling a couple walking the grounds. He put his hands on his knees and did nothing but breathe for a moment, waiting on a bullet.

None came.

He stood upright, thinking, **This is the last one. The last time you have to risk your life.**

The mantra went through his head over and over as he circled the gothic spires of St. Pierre Cathedral. He reached a sign proclaiming an archaeological site before the main doors to the chapel, and licked his lips. This was it. Commit, or go home.

He opened the double doors, walking down the stairs. The cathedral had been built on the ashes of the creation of Geneva, dating back to the fourth century. The very heart of the city was buried underneath the granite of the church. It had been excavated and subsequently turned into a museum of more than three thousand square meters of underground tombs and narrow hallways delineating the history of the city.

It was an area that could be completely controlled by a surveillance team, with only one entrance and one escape. Meaning he'd be trapped if the surveillance team decided to go kinetic. It wasn't a place he wanted to enter alone. But he had his orders.

He walked down the stairwell, entering a lobby with a caretaker manning a desk. As instructed, he paid for a headset, and then began his tour, walking from one point to another, the old stone, wells, and skeletons describing the advent of the city of Geneva from the Celtic era through Roman times. He fought the urge to glance around him, wondering if he was being watched in the claustrophobic confines.

Eventually, as he'd been warned, he entered a small room with four benches and a wide-screen television. He noticed two people in the rear, but as instructed, ignored them. He took a seat on the bench at the front, pulled out his cell phone, and tapped the application with the wire transfer for the money. He punched the next number on his headset, and watched the movie on the television, staring rigidly ahead, but not assimilating anything that was coming through the headphones on his ears. Five minutes later, the movie was over. He glanced at his cell phone, seeing it was now upside down on the bench. Someone had moved it. He whipped his head to the rear, and realized he was alone.

He picked the phone up, tapped the screen, and saw a new application had been added. A commercial one from a specific bank, with a Bluetooth key. He checked his wire transfer, finding it empty. So they'd taken the money, but they didn't know he'd told his command the price was much higher than what the North Koreans had dictated. He went into his account, seeing that 750,000 US dollars still remained. That, with the money he would get from the CIA, would be enough to get him the life he wanted.

He dug into the hidden BIOS of the phone, powering up the program he'd originally received, and found new instructions for a bank on the other side of Lake Geneva.

He put the phone in his pocket and left the museum, ignoring the rest of the tour, glancing left and right and not feeling safe until he was back in the daylight. The man at the counter took his head-set, sensing something was wrong. Yasir caught his look and ran a hand across his brow, finding sweat. The man asked if he was okay, and he said yes, but he didn't feel that way. He felt he'd come within a hair of dying.

He'd run many intelligence operations, and he knew what he'd just experienced was one of the best he'd ever seen executed. It was pure, giving the North Koreans every opportunity to eliminate him had he been deemed a threat, and giving him no opportunity to protect himself or even identify his enemy. They may have been a pariah state, but apparently they could operate within Switzerland with impunity.

He'd gone back to the hotel, locked his room, and spent the night staring at the door. Waiting for someone to knock. It never came.

When dawn had broken, he'd taken the ferry to the courtyard, and now stood outside, wondering if it was another possible trap. But he knew he could never have the life he wanted if he didn't follow through. If Bashar al-Assad didn't kill him, he was sure the North Koreans would. And as much as he feared Assad, he feared the Koreans more.

He walked up to the door, rang the bell, and waited. A prim, older woman answered, saying, "Yes?"

"I've come for a safe-deposit box. I need the contents."

He waited for her to ask for identification, or an account number, or some other proof that he'd been here before. Instead, she simply smiled and said, "Of course. May I see the key?"

He tapped the Gausture Holdings application on his phone, and the bar code appeared. She scanned it. Her device blinked green, and she said, "Yes, yes. Follow me, please."

He entered a plain lobby, the room devoid of pictures, the only thing in sight a desk with a computer. Behind the desk were four oak doors. She said, "You have room three. Do you know how to use the key?"

And he realized that she dealt with people all the time who showed up without knowing what they were supposed to do. Meaning she dealt with the shady side of the Swiss banking laws. He said, "Not really."

She opened the third door, and he saw a small anteroom, with four large safes set into the wall. She said, "It's simple, really. I'll activate the security code, then leave you alone. All you need to do is synch your Bluetooth key to the safe. It'll be called Gausture One, Two, Three, or Four. I don't even know which one you have. Once it's synched, just press the button on your phone, and the safe will open. Okay?"

He was amazed. He said, "Sounds good."

She fiddled with a device in her hands and said, "It's on. You have one minute before it resets. If you can't get your key to work, come back outside."

She left the room, closing the door behind her. He synched the Bluetooth without issue. He pressed the button, and the second door from the right opened. Inside, he saw a backpack. He pulled it out, finding two cylinders that looked not unlike coffee thermoses.

His Red Mercury.

He shouldered the backpack and left the room, thanking the woman for her help. He exited to the street, walking to the ferry again, smiling, the fear falling away. His plan was working. His terrorist "friends" should be safely in Zurich, but they offered no threat. He knew exactly how to deal with them. He'd need to set up a meeting to transfer the weapon, but first he needed to solidify his last bit of retirement with the United States.

He pulled out his special flip phone, the one given to him by that ass in the CIA, and dialed a number.

23

★★★

David Periwinkle heard a vibration and stopped typing. It came again, and he turned from the computer, cocking an ear. The rattle filled the room. He touched the phone in his pocket, but didn't feel the vibration. Realization dawned on him, and he frantically jerked open the second drawer of his desk, seeing the burner flip phone sliding back and forth, the front screen illuminated. He snatched it up, punching an intercom button on his desk, saying, "Get in here."

He flipped the phone open and put it to his ear. "Yasir?"

He heard laughter, then, "Yes. Who else would this be? Are you giving this number out to many men from Syria?"

The door opened, and a ginger-haired man of about twenty-five stuck his head in. Periwinkle pointed at the phone to his ear, then back at the man in the door. He nodded, then slowly let the door close.

Periwinkle said, "Sorry. You never know if someone has taken the phone from your dead body." He paused, then said, "How is your sister?"

The case officer leaned forward, waiting on the answer. He heard, "She's still trying to get her degree. Still studying."

Periwinkle relaxed. If he'd heard **She's quit school**, he would have known Yasir was under duress. He said, "So what do I owe the pleasure of this call? If I remember right, you decided to cut us off. You cut **me** off. I figured your friends in Syria were worth more than your friends in the United States."

Periwinkle had run Yasir for two years, gleaning high-level intelligence from the Assad regime, and then, inexplicably, Yasir had stopped all contact. Periwinkle had chalked it up to the spy game, and had devoted his time working other assets. Then, one month ago, Yasir had surfaced again, promising a load of intelligence that would dwarf anything the United States had on the Syrian regime. That promise had come with a bill that was very steep, and so far, Periwinkle had seen nothing.

Yasir said, "David, David, that was never the case. You know my life is precarious. I have never let you down."

Periwinkle chuckled and said, "Shit, Yasir, most of the intelligence you've given me was good, but it was always too little, too late. If I didn't know better, I'd say you were selling me old information just to get the money."

Yasir said, "I can promise you this isn't old. What

is it you people want above all else? What would make your intelligence community happy?"

Periwinkle felt his pulse increase, but didn't betray it on the phone. "Yasir, I don't have time for games. Talk to me or disconnect. I've already hung my ass out way too far for you. I should have just let you get rolled up in Monaco and then gotten the information."

"That would have been a mistake, because I didn't have the information a few days ago."

Periwinkle waited. When he heard nothing else, he said, "What the fuck is it? I'm about to hang up."

"I have the locations of every single chemical facility the regime owns. Every one."

Periwinkle said nothing, considering the breadth of what he was being told. Chemical weapons had been the bane of the United States since the start of the Syrian civil war. From one red line to another, Assad had continued to use the weapons, dodging missile strikes and confounding all who tried to remove them.

Yasir said, "Hello? Is this worth something? Or do you want to keep striking empty buildings in a pathetic attempt to show strength?"

Periwinkle said, "How did you come across this?"

"I am a general in Air Force intelligence. How do you think I came up with this?"

"From some whore in a Lebanese flophouse. That's what I think."

Yasir laughed and said, "Maybe. But maybe not. Is this something you want?"

Periwinkle couldn't reflect it on the phone, but of course it was something he urgently desired. It was the very reason he'd decided to alert Yasir ahead of that stupid assault against him by the Neanderthal SOCOM direct-action team. He'd used his instincts, and he'd been proven right.

He said, "Yes, of course we want it."

"It will cost you. This is it for me. I'm taking your payment as retirement, and you'll never hear from me again."

The comment gave Periwinkle pause. He said, "You're going cold?"

"I am. I know I shouldn't say that, but I want to show you my honesty."

Periwinkle said, "I understand. If it's what you say it is, money is no object. How will you pass?"

"I have a trip out of Damascus to Istanbul in seven days. I'll meet you at the usual location? Back when we were friends?"

Periwinkle looked at his calendar and said, "That would work for me. I'm not in Turkey now, but I'll be back by then. I'll call with details."

"Sounds good, my friend. You did the right thing in your call to me earlier. I wouldn't have this information without it. I expect the same loyalty, because I'm taking significant risk."

"You'll have it. Don't do anything else inside the regime. Just get out."

"See you soon, **inshallah**."

The phone disconnected, and Periwinkle placed it back in the drawer. Five seconds later, the door opened and the young ginger entered, his face grim.

Periwinkle said, "What?"

"He's not in Damascus. He's in Geneva, Switzerland."

Switzerland? What the hell?

David Periwinkle felt the first tendrils of fear that maybe he wasn't the player, but was being played.

The thought made his gut clench. If he **was** being played, he'd made a significant mistake warning Yasir about the SOCOM hit. He would need to mitigate the damage that could cause. Maybe he should tell those men where Yasir was. Let them roll him up, then use his information as leverage for his release.

No, that wouldn't work. If they interdicted him, Periwinkle wouldn't be able to explain how he knew who Yasir was after being shown a photograph of his face and claiming he didn't recognize him.

He took a couple of breaths and began to calm down. Just because Yasir wasn't in Damascus didn't mean he wasn't telling the truth. He'd claimed to have incredibly important intelligence—and that was something worth the expense of preventing that asshole Pike from taking him down.

He nodded, convincing himself he was correct. The best course of action was to conduct the linkup with Yasir. The man wanted to get paid—and had said so explicitly. He wouldn't be calling a CIA case officer if he were doing something heinous.

Don't read into the NSA trace of the phone. Don't get paranoid.

But he **would** need to let HQ know that Yasir was active again. Along with the nugget of intelligence he was willing to provide that would make Periwinkle a legend in the CIA.

He began shacking up a cable, parsing his words and leaving out selected tidbits such as locations and timing, directing it to the chief of station in Turkey. He would need to get authority for the funding, but with as much as the CIA had bled into Syria for everything from TOW missiles to twelve-year-old sources, he knew that wouldn't be an issue. The intelligence community would definitely want what he was buying.

He just had to protect how he'd received it.

24

★ ★
★

President Hannister leaned back behind the Resolute desk and said, "So you didn't get any of the OPM data breach? We risked that entry into the data storage facility in a sovereign country for nothing?"

Kurt Hale could tell the president was aggravated. As an extrajudicial force, he didn't take employing the Taskforce lightly—especially when it failed.

Or ostensibly failed.

Kurt said, "No, sir, it wasn't for nothing. It's true we found no evidence of the Chinese hack of our OPM databases, but we did find something else. I believe we were misreading what was actually happening. I looked through the transcripts, and when I was done, I came to the conclusion it was much worse. They might actually be selling WMD."

"What makes you think that?"

"Two words: Red Mercury."

Amanda Croft said, "What is that?"

Kurt turned to the director of the CIA and said,

"Kerry? You want to explain? You guys did the translation of what Pike retrieved from the server."

Kerry rose slowly from the couch, turning to the four members in the Oval Office, taking the time to frame his words carefully. Because it was a joint CIA/ Taskforce operation, Kurt and Kerry had coordinated in advance, debating on how to proceed. They'd agreed to alert what was colloquially called the "principals" of the Oversight Council, letting them hear the evidence before bringing in the rest of the members. The secretary of defense, the secretary of state, the director of the CIA, the national security advisor, and the president. It was a group that held the outcome of Council votes, and a way to float their trial balloon—although Kurt knew this was a decision brief. What they were doing would never make it to the full Council. He'd seen that play out in the past. It was a subterfuge, and a risk, but working within an organization that had no statutory requirements had its benefits.

Kerry said, "Red Mercury is a myth. It first appeared in intelligence data at the end of the Cold War, when everyone was worried about losing Soviet nukes. According to the legend, it was a Soviet chemical agent that would have the effects of a nuclear strike without the blowback of fallout."

Amanda said, "If it's a myth, why do we care?"

"Because the North Koreans used that term. It's a myth to us, but not to terrorists. Since 1991, terrorists have been fanatical about obtaining Red Mercury, so much so that we've captured a few just by dangling that term in the wind. They fully believe it's real, and the quest to find it has taken ludicrous turns. At one point, when we were in Iraq early on and the insurgency was heating up, the bad guys determined that Singer sewing machines were hiding the substance, with a subsequent drop in tailor-shop productivity when every machine was stolen and stripped looking for it. It's a myth, but also a real thing to unsophisticated psychopaths who want to kill. And the North Koreans have used that term in an official communiqué."

Alexander Palmer said, "So you think that they've developed this Red Mercury?"

Kerry laughed and said, "No way. There are a thousand scientists both on our side of the Atlantic and the other who have shown conclusively that it's just a legend. Red Mercury doesn't exist."

"Why does this matter, then?"

Kurt spoke up, saying, "Two reasons. One, it means whatever they're selling, they know it's deadly. It's something new and unique. It's a killer, which should be enough to cause us concern, but two, as Kerry said, they used that term. They know it's like catnip to terrorist groups, which means they aren't selling it to a state. No state would buy it because they know Red Mercury is a myth. North Korea would have called it what it was, like Hwasong-17, or something else official. But they didn't, which leads me to believe North Korea is selling a WMD to a terrorist group."

President Hannister said, "But I thought we were tracking a Syrian? A member of the Syrian state? Not a terrorist group."

Kurt said, "That's true, sir, but let's face some facts: The Syrian regime is rife with the same mentality of the terrorists they're fighting."

Palmer said, "I don't know. There's not a lot here. Just a translation from Korean with the words 'Red Mercury.' Why would North Korea do such a thing?"

Kerry chuckled and said, "Because they need money. Because you're crushing their nuts with sanctions. The correct question is why **wouldn't** they do it. They helped build the Syrian nuclear reactor that the Israelis destroyed in 2007. Kim Jong-un himself ordered the killing of his half brother in Malaysia with nerve agent. They aren't exactly hewing to societal norms."

"Yeah, but even given they're bad actors, aren't you guys stretching things?"

Kerry said, "As much as I hate to admit it, being a CIA man, the Taskforce has found something else in the data dump. Kurt?"

Kurt grinned at the good-natured jab and said, "Along with the Red Mercury description were two separate cell phone numbers. We believe that those numbers are connected to the sale. We don't know who they are, or even if it's two separate people, but they are real. We believe it's the Syrian."

Amanda Croft said, "Why?"

"Because we've geolocated both numbers, and both of them are in Geneva, Switzerland."

The room became quiet. After a moment, President Hannister said, "Okay, let me get this straight. You penetrated a data center, found information leading to the sale of a WMD called Red Mercury, and in that same extraction you collated two cell numbers that were associated with the sale, and **both** of those numbers are within spitting distance of the data center?"

"Yes, sir."

Amanda Croft said, "And why are the numbers being in the same country relevant?"

Kurt looked at Kerry, surprised at the question coming from the secretary of state. Kerry said, "Ma'am, Switzerland is a neutral country, and because of it, the North Koreans travel freely. It's one of the few places in the Western world where they can. The leader of North Korea, Kim Jong-un, went to boarding school there. Shit, the Swiss population just had an outcry about the Swiss military conducting target practice with North Korean officers."

Kurt said, "In addition to that, Switzerland has a history of secrecy. In the old days, a Swiss bank account guaranteed monetary discretion, but not anymore. They recently softened their banking laws, but have also started renting out their bunkers for safe storage. Nobody checks what's stored, because the bunkers are outside the purview of banking regulations. It's a way to avoid scrutiny, and the perfect place to transfer the weapon."

President Hannister fiddled with a pen on his desk and said, "That's what you have? That's the evidence? Swiss banking laws and a phone number?"

Exasperated, Kurt stood up and said, "Sir, we're not asking to invade Switzerland. All we're asking is for Alpha authority to explore. Before this becomes something we can't control. Before there are a lot of dead bodies."

Hannister tapped his pen, looking at Kurt. Finally, he said, "And how would you do that?"

"Pike's team is in Switzerland. We can track the phones. Let him investigate. Let him interdict, if necessary."

President Hannister scoffed and said, "Pike Logan. Every time I get him involved somewhere, things seem to go to shit."

Kurt smiled and said, "No, sir. That's not correct. Things go to shit all on their own. All Pike does is prevent the splatter."

The room collectively winced at the analogy, but Hannister chuckled. He said, "So how would this work?"

"We'll pick one number and track it. If it doesn't pan out, we'll pick the other. No high adventure here. Just investigate. As you say, it might be nothing. But it might not."

Hannister nodded, tapped his pen again in thought, then said, "All right. Let's vote. I'm okay with it."

Palmer said, "Sir, we need to think about operating in Switzerland with so little information. We should develop the intelligence more fully before we—"

Hannister cut him off, "That's exactly what Kurt is asking to do. I understand the implications. I'm sure it would be better for our relations with Switzerland to do nothing, but they don't care about American deaths. I do."

Kurt was shocked at the rare rebuke of the national security advisor, but it solidified his trust in the president.

Palmer backed down, chagrined, crossing his arms and looking petulant. Kurt knew he was a no-vote and hated the politics of the entire debate.

Why can't we just make a decision based on the risk to lives instead of our egos?

He glanced at Amanda Croft and saw a small grin on her face. She was all in.

Well, there's that. Knuckles is paying off in more ways than one.

Hannister asked for those in favor, and all agreed but Alexander Palmer. The hands dropped, and Hannister said, "You have the authority, but only Alpha. Only to explore what those phones are doing. Is that understood?"

"Of course, sir."

"Yeah, I get **you** understand. What I mean is, does Pike understand?"

"Sir, he will."

Hannister stood up, indicating the meeting was over, and the people began to file out of the Oval Office. Kurt went to follow and Hannister said, "Kurt."

Kurt turned to him. Hannister said, "I mean it. This is very weak. Pike explores, and that's it. I can't afford a diplomatic row with Switzerland because Pike went nuts. And I certainly can't afford looking like the bad guy in a dispute with North Korea. Pike can't make them the aggrieved party at the end of any action. You understand that, right?"

Kurt said, "Sir, I understand the risks. I wouldn't have asked if I didn't think they were worth it."

Hannister chuckled and said, "It's not you I'm worried about. Make sure Pike knows. He has a habit of getting into trouble."

Kurt shuffled his feet, wondering if the president was asking him to back off, even after the vote. He said, "He does, sir, but it's never of his making. Pike solves problems, period."

Hannister walked to the door, saying, "I know. Just tell me he isn't going to do something stupid."

25

★
★ ★

Brett said he had a weak signal, but that wasn't good enough to pinpoint anything. I saw the size of the crowd and thought about doing something stupid just to make our target show his hand. Something to get the crowd to break up so I could locate the phone.

I looked over at Jennifer, who was giddy over the history surrounding her. I leaned into her ear, whispering, "I'm thinking of calling in a bomb threat. Just to separate our phone."

She whipped her head to me and said, "Don't you dare. No reason to rush things. We'll find him sooner or later."

"Meaning we have to tour this entire place, right?"

She raised an eyebrow and said, "Well, if it comes to that, what's the big deal?"

We were inside a castle from the twelfth century called Chillon. On the shores of Lake Geneva, near the town of Montreaux, it was a forbidding fortress exactly like one would expect from a King Arthur movie. Because of that, Jennifer was hell-bent on exploring every inch of its history. I have to admit, it **was** pretty cool, but we also had a mission to accomplish.

Kurt had contacted us in Zurich, and I anticipated he would tell us to get our ass back to Eze, because we were still under contract for the work at the church and we'd left pretty abruptly. We had a convincing story about a death in the family, and had left on good terms, but still, I expected Kurt to tell us to return. After all, a funeral only takes so long.

He hadn't. Apparently, our little B and E of the bunker had gotten the Oversight Council's panties in a knot, and we'd stumbled on something more than just a theft of data. It wasn't a possible exposure of US covert intelligence personnel; it was something called Red Mercury. Just like Kurt, I knew no such material existed, but—like him—the fact that the North Koreans had used the term was a flashing red light.

He'd given us two numbers to explore, both in Geneva, telling me it was a shooter's choice. Meaning me, as the gunner, could pick. I chose one and immediately got the team moving to Geneva while Kurt got the massive architecture of the NSA to geolocate the number beyond just a city. By the time we'd arrived, the number had left Geneva and traveled about an hour north, along the lakeshore, to a tourist destination called Chillon Castle. And now we were trying to identify the man who held the phone.

We had an iPad-looking device called a Growler that could pinpoint the phone's signal—basically tricking it into thinking we were a cell tower—but that was only good enough to say you were close to the target. It couldn't pinpoint a person in a crowd, and this castle was crawling with tourists. Which is why I was considering the bomb threat. We could survey who was near us, call the threat, make everyone scatter, then locate the phone again. Once we surveyed **that** crowd, we'd be able to identify who was in the original location. Maybe we'd have to wait until the phone jumped one more time, but eventually, we'd correlate the person with the handset.

Right now, in the courtyard of the castle, I had no signal on the Growler, but Brett and Knuckles had one on the second floor. It was weak, but they were closing in.

The phone was here. We just needed to find the owner.

Amena studied the tourists, looking for an easy mark. There was one fat man with two kids who were constantly distracting him, along with a wife who clutched her purse a little too loose, but Amena held back. She no longer had her brother to help, and she needed to get out clean. Within this castle there would be no running to safety if she was caught, but she most definitely needed money.

Outside of some stale bread she'd found in a trash bin behind a Nice train station bakery, she hadn't eaten in a day and a half.

On the night of the horror, she'd fled the police station blindly, running straight back down the hill toward the Mediterranean coast, no other thought than to get away from the killer chasing her. She'd gravitated to the familiar, not knowing what else to do, running to the Eze train station. By the time she'd arrived, she was ragged and sweaty, but thinking more clearly. She'd originally intended to take the train to Monaco, but decided to go to Nice instead. She didn't know it nearly as well, but she was convinced the killer knew she frequented Monaco, and he would find her there.

She'd boarded the final scheduled train, hiding in an empty car. She'd made it to Nice without any problems, and had spent the night curled up in a restroom in the station, the door locked behind her. She'd slept fitfully, nightmares of her travails snapping her awake, causing her to sob uncontrollably until the exhaustion took over again. When dawn arrived, she was stiff and hungry.

She'd cleaned the blood off her clothing as best she could in the bathroom sink, then had dumpster-dived behind a bakery, finding yesterday's bagels in the trash. She'd eaten in the shadow of the bakery, seeing the sign for departing trains in the distance, watching the numbers flip as the trains came and went. And an idea formed.

She could take a train from here and go deeper into Europe, to a nation more welcoming of refugees. She scanned the sign and was dismayed to see that all of the trains went to either Italy or somewhere else in France. That was no good. She'd lived like an animal in the Italian refugee camp for weeks, and she'd experienced the disdain of the French since she'd escaped that hell.

Leaving here for another French or Italian town would not solve anything. She'd be in unfamiliar territory with the same hatred. The numbers flipped on the screen, and she saw one train leaving for Geneva, Switzerland, in twenty minutes. **Switzerland.** She knew nothing about the country, barely knew it even existed, but it wasn't France or Italy.

She'd had no money for a ticket, but from what she knew on the train that ran to Monaco—and had allowed her to escape to Nice—nobody ever checked for a ticket. She'd never once been questioned. Everyone seemed to buy a ticket out of honesty, but no authority ever confirmed. Supposedly there was a system to catch cheaters, but she'd never seen it.

She'd tossed the final bagel in the trash and went to the platform only to see a man in a train uniform checking tickets before letting anyone board. That was something new.

She watched for a moment, seeing him look at a ticket, then direct one couple back outside the ropes to the front of the train, where the first-class section was located. She watched closely, and they boarded without any further involvement from the train personnel. She walked down the platform, smoothing her hands against her jeans, attempting to clean up her appearance.

She'd sidled forward, took one look back at the conductor, then scampered on the train, seeing the first-class cabin mostly empty. She'd taken a seat in the back, and the train had rolled. Four hours into the trip, she traveled down the car to the bathroom and had seen a conductor punching tickets in the following car. She'd felt the blood drain from her face, the fight-or-flight instinct erupting within her, but there was nowhere to flee, and fighting would do nothing but get her arrested again.

The conductor advanced through the cabin, and she took a breath, entering the bathroom, praying he would pass. He did not. He knocked on the door, startling her. She flushed the toilet and exited, acting scared at the intrusion—although it wasn't really much of an act. She prayed her young age would save her.

It did. He glanced over her head, saw the bathroom was empty, and after a few words, she was allowed to scuttle past him to her "family."

She'd arrived in Geneva just as scared as when she'd landed in Italy on the Navy ship. But at least in Italy, she'd had her brother and father. Now all she had was herself.

She'd stopped in the station, sat on a bench, and pulled out the stolen phone. She googled the city, familiarizing herself with it.

In her heart she knew she should have thrown the iPhone into the trash or destroyed it outright, but she hadn't. They'd killed her family for it, and so a stubborn part of her had kept it. It was a touchstone to her father and brother, like an unspoken oath. The murderers wanted it badly enough to take the lives of her family, and so she would keep it from them. Besides, she'd killed one of them. She was sure they wouldn't quit trying to find her whether she had the phone or not.

She was too young to realize that the phone itself was a threat. A beacon guiding her enemies to her.

She'd spent the morning wandering around Geneva, looking for a mark to rob, the hunger growing stronger. She had no luck, because she was too afraid of hitting a local. She wanted a tourist. Someone who wasn't familiar with the police system and how to alert them.

She realized what she truly needed was a target-rich environment. A place where only tourists would go, minimizing the risk of robbing someone who lived in Geneva.

She'd used the phone, and had found the Chillon Castle. She'd taken the train up the coast of Lake Geneva, happily finding it like the train from Eze to Monaco. Nobody checked for tickets. She'd left the train at the Chillon stop and walked to the castle entrance, taking a seat on a bench next to a trash bin, watching the people exit. Sooner or later, someone would use the trash can. She didn't have to wait long. Within twelve minutes, a thin man with a sun hat had thrown his ticket away. She waited until he was across the road, then dug it out. From there, it had been a small matter to claim she was going back into the castle to find her parents, showing the ticket with the bar code. The lady at the entrance hadn't even bothered to scan it.

She'd passed through the gate, the walkways flush with tourists, looking for a mark that would give her enough of a stake to eat for a few days. She decided on the fat man with the obnoxious kids. She patiently followed them through the castle until they rose to the second floor, entering a great room.

A granite dining hall, the space was huge, complete with a giant wooden table and a fireplace large enough to park a car. Tourists wandered about, looking out the window toward the lake, or taking pictures of a sixteenth-century toilet that dropped the waste straight into the water below.

She closed within four feet of her target and caught the eye of another man who was looking at her. Tall, with a hatchet face and some sort of tattoo on his back crawling up his neck, he didn't give off the vibe of a tourist. She backed off, pretending to read a plaque describing the fireplace. The man didn't continue on. She went to the other side of the room, toward a sign with an arrow showing the way for the self-guided tour. The man followed, sending a bolt of adrenaline through her, her hunger forgotten.

She wasn't the only hunter in the room. He was stalking her.

26

★★

I found it." The three words came through his cell phone, bringing a smile to Tagir Kurbanov's face for the first time in days.

Finally. He said, "You sure?"

"Yeah. The phone signal's sky-high, and the device you gave me has tightened to fifty feet of probable error, meaning it's in the same room as me."

"How many people in the room?"

"Probably thirty. It's a big room."

"So how do you know who has it?"

"It's the girl."

"The kid? She kept the phone? She didn't sell it?"

He couldn't believe it. He was convinced she would sell it as soon as she could, but when it had remained in the Nice train station for close to seven hours, he'd feared she'd simply ditched it in the trash for anyone to find. During that time, Tagir had had his hands full dealing with his actions at the police station—sterilizing the area as best he could, ditching the rental car that was under his now-dead partner's name, and calling for further instructions from his Wagner bosses.

He'd awoken Dmitri Pavlov before the sun crested the horizon, hoping the search for the phone was no longer relevant, but that was not to be. Dmitri was still fanatically adamant about retrieving it, and he'd given Tagir an earful about his "wasting time" instead of chasing it down immediately.

Disgusted, Tagir had listened to Dmitri rant, thinking, **Clearly the company has my welfare at heart.**

He'd said, "Dmitri, I just slaughtered an entire French police station and lost the partner you gave me in a single night. There were precautions I had to take. Some cleanup to execute."

"We don't have time for that. Every minute that phone is loose is a risk. You worry about being caught for what you did to find it, but you should be worrying about what will happen if it's lost."

"I'll find the phone. It's in Nice, and it's been there for the night. My bet is the girl threw it in the trash."

By the time he'd cauterized his connections in Eze and made it to Nice, the phone was on its way to Geneva, Switzerland. The second call to Dmitri hadn't been as pleasant as the first. Dmitri started screaming, and through the projected anger, Tagir heard something else: fear.

He'd interrupted and said, "I need a crew. And not that Russian gangster crap you gave me in Eze. I need Wagner men."

Dmitri started to protest, and Tagir had had enough. "Get me the men, or get the phone yourself."

He'd hung up, then went into a bathroom to clean off the grime from the last twenty-four hours. He'd splashed water on his face, having no idea he was within arm's reach of where his target had been less than three hours earlier. He caught his reflection in the mirror and paused, wondering what he had become.

A recollection of his childhood floated up, when he'd been about the same age as the target he was chasing. His brother hounding him through the woods, his mother hanging clothes in the summer air, his father chopping wood. Not a care in the world.

It was the last good memory he owned.

Shortly thereafter, Grozny was leveled and his family wiped out. And now he was hunting a girl not unlike himself. An orphan. A daughter of war. The difference was that **he** had created her condition. Regardless of what horrors had driven her to flee her country, he had been the one to wipe out her family.

He stared at his reflection, wanting to feel revulsion. Wanting the remorse to flow. It didn't. All he saw was a man executing a mission, like so many others in a savage world.

She was nothing more than collateral damage. It wasn't his fault she'd stolen the telephone. It was hers. He'd faced much worse in Grozny than he'd given her here, and he'd lived. Some are predators, and some are prey. That was simply the way of the world. She could live, too, if she wanted to become a predator. Like he had.

He saw the reflection grin back at him like an out-of-body experience.

That isn't happening. Especially after what she's put me through.

He left the bathroom and took a seat on a bench next to the entrance, waiting for a special arrival. At ten in the morning, four men walked into the lobby of the station, all heads on a swivel, analyzing the atmospherics. One was tall and lean, with a tattoo crawling up his neck. Two had bands of muscle rippling all over, to the point of being almost caricatures from a superhero comic, one with a ponytail and the other with a crew cut, giving them the look of identical twins who their parents were trying to keep distinct. The last was older, with glasses, a bulbous nose, and a shag of salt-and-pepper hair.

To the uninitiated, they simply looked a little rough, but Tagir knew who they were as soon as they'd opened the door. He could see the same aura of death surrounding them that he'd seen in the mirror earlier.

He'd given them an overview of what had transpired, and they'd taken the next train to Geneva. From there, it had been a simple matter to geolocate the phone to the Chillon Castle, making up for the trouble the girl had given him earlier. And now they'd pinpointed it.

Tagir said, "Are you sure it's her? Do you see the phone?"

"I don't see the handset, but it's her. She's not from here, she's acting skittish, and she has shown no connection to anyone else. I mean, what's she doing here by herself? Makes no sense. It's her."

From inside his rental car, Tagir looked at the castle entrance, thinking. They could end it right here, if they could get the girl alone. He said, "Okay, vector in the others. I'm no good for this. If she sees me, she'll bolt. She knows me by sight."

"Tagir, we can't take her here. There's no clean area. It's all tourists, and there are cameras all over the place. I'd recommend waiting."

Tagir grimaced, but understood. He knew the urgency behind the mission, and didn't want to wait, but it was good to finally have a team that knew what they were doing, instead of a jerk-off who thought gold chains and intimidation was a winning strategy.

He said, "Understood. If you get the chance, execute. If not, just keep eyes on and wait until she leaves. She's not getting away. She's alone in a world where she doesn't belong. She has no friends to help her."

27

⋆
⋆⋆

Jennifer wanted to inspect every inch of the courtyard, reading one boring plaque after another about life in the Middle Ages, but I was itching to get into a position to support our other surveillance team. I said, "Blood, Blood, you got a vector yet?"

"Yeah. Well, no, but yeah. Knuckles and I are in the main dining hall, second floor. The Growler is pinging red, but the room's full. He's here."

"And?"

"Looking at the crowd, there is no Syrian man in here. But I've got two jokers acting strange. They aren't tourists. They're something else."

"Something else how?"

"Not sure, but they're giving off a vibe. They aren't here for the castle."

Veep cut in, saying, "It's more than two. It's four. I saw two muscle heads enter who definitely weren't tourists."

I'd placed Veep at the entrance as rear security,

telling him to analyze anyone who entered or left. I usually gave him a ration of shit about being a millennial, but he was very sharp on reading a crowd. On a mission in the past, he'd spotted men that I had missed. If he called them, I believed it.

I said, "Knuckles, what do you make of this? What's going on? The phone was here before we entered. If Veep's right, then those guys he saw don't have it."

"Maybe they're hunting it, and my guys have it. They aren't muscle heads. One's thin, with a tattoo crawling up his neck. The other's an older guy, but he's hard."

Which was exactly what I didn't want to hear, but it was what had sprung to mind before I asked the question. I said, "Okay, so we have two targets that we think have the phone, and two targets that may be hunting it. I need a lock-on to both sets."

Knuckles said, "Just sent you photos of our targets. You need to locate the other two."

My phone dinged, and I pulled up the picture, seeing a lean guy with some sort of tribal art on his neck and a man with glasses and a shag of salt-and-pepper hair who might've passed for a college professor if not for his dead eyes.

I said, "Got it. Koko and I are going hunting. Keep eyes on. Veep, keep alert out there."

He said, "Roger all."

I turned to find Jennifer, and bumped into her

standing right next to me. She looked at me expectantly and I said, "Done with the archaeological work?"

She smiled, now into the mission, holding out a map. She pointed and said, "This is Knuckles and Brett's location. I say we go to the keep."

"Because it's more cool than that great room they're in?"

"Yep. It's the final battle position for the last stand of the castle. I figured you'd like that. And because they'll see the muscle heads before we will on that side. The side with the keep is clean, no eyes on."

I smiled. "Lead the way."

I gave an update to the team, and we walked across the courtyard, the castle keep rising in front of us like a granite tube puckered with slots for archers. We went up level after level, passing tourists along the way and clearing the small rooms and hallways that led off of the keep, not seeing our targets. Eventually, we went higher than the roof of the castle, reaching the top of the keep with an expansive view of the entire compound and the terrain beyond. We hadn't seen the muscle heads.

I leaned out, searching the tourist crowd four stories below, and Brett called, saying, "The two suspects left my room, and the Growler dropped. It's them."

Knuckles said, "I'm on them. They're heading to the prison in the basement."

Out of the corner of my eye, I caught movement,

going much faster than the leisurely tourists gawking at the sights. Two men forcing their way through the crowd, moving to the exit. And they were big.

I caught Jennifer's attention, pointed at them, and said, "Keep eyes on."

I got on the net, saying, "Got the muscle heads. They're in the courtyard, heading toward the front exit."

Jennifer glanced up and said, "That's also the northern exit from the prison. You can get in from the north on the outside, or the south from the inside."

I said, "Where are they?"

"Unsighted. They're either headed down, or exiting."

I turned to the stairwell, taking them two at a time, Jennifer right behind me. I said, "Veep, Veep, status?"

"Pike, they didn't exit."

"Knuckles, Blood, you copy?"

"This is Knuckles. We copy. What's the ROE if they go kinetic?"

Meaning, what do you want us to do if the muscle heads try to take out the phone crew? Technically, there was nothing I could order them to do. We had Alpha authority only, which meant no interdiction of the target. But I could at least put my guys in harm's way to prevent that. I was sure they were itching for such a thing, and more than willing to risk life and limb without the ability to do anything back.

Because they couldn't imagine a life without me as a leader.

I said, "No kinetic action. What I want you to do is stick close to the targets. Remain in eyesight so that the muscle heads will have to take you into account if they try anything."

I got back, "Are you shitting me? So just put me and Blood in the room as a deterrent, but if that doesn't work, run?"

We reached the bottom and I said, "Yeah, that's pretty much it. You always have the right of self-defense. Koko and I are on the way."

"Pike, if they execute here, we're going to lose both the target and the phone."

I raced across the courtyard, moving as fast as I could without running flat out and alerting anyone that something strange was happening. The last thing I wanted to do was be on a highlight reel from a surveillance camera if something did go down.

I heard, "In the dungeon. Few tourists. Just a child, us, and the targets. We're burned for further work."

I posted Jennifer on the outside of the entrance stairwell and said, "I'm on the way down. Meet you in the middle."

I reached the bottom, the area more like a cave, with rough stone walls carved straight out of the earth and iron grates looking out onto the lake, the pillars inside crowned in chains, replicating what life was like for prisoners eons ago. I saw a group of tourists headed my way, and knew Knuckles and Brett must be deeper in.

I started down the path and heard, "Muscle heads in sight. They're closing on us."

I entered an empty room with a gallows, a hangman's noose blowing in the breeze coming off the lake, and began sprinting. I reached the open door to the next room and heard, "Muscle heads walked right by us. Kept going."

I halted and smiled, saying, "Looks like you two badasses stopped them with just a glance."

I pulled into an alcove, hearing, "Yeah, yeah. I love being your bait."

I waited and a little girl of about thirteen exited, looking scared for some reason.

Probably lost her parents.

Thirty seconds later, the targets exited, not seeing me. They moved fast to the stairwell, and Jennifer called, "Targets out, moving to the exit."

Knuckles appeared and I stepped out. He said, "You are a piece of work."

I keyed my mic and said, "Veep, they're headed your way. Don't lose them. Koko, back him up."

I heard, "Got them. Headed to the train station. Want me to follow?"

I grinned at Knuckles and said, "Mission accomplished. And all it took was a little heat glare from you."

I keyed the radio and said, "Yes. You and Koko have them. We're moving to the rentals. Just vector us in."

I heard, "Roger," then Knuckles said, "What about the beef that's still here? They wanted the target. Should we keep eyes on them?"

I thought about it, and couldn't decide. On the one hand, they were a threat, but on the other, I'd need everyone we had to run a proper surveillance of the new targets. I said, "What do you think?"

Brett cut in, saying, "Let 'em go. We know what they look like, and if they enter our bubble, we'll see them. Don't split the team just to follow them. It'll burn us with them if we need the element of surprise."

I nodded and looked at Knuckles. He said, "I agree. Let's get to the cars."

28

★★
★

Amena walked out of the castle and up the tracks to the platform, seeing a train approaching. She jogged forward, reaching the platform just as it pulled to a stop. She waited for the passengers to exit, then boarded. Normally, she would seek out an empty car, but today she wanted people. The risk of getting killed far outweighed getting thrown off for not having a ticket.

She took a seat facing the platform and saw the tattooed man approach with his partner. They both entered, but didn't come into her car.

The doors closed, and the train pulled away for the short ride to the town of Montreux. She used the time to google the town on her phone. She'd looked once before, but had decided to go farther to Chillon Castle. From what she remembered, the lakefront was where all of the tourists were located, with a lakeshore path that meandered through parks and restaurants. Exactly what she needed.

If the men stayed on the train, she might be able

to execute her original plan and garner money for food. If they got off, she would use the crowds to prevent them from doing anything.

She thought about going to the police, but she wasn't sure if she was just being paranoid. Turning herself in simply because someone had looked at her strangely might lead to her being shipped back to France, or worse, Syria. And she remembered what the killer had done the last time she'd been in police custody. No way was she going to let herself get locked up again, like a goat on a stake.

The train pulled into the Montreux stop, and she hesitated. The doors opened, but the men didn't move. She waited until the last moment, then exited. She went down the platform, then took an escalator up to the station. When she reached the top, she went left and stole a glance back down. She felt a sledgehammer of fear.

The two men were on the escalator, leading a group of passengers who had all exited late. She snapped her face to the front, controlling her emotions, and entered the station. As soon as she was through the door, she began running, wanting to get to the waterfront.

She exited onto a street, unsure of where she was. She saw a sign proclaiming Avenue des Alpes, and went left, walking fast and looking at her phone. She saw she was basically traveling parallel to the lake, with the avenue getting closer to the shore, but never reaching it.

She glanced behind her, and recognized the men. They were walking in the same direction she was. The fear returned. She went through three blocks, not wanting to wait on a crossing light and let the men catch up to her.

Eventually, she reached an intersection where the light was in her favor. She ran across the street, praying the signal would change before they could follow her. She didn't bother glancing back, but kept jogging toward the lakeshore.

She entered a section of restaurants, with more and more pedestrians on meandering walking paths. She was close.

She burst out into a courtyard, with a statue of a man holding his fist in the air, tourists surrounding it, taking selfies.

She went by them, reaching the large concrete path that snaked left and right against the shore of Lake Geneva. She continued south, looking for a place to hide. A restaurant was out, because she had no money. They wouldn't let her stay. She needed a place that was free of charge, where people could come and go.

She kept walking, working her phone and hoping she looked like every other teenager in Switzerland. The thought brought a nervous giggle. How many other teenagers were using their phones to escape a violent death? Answer: none.

Using Google Maps, she zoomed in on a casino, just a hundred meters ahead. A place where tourists milled about, visiting at all hours. She put the phone away and picked up her pace.

She saw the casino ahead, walked by an alley, and circled toward the lakefront entrance. She opened the door and stepped inside, hearing the clanging and ringing of slot machines, the space full of people meandering in all directions. And a security guard at the door.

She felt relief. She took two steps forward when the security man stopped her, saying in French, "Hold on there, little lady."

She stopped and said, "Yes?"

"You looking for your parents?"

She shook her head, now wishing she hadn't entered.

He said, "I'm sorry, but you're too young to enter."

Next to him was a poster with a picture of a man holding his fist in the air and screaming into a microphone. She recognized him. It was the statue she'd passed earlier. Underneath him was printed THE QUEEN STUDIO EXPERIENCE, FREE. She pointed to it.

The guard smiled and said, "Oh. Yeah, that's here, but it has its own entrance around the front. You can't get there from here. You'll have to go back out."

She nodded and exited the casino rapidly, feeling the sweat growing on her neck. **This isn't going to work**. She was squeezed between men who wanted to harm her and her own illegal status. She closed her eyes, feeling the tears well up. She wanted her mother.

If it is to be, it is up to me.

She opened her eyes and retraced her steps, seeing the tattooed man coming up the lake path, now by himself. Before he could see her, she darted into the alley she'd passed earlier and ran to the end, bursting onto the city street fronting the casino. She went down it until she saw a sign for the exhibit, and entered, finding herself on a balcony above the casino floor, the cacophony of ringing and clanging returning.

She went down the balcony until she reached an open door. She glanced inside and saw some sort of museum.

What is Queen?

She entered, seeing multiple tourists wandering about the small space, pictures of the man from the statue all over the walls and inside individual exhibits. She assumed he was some sort of statesman. Possibly someone who worked for the queen of Switzerland.

She went in deeper, seeing a photograph of the man standing behind a row of women on bicycles, their breasts exposed.

What in the world?

Switzerland royalty was not what she had expected.

And neither was this "experience." It was much too small for her to stay for any length of time, even with the crowds. Eventually, someone would wonder what she was doing remaining in the exhibit room.

She went down a short hallway, parted a curtain,

and found a tiny theater showing a silent movie, the man from the statue on the screen. The theater only housed about eight or ten people, and she saw they all had on headphones. She looked around, but no other headsets were available.

She sat in the back, wondering how long the movie would run. No sooner had she'd thought it than the movie ended, and people began to leave. She slid to the right rear seat, where she could see the door without being immediately seen, and put on a headset, pretending to wait for the movie to start. She was petrified the tattooed man would appear, but after several minutes alone, she began to relax. She could stay in here all day long.

Three people came in, including a man with a ponytail she thought she recognized. Bristling with muscle, his arms threatening to split his shirt, she'd seen him somewhere.

He put on his headphones, glanced her way, and in that single look, she knew.

29

★★★

Tagir got the call that the girl hadn't traveled back to Geneva, but had exited at Montreux, and began to feel she was somehow outsmarting him. He'd already assumed she was returning to Geneva and had raced down the highway to meet the train. His patience was wearing thin with her antics.

He whipped his car around, heading back toward Montreux, and said, "Tell me someone has her."

"I do. Me and Simon. She's walking down the street right now, headed toward the lakefront."

"What about Markov and Luca?"

"They're on the ground, but we've got the eye."

"Okay, keep on her. Control the team until I get there."

"Got it."

"Listen, if you get the chance, take that bitch out. I don't care about surgical. I want her dead, and the phone in our hands."

"Will do."

By the time he'd found a place to park, the girl was inside a casino, with Simon still on her tail. He got an update, hearing that she wasn't in the actual casino, but inside some exhibit attached to it. Simon was waiting outside.

Tagir said, "Hold where you are. You've been behind her for damn near an hour. I'm switching you out. Markov, Luca, you on the net?"

"This is Luca. I'm outside the casino. Markov is down the street, locking down the exit."

"Okay, get inside and trade out with Simon. Go into the exhibit and get me a readout of what she's doing."

"Moving now."

Seven minutes later, Luca called back, saying, "She's in a small theater, watching a free movie."

Bad for her. Good for him.

"Get in there with her. If it's dark enough, eliminate her right there and leave the body."

Luca said, "I'm inside, but it's not that kind of theater. I mean, it's small, like for only ten people, and it's not dark. It's fully illuminated. It's more like a living room than a theater."

Tagir pounded his steering wheel and said, "What does it take to get you guys to execute? Kill that bitch."

"She's moving. She's going past me. She's out of the theater."

"Follow her, and when you get a shot at her, take it."

From the casino floor, wasting Taskforce money in a slot machine, I spotted Tattoo Guy. For whatever reason, he had entered the balcony to the Queen exhibit, but refused to enter the museum. The Growler was pinging, so I figured he had the phone and not his professor-looking partner. I'd left Knuckles to keep eyes on him at the lakefront, and then had staged Brett and Veep left and right of the casino entrance to pick up the follow when Tattoo left. I was running short of personnel, but I had Jennifer as my reserve. From our position, I could throw her out the back toward Knuckles or out the front toward the surveillance box.

I said, "What in the world is this city's fascination with Queen?"

We'd seen the Freddie Mercury statue as we tailed Tattoo and Professor, and now I was in a casino that proclaimed a Queen "studio experience."

Jennifer shoveled money into her machine and laughed, saying, "Are you serious?"

I pulled my slot arm, getting nothing, but keeping an eye on Tattoo. A little miffed, I said, "Well, yeah, I guess I am."

"This is a famous place. It was his recording studio. All of Queen's popular songs were recorded here. In fact, the casino itself is famous. It burned to the ground once, while Deep Purple was here making a record. They sat outside and wrote 'Smoke on the Water,' which was about this place burning down. Freddie Mercury rebuilt it and began recording here. The museum is his old studio."

I turned to her and said, "No shit? You some sort of Queen groupie or something?"

She grinned and said, "No shit. But I'm not a groupie. I just do my research beforehand."

"Well, what's that research telling you about Tattoo being in here?"

She pulled her slot arm, hit a bingo, collected her coins, and said, "I have no idea. This thing is getting stranger and stranger. First the Chillon Castle, now this? It's almost like they're trying to confuse **us** about their intentions."

"Or confuse those meatheads who are following them."

No sooner had I said that when Brett called, saying, "Pike, Pike, I've got Ponytail Meathead coming in. I say again, hunters are closing in."

How are they tracking this guy? They weren't on the train with Veep, and yet here they are.

I said, "Is he printing?"

Meaning, **Can you see a weapon under his clothes?**

"Not that I can tell, but he's about to breach. Want me to follow?"

I was relieved to hear it. I'd decided not to bring any weapons on our surveillance effort because having one on a recce usually caused more problems than it solved. It was a straight Alpha mission, and I had no idea about the security posture of Switzerland. Potentially, we could lose the guy if he went into a courthouse or museum that was armed with metal detectors like in the US, so I'd made the call to leave the guns behind.

I said, "Negative. No follow. Tattoo is on the balcony in full view of the casino. He won't do anything here."

We watched the upper entrance, and saw the mountain of a man silhouetted in the light of the doorway. He turned, walked straight to Tattoo Guy, and they exchanged words. Tattoo Guy patted Meathead on the shoulder, and left. Meathead entered the exhibit.

I checked the Growler, and it was still pinging.

What the hell?

I called, "All elements, all elements, the muscle heads aren't tracking the other two. They're working together. Tattoo just passed the phone to Ponytail Meathead. Hold your positions. Ignore Tattoo. Ponytail is the new target."

A group of tourists exited the exhibit, chattering and laughing on their way out. I saw a small girl dart between them, running toward the door. I'd seen her before, in Chillon, right in front of Tattoo and Professor. She wasn't moving with childlike innocence, as if she were attempting to annoy her parents. She was running scared.

She exited the casino, and Ponytail Meathead appeared, walking with a purpose toward the door and talking into a cell phone. I checked the Growler, and it was zeroed out. No signal at all.

It took the wind out of me, the realization slamming home.

Jesus Christ. It's the girl. They're tracking the girl.

I watched Meathead disappear out the door and knew that little girl had minutes to live. I had to make a decision. One I hadn't been given the authority to make.

Fuck it.

I keyed my radio.

30

★
★ ★

Amena cracked open the casino door, glanced up and down the street, then exited, her heart beating as fast as a hummingbird. She didn't see the tattooed man or his partner, but that was little consolation. The ponytailed man in the casino told her that she had no idea how many were out here hunting. She began walking rapidly toward the alley, wanting to get back to the lakeshore path and the tourists from around the world. Her first thought was to return to the statue, where she'd seen the throngs taking photos.

She slipped into the alley, seeing the lake seventy meters away. She began running, her little legs pumping as hard as she could make them. She was within twenty meters of the exit when the tattooed man appeared at the end.

She skidded to a stop, her mouth open in a silent scream. He bared his teeth at her and began walking up the alley. She whipped around and began running back the way she had come. She managed seven steps before the giant with the ponytail appeared, coming down the alley from the other end, holding his arms out as if he were catching a loose chicken, the veins crisscrossing his forearms highlighting the muscles.

She turned back, seeing the tattooed man closing in on her. She backed up against the wall, holding up her hands and saying, "Don't, don't, don't."

With an accent so strong she could barely understand his English, he said, "Where is the phone?"

Her legs failed her. She slid down the wall until she was sitting down, her arms over her head.

The giant man grabbed her hair, jerking her back up. She squeezed her eyes shut, silently calling for her mother.

She heard what sounded like meat being slapped in a butcher's shop, then was unceremoniously dropped to the ground. She opened her eyes and saw a black man above her, striking the giant with blows so fast they were a blur, the giant's hands always a split second behind as his head snapped back, absorbing every punch.

The tattooed man shouted, raising his fists. She threw her hands over her head again and a form jumped over her body, colliding with her enemy. Wide-eyed, she watched the struggle, both grunting, the sweat flying off from the fight. Two seconds later she saw the tattooed man flying over the back of the other man, her rescuer holding his elbow as her enemy slammed into the wall next to her head.

The body crumpled to the ground, unconscious, and her benefactor turned to her, holding out his hand. He smiled, and she leapt up, running toward the waterfront, expecting him to grab her. He did nothing. She exited the alley, her lungs sucking in great gouts of air. She began sprinting blindly back to the statue, her brain reverting to a primordial instinct of survival.

She cut into a park, racing down a path that wound through the trees, and ran headlong into the older man. The tattooed man's partner. She struggled to escape his grasp, and he snatched her up by her neck. He held her high with both hands, her feet twitching in the air, and then something slammed into him with the force of a freight train. She bounced on the ground, rolled upright, and saw a chiseled man with shaggy black hair cradling the older man's head in his arms, Tattoo's partner thrashing like a shark on a line, his glasses askew, and spittle flying from his mouth.

She leapt up again, her own mouth agape, and raced out of the park, her mind unable to assimilate what was happening. She broke out into a street and realized, in her disorientation, she'd run **away** from the lake. She glanced down the avenue and saw another giant of muscle stalking toward her, this one with his head shorn close to his scalp.

They're everywhere. And I'm going to die.

She ran up the street, now without a plan. Like a car thief sprinting from police after wrecking the ride, her only thought was to get away.

The road took a turn, and she was out of sight of the mountain of muscle, hidden by the buildings along the road. Ahead of her, the avenue bridged a canal. When she reached it, she stopped, looking toward the lake.

The canal went under one other road before emptying at the shore. The channel was deep, but it only held what looked like three feet of water, and had a raised path on both sides. An idea formed. She glanced back to make sure the muscled giant hadn't made the turn, then scrambled over the railing, landing in a heap on the path. She scrambled underneath the bridge, wrapped her arms around her legs, and waited, trembling.

She heard cars passing over her, then laughter floating out from a group of tourists walking across the bridge. She began to hope. To believe the giant man had kept running down the road, trying to find her.

Her brain engaged again, the panic dissipating. She pulled out the cursed phone, feeling both loathing and love. It had killed her family, but it had also saved her life. She began googling the rail system out of Switzerland. She needed to leave behind anything these men knew, go someplace completely different. Maybe make it into Germany and turn herself in to the authorities.

The iPhone diligently searched for her request, then cleared. She clicked on a link for the Eurail website, and heard a thump to her left. She looked that way, and her world collapsed.

It was the giant. He stood on the other side of the bridge, grinning. He walked underneath, crouching low, and said, "Neat trick. But not good enough. Give me the phone."

She screamed and leapt up. He snagged her shirt and she jerked it free, running as fast as she could toward the lake, hearing his footsteps behind her, her conscious mind shutting down. She'd reached her breaking point, the whipsaw of repeated fear cracking her. Her mother had not been correct. **If it is to be, it's up to me** ended up being nothing more than a saying. It hadn't saved her life, just as it hadn't her mother's. Her father had also been wrong. His search for a better life had ended in a rain of blood.

And she was next.

She ducked under the next bridge, cleared the other side, and saw her worst nightmare standing on the path. The man who had murdered her family. The one who had slaughtered an entire police station.

Her legs faltered, and she fell to her knees. She was done.

He walked to her and said, "Hand me the phone."

She pulled it out of her pocket, her hand trembling. She said, "Take it. Take it and let me live. Please."

He didn't reach for the handset, instead looking

into her eyes. He said, "I wish I could, but you've used that phone. Which means you've seen what's inside."

She started sobbing, shaking uncontrollably, holding the phone out as an offering with her head bent down. She said, "This isn't right. You killed my entire family. Isn't that enough? Take it. Please. This isn't right."

He said, "I'm sorry, but right's got nothing to do with it."

He took a step forward, and a shadow blotted out her vision. A man thumped to the ground in between her and the killer. He turned to her, and she saw another predator. A man with close-cropped hair, ice-blue eyes, and a scar tracing a path through his cheek.

She was dead.

He rotated until he had one man on the left, and the other on the right, his back to the wall of the canal, then said, "Get behind me."

What? She didn't move, still trembling on the ground.

He flicked his eyes to her, then returned to the two men, his voice like steel. "Get behind me. Now."

She recognized the accent, and the clock of her life began beating again. **He's American!**

She scampered behind his back, cowering and using him as a shield. The killer said, "I have no idea who you are, but this isn't your concern. You are making a huge mistake."

The predator said, "Am I? Because I only caught

the last part of the conversation. Did you really murder her family?"

The killer shook his head, as if he disdained the conversation. He said, "Yes. Just like I'm going to kill you."

The man in front of her changed in that moment. Becoming something else. Something unworldly. Amena saw it, and was frightened, even with the others trying to take her life.

From the left, the mountain of muscle charged forward, swinging a knife at the predator's chest. Like a magic trick, the predator trapped the giant's arm and rotated down, leveraging the momentum and causing all of that muscle to flip through the air. The giant of a man slammed into the stone, and the predator bent his arm forward, using the man's own knife to stab him in the heart, leaning over him to make sure it penetrated.

The murderer of her family launched himself at her protector, and Amena ran. Even if the American showed talent at fighting, she knew what the killer could do. The man with the scar wouldn't win. Nobody could win against the killer. She went twenty meters, cleared the other side of the bridge, and then turned, seeing them locked in combat.

She took one tentative step back, believing she should help—wanting to help. She saw the killer gain the upper hand, rolling on top of the American, and she turned, racing back up the canal the way she'd come.

31

★★

Jennifer and I were running toward the lakeshore path to Knuckles's location when he cut in on the net. "Pike, Pike, target is down, and the girl is in the wind."

Shit.

I held up, saying, "What happened?"

"She was attacked by that older asshole from the castle, the one we originally thought had the phone. He was holding her by her throat. I had to interdict."

Against all authority I'd been given, I'd made the call to track the girl and protect her, hoping against hope that we could follow all of them, then whisk her away from under their noses. Praying they weren't willing to execute an open-air interdiction, but would try to get her when she stopped for the night. That hadn't worked out. Within seven minutes of her leaving the Queen museum, she'd been assaulted.

Brett and Veep had stopped that idiocy, but she'd escaped because Veep "didn't want to scare her." I understood his sentiment, but it royally pissed me off. Brett calmed me down by saying they were better off searching for the men here than chasing after her. And he had a point.

Jennifer and I had exited out the front of the casino, moving up the street, waiting on a lock-on from anyone to tell me where she'd gone, and Knuckles had just given it.

I said, "You don't have control?"

"No. Sorry. I had some issues with the professor guy. Turned out, he could fight. I had to put him down."

"Permanently?"

"Yep. He wouldn't quit."

It raised my worry about what was happening. These guys weren't random human traffickers out to score a child. They were trained and had someone behind them. If Knuckles said the guy could fight, it meant he had to exert some energy to put him down, which meant that the guy could have probably destroyed 90 percent of American males.

I said, "No issue. Can you break from the body?"

"Yeah, no worries. He's in some bushes. No attachment to me. Nobody was in eyesight, and I scanned the area for cameras. He's got my DNA on him, but no connection."

That was basically the same story I'd received from Brett and Veep, except their guys were still breathing. So far we were in the black. I said, "Give me a vector."

He said, "She took off straight north, away from the lake. Right toward you, but she was running like a scalded monkey. You need to be quick to get her."

I glanced at Jennifer, who was already working her tablet, and said, "Koko's looking. Figuring out a search pattern."

She raised her tablet, showing me the screen, and, off the net, said, "I've got it."

Knuckles called back, saying, "I'm moving north in her last known direction. I just have no idea where she went. I don't have a Growler."

I said, "Hold what you have. She might double back. We've got the lake secure, and the east secure. We're going to take the west. Out."

I looked at Jennifer, and she said, "She's running straight into the city. If she deviates, it's going to be on this road." She pointed at the one we were on, "Or the one farther up. I'll take the high road. You take the lower. We push west, and see what we can find."

I nodded and said, "Okay, but if you locate her, call me. Don't try to interdict. There are enough assholes involved here that I don't trust a singleton assault. Get two or more, or back off."

She read right through me. "Meaning I might get my ass kicked?"

I looked into her eyes, knowing she thought I didn't trust her skills, but that wasn't it. I gave her the hard truth. "Meaning you might be killed. If Knuckles had trouble, they're experts. Call me, no matter what."

She squinted at me, not liking what I had said, then nodded and took off across the street. I started walking at a rapid pace west down the avenue, and then heard, "Pike, this is Koko, I'm on the parallel. Moving west now."

I acknowledged, and kept going, peering into shop windows and looking for anyone running on the street. I saw nothing. I checked my Growler, and had no signal, which frustrated the shit out of me because we had a much better capability to find that damn phone, but it required a spool-up. The girl was on the run, with probably about thirty minutes worth of life left, but it would take me three times that to get the giant bureaucracy to geolocate her handset. If she made it into the night, I would be able to track her again.

But I didn't think she had that long.

I reached a bridge across a canal, still seeing nothing. I began to jog across it, and felt my Growler vibrate.

Huh?

I stopped and brought it up. The signal was strong. I looked up and down, seeing nobody on the road. I went to the rail of the bridge, looking north. Nothing. I went to the south, and saw the girl.

She was on her knees in front of a man towering over her. A man who radiated skill. I'd seen his type before—every damn time I looked in a mirror.

She was holding a phone in the air and trembling, catatonic in fear. The sight brought a spasm of rage.

I whispered on the radio, saying, "All elements, all elements, I have her. She's with a hostile. Sending grid. Close on me now. As fast as possible."

I knelt down, pulled out my cell phone, and sent my location. I heard the girl offer a message of mercy. "This isn't right. You killed my entire family. Isn't that enough? Take it. Please. This isn't right."

The man said, "I'm sorry, but right's got nothing to do with it."

I'd told Jennifer not to interdict without backup, and I had fully intended to do the same, but the words ripped through me, tearing open a scab that had never healed.

Enough.

I vaulted over the railing, slamming into the ground between the girl and the man. I stood upright, caught movement over my shoulder, and saw the crew-cut mountain of muscle crouching underneath the bridge, a knife in his hand.

Shit. Bad decision.

I rotated my back to the stone of the canal and said, "Get behind me."

The girl looked at me like I was Freddy Krueger, her fear burning bright.

I put a little steel in my voice, locked eyes with her, and said, "Get behind me. Now."

I saw recognition on her face, of what I wasn't sure, but she scampered behind my back, holding on to the legs of my pants.

The man to my front said, "I have no idea who

you are, but this isn't your concern. You are making a huge mistake."

I kept one eye on the muscle and said, "Am I? Because I only caught the last part of the conversation. Did you really murder her family?"

He tossed his head left and right, like this was nothing but an inconvenience, then said, "Yes. Just like I'm going to kill you."

I heard the words and felt a crack in the blackness of my soul. Something I'd buried in years of scar tissue split, the evil slithering back out. The worm wanting satisfaction. Wanting to feed.

The man-mountain charged. He came forward at a dead run, swinging his knife, sure that all those hours in the gym would translate to an easy win. I dodged the blade, trapped his arm, locked up the joint of his elbow and wrist, then whirled in a circle, using his own momentum to flip him to the ground. He hammered hard onto his back, and I immediately torqued his arm over his chest, falling on the blade with my body and ramming it into his heart.

I whirled to the other threat, but I wasn't quick enough. The killer hit me in the shoulders, wrapping his arms around me and taking me to the ground. Within a split second, I knew he could fight. Everything was an economy of motion, designed to protect his vital parts while harming mine. He tried for a quick-finish arm bar, but I evaded his hold, and then we started swimming, arms and legs all fighting for dominance. I saw his eyes widen, realizing the same thing I had about him.

Yeah, asshole. I can fight, too.

He mounted on top of me, crossed his wrists, grabbed my collar, and jerked outward, trying to choke me. I broke one hand free and punched him with an ineffectual hammer fist to the head. He leaned forward, his head tucked, and slammed me with his elbow, ripping my face. I locked my legs over his and torqued, flipping him onto his back. He countered, wrapping his legs around my waist. I swam a hand under his thigh, broke the hold, and punched him directly in the face. He rolled away from me and I scrambled to keep up the pressure. I wrapped my arms around his body, attempting to gain a rear naked choke, and he threw another elbow, catching me in the nose with the force of a jackhammer. I saw sparks, and lost the momentum. I continued to hold him, but my head was in a fog from the blow. He spun on his back, grabbing my arm and jerking me close to him. He whirled his legs and locked them around my neck in a triangle choke. He began squeezing. I felt the pressure and knew I had seconds before I passed out from the lack of oxygen to my brain.

The son of a bitch is going to win. Kill me.

I huffed like a bull, the blood snorting out of my nostrils. I heaved off the ground, his legs still locked around my neck, his hands holding my shirt. I staggered to the edge of the canal, him still squeezing, a maniacal look on his face. I dropped forward into the water, falling on top of him.

I saw his face under the surface, eyes wide, his legs squeezing harder, his body thrashing to get oxygen, realizing it was a race. The fight had left us both heaving, but I could still get air even as he cut off my blood flow. I felt my vision tunnel, saw his head break the plane of water, and I slammed my hand on his face, pushing it back below the surface. I hammered his stomach, saw an explosion of bubbles, and my vision closed to black. I lost consciousness for a split second, and then felt the legs leave my neck. The blood flowed, and my vision opened again, like a curtain being drawn back.

He had given up and was now trying to escape. He broke the surface, coughing water and gasping for air. I grabbed his neck, the demon consuming me, the need for vengeance overpowering. He slapped his hands on my wrist, and I drove him back under the water. He struggled for a blissful amount of seconds, thrashing about, his legs kicking above the water while I held his head below, bringing me joy. The legs sank under the waterline, now only twitching. And then he stopped moving, his eyes staring at me from under the surface. Two small bubbles popped out of his open mouth and lazily floated upward.

I released my hands, feeling a tendril of shame at what I'd done. I'd let the blackness take me. Like an alcoholic sipping a drink, I'd failed. I crawled to the path above the canal, then collapsed, staring at the sky.

I heard running feet, then a shout. "Hey, you okay?"

I saw Knuckles on the bridge, bringing me back to the mission. Forcing me to be a team leader. The blackness could wait.

I remained on my back, saying, "Yeah, I'm okay. No thanks to your slow ass."

He laughed and said, "Well, get up here. Koko's got the kid."

32

⋆
⋆ ⋆

Amena sprinted back the way she'd come, her legs trembling in weakness at every step. The constant adrenaline and lack of food were taking a toll. Along with the deaths she'd caused. She reached the first bridge, crawled up the slope of the canal, and peeked out, turning her head left and right. She saw a couple with kids, a blond woman peering into a coffee shop, and two men of about seventy-five. She scrambled over the bank, then began walking rapidly down the street toward the train station. She didn't care what was leaving or where it was headed, she was going to be on it.

She passed a candy store, and a door slammed behind her. She jumped at the noise, then reacted by instinct, her body immediately running like a rabbit in a field. She caught her head on an outdoor sign, tearing her scalp and flipping her onto her back.

She rolled upright and started crying, wrapping her arms around her knees and rocking back and forth. She put her head down, her breath hitching.

She closed her eyes, and saw nothing but slaughter. Her mother. Her father. Her brother. And the man who'd just allowed her to escape.

She no longer wanted to continue. She wanted it all to end.

Someone tapped her crown and said, "Hey, are you okay?"

She snapped her head up, seeing a tall blond woman with kind, liquid eyes. Her first instinct was to run, but the woman's gaze held her in place. She remained mute, simply staring upward.

"My name is Jennifer."

Amena said nothing. The woman persisted, saying, "Are you lost? Did you lose your parents?"

The simple declaration brought a well of tears, Amena unable to stop herself, the sobs uncontrollable.

The woman sat down next to her, putting a hand on her shoulder, saying, "Whoa, whoa. What's that about? We can find them. Don't cry."

The words only increased her pain. The woman put her arm around Amena's shoulders and whispered, "Shhh. Stop. It's okay. Everything is going to be okay."

It was the first bit of kindness from a stranger she'd experienced since fleeing Syria. Without conscious thought, she leaned in, burrowing into the woman's side. She felt the woman rub a hand over her back, then wrap the other arm around her in a hug, saying, "It's okay. Nothing is as bad as it seems."

Amena sniffled, thinking, **This is.**

Her stomach growled loud enough to be heard ten feet away. The woman leaned back and said, "Was that you?"

The joke brought a weak smile to Amena's face. She looked up and nodded.

"Are you hungry? You want to go get some food?"

Amena said, "You mean, with you?"

Jennifer smiled and said, "Yes, of course with me, silly. It's called an invitation."

Amena hesitated, wanting desperately to go, but not wanting to put the woman in danger. The men chasing her would kill Jennifer as easily as they would her. She said, "I . . . I don't know. I should probably go. I have to get back."

"Back where?"

"Back . . . Just back."

"Well, you can go 'back' after you've had some food. Your stomach sounds like a lion roaring."

Amena sighed, the thought of a full belly too much. She said, "Okay, but we need to eat quickly. I can't stay long."

Jennifer stood up and held out her hand, saying, "That's fine by me. There's a deli right down the street. It looked good."

Amena took her hand, standing up, then realized something. "You're American?"

"I am. And you?"

"I'm not American, but I will be."

Jennifer laughed, an easy, relaxed sound that was

soothing. They walked down the street and Amena heard her say, "Pike, Pike, this is Koko."

Amena looked at her, and she said, "Sorry. My boyfriend's wandering around here somewhere. I need to let him know where I am."

Amena nodded, saying nothing. Jennifer listened to something, then said, "Hey, Knuckles, I'm headed to a deli with some precious cargo. I'll shoot you the location when we get there."

Amena scrunched up her eyes, and Jennifer said, "He's a friend of my boyfriend's. That jerk didn't answer the phone."

"His name is Knuckles? Is he American, too?"

Jennifer's laughter floated out again, causing Amena to shyly smile, proud she'd caused the reaction. Jennifer said, "It's a nickname. Don't ask me how he got it. They seem to tease each other with them."

They reached the deli, and Jennifer opened the door, letting Amena in first. Amena said, "Do they tease you? Do you have a nickname?"

Jennifer followed her and rolled her eyes, saying, "Yes, unfortunately, they do. But I don't let them use it unless we're on the phone."

"What is it?"

"Koko."

They reached the counter, and Amena said, "Like the talking gorilla? The one that does sign language?"

Jennifer's face flashed surprise. She said, "Yes. That's exactly what it is. How did you know?"

Miffed, Amena said, "I can read. When she died a few months ago it was all over the web."

Jennifer appraised her for a moment, then looked up at the menu on the wall and said, "Order whatever you want. It's on me."

Amena did, buying much more food than she could possibly eat. Jennifer said, "Is that it? Or do you want to order something for the town as well?"

Amena grinned and said, "And a chocolate milkshake."

They took a seat, waiting for the food to arrive, and Amena said, "Why do they call you a gorilla?"

"It's a long story. Let's talk about you."

In that moment, Amena wanted to tell her everything. Put herself in the hands of someone who might help. Relieve herself of the burden of survival. But she didn't. She couldn't place anyone else's life in danger. She'd been the cause of death for too many already.

"I don't want to talk about me."

"Why not? I'd like to know where you're from. You know I'm from America, what about you?"

Amena stared out the window, and before she could stop herself, she said, "I'm from nowhere. I have no home."

Her eyes welled up, remembering the American

who'd helped her. The one she'd run from. The one now dead because of her.

She started crying and said, "I saw someone killed today. He was helping me, and they killed him. They might kill you, too. They kill **everybody**."

She felt Jennifer take her hands, and looked up. Jennifer showed no surprise at the statement. Only pity for the pain Amena felt. She said, "He's not dead."

Amena pulled her hands away, shocked. **How would she know that?**

And the realization hit her with the force of a punch. **She's with them.**

33

★★

Amena leapt up, saying, "I have to go. Right now."

Jennifer said, "Wait, I don't even know your name."

Amena turned to run, and the predator came through the door, his left eye swollen almost shut, his cheek torn and bleeding. Behind him was the man who had saved her in the park. The one with the shaggy black hair.

She started to back up, her head flicking left and right. Jennifer stood and said, "We aren't the enemy. You know that."

She spat out, "Then why are you chasing me?"

The predator advanced, towering over her, and she defiantly looked him in the eyes. She saw no hate. Only kindness. And sadness.

He said, "We weren't chasing you. We were chasing someone else. We just found you in the middle of it." He held out his hand, saying, "My name is Pike Logan."

The food arrived, breaking the tension, the waiter looking at them strangely. Pike said, "Not going to waste that, are you? 'Cause I'm a little hungry."

She sat back in the booth, eyeing them warily. Jennifer sat next to her, putting a hand on her shoulder and saying, "It's okay."

Pike and the black-haired man sat across from her. Pike pulled out a couple of French fries and popped them in his mouth. He said, "You wait any longer, and I'm devouring this stuff."

She reached for her sandwich, not saying a word, but keeping her eyes on them. She saw Pike glance at Jennifer, and Jennifer raise an eyebrow, then smile. It was genuine, and she could see the affection.

He really is her boyfriend.

Jennifer said, "I have to tell you, you looked a hell of a lot better this morning."

Pike looked at Amena and said, "I had a little issue at the canal."

And it dawned on Amena what had occurred. If the predator was eating her French fries, that meant the killer was . . . what?

She interrupted for the first time. "Where is the man you fought? Is he . . . Can he find us? Did he follow you?"

Pike looked embarrassed. He said, "No. He won't find us. Ever."

Amena slitted her eyes and said, "Did you kill him?"

"No, no. I just made sure he couldn't follow us."

Amena leaned back, looking at the ceiling, her voice flat. "He killed my father. Cut his throat right in front of me. And he broke my brother's neck. Murdered them both."

She dropped her head and looked the predator in the eye, waiting.

He said, "Yes. I killed him."

Jennifer exclaimed, "Pike! That's not necessary for her to hear."

He glanced at her and said, "Yes it is." He turned to Amena, his eyes boring into her soul. He said, "He will never harm you again. He's gone, and so is his partner."

Amena slowly nodded, saying, "Did he suffer?"

She saw Pike's face twitch, reliving what had happened. He said, "Yes. He did."

She saw the pain and felt a connection she couldn't explain. She said, "Thank you."

He said, "Eat. You must be starving."

And she realized she was, in fact, ravenous. She started tearing into the sandwich, and the door opened. She saw the black man and his partner from the alley. Her mouth fell open.

Pike said, "Don't worry. They're just more friends."

They walked up and introduced themselves. She said, "Do you guys have nicknames like everyone else?"

They glanced at Pike, then the black man said, "Yeah."

"What's yours?"

"Uh . . . Blood."

She scrunched her eyes and said, "Because you're black? Is that an American gangster thing? I've seen it on YouTube."

He rolled his eyes, then stared at Pike, saying, "Noooo . . . but that's sure as shit what everyone thinks."

She giggled, then said, "And you?"

"It's . . . well, it's Veep."

"Veep? What does that mean?"

Pike cut in, saying, "It's an inside joke. That's all."

She could tell he was hiding something. She continued eating, then said, "Why would you help me? Why did you follow me, protecting me?"

She saw them all look at one another, and knew they were trying to come up with a story. It was the same thing she used to do with her brother when they were confronted by her father.

Pike leaned back, running his hands through his hair. Finally, he said, "Funny you should ask. You don't, by chance, have a cell phone on you, do you?"

The phone.

She snapped her head to him, the sandwich halfway to her mouth. "Why would you ask that?"

He said, "Because I know you do, and I know it's not yours."

She continued chewing, not saying anything.

"Look," he said, "I don't care if you stole it. In fact, I'm pretty sure you were going to sell it, and I'm here as a buyer."

She put the sandwich down and said, "What does that mean?"

"It means I'm willing to pay top dollar for your phone. Better than any fence will."

"Why?"

"That's not your concern. Can I see it?"

She cocked her head, then pulled out the phone, setting it on the table. She said, "It's brand-new. I haven't done anything to it. Just used what was on it."

Pike said, "An iPhone Ten? Impressive. I'll tell you what, I'll give you retail for it right now. One thousand American dollars."

The amount floored her. The most she had expected to get was one hundred, knowing the fence would pocket the rest. It was the price she paid as a refugee with no other options. With a thousand dollars, she could travel anywhere. She could actually sleep in a bed. Her voice excited, she said, "You have that much? Right now?"

"No, but if you wait here for fifteen minutes, I will."

She could have everything she wanted. She could get to Germany, and maybe all the way to the United States. And then it dawned on her. They were Americans, and they wanted her phone. They didn't want it because it was a new iPhone. They wanted it for something else. Something she didn't understand, but they did.

She said, "No. That's not good enough."

Exasperated, Pike said, "What the hell do you mean?"

"I want to go to the United States. I don't want your money, and I don't want your pity. I want to go to the United States."

Pike scoffed and said, "That's insane. Look, I have no power to get you to the United States. You might as well ask for a spaceship. Take the money, and that's it. We leave, and you go do what you do. You're safe now."

She sagged back, realizing her gambit had failed.

Jennifer said, "Pike, we can't just give her money and then throw her into the street."

Pike glared at her and said, "Yes, we **can**. We're not running an orphanage. With a thousand bucks and her smarts, she'll be fine."

Jennifer leaned forward, and Amena could feel the heat coming off her. So could the other men. They backed up, not wanting to be in the fight.

Jennifer said, "No, she **won't** be fine. This is ridiculous."

In that moment, Amena fell in love with her. But she knew she had lost. Whatever Jennifer said wouldn't alter Pike's decision. He was here doing something else, and he needed the phone to complete it. Amena was just a distraction.

And what Pike had said earlier clicked. **We weren't chasing you. We were chasing someone else.**

Pike started to snarl something back at Jennifer

and Amena said, "Wait. You don't want that phone, you want the man who had it, don't you?"

Pike closed his mouth. Every single person focused on her. Nobody said a word. She said, "I don't want your money. Just let me stay with you for a few days. Take me with you, wherever you go."

Pike glanced at Jennifer, then at Knuckles, and said, "Why would we do that?"

"Because I want to go to America."

Pike started shaking his head, and she said, "And because I know what the man who owned this phone looks like. A Syrian. A member of the regime that killed my mother. I know him on sight."

She saw Pike's eyes widen, and felt a smile leak out, realizing that the cursed phone had just saved her life. She looked into the predator's eyes, not flinching, holding her own.

She said, "Since you were chasing **me**, a thirteen-year-old girl, I'm assuming you don't know who he is, but I do. Is that worth a few days with you?"

34

★★

Yasir took a seat at a corner table on the patio, putting his backpack under his feet and watching for a moment. He didn't want to be inside, where his escape options were limited, but being outside held its own risks—namely that anyone in the small square, from any of the numerous restaurants or apartments, could see him and those he was meeting. Since he'd already been paid for the mission, he preferred the outdoor seating. Better to be able to escape than worry about whatever trouble he might be causing his new friends by someone watching.

After seeing nothing but students and the occasional tourist couple milling about, most under the age of twenty-five, he pulled out the burner flip phone Periwinkle had given him, secretly satisfied that he was tainting it with this call, leaving the CIA to explain how his sole contact with a case officer was also involved in terrorist activity. One more mirror he wanted to build in the wilderness.

Someone answered, and he said, "I'm here."

Nothing more. There was no way he was going to discuss operational details on a cell phone provided by a CIA case officer.

The other end said, "On the way."

Yasir heard a bleat from a horn, the noise causing him to whirl. He saw a bunch of college kids playing in the square, one juggling, another blowing into what looked like a fake seashell, both annoying a driver trying to complete his delivery.

Yasir relaxed. He'd directed the team here precisely because this section of Zurich was a little bit of a free-fire zone, run amok with students who lived in the cheap apartments, but also frequented by tourists attracted to the history. Situated just across the Limmat River from the swanky Zurich shopping district, it was an eclectic mix of young and old. The students who lived in this area were more than willing to turn a blind eye to anyone staying here—because not doing so would be tantamount to racism in their eyes—and he leveraged that.

He ordered a beer and waited, looking at the entrance of a tunnel that led to the claustrophobic apartment he'd rented for his "friends." Right above the archway was a sign reading ASS BAR. He chuckled. This place was so outside the caliphate his contacts fervently searched for that he wondered if their heads had exploded upon checking in.

He watched the tunnel, seeing young women and hipster men with goatees, students he was sure were begging someone to ask them what music they listened to or beer they drank so they could opine about their ironic taste. He wondered which of them was his contact.

Nobody approached the café. He checked his watch and saw eleven minutes had passed. He glanced left and right, then stood up to leave, anxious that he'd been led into a trap. Before he reached the square, two men exited the tunnel, funneling through the crowd. Both looked like damn terrorists.

One was thin as a rail, with a thick, coarse-spun Moroccan hooded jacket. Something out of a hippie commune in the 1960s, except it was real. The other was tall and brooding, with a shaggy neck beard and heavy eyebrows, wearing billowing linen pants cinched at the ankles and sandals that looked like they'd come from Disney's **Aladdin** movie—or an ISIS recruiting video.

Is this a joke?

They crossed the plaza, and he held up a hand. The rail-thin man saw it, and they veered over. Yasir returned to his table.

He'd expected to be surprised when they arrived, with him not able to tell who they were until they introduced themselves, but that was not the case here. Which gave him no small amount of concern. If anyone had any indication of what was to occur, they would be found out in a heartbeat.

Thank heavens they're going back to Syria, because that is the only place they will blend in.

The two sat down, looking uncomfortable. Finally,

the thin man said, "I am Bashir. This is Sayid. Thank you for seeing us."

Yasir said, "My name is Farouq, and it is you who deserves the thanks."

Sayid said, "You have something to help us, yes?"

"I do, but first, how are you here in this country? How did you cross?"

Sayid said, "I have a passport from Egypt. Bashir's is from Tunisia."

"So no Syrian connection?"

"No. Is that an issue?"

"Yes, a little bit." He passed across a thick envelope, a key rubberbanded to the top of it. "Here are your instructions. I've arranged for a boat to take you from Nice to the Syrian port of Tartus. Having a Syrian passport would help, but it's not insurmountable."

"The port with the Russian base? The country helping Assad? Why would we go there?"

"Because it's the way I've developed to get you in. Don't worry about it."

Bashir spoke up, saying, "Why aren't we going through Turkey?"

Yasir said, "Take that ridiculous hood off. You look like a jihadi."

Bashir snapped his head back at the rebuke, but removed the hood.

Yasir said, "Look, you men are on an important mission. I don't know what your command told you, but you can't wander around here looking like bedouin tribesmen. Try to blend in."

Sayid said, "We don't bow to the whims of the kaffir just because we want to 'blend in.'"

Yasir leaned forward and said, "You will here. Remember what the Prophet said, peace be upon him. You can act like an infidel in order to survive. That's all I'm asking."

Bashir nodded and said, "We'll consider it. Khalousi says you are a man we can trust."

"I am."

Khalousi had been a lieutenant inside the Nusra Front before jumping ship to the Islamic State. Through all of that time, no matter how much terrain they took, Yasir had been his contact with the Assad government, and Khalousi had facilitated selling oil and other supplies to the administration in order to be left alone.

There was a reason that the regime focused all of its efforts against other rebel groups, and it was precisely because Assad preferred ISIS to live. Having them exist, chopping off heads on the world stage, gave Assad a legitimate reason to fight. Gave him the ability to pronounce that his war was all about terrorist brutality, not his own. The relationship was strangely symbiotic, because Assad's neglect allowed ISIS to flourish even as it gave Assad the ability to say he was fighting terrorism, not a civil war. Through it all, Assad had bought fuel from the very terrorist group that had stolen the oil fields.

Eventually, the self-proclaimed caliphate of the Islamic State had collapsed, not at Assad's hands, but at the fighting prowess of the Kurds and the firepower of the United States. Like many other roaches fleeing the light of the sun, Khalousi had run from the capital of Raqqa, and then had started a new group—the White Flags, comprised of Sunni resistance fighters. Yasir wasn't sure what their agenda was—nationalism, freedom from persecution, or the usual desire to build a caliphate—but Khalousi had stated that he wanted to put the group on the world stage.

And Yasir was more than willing to facilitate that goal, because it would once again help the regime in the propaganda fight.

Bashir said, "What do you have for us?"

Yasir leaned forward, glanced left and right theatrically, and said, "Red Mercury."

Bashir's eyes went wide, and Sayid said, "You have the real Red Mercury?"

Yasir removed his backpack, opened a latch, and showed them the two thermos-like containers. He said, "Yes. From North Korea."

Both of their eyes glistened, like cocaine addicts seeing a mountain of white. Making Yasir wonder how on earth such men were created. It was just like the interrogators he'd commanded in his prison. Some short circuit that allowed—no, encouraged— a savagery he didn't understand. He did what he did out of survival. The men in front of him did it out of pleasure.

Sayid reached for the backpack, and Yasir pulled it away, saying, "First, there are conditions."

Bashir said, "We know. Only use it inside Syria."

"Yes. You must use it against a US Special Forces outpost. Can you do that?"

"Of course. We have one pinpointed in Manbij, at their base. The one that the Turks are threatening to destroy. The French have shown up, and they do joint patrols."

Yasir thought, **Talk about a mess. There are more factions fighting than there are sides.** He said, "That would be perfect. Kill both the French and the Americans. If you kill some Turks as well, it would be even better. Good target."

He passed the backpack across, saying, "It's two self-contained units, with an aerosol propulsion system. You press the switch, and it starts spraying like a fumigation can for insects."

"So we press the button and it starts killing?"

"Yes."

Bashir looked at Sayid, then said, "How will we initiate and get away?"

Yasir smiled and said, "That's up to you. But I suspect you won't be getting away."

35

★★

I handed my company credit card to the guy at the desk, letting him run it. I turned to Knuckles and said, "Me paying for all of this shit is getting old."

He laughed and said, "Maybe you need to fire a few of us. Make it cheaper."

I started to reply when Brett tapped me on the shoulder and said, "Turn back around. Now."

I did so, hiding my face, and said, "What's up?"

He ducked his head as well, saying, "The North Koreans just entered the hotel. The targets from Monaco."

What?

"Are they checking in?"

"Don't know."

We were at the Park Hyatt in Zurich, attempting to locate the second phone from our original theft of data—after wasting precious time in Geneva. We'd hooked Amena's iPhone to our computer, and the reach-back hacking cell had drained it of everything it could, and, deep in the BIOS, had found instructions for a meeting that had occurred at an archaeological site in the basement of a church two days ago.

That told me all I needed to know. The Syrian owned both phones. It wasn't two people, it was one, and Amena had interrupted whatever had been planned by stealing the first phone. We'd searched the men who'd attacked her, finding absolutely nothing. They were completely sterile, but I had no doubt why they were chasing her. They were trying to protect the Syrian.

We'd managed to stop that, and had to wait an agonizing amount of time to continue. Truthfully, after what I'd executed, I was a little amazed that the Council let us go forward at all. Kurt had thought I was joking when I'd told him about the interdiction and rescue. Right up until I put Amena in front of the computer. Then he'd become apoplectic.

I'd had Jennifer take Amena out of the room, and he'd shouted, "I promised the president you wouldn't do anything stupid!"

Calm as ever, I'd said, "Sir, they were going to kill her. And she had the first-target handset. I had to intervene. It's in the Taskforce charter—the right to protect. I couldn't let her die."

He'd rubbed his face with his hands, clearly not wanting to hear what I was saying—but he knew I was right. He said, "Tell me she can give us something. Some reason for saving her other than that phone."

A little miffed, I said, "You mean other than her damn life?"

Curtly, he said, "Yes. You know the drill. Anything would be nice when I brief the Council."

And I did know the drill. He was going to need everything he could get to continue operations, and he would spin anything I gave him in our favor. I said, "She knows the Syrian on sight. She stole the phone from him."

"We have a picture of him from Johnny's team. Why is that a help? Is she going to describe him better than a photo? Does she know something the picture doesn't show?"

"No, sir, but that photograph is a half-profile shot from a distance. It's a good start to locating this guy, but she's a sure thing. Tell the Council that."

He nodded, and then what I'd said sank in. "Are you implying you're taking her on the operation if I get approval?"

"Well, of course. She's just an asset at this point. Same as we use in other operations."

Up went the hands again, rubbing his forehead. He should buy stock in aspirin, because I was pretty sure I was giving him a monster headache. He said, "Pike, Pike, there is no way I can sell that. I'm going to have a hard enough time getting approval just for continued Alpha in Zurich. I can't tell the Council that you're now using an uncleared **child** as an asset on an operation."

I said, "Look, sir, you know how to spin this.

Don't mention an age. You wouldn't if she were an adult, so why do it here. You wouldn't go in and say, 'Pike was forced to interdict, saving a thirty-two-year-old male.' You'd just say, 'Pike interdicted under the R2P protocol of the charter, saving a male.' Do the same here."

"That's tantamount to lying."

I said, "No it's not. You're telling them everything except her age. Is there some age restriction in the charter for assets we use?"

He leaned back and said, "I'm pretty sure there damn well should be."

He acted aggravated, but he'd known I'd given him his only out, and he'd taken it. The Oversight Council had wrung their hands, fearful there would be blowback from our actions in Montreux. It made me impatient, but, given what we'd done, I understood. We'd managed to get out of Montreux clean, but leaving dead bodies around was never a good idea.

After a day and a half, they'd agreed to let us continue with Alpha in Zurich, where the second handset had been located. We'd pinpointed it to the Park Hyatt, and we'd arrived attempting to neck it down. I'd wanted to ask Kurt if he'd told them we were taking along a prepubescent teenager as our asset, but figured that was probably poking the bear. With the arrival of the Koreans, I was pretty sure this second phone would be tied to our target.

Thankfully, the lobby of the Park Hyatt was a little chopped up. You entered a foyer, then had the choice of left to reception, right to the elevators, or straight ahead into a restaurant. If they were already booked, they'd pass by us.

But they'd run into Jennifer.

She'd taken Amena to the bathroom while I checked in, and that was located near the elevators. It would be just my luck Jennifer would pop out, right in view of the Korean whose ass she'd kicked.

None of us were wired for sound, because all we were doing was checking into a hotel, forcing me to hastily pull out my cell phone and call her. I told Veep and Knuckles to handle the rest of the check-in, then Brett and I scurried to an alcove while I gave Jennifer the threat information. She acknowledged, saying Amena was wondering why they had to stay in the bathroom.

Because people want to kill you.

We remained in place for a few excruciating seconds, then I felt my phone vibrate with a text from Knuckles. **Clear. They went straight to the elevators.**

Which made our life significantly more difficult. If they were staying here, we stood a good chance of being compromised, but it also told me that we were in the right place.

We returned to the front desk, finding Jennifer holding Amena's hand, the girl looking at me like she wanted to say something.

I said, "What?"

She said, "What, what? I'm just standing here."

I said, "Oh. I thought you were going to ask me for ice cream or something."

She looked up at Jennifer and said, "You're right. He **is** sort of an asshole."

Jennifer put a hand over her mouth to hide a smile, then leaned over the girl, whispering in her ear.

Knuckles started handing out key cards and I gritted my teeth, saying, "Jennifer, take our stuff to the room. Knuckles and Veep, start your magic on the elevators. Brett, you and I are going to recce this place for other exits."

Amena said, "Do I get a key?"

Jennifer said, "No. You're in our room."

She looked concerned, and I said, "Don't worry. You'll be safe."

She said, "I know. Do I get a bed?" And the comment brought a smile. "Yes, little Jedi, you'll get a bed."

She grinned, and it truly affected me. She was willing to finger the Syrian, knowing it put her life at risk, and all the payment she wanted was a bed. I ruffled her hair and said, "Help Jennifer with the bags. Since you don't have any."

She said, "Yeah. We need to talk about that. I figure helping you might be worth some clothes."

I smiled at her words. She was sharp, and she was going to bleed me for all I was worth. I said, "Just take the bags. You have to earn the new wardrobe."

She slitted her eyes, and I said, "Everyone meet in our room in one hour. By then, I want to be operational."

36

★
★ ★

Yasir exited his cab in front of the Park Hyatt, walking through the lobby with his head on a swivel, surveying the room in a practiced manner. He saw nothing to cause concern. But he was experienced enough to realize that anybody worth their skill wouldn't raise a signature.

He went rapidly through the reception area, entered the elevator, and touched his key card to the small knob that allowed the elevator to work. It flashed a green light, and he hit the ninth floor. He rode up in silence.

The door opened, and he glided down the hall, happy at how the mission had proceeded. He'd passed the Red Mercury, alleviating any repercussions from the North Koreans, and now all he needed to do was get the final payment from the Americans. From that ass Periwinkle. He wondered what would happen to that guy once the attack happened, and the subsequent investigation revealed his complicity. But he didn't really care. By that time, he expected to be in a whole new life, his past behind him, experiencing the real-world promise of the Quran. Seventy-two virgins and a daiquiri.

He grinned at the thought.

He reached his door, keyed it for entrance, and pushed it open. The first thing he saw was the same Korean security man who'd given him the second phone, now sitting in a chair, facing the door. He had bruises on his face, like someone had used it for punching practice. And he wasn't pleased.

Yasir entered, let the door close, and said, "To what do I owe the pleasure?"

A voice from inside the room said, "Come in."

He did, seeing Song Hae-gook, the same Korean "investor" from Monaco. He immediately whirled around, looking for the killers who had passed him the information in Geneva, convinced he was about to be gutted.

Song smiled and said, "Stop it. If I wanted you dead, I wouldn't have sat here in your room. You'd have died in the elevator."

Yasir looked at him warily and said, "How did you get in?"

"We have our ways."

Yasir nodded, then said, "Okay. So what brings you here?"

"There has been some trouble with your transfer. We just want to make sure the passing went satisfactorily."

"Trouble? How?"

"Did you really destroy your phone by accidentally dropping it in a toilet?"

Yasir felt the sweat break out on his forehead, but used his training, keeping his face stoic. "Yes. Of course. Do you think I gave it away or something?"

"No. I don't think you **gave** it away, but I do think you lost it."

Yasir advanced into the room, taking a seat on the bed across from Song. He said, "Why do you say that? The phone was ruined. Why else would I come back to you for another?"

Song scoffed and said, "Do you not think we have ways of tracking the handset? It wasn't destroyed, and there was significant activity around it." He leaned forward and said, "Activity leading to dead people."

"What are you talking about? That phone is gone."

"It is now, that's correct."

"Quit the games. What's going on? Why are you here? I just passed the Red Mercury, like we agreed."

Song rubbed his index finger against his thumb, like he was scrapping something off of it. He said nothing. Yasir waited, then said, "Tell me what this is about."

Song gazed at him with hooded eyes and said, "There were several Russians killed in Montreux, Switzerland, a few days ago."

"So?"

"They were killed in the last known vicinity of your original handset. So I know you're lying. What I want to know now is why."

Yasir felt his head spin. He'd alerted his Russian contacts just to cauterize a wound, and now it was coming back to burn him. **What the hell had they done?**

He had to tread lightly, because he understood the man in the room wouldn't believe him. He wished he'd never called in his Russian chit.

He said, "Okay, okay. I lost the phone. I was afraid to tell you that. I asked some friends of mine to retrieve it even as I executed your mission. I made a mistake."

Song nodded his head and said, "Good. Honesty. That's better than the lies you gave before."

Yasir waited. Song seemed to study the drapes, scratching his chin. Finally, he said, "Did the pass go as expected?"

Now wanting to curry favor, Yasir gushed, "Yes. Yes it did. They'll head to Nice in the next day or two, and link up with a boat I've arranged. I have the itinerary and their safe house, if you think I'm lying."

Song stood and said, "No, I don't think you're lying, but you need to understand that we didn't give you the Red Mercury for money. We gave it for other reasons. We need that attack to occur, and you haven't given us a lot of confidence about execution."

Confused, Yasir said, "We paid you for it. You got what you wanted. Money."

Song leaned over him and said, "Money is not what we want. We want your tribe to kill people with that weapon. We want a statement. Do you understand?"

Yasir nodded, saying, "Of course. They'll do it. They even have a target already planned."

Song said, "Good. Very good. Now all that remains is the mess you created."

"What do you mean?"

Song looked at him and said, "Someone killed those Russians. Someone with skill. And now I'll have to alert my own kill team to repair your failure."

Song and the security man left the room, and Yasir glanced at the iPhone on the table. The one implanted with the instructions.

Those bastards have been tracking me forever.

He turned it off, and realized why they'd specified an iPhone. One couldn't remove the battery, so turning it off did nothing if there was malware involved. And Yasir was sure that was the case.

He rose up, sweating. He needed to leave here tomorrow. Check out. Get away from the last place the North Koreans knew. He sat down, took a deep breath, and exhaled, letting the air go like a leaked balloon.

And then he remembered what the Korean had said. Who had killed the Russians?

37

★
★★

Amena sat in between Jennifer and Pike on a bench facing the elevators, wondering what she was doing. They'd told her to simply point out the Syrian, but that was the easy part. She wondered why. And they weren't talking. Not only that, but they definitely were scared of others finding out what they were doing. She'd seen that when Jennifer had told her to remain in the bathroom. She wondered if they were criminals.

Earlier, three Asians had entered the elevator, and you would have thought they had the plague by the way Jennifer had jerked her back into the bathroom. It made her wonder what was going on. What she'd gotten herself into.

After five minutes, she'd been allowed to leave the restroom, and then Pike's team had turned into a whirlwind of activity, with everyone doing something—Veep and Knuckles pulling out electronic gear from a suitcase, Blood and Pike disappearing into the lobby, and her being led to a room by Jennifer. Eventually, Pike had arrived at the hotel room with everyone else, and they'd gone back down to the ground floor. Sitting in between the two, she looked up at Pike and said, "You guys don't like Chinese people?"

Pike laughed and said, "No, it's not that. Just keep eyes on the elevators and maybe I'll buy you some new shoes."

She said, "I don't know why I'm doing this. Maybe I should just walk away."

Pike glanced at her and said, "Maybe you should. I'm not keeping you. You're the one who said you wanted to tag along."

She looked at Jennifer and saw compassion. Someone who wanted to help her. She decided that Pike was the enemy. She'd need to work on Jennifer for her goals.

Jennifer said, "Hey, you're helping to stop something bad, like what happened to your family. That should be enough."

She said, "You guys are dating? Is that right? I've seen American dating on the web with Kim Kardashian. I know all about it."

Pike gave her an exasperated glance and said, "Yes, damn it, we're dating. Just watch the elevators."

Truculent, not knowing the grenade she was setting off, she said, "You don't have to be a jerk all the time for my help. My father was a jerk sometimes, but he understood what it meant to raise a child. He was kind when it mattered. He loved me. I know you don't get that, but trust me, being nice is a good thing."

She saw Pike fold into himself, and then look at her with unadulterated pain. He stood up and walked away.

She looked at Jennifer and said, "What did I do?"

She saw a hint of a tear in Jennifer's eye, which confused her further. She said, "What?"

Jennifer said, "He had a child. A girl. Younger than you. He had a wife, too. They were both murdered. Don't judge him. He's walked your path, and he wants to do the right thing."

It was the last thing Amena expected, the words a physical blow. She'd believed that none of the horrors of Syria could possibly translate anywhere else, and she'd been wrong. She looked at Pike across the lobby, seeing the pain she had felt for the last eighteen months. Seeing the scab she'd ripped off. She then realized the cause of the change she'd seen on the bridge, when the killer had admitted to murdering her family. Right before Pike had slaughtered him.

She felt a kinship.

She took Jennifer's hand and said, "This was meant to be."

Jennifer squeezed back and said, "Don't do that. It is what it is. It means nothing for your future. We can give you money, but that's it. You need to understand that."

Amena locked eyes with her and said, "No. If it is to be, it is up to me. And this is up to me."

In the background, she heard an elevator ding. She saw that Jennifer didn't believe her. Didn't understand the depth of her mother's words. Jennifer showed the hurt of what was to come, knowing they would abandon her. But that was just because Jennifer didn't understand her. She was not going to be abandoned. **Ever** again.

The elevator opened, and a group of men exited, all walking with a purpose. Still focused on her, Jennifer said, "Honey, this **isn't** to be. Don't get your hopes up."

Amena looked at the group, and felt her world harden. She said, "That's him. That's the Syrian."

Jennifer whipped her head to the right, then began working her radio.

I stomped away from Amena, not wanting to admit how much saving her had meant to me. Not wanting to acknowledge how much I wished I'd been home when my family had been slaughtered. I knew it wasn't fair to put that on her, and I hadn't saved her life out of a duty to my own. Well, not entirely anyway.

She was confusing to me. She was a smart-ass of the first order—which I sort of liked—but she was also feral, not trusting anything anyone said. It meant she could bolt at any moment, screwing us just to save herself. Selling us out to the police or the enemy if she thought she'd get more favorable treatment. She was the worst asset I'd ever run. But she was also key to identifying our target.

And, truthfully, I liked her as a person, no matter what she could provide.

I leaned over a railing to the hotel restaurant, letting the steam dissipate from her comment to me, knowing she would never understand how deep her words cut, and my radio went off.

"Pike, Pike, this is Koko, target in sight. He just left the elevator."

My first thought was, **Are you kidding me? The second I step away?**

Brett cut in saying, "There was no Growler activity. If it's him, he doesn't have the phone."

I said, "Are we sure it's the target?"

Jennifer said, "This is Koko. It's him. I say again, it's him."

"Veep, Veep, did you get an elevator car?"

Veep said, "I've got two elevators he could have used."

I said, "Get on them, now. Lock them down."

We only had Alpha authority against this asshole, which meant I couldn't thump him in the head and squeeze it for information, even if that was the best course of action in my mind. Instead, I had to do the cowardly surreptitious answer—which meant cracking into his room. But, since I didn't even know his name, I had no idea what room he was in. To the uninitiated, this would seem to be an insurmountable obstacle. But not to the Taskforce.

The elevators in this Hyatt used an RFID key card to actuate, meaning if you wanted to go up or down, you had to prove you were staying in the hotel, giving us a vulnerability. While I was conducting a recce with Brett, Veep and Knuckles had installed a skimmer on the elevator key access, basically duplicating what criminals did all over the world at gas pumps, skimming credit card information for nefarious use.

Whenever someone touched their key to the pad, it was recorded in the official hotel database, to include name and room number. All we had to do was short-circuit that, giving us the information. But that also required us to halt the elevators before anyone else keyed the pad. We had to know that the last keyed one was our target. So I had both Veep and Knuckles staged to "ride" the elevators and shut them down, until they could read the skimmer, based on our alert.

Veep called and said, "I'm in elevator four, and the last is the twelfth floor. A guy named Sheetston."

That isn't it.

Knuckles called and said, "I've got a guy on the ninth floor. His name is Yasir al-Shami."

Bingo.

38

⁂

I said, "Okay, we're in motion. Blood, remove the skimmers from the elevators. Knuckles, you've got security. Let us know if he comes back up. Koko, take Amena back to our suite. Veep, you're with me. Let's crack the room."

Everyone started moving in a practiced motion, me meeting Veep holding a door at the elevator bank. I entered, let the door close, then said, "Room?"

He pulled off a backpack and said, "Nine thirteen."

He withdrew a handset with a USB plug dangling out of it, and started cycling through programs. I said, "Creed online?"

"Not yet. I want to get it in first." He handed me a thin folded metal rod and I snapped it into place, forming an L shape.

We reached the ninth floor and I said, "You good?"
"Yeah."

"Don't fuck this up. We need to be in and out."
He said, "You want to do it, Grandpa?"

I laughed and the door opened. We exited and speed-walked down the hallway, reaching room 913. I saw a DO NOT DISTURB sign on the handle and went past it, walking to the end of the hall, searching for cameras or other exits. I saw none. I returned to the door and said, "Radar scope."

He handed me what looked like a cell phone from an eighties movie. The gadget could penetrate the walls and let us know if something was alive inside. It didn't matter how still you were, it would sense something as tiny as a heart beating.

I put it against the wall to the left of the door, then began scanning, looking like I was trying to find a stud. I got nothing. I repeated the maneuver on the far side of the door, and said, "Room's clear. Elevator."

He jogged back, positioned himself, and keyed his radio, "Clear, but there's a camera here. It saw us exit."

I pulled a spool of cable from the handle of the tool he'd given me, forming a loop, and said, "No issue. As long as it can't see me."

"You're good."

I slid the rod under the jamb, holding the running end of the wire. I pulled the rod up against the door, then leaned it toward the handle. It missed, rotating all the way to the floor. I withdrew it, then began again. This time, I felt it seat, and slowly pulled the wire running out from under the door. I got nothing.

Shit.

Every hotel door opens from the inside—even if the bolt lock is engaged—to prevent someone from being unable to escape in an emergency, such as a fire. The tool I was using was basically a loop that would engage the handle and release the lock as if a guest were in the room—but getting it to seat correctly while being on the outside wasn't a sure thing. It was like trying to insert a key with a blindfold on. I began to feel the heat of time. If anyone popped out of their room in the hallway, I'd look like an idiot.

I pulled the rod out a bit, then let it fall back in place, gently tugging the wire. I felt resistance. On my radio, I heard, "Elevator. Not the target, but two people exiting."

I gave up on gentle, yanking the wire hard. I felt the door pop open, and slipped inside just as two people rounded the corner. I put my eye to the peephole, seeing them pass without incident. I said, "Inside. Come on."

Ten seconds later I saw Veep in the peephole. I let him in, and pointed at the television. Mounted on a swivel bracket designed to swing so that guests could see it on the bed, I pulled it away from the wall while Veep set up the penetration device.

Before we'd checked in, the Taskforce had given us a complete readout of the vulnerabilities of the room, and the biggest one was the television. A flat-screen Samsung model, it had built-in voice commands that could be used to change channels or search for programs, routed through the internet to a server at Samsung corporate. In this case, the hotel hadn't activated voice command, but the hardware still existed and was something we could exploit. Using a program called Weeping Angel, we could turn on the voice feature no matter the status of the television, then slave the TV's Wi-Fi function to our own servers, in effect turning it into a giant microphone that would hear everything spoken in the room. Yay for the Internet of Things.

I found the USB port, pointed it out, and said, "You got this?"

"Yep."

"Give me the Dragonball. He left without his phone."

He passed me another device, this one smaller, looking like a scientific calculator with multiple dongles hanging out of it. I left him to his work, then began searching the room, careful not to disturb anything. After checking the bedroom, I went into the bath and found another iPhone X on the counter, in plain view, but turned off.

I fired it up, then selected the Apple lightning port dongle of the Dragonball. I plugged it in, turned it on, then saw the iPhone screen go blank, showing a battery charging symbol with zero percent. It jumped to four, and I knew the device was working, cloning the phone.

I went back to Veep and said, "What's the status?"

He said, "Done. Just need to test."

He pulled out a cell phone, dialed a number, then said, "Creed, we're live. Want to test."

He listened, then muted the phone, saying, "Test, test, test" into the room.

He unmuted the cell, put it to his ear, then looked at me and smiled. He said, "Good work," and hung up. "We're live."

"So if I say Creed's an asshole, he'll hear me?"

My cell vibrated in my pocket. I pulled it out and saw a single text: **Yes.**

I laughed and said, "Okay, good to go. Just know that I'm going to need the transcript first thing in the morning. By six a.m."

Will do.

"Thanks, Creed. Never had a doubt." I went back to the bathroom, checked the Dragonball, and saw it at 97 percent. My phone vibrated again.

Koko there?

It went to 98 percent, and I said, "Yep. But she's wearing a bathrobe."

Creed had a massive crush on Jennifer, even as she treated him like she was a babysitter tolerating the affections of a kid. He ate it up, relishing her attention, not realizing she was far out of his league. Or understanding the fact that I was dating her. Then again, maybe he did understand that, which made him a braver man than I would have been if the roles were reversed.

Veep came into the bathroom, a question on his

face, and I held up my phone. He read the texts, grinned, and it vibrated again.

She's in what? Say again?

We hit 100 percent, I unplugged, and said, "Creed, get your head out of the gutter. I'm in a hostile room. She's not here. She's babysitting someone besides you."

My phone went crazy with three texts.

That isn't what I meant.

You are cruel.

I might not monitor.

I moved to the door and looked out the peephole, saying, "You'd better, or you'll never see her in a bath-robe."

I cracked the door and my phone vibrated a final time.

I'm telling her you said that.

I let him hear the door slam closed.

We started to leave, and I saw a piece of tape torn at the base of the door. Something I'd missed before in my haste to get in.

I thought, **You are sly, but so am I.**

39

⭑
⭑⭑

Yasir entered the lobby to the Park Hyatt convinced he wasn't under surveillance, but he surveyed anyway, with a practiced eye. He made the right turn to the elevators, and saw nobody take any interest in him. Just as had happened outside.

He'd given the Koreans about a twenty-minute head start—enough time to set up a surveillance box if they were so inclined—and then had left, the sole purpose to identify those following him. He'd conducted a two-hour surveillance detection route on foot, running all over the shopping district of Zurich before finally stopping for dinner. He'd repeated the task coming home, and had found no indication of anyone following him.

He entered the elevator, thinking, **They found me because of that damn phone. No telling what malware they have on it. That won't happen again.**

He exited and went straight to his room. He reached the door, checked down, and saw the tape still in place. He entered and stood still. Sensing.

Feeling if anything was out of place. He used his eyes and ears, but really, he trusted his subconscious brain to tell him.

He felt nothing.

He went straight to the bathroom, seeing the iPhone X on the counter. He picked it up, set it carefully on the marble floor, and smashed it with his heel. He crushed it repeatedly, then took the pieces and tore them apart, until the phone was reduced to a shattered screen, a battery pack, and loose circuit boards.

He brought the mess into the bedroom and sat in a chair, thinking. He went through his options, but really, there was only one: He had to leave first thing tomorrow. He had a reservation for two more days, but staying here was just asking for the return of the Koreans. He was sure they had his reservation, expecting him to remain, and walking away tomorrow morning, while they still thought they had an anchor, was the only way to remain clean.

He'd conduct another SDR on the way to breakfast, and if he was free of surveillance, he'd just keep going.

His thoughts turned to other ways that the Koreans could find him, and he realized he needed to alert the team. They could still compromise him. He had no idea what games the North Koreans were playing, but he wasn't going to give them any opportunity to affect this mission. They'd said they were going to alert their killers because of the dead

Russians, but the last thing he needed was a kill team from Assad hunting him because he'd supposedly taken regime money and fled. He needed the attack to occur so that—ironically—he could take the money he'd skimmed and flee.

He pulled out the CIA flip phone from his pocket and dialed. When a man answered, he said, "Hello, we have a problem with your credit card."

He heard, "You'll have to talk to the owner of this phone. It's not me."

Yasir smiled at the bona fides, glad they at least understood operational security. He said, "Is this Bashir or Sayid?"

"Bashir."

"Listen, you both need to leave tomorrow. Head to Nice."

"Why? You said we had three days."

"Something has come up. The people we gained the product from have been acting strange. They showed up at my hotel, which means they might have seen me with you. I don't think they did, but they might have."

"And? Why does that matter? They received their payment, yes?"

"Yes, of course. I don't know why, but it would be better to get away."

"Get away from what?"

"From the North Koreans. They may have another plan in motion. They said as much. Just get out."

Yasir heard nothing for a moment, then Bashir

said, "Okay, but I'm not sure about using the original plan. Are the assets in Nice compromised?"

"No. Not at all. That was all me. They had nothing to do with it."

Bashir said, "We'll leave tomorrow, but we won't talk to you again. This phone will no longer exist. **You** no longer exist."

Yasir heard the words, but didn't blame Bashir. He would have done the same. He said, "I understand. I'll keep the phone open, but won't try to contact you. I'm out of here tomorrow morning as well."

"Don't expect to hear from us. Forget we ever met." And Yasir heard the phone connection close.

He sat for a moment, contemplating his situation. The North Koreans had something more in play, but beyond their money, he didn't really care. He had the slice of his payment in a Swiss bank account. It was safe, but it wasn't enough to support his retirement. Not with the luxury he wanted.

He needed to speed up his meeting with the CIA, before the Koreans did something stupid. He dialed a second number, hearing it connect, then: "Twice in one week. That's a record. What do you have now? The plot that killed JFK?"

He came in hard, saying, "Stop the joking. We need to meet sooner than later."

"Oh, you having issues in Syria?"

"Yes! I am. We need to meet in Europe, not Turkey. I can't get to Turkey in the time I need."

"Because you're in Switzerland? Seems that would be an easier connection."

Yasir felt his head swim. **How does he know where I am?**

He felt his cheeks flush, staring at the phone, realizing he'd been stupid. He maintained a steady voice. "So you're tracking me?"

"No. Just checking up on you every once in a while. As I'm sure you would want me to. For protection."

"Well, I need protection now. I have people hunting me, like you warned me about in Monaco, but they aren't Americans."

He heard nothing but sarcasm. "Honestly, I would expect as much. I've given you all the protection I can, and I don't like being lied to. You told me you had information we would like, but said you were in Syria. Now you're asking for my help."

Aggravated, knowing how this game was played, Yasir said, "I never told you I was in Syria. All I said was I have WMD intelligence. Does the agency want to pay for that information or not?"

Yasir felt the anger coming through the phone. "Don't say that shit on an open line, you dumbass. I'll meet you in Turkey, like we agreed."

Yasir heard him hang up.

He threw the phone on the bed, wondering what to do now. Periwinkle was an issue, but that was something he could deal with tomorrow.

After he ditched the North Koreans.

40

⋆⋆
⋆

Bashir put his shoulder bag on the floor and said, "You're still going to wear that Berber coat?"

Sayid said, "Yes, I am. I don't need these kaffirs telling me how to dress. It just proves why we're here. If they hate us for it, they'll reap what they sow."

Bashir smiled at the reference to the Quran. Now clean-shaven, wearing jeans and cheap shoes he'd bought at a thrift store, he said, "That is true, but we want to be the ones who cause the pain. Not wait in a jail cell for paradise because we were stubborn."

"I'm not changing my mind. What time is the train?"

Bashir said, "We've got three hours before it leaves. Do you think we need to go now? Get out of this apartment?"

It was an hour before dawn, and Yasir's call had left them little sleep. After that contact, all night long they'd expected someone to break into the room, unsure of Yasir's loyalty. But they had nowhere else to go. Yasir had arranged the room, and sleeping on the street would do nothing but invite more scrutiny. They didn't even know what the threat held. All they knew was that Yasir had been scared, and because of that fear, they, too, worried about the boogeyman.

Sayid paced about, then said, "Yes, we need to leave, but I'm not sure that will solve the problem. I'm not sure of this plan. Not at all."

Bashir said, "You think he's setting us up?"

"I don't know, but he's not with **us**. For all we know, he works for Assad."

The words hit Bashir like a slap. He said, "The regime? That's insane. What are you saying?"

"He's not one of **us**. That I'm sure of."

"Khalousi said he was a friend."

Sayid glanced out the window, then fiddled with his bag, saying nothing. Bashir said, "What?"

Sayid said, "Being a friend in the past doesn't make one a friend now. You know that as well as I do. We have both been betrayed in the past."

While each held passports from different countries—Egypt and Tunisia—they were both from Syria. Born and raised. The sons of simple merchants, Sayid from Hama and Bashir from Manbij, they had joined the secular protests at the beginning as students, and had suffered the pain from the Assad regime.

Fighting against a despot, having their relatives arrested, tortured, and killed, they'd initially joined organizations that had used peaceful protests, begging the world to stop the slaughter. And the world had turned a blind eye, forcing them to turn to others. Those who would fight, but who also had an agenda. Bashir had fallen into the Nusra Front, while Sayid had embraced the Islamic State. The methods of both were horrific to them, but their commitment to the fall of Assad was resolute, and the deaths each group caused were paltry compared to the regime itself.

It was only a matter of time before the tendrils of hate emanating from the groups corrupted their thinking. What had once been a fight against a brutal regime became a crusade against anyone who thought differently than them, twisting the two into something beyond human comprehension. Turning them into killers who would slaughter just because of a different faith—or even the same faith, if they didn't pledge allegiance to the cause.

Bashir said, "You think we shouldn't take the boat to Syria?"

"I think taking a boat to a port controlled by the Assad regime, right next to a Russian base, using passports that are at best sketchy, is not a good idea. Especially since a man we don't know coordinated it all."

"What do you want to do? We can't stay here. The very man you distrust alerted us to the danger."

"Contact Khalousi. Let him give us guidance."

Bashir said, "I don't want to worry him. He believes everything is working."

"Send the imam a message. See what his thoughts are."

Bashir put his palms to his eyes, pressing down and attempting to subdue a headache. He sighed, dropped his hands, then bent down to his bag.

He pulled out a laptop, booted it, then double-clicked on an app called Telegram. A unique program developed by a Russian entrepreneur after Edward Snowden had hyperventilated about state surveillance nets, it was an end-to-end encrypted system that allowed them to communicate securely, both to have point-to-point communication and to disseminate propaganda out to a broader audience. Ironically, far from protecting innocents, Snowden's revelations had only helped those that meant harm. Developed from a misguided fear of the surveillance state, Telegram had become the primary method used by terrorist and criminal groups all over the world.

Bashir clicked on the contacts, chose one, then clicked "Secret Chat"—a way for him to send a message that would self-destruct after the recipient viewed it, and one that would not pass through the Telegram cloud server. Once he hit send, the message traveled with unbreakable encryption, leaving only one way to intercept it—standing over the shoulder of the recipient and staring at the screen. No amount of technology the United States mustered could penetrate the program, and once the imam clicked on the message, it would only exist for two minutes.

He typed out a concise message, stating their predicament and asking for guidance, then waited. Khalousi would have to connect on the secret chat channel before he could do anything else. Bashir looked up from the computer and said, "We should at least start on our journey to Nice."

"Maybe. Maybe not. I think we should head to Turkey, like we planned. There is no way we're going to take a boat to Tartus and be able to penetrate hundreds of kilometers of regime-held territory, and then penetrate hundreds of kilometers more through Rojava. If Assad doesn't torture us to death, the Kurds will skin us alive. We should come from their rear, through Turkey."

Telegram beeped, and Bashir leaned over, reading the message. "The imam says to go to Nice, but not to travel to Syria. He'll give us further instructions from there."

Sayid said, "What? Why?"

Bashir finished reading, then looked at him and said, "He doesn't trust our contact."

"Meaning that guy is bad?"

Bashir stood, shutting down the computer. He said, "No. Meaning that guy is a risk because he knows what we're trying to do."

"But that was always the case. Why is it a problem now?"

Bashir stuffed the computer into his bag, shouldered it, and said, "Because Khalousi thinks he's going to be captured."

41

★★

I looked at the transcript on the screen, and knew we'd lost our target. He was in the wind. I sagged back and said to Veep, "Call them home. Break down the box. He's gone."

Earlier, our target had entered our surveillance box in the lobby and we'd begun to track him. Within minutes, Brett had called, saying he feared the target was conducting an SDR—which was basically a route over time and distance to smoke out a surveillance effort, all the while making it look like a natural flow of travel. Done correctly, it was damn near impossible to tell if it was an SDR or just a normal route.

Five minutes later, he'd called, "I'm off, I'm off. Target is definitely conducting an SDR."

Jennifer had cut in, "This is Koko. I have the eye. Knuckles, run a parallel."

In our TOC, as surveillance chief, I'd called, "Blood, Blood, how sure are you?"

"I'm positive. He's tracking for surveillance, and

he's been trained. He's using reflective surfaces, choke points, channeling, the whole nine yards."

I'd then made the decision I was now regretting. "Koko, Knuckles, break off. We know his bed-down. Let him go. Build the box back here for a follow-on effort. I don't want to burn the mission. He'll be back."

Hindsight, as they say, is 20/20, but I knew I'd made the correct choice with the information we'd had. We were building an intelligence package for the Taskforce, and getting burned by the target would be, to put it mildly, less than a good outcome. Not only would my team no longer be of any use, but the target himself would realize he was being hunted, making any follow-on effort by a second team that much harder. But now, with the transcript in front of me, I knew I had made a bad decision.

Creed had promised it by six in the morning, but it had taken longer than that, because part of the transcript was in Arabic, forcing the Taskforce to translate, and that had meant waiting until some nine-to-fiver linguist showed up. Eventually, they had, and the transcript was damning. Through our television hack, we could only get one-half of the conversation, but two bullets in the report stood out.

```
* Something has come up. The
  people we gained the product
  from have been acting strange.
  They showed up at my hotel,
```

```
  which means they might have
  seen me with you. I don't think
  they did, but they might have.
* From the North Koreans. They may
  have another plan in motion.
  They said as much. Just get out.
```

So that asshole most definitely was doing something bad, and had terrorists he was controlling. This was enough evidence to go to Omega immediately, as I had no doubt the appearance of the North Koreans yesterday was what he was talking about, and had been what spurred the panic. Unfortunately, it was too little, too late, because a final bullet told me he was in the wind.

```
* I understand. I'll keep the
  phone open, but won't try to
  contact you. I'm out of here
  tomorrow morning as well.
```

He was gone, and with it, so was our ability to prevent whatever was about to occur. The handset we'd tracked to the Hyatt had dropped off the face of the earth, and it was hoping against hope that he would be stupid enough to turn it back on. We could crack into his room and do an in-depth search of the luggage he'd left behind, but I was positive we would find nothing. He wouldn't be smart enough to trick us by leaving before his reservation was complete, walking out without his luggage, only to hand us a golden egg when he knew we'd search the room.

There were still the North Koreans, but from his conversation, it didn't sound like they were exactly friends. We could take them out, but it wouldn't lead to the men he'd passed the weapon to, even if we found them again.

Jennifer and Knuckles entered the room, saying, "What's up?"

The bathroom door opened, and Amena stuck her head out, saying, "Are you guys done? Can I come out?"

I said, "Not yet. Did you finish your game?"

I'd given her an iPad, pumping in twenty dollars on iTunes for her to purchase whatever she wanted, then made her wait in the bathroom with the television cranked up to mask any calls that came in. She said, "You can't finish this game. You can only keep playing it, and I'm getting tired of it. I can't get past a level."

She saw I wasn't moved, and said, "Okay, okay. I'll go hide in the bathroom again."

I smiled, and she closed the door. I stood up, giving Jennifer the seat and letting her read the screen. I said, "He's gone. Done. He's not coming back. Knuckles, you and Veep head on up to his room and search it. I don't think you'll find anything, but let's cover the bases, and I want to get in there before the maids do."

They started collecting the necessary gear, then Brett arrived, saying, "Why'd you call us back? He's looking for surveillance, but that doesn't mean we need to hide. Static surveillance is impossible to detect—especially in a hotel we're staying in. It's only natural to see the same people over and over again, and eventually, he'll let down his guard."

Knuckles and Veep left, headed to the ninth floor, and I pointed to our computer, saying, "He ain't coming back. And we're out of options."

Jennifer turned around and said, "Creed just sent a second transcript. This one is in English."

```
* Stop the joking. We need to
  meet sooner than later.
* Yes! I am. We need to meet in
  Europe, not Turkey. I can't get
  to Turkey in the time I need.
* So you're tracking me?
* Well, I need protection now. I
  have people hunting me, like
  you warned me about in Monaco,
  but they aren't Americans.
* I never told you I was in Syria.
  All I said was I have WMD
  intelligence. Does the agency
  want to pay for that information
  or not?
```

What in the world? It took a few seconds for the words to sink in, but when they did I felt an unbridled rage. Jennifer realized the import of the transcript at the same time I did.

She said, "That bastard is working with the CIA."

42

★★

I shook my head at the screen and said, "Sir, no Oversight Council on this one. I want to brace him one-on-one."

Kurt said, "Pike, I can't turn you loose on a CIA operations officer. Come on. You don't even know if it's him. Shit, you don't even know if it's the CIA. He could have been talking to a German or a Russian."

As soon as I'd realized what Creed had sent, I'd ordered everyone out of the room and dialed up the Taskforce, demanding to see Kurt Hale immediately on our VPN. I'd expected the pushback, but I could also tell he realized how pissed off I was if the subterfuge from the CIA was real.

I said, "Sir, he talked about a meeting in Turkey—where that asshat Periwinkle was pulled from—and he's speaking English."

"Maybe he's speaking English because it's the only common language they both have. Maybe the Syrian doesn't speak German, and the other guy doesn't speak Arabic."

Exasperated, I said, "Did you read the transcript? He said he was warned in Monaco. Remember when he disappeared and we didn't know why? **That's** why. And the only person outside of the Taskforce who knew we were about to interdict was the CIA case officer Periwinkle. It's him. Not Germans or Russians. It's Periwinkle, and that asshole knew who the Syrian was from day one."

Kurt pursed his lips, and I could tell he believed me. But that didn't mean I'd won. He said, "I still can't authorize this without the Council. Kerry Bostwick is a good man. He wouldn't sanction what Periwinkle did—**if** it's true. I need his concurrence to roll up his guy. This was the first joint CIA/Taskforce operation, and you want it to end with a unilateral Taskforce hit on the CIA? Look where I'm at here."

"Sir, I understand that, but remember Standish? Remember what that asshole did? Kerry may be a good man, but we have no idea how rotten this is. You brief the Council—you brief Kerry—and it's going to get back to Periwinkle. He's going to start building a cover story. And we're going to miss the terrorists."

"Pike, you're talking about an Omega operation against a United States citizen. Not only that, but a clandestine officer in the CIA."

"Come on, sir. You officers make things a hell of a lot more complicated than they need to be. I'm not talking about kidnapping his ass and waterboarding him. I just want to brace him. Use Johnny's team. We'll stay here. Just send them in and scare the shit out of him in an office visit."

"Johnny's been pulled out. He's no longer in Europe."

Crap.

"Carly, too?"

"No. She's in Paris. I've got her on something else."

"Okay, well, I can be back in Monaco in an hour. The Rock Star bird is standing by. Give me Carly and I'll do it with my team."

"What, exactly, does 'do it' mean?"

"The Syrian is in contact with the terrorists, and he's disappeared. Periwinkle is in contact with the Syrian, and that guy wants a meet—in his words 'sooner rather than later.' Let me rip Periwinkle a new asshole, and we'll set up a meeting, rolling up the Syrian."

"Why do you need Carly?"

"Because that asshole trusts her. She's in his tribe. She'll be the calm before the storm. He'll have his guard down if it's her."

Kurt rubbed his chin, and I felt the tide turning in my favor. I knew better than to push it, though. It had to be his decision.

He said, "If your plan works out, I'll have to brief Omega anyway. You can't unilaterally set up a meeting with the Syrian and take him down."

"I get that, but if my plan actually works, it'll sell

itself. And I know you're worried about hiding this first phase, but blame my ass. Tell 'em I unilaterally did it. When the smoke clears, nobody is going to question it."

"I'm not going to sell you down the river. I'm the commander. But it does beg the question. Why aren't you unilaterally doing it anyway? Like you did in Lesotho last year?"

He was talking about a mission where I'd used a little subterfuge to accomplish our objective, doing what was right even without his permission. But that was precisely the point—it was the right thing to do, and it hadn't altered our outcome. I'd even tacitly hinted that I was going to do it anyway—and I'm sure he knew it at the time. The question was a little offensive.

I said, "Come on, sir. I'd never do anything to put you or the Taskforce in jeopardy. Lesotho was a mission inside a mission. It wasn't this. I know where the line is drawn."

He laughed and said, "Yeah, sure. Okay. I'll get Carly moving, but it's just an office meeting. Right?"

I grinned and said, "Sure. But it's going to be the roughest office meeting that asshole has ever seen."

43

★
★ ★

Dr. Chin Mae-jung felt the unease rise as they left the central portion of Pyongyang, heading north. He'd had a spike of fear as they'd approached the gigantic presidential palace complex, bristling with wire and armed men, and then had relaxed as it faded in the rearview mirror. Now, as they left the elite neighborhoods and government buildings behind, he began to grow more concerned. Not that there was anything he could do about it, and the driver wasn't talking.

He'd been summoned to a long black Mercedes that looked to have been built four decades ago, the driver simply telling him to get in. Within the world of North Korea, that created instant compliance. Having no idea who the car belonged to, but fearing it represented the regime, there was no way he was going to disobey. Simply not clapping loudly enough at the Supreme Leader's proclamations could be a death sentence. Refusing to enter a car would mean death by instruments that weren't instantaneous.

Eventually, they reached a more rural area, passing through a gate manned by the ubiquitous armed soldiers who were everywhere. They raised the drop bar, refusing to even look inside the car for fear of repercussions, the appearance of the Mercedes itself granting instant access.

So he'd made the right choice. It was most definitely the regime.

In the distance he could see a sprawling, four-story granite structure built in a plain, utilitarian style. One befitting its communist heritage. Behind that building, he could see what looked like a prison, a squat, ugly one-story cement structure with bars on the windows. They passed a sign, and his heart almost stopped beating.

STATE SECURITY DEPARTMENT GENERAL HEAD-QUARTERS.

It was the infamous SSD, the Democratic People's Republic of Korea's chief security and intelligence agency—meaning the Supreme Leader's personal praetorian guard. The single most important agency tasked with enforcing the monolithic ideological system of the Kim regime. At first, he believed he was dead, or worse, going to a gulag for some unknown obscene transgression. Then he realized that made no sense. As a scientist in the research bureau, he already fell under the General Staff

Operations Bureau, and thus would have simply been arrested by them. There was no need for the vaunted SSD, as he worked in a compound that had plenty of security all on its own.

The Mercedes pulled to the steps in front of the building, and he saw the two men who had witnessed the very first live test of what they now called Red Mercury. The ones who had made him remove his protective gear to prove it had become inert. They now had on military uniforms, both colonels.

The driver said nothing, simply turning around and looking at him. Chin exited the sedan, then stood hesitantly, waiting on a command.

The first man said, "Dr. Chin, good to see you again. Have no fear."

Chin advanced up the stairs, and he said, "I'm Colonel Lee Dae-jung. This is Colonel Park In-young." Chin was off-kilter from the niceties. They'd not introduced themselves at all when he was about to die. Now they acted like they were old friends. He pushed his glasses on his face and nodded rapidly.

Colonel Park opened the door to the building, and Colonel Lee said, "Come. We have operations involving your invention, and a man wants to meet you about them."

They entered a sterile hallway, wide enough to drive a tractor down, the floor polished to a high gleam. Colonel Lee said, "Don't do anything other than answer the questions you're asked. Don't offer anything."

Chin nodded, and they stopped at a door flanked with flags. Colonel Park knocked, and Chin heard, "Come in."

The door swung open, and he saw General Kim Won-hong, the minister of state security. One of the most powerful men in the DPRK. Gruff, without any pleasantries, Kim said, "Is this him?"

Park said, "Yes, sir."

Kim pointed at a cluster of metal chairs and said, "Take a seat."

They did, and Kim said, "These two tell me that your invention does what you reported. It kills on command, and then becomes inert. I wanted to hear it from you."

Chin nodded and said, "I tested it myself."

"How?"

Chin glanced at the two colonels, then said, "I conducted a live-tissue test, first proving lethality, then, after the period for safety had passed, I introduced more live tissue. The new tissue lived."

Kim smiled and said, "I know who the first test was conducted on. What 'live tissue' did you use for the second? A dog?"

"No, sir. I did the test on myself."

Kim was mildly surprised. He said, "**You** did it? I'm impressed with the dedication. If we only had more like you."

Chin nodded, not saying that his "dedication" came from the barrel of a gun. General Kim turned to the other officers, his interest in Chin gone.

"So, we know it works, and you have sent the second batch?"

"Yes, sir. It's in Switzerland waiting for pickup."

"Where? Is it secure?"

"Completely. The Swiss are nothing if not tight-lipped about privacy. The only ones who have access are our men."

"And the Syrian? He is accomplishing what we need?"

"Yes, sir. He said the pass went fine, but there is still the issue of him lying about the phone."

"Do you think there is a breach? We need that attack to occur before we do our own."

"I don't know. We never recovered the phone, and there was the matter of the Russians. He claims he asked them to retrieve the phone, but at this point, it's just a claim. It's not optimal. I know we're clean, but I don't know about him. We paid him a visit, and it seems to have scared him. He's left Zurich."

"How can you say we're clean? He met us, did he not? He knows where the device came from, does he not?"

Colonel Park fidgeted, not liking the turn in the conversation. "Well, yes, sir, but that was un-avoidable."

"So if he talks, either to the Russians or anyone else, they will make the connection, which will completely destroy our attack. We want **them** to be blamed, not us."

Park said, "Sir, interdicting him might be messy. It might compromise our own status in Switzerland, which will eliminate our ability to execute our own plan. We're watching him. He can't do anything without us knowing."

"I don't think that's good enough. We might end up watching him get captured by a hostile power. You think removing him is messy, think about trying to silence him after he's in someone else's hands."

Park nodded, subdued. Kim continued, "The member states of the Conference on Disarmament convene in one week, and I don't have to tell you what they'll be discussing. More resolutions against the DPRK. The Syrians' attack must occur before then."

Kim thought for a moment, weighing his decision, then said, "Where is he now?"

"He's in Lucerne, at a cheap hotel. We have the ghost team on him. He thinks he's broken contact, but we've already wired his room. We know his every move."

"Kill him. I don't want him captured or questioned. Just eliminated."

Knowing that anything less than compliance could be viewed as insubordination, Park simply nodded.

Kim said, "I expect the same dedication Dr. Chin has shown, is that understood? Anything less than success, and you two will be live-tissue samples for the next round of tests."

44

✦
✦✦

David Periwinkle sat underneath a table umbrella on the south end of a small square called Place d'Armes, hidden behind a crowd of shoppers milling about at a farmers market. It was the best vantage point he could find. Even though someone could enter the square from multiple directions, then disappear into the market, they'd have to continue east to the pizza restaurant, crossing open ground, and he'd see them.

He had two more days on his forced assignment in Monaco, and as far as he could tell, it was going nowhere—mainly because he'd protected their target. But there were worse places to spend some temporary duty.

Yesterday, he'd received a call from Carly—the CIA case officer acting as the liaison for those SOCOM Neanderthals—asking for a meeting. He'd thought about blowing her off, because he knew the meeting was going to produce nothing, but he remembered she was fairly cute. Maybe there was something more to be gained.

As the chief of the CIA side of this worthless joint endeavor, she technically worked for him, and it wouldn't be the first time such a situation had turned in his favor. After all, it wasn't like she was going to get a lot of credit working on the Syrian case, and he could leverage his position as a bargaining chip, ostensibly to help her career.

It was worth a try.

He'd arrived thirty minutes early, casing the meeting site, then taking a seat with a view to the entrance. He was sure it wasn't necessary, but old habits die hard.

Seven minutes before the meeting time, he saw her, wearing sunglasses and a yellow sundress, her tanned legs running down to her bare, sandaled feet. The sight energized his imagination.

She took a seat at a stool next to a table of produce, not proceeding into the restaurant. She glanced around, but she wasn't looking for him. She was looking for someone else. And then she stood. He could tell she was hesitant about something, clutching a purse, making him think she might have a weapon and was looking for a threat.

He leaned forward.

A tall man with shaggy black hair and a two-day growth of beard approached, his T-shirt tight enough to showcase the rope of his muscles. She knew him, but seemed scared. He hugged her, then kissed her cheek.

What the hell?

Carly took a seat on a stool just to the edge of the farmers market, knowing that Periwinkle was probably lurking about somewhere, but more concerned with whom she was bringing to the meeting. She brushed her hair with her hand, an unconscious gesture to ensure she was presentable. She'd told herself she was just blending in by dressing as a tourist, but if she were honest, she'd chosen the sundress because it was flattering.

She waited, and then saw him in the crowd, half a head taller than everyone else. She stood, feeling an uncharacteristic hesitation, like a child caught for shoplifting and forced to apologize to a store owner. She felt a tinge of shame she knew wasn't fair.

From the day she'd VW'd selection, she'd spoken to him only once, on the phone. She hadn't seen him face-to-face, and she knew how much Taskforce selection meant to him. How much he'd put on the line for her, only to have her quit.

He stalked through the crowd, and she saw he was still a magnet. Women young and old surreptitiously glanced at him as he passed, drawn to him. If the gender roles had been reversed, they would have catcalled.

She waited, wondering if he would treat this as

the CIA operation it was—all business—or acknowledge their previous relationship. Truthfully, she wondered why that asshole Pike had sent him. Surely there was someone else on the team who could do the operation. But she knew why. That asshole Pike was getting closure. Ensuring she was accepted. It didn't make this meeting any easier.

He broke through the shoppers, glanced around, caught her eye, and his face split into a radiant smile. Before she knew it, he had his arms around her, kissing her cheek.

"Hey, you're a damn heartbreaker in that dress. Not sure how you're going to run in those sandals, though."

She laughed, genuinely relieved, and said, "Just a meeting. We won't be running, and I certainly don't want to look like a G-man on any surveillance cameras."

Knuckles passed her a manila envelope and said, "Here's the photo and transcript."

She took it and said, "We have about five minutes. The meeting site is across the square, in a back booth at that pizza joint."

They walked toward the entrance, and she said, "How are we going to play this?"

"You do all the talking. Bury him with the evidence, but give him an out. Get him to play ball as if he's helping. Give him a Get Out of Jail Free card. If it seems futile, and he's not budging, just tell me to step in."

They passed through the outdoor tables, reaching the door for the inside section. She pulled the handle and said, "Which means what?"

"It means I'll go a little Pike on his ass. He'll play. Remember, the end state isn't us building some prosecutor's case against him. It's getting to the Syrian."

She said, "Fine by me. This guy is kind of a creep. Never looks in my eyes."

They entered a narrow corridor, the left crowded with pizza makers whirling dough or cooking pies. Farther in, the place opened up to a section of booths, two occupied, the others empty. Carly took the last one on the far side, near a hallway for the restrooms, putting her back to the wall. Knuckles slid in beside her, bringing out a grin.

She said, "You trying for something?"

He chuckled and said, "I'm not leaving my back to the door."

She nodded, then looked at him, saying, "You're not going to ask?"

A waitress brought menus, and, after she'd left, Knuckles said, "Look, I'm not going to lie, it hurt. I took a hit with the team laughing at me. Actually, laughing at **you**, which hurt even more, because I knew it wasn't about capability or skill." He dropped the menu he was reading and said, "It was your decision, and I'm good with it."

She exhaled and said, "Thank you. That means a lot to me. You kept putting up so much pressure to do it, and I don't think I was ever all in."

Surprised, he said, "Why didn't you say something?"

"I don't know . . . Decoy . . . You . . . Pike . . . Jennifer . . . It was a lot of pressure. I just didn't say anything. But I should have."

He played with a napkin, then said, "Is that why you broke it off? Because I was pressuring you, and you didn't want to do A and S?"

She hit his arm and said, "Oh, stop it. Don't flatter yourself. It wasn't that. The decision we made was the decision **we** made. I didn't mean to imply something about our relationship. It is what it is, and I just like being a case officer more than some commando."

He grinned, and she said, "Besides, I hear you're boinking the secretary of state now. That didn't take long."

His mouth dropped open and she looked at the door to the restaurant, saying, "That's him."

Knuckles saw the man in the doorway and bit back a reply to what she'd said. A thin guy wearing baggy khakis and a knit polo, with expensive sunglasses on the crown of his head, Knuckles thought he looked like something out of a **Miami Vice** remake. He whispered, "Remember, I'm just security. You do the talking until you don't want to talk anymore."

Periwinkle slid into the booth opposite them, immediately saying, "Who's this?"

Carly said, "Contract security. Just in case. Don't worry, he's cleared."

Periwinkle said, "This isn't Iraq. It's Monte Carlo. Who **is** he?"

Carly deflected, snapping her fingers and saying, "Hey, my eyes are up here."

Knuckles glanced at Periwinkle, and saw his face redden. He couldn't believe it. The jerk had actually been looking at her breasts. At an official CIA personal meet. He wanted to wring Periwinkle's neck immediately, but Carly's tactic was masterful, setting the case officer on his heels for being an ass and shutting off any discussion of Knuckles's status.

She continued the pressure, not letting Periwinkle recover, saying, "Look, this won't take but a minute. We need you to set up a meeting with the Syrian we're chasing."

Periwinkle leaned back in the booth, saying, "What are you talking about?"

Carly pulled the photo out of the manila envelope, laid it on the table, and said, "This guy. Yasir al-Shami."

He glanced at it, then said, "I told you before, I don't know who he is."

She pulled the transcript out, laid it on the table, and said, "Well, maybe he's got a different name, but that's the one he was using when you talked to him in Zurich."

Knuckles watched him closely, and saw a tie in his left eye. He **was** the one.

Periwinkle picked up the sheet, read it, then said, "This isn't me. You need to go back to wherever you got this for a new thread."

"That's the whole point. Yasir—or however you know him—has passed what we believe is WMD material to a terrorist cell, and now he's in the wind. We've lost him, but he wants to meet with you, and we want you to set that up."

He balled up the paper and dropped it on the table, saying, "I don't know him."

Carly said, "David, we're not here to turn this into a CIA shit storm about missing links to 9/11, but if this attack occurs, that's exactly what will happen, and it won't be just finger-pointing about being lazy or missing the dots. It's going to be crossing into the accomplice range."

He snarled, "You little shit, pretending to be a case officer, bouncing around Monte Carlo in a sundress. Do you know who I am? Who has my back on the seventh floor? **Everyone.** You'll be lucky to get an assignment to the Congo after the cable I'm about to send."

She crossed her arms under her breasts, and Knuckles saw Periwinkle's eyes slip again, focused on something other than her face. Carly saw it as well, and looked at Knuckles, disgusted. She said, "I'm done. Your turn."

Gladly.

Periwinkle had a flash of confusion on his face, and Knuckles said not a word. He reached across the table with both arms, grabbed the back of Periwinkle's head by his hair, and bounced his face on the table. Periwinkle snapped upright, holding his nose and shouting, "What the fuck are you doing?"

The waitress came over, alarmed, and Knuckles said, "Nosebleed. Can we get some napkins?"

She nodded and scurried away. Periwinkle said, "You two fucks—"

Knuckles repeated the maneuver, snatching Periwinkle's head and slamming it into the table again. Periwinkle screamed once more, then snorted blood. Knuckles said, "We can do this all night, but at the end, you're going to set up that meeting."

Through his hands, Periwinkle said, "Who are you? I saw you two hug. You're no contract security."

Knuckles leaned over, getting into his face. "Who I am is irrelevant. **What** I am is what you should be concerned with, because if that terrorist attack occurs, you won't have to worry about interagency repercussions. **I'll** fucking kill you."

They locked eyes, and the waitress reappeared, dropping a sheaf of napkins on the table, glancing between them. Her voice trembling, her pencil vibrating from her shaking hand, she said, "I'm so sorry about the nosebleed. Can I get you guys anything?"

Knuckles kept his eyes on Periwinkle, saying, "I don't think so. He's going to need an ice pack. We're probably leaving."

She nodded, immensely relieved to hear they

would be gone, then walked away, snatching looks back at them as she went. They sat in silence for a moment, then Periwinkle glanced at Carly. Knuckles snapped his fingers, saying, "Hey, my eyes are over here."

Carly tried to hide a grin, and Periwinkle stuttered, "I might know how to find him. It might take some time. But maybe I can help."

Knuckles relaxed, putting his elbows on the table. He said, "Good. That's my boy. Get the fuck out of here and pack your bags. You're going to Zurich. So you know, nobody knows about this but us right now. Nobody on your vaunted seventh floor knows you've withheld information. You send a cable, and you'll open up your own shit storm."

Periwinkle nodded, then staggered out of the restaurant, holding a napkin to his face.

Carly exhaled, then said, "I think that went well."

Knuckles knew it was sarcasm, but said, "Me too." He looked at her and said, "Good to be working with you. I mean it."

She smiled and said, "You too." She pecked his cheek and said, "I mean it."

He put a hand on her thigh, saying, "Well, as long as we're waiting for him . . . what are you doing for dinner? We could get some room service."

She felt the rub, raised her eyebrows, and said, "You're kidding, right?"

He jerked his hand away, shamed, and said, "At least I was looking into your eyes."

She laughed and said, "I'll get dinner with you, but I'm not going to your room."

He saw her eyes, and where there had once been fear and shame, there was now a bubbly life. He realized, in his own ham-handed way, he'd done something right.

He'd validated her choice.

He said, "I'd like that. I really would."

45

✦✦✦

Sayid exited onto the platform of the Gare de Nice–Ville station, disoriented. He looked left and right, wondering in which direction they should go. Bashir pointed left, and they walked to a broken escalator, pulling their bags up as they advanced.

Sayid said, "Of course the up escalator is broken. Perfect."

Bashir said, "We're lucky there is an escalator."

Sayid laughed and said, "Why, exactly, is this a good thing? A broken escalator is the same as having none at all."

Bashir said nothing, realizing Sayid had missed his point.

They'd had no trouble getting from Zurich to Nice, nobody checking any baggage, and only one conductor looking at Sayid strangely when she'd punched his ticket. Before leaving, Bashir had begged him once again to assume the dress of the infidel, but he had refused, saying that the kaffirs were too stupid to see the threat. And Bashir had to admit he'd been right. They had been allowed to continue straight into Nice.

They reached the top of the platform, Bashir read a sign, then led Sayid to a section of lockers, some big enough for full-size luggage, others smaller, built for carry-ons. He looked at a sheet, then advanced to a smaller locker, putting in the key given to him by Yasir. The door swung open, and he found a sheaf of papers, along with keys for an apartment. He smiled.

As much as they didn't trust Yasir, he was proving true to his word. Bashir clenched the keys and said, "Let's go."

They exited the front of the old station, the eighteenth-century facade projecting a veneer of respectability that was probably true back then, but was wholly unearned in the modern day.

They looked at the expanse of pavement in front of the station, bustling with travelers, the road beyond full of traffic and bleating horns, and Bashir's enthusiasm waned. Sayid said, "Take a cab? We have no idea where that apartment is."

Bashir said, "No. Remember the cabdrivers in Damascus? They were snitches for the regime. It might be the same here. Let's Uber. Get some kid here that won't talk."

"Uber is just as bad as a cab. Doesn't matter who picks us up, it's all on computer now. For all we know, France is monitoring that system."

Bashir said, "Then we find someone. Someone that's not either. If this is like every other city in

Europe, there will be unregistered cabs. Someone who is illegal to begin with. That's what we want." He pointed, then said, "Someone like them."

Sayid saw a clutch of unmarked cars with men leaning on hoods and smoking cigarettes, while others badgered the travelers exiting the station.

Bashir began walking toward them and someone shouted in Arabic, "You! You! Need a ride?"

Bashir turned to him and, in Arabic, said, "How do you know we speak the language?"

The man pointed at Sayid's Berber jacket and said, "I just guessed. But I'm one of the faithful. Where would you like to go?"

They loaded the car, and Bashir gave him an address, picking a number at random along the shoreline. He wanted to be dropped off near where they were going to stay, but not on top of it. The driver plugged the address into his GPS, and they left the station.

Twenty minutes later, the car stopped on the famed Nice waterfront, adjacent to a public toilet. The driver said, "This is it? But there's nothing here. Did you give me the right address?"

Embarrassed, Bashir told him that he had and exited, stepping out into the same space where another true believer had slaughtered eighty-six people in 2016. Celebrating Bastille Day, they had been mowed down by a truck, the vehicle grinding the revelers apart like a scythe, staining the promenade in blood. That had been wiped clean, all traces removed, and today most tourists had no idea about the attack, the promenade clogged with people enjoying the sunshine and the shore, unaware of the history.

Bashir watched the unregistered cab drive away, then surveyed the throngs of people flowing around them. He said, "It's amazing they don't learn. We attack, and they still come back, like roaches."

Sayid said, "It takes a breaking point. A truck wasn't it. But maybe we are."

Bashir smiled and said, "Yes. Maybe we are."

They began dragging their luggage into the old town, the road they were on narrowing into what appeared to be nothing more than an alley. Bashir kept checking his sheet of instructions, looking for a church. Eventually, he found it—an ornate cathedral with a bell tower, surrounded by outdoor cafés and gelato shops. He turned in a circle, then pointed down another alley.

They wound through the narrow lane, Bashir glancing at numbers every few feet. Sayid followed him patiently, then Bashir cursed, looking at his sheet. He retraced his steps, eventually stopping and saying, "This should be it."

They went up a small flight of stairs to a simple wooden door, and Bashir put in the key. It worked, causing them both to exhale.

They searched the flat, finding it empty. A one-bedroom place with a small kitchenette and a balcony off the bedroom, it didn't take long to clear it. Sayid said, "So we have a place to stay. What now?"

Bashir said, "We left Switzerland early. The boat doesn't show up for three days. So I guess we have three days to wait."

"That's not my question. Are we doing the original plan, or something else?"

Bashir said, "We can't do anything without that boat. We can't attack anyone in Syria until we get there."

"Maybe we aren't attacking in Syria. Contact the imam."

46
⋆⋆⋆

Burning off time before his meeting, Yasir took a seat inside a large candy store just to the north of the bridge across the Reuss River, with Lake Lucerne in view across the plaza out front. He watched the tourists buying pounds of chocolate and other treats and wondered if it was worth the sky-high prices.

He was nervous. More nervous than he should have been, given his history. It was just another meet, like the hundreds he'd done in lands that were decidedly more dangerous—including his own. Maybe it was because he was so close to achieving his dream. Or maybe it was because he was walking into the arms of a CIA man who just a day and a half ago seemed not to care a whit about what he had to offer.

After making significant efforts to obscure his plans, leaving his hotel room with nothing more than the clothes on his back, he'd fled Zurich, traveling to Lucerne—a location he'd never been to before and had absolutely no reason to travel to now.

It was a complete break from any known connections in Geneva and Zurich, and a city where he could settle for a bit, planning his next moves. On the first night in his hotel, Periwinkle had called, surprising Yasir, saying he'd been given a different assignment and was leaving Europe. If Yasir wanted to pass the information, they needed to meet immediately.

It had raised Yasir's suspicions, but the money Periwinkle was offering was too much to pass up. Yasir had set the meeting location and time, while Periwinkle had dictated Yasir's route, saying he'd provide countersurveillance to ensure he was clean. It was an SOP that Yasir had habitually used when meeting his CIA contact, but this time it made him uneasy. In the past, he knew the CIA man was on his side. He wasn't sure anymore.

Yasir checked his watch, then stood. He'd rehearsed his route this morning, wanting to make sure he knew precisely how long it would take. He needed to arrive at his selected site plus or minus thirty seconds from the meet time. Anything outside that envelope would cause Periwinkle to worry that something had gone wrong, and maybe he'd been compromised or interdicted en route. He couldn't give Periwinkle any reason to be wary.

He tossed his coffee into the trash and threaded past the crowds buying candy, seeing an entire tour of Asians exiting a bus outside, a guide in front with a flag. He sank against the wall, thinking of the North

Koreans. Surely they couldn't stage something so bold, infiltrating an entire group on a tour bus, could they? He waited until the last one entered, checking each individual as they passed. Nobody paid him a bit of attention, and he began to feel foolish. He had taken great pains to vanish. There were no North Koreans in Lucerne.

When the final tourist entered, he exited through the open door, walking into the plaza fronting Lake Lucerne, the roundabout clogged with tour buses. He checked his watch, and saw he was running late.

He jogged toward the river, paralleling the shore of the lake on the avenue. He reached the intersection of the Reuss River and Lake Lucerne, and took a right, seeing the famed Chapel Bridge, the first segment of his designated route. Built in the fourteenth century, it was a covered pedestrian walkway made of wood that traversed the river—a choke point that would allow countersurveillance to identify anyone following him. Or allow someone to track his movements.

A necessary risk, if he wanted his payout.

He passed several tourists going the other way, with only an elderly couple taking an interest in him. He went by a souvenir stand built into the bridge, then exited on the far side. He paused, seeing nothing but a child kneeling next to a bench with a stick of chalk, doodling on the pavement.

He went west, following the bank of the river,

walking rapidly past outdoor cafés and shops. Eventually, he reached a restaurant that was larger than the others. Called Opus, it had both an inside and outside eating area and multiple escapes, north, south, and east. It was his choice for the meeting location for that very reason. He checked his watch, saw he was fifteen seconds early, and pulled the door open.

My radio broke squelch, and I heard a voice attempting to sound official, but coming across as something from a bad television movie. "Pike, this is Rogue, Tango One in sight. Over and out."

I grimaced, seeing a smile play across Jennifer's face. I keyed my radio and said, "Roger all. Stay off the net now. Everyone else acknowledge."

I got a call from my team and saw Periwinkle, four tables up, surreptitiously hold a finger in the air, then drop it.

The call told me we had about five minutes before the target arrived. A waiter showed up, pouring us water—an Asian guy, which was about as weird as seeing a Swiss citizen serving falafels in Fallujah, Iraq. He left, and I said, "You know we have to do something with Amena."

"We're not going to drop her on the street with a wad of bills. I've told you that."

I raised my hands and said, "I'm not talking about

dropping her on the street, but there's gotta be some-where we can send her. I mean, surely there's a refugee place around here."

She crossed her arms, and I saw the granite wall. "We're **not** going to abandon her. Her entire family was slaughtered. She's traumatized. I will **not** just drop her at an orphanage like in a Dickens novel. I see you with her. Tell me you don't like her. Tell me you think that's right."

And she hit a chord. I **did** like her, but I wasn't running a daddy day care. I was catching terrorists. Even so, I knew to back off. I demurred, saying, "She can't even use a correct callsign."

Jennifer chuckled and said, "It was your decision to use her. Maybe I should have fought you on Koko."

Rogue was the callsign Amena had taken for herself. It wasn't one that I would have given her for this mission, and she didn't seem to understand that you couldn't pick your own callsign. Someone else picked it.

In the hotel the day before, when we'd developed our plan, I'd simply run out of people. I needed a capture team—which meant at least a three-to-one ratio to ensure dominance over the target. With Jennifer and me inside the restaurant to handle any-thing crazy this guy could do, or other contingencies, that left the rest of the team on the street—and no trigger. I most assuredly wasn't going to trust Periwinkle to help.

Sitting in the corner, Amena had said, "I can spot

him. It's not that hard." Of course I'd said no, because I couldn't put her on the street to trigger a counterterrorist operation for the United States of America. She was a child, for God's sake.

She'd answered by saying, "I've already done it once. What's the big deal?"

She didn't get what the "big deal" was, but she absolutely had a point. I'd looked at Jennifer, and she'd nodded. Knuckles chimed in, saying, "Same thing as before. There isn't a threat."

I said, "Okay, okay, but this is the last time." Amena's face had split into a smile, and I had to admit, a part of me admired her spunk.

We'd received the call earlier that Knuckles had convinced Periwinkle to play ball, and working with that asshat, we'd had him set up a meeting, along with developing a route for Yasir to follow. One segment would walk him in, the other would walk him out. What he didn't know was the route walking him out would be into a kill zone for capture.

This initial meeting was supposed to just delineate the exchange of money for Yasir's information—and I didn't really care what they talked about, as long as it looked real and lulled the guy into thinking that we were on his side. Once I had my hands on him, we'd get every bit of information he had for free.

And so I'd made Amena a Taskforce member for this one operation, but she had to talk on the radio, meaning she needed a callsign. Amena had said, "I have one. I want Rogue."

Just teasing her, not really caring what she was called, I said, "Look, kid, you want to be a part of the team, you don't pick your callsign. We get to pick it."

She said, "I'm not going to be a talking gorilla or named after a drug gang."

Incensed, Brett said, "Hey, wait a minute. I told you, that's not what my callsign means."

She'd looked at me with her liquid brown eyes and said, "I am Rogue."

I said, "Why?"

It turned out, she'd watched a bunch of bootleg DVDs with her brother, and Rogue was some **X-Men** character that she identified with. I'd scoffed at that and said, "You're picking a comic book character? Be original. Something like Raghead would be much better."

She'd looked at me solemnly and said, "I'm not being anything other than Rogue." She then began talking about how Rogue couldn't touch anyone because she'd harm them, and how she was always looking for some place to be where she could finally find a home. How her entire life was searching for a connection that she could never find.

As dumb as it sounded at first, her words were profound. I couldn't tell if she was talking about herself, or the comic book character. Rogue she had become.

Inside the restaurant, I realized I should have

spent my time teaching her proper radio procedures instead of arguing about her callsign.

Four minutes and thirty-eight seconds after Amena's call, Yasir appeared outside the glass front door, right on time. He looked at his watch, then broke the threshold. I called, "All elements, all elements, target is inside the box."

I got a "Roger" from my kill team, and then, "This is Rogue. I copy last transmission. Tango inside the box. This is Rogue, over and out."

I rolled my eyes, and Jennifer chuckled. I said, "Sooner or later, we're going to have to leave her."

She said, "Later. No need to decide right now. You're the one using her."

Which was a good point.

Yasir came inside, glanced left and right, saw Periwinkle, and walked straight to his table. Which sort of crumbled Periwinkle's whole alibi of "I'll set it up, but I **really** don't know the guy . . ."

He was a damn liar.

47

★
★ ★

Yasir took a seat, and they began talking. The same Asian waiter walked over to them, pouring water from a pitcher. Yasir did a double take at the waiter's heritage, then held out his glass.

The waiter left, and I saw Yasir begin waving his hands, clearly trying to make a point. Periwinkle countered with something, knowing his whole job was to make this look good. Understanding that Yasir's ass in a cage would be the only thing that saved him. Yasir became animated, and Periwinkle took a sip of water, holding his other hand out as if to say, **No good.**

Yasir sagged back in his chair, saying something, then picked up his own glass. Periwinkle's face grimaced in pain. Yasir raised his glass to his lips. Periwinkle clutched his chest, and I saw the Asian waiter staring at the table hard, and not because he was concerned.

I leapt up and charged across the floor, my chair

falling over in a clatter and startling everyone in the small dining room. Periwinkle fell face-forward onto the table and I slapped the water glass out of the Syrian's hand. It shattered against the wall and he flopped out of his chair, holding his arms over his head. I whirled to the "waiter," and he snaked his hand into his jacket. I reached for my waist, underneath my own jacket, gripped the butt of my weapon, and stared at him.

We locked eyes, and he saw I was a killer, too. He backed up into the kitchen, his hand still on his weapon. The door swung shut and I glanced to the front, seeing the Syrian fleeing the way he'd come. Away from our planned kill zone. Jennifer reached the table and I said, "Start CPR. See if you can keep him alive," then leapt up the stairs to the front exit, breaking onto the net.

"All elements, all elements, the meeting was interdicted, the target is on the run, out the river side."

My team was one block away from the river, in an ambush site complete with a vehicle for escape, and I knew I had to get them moving immediately. We had no idea where this guy was staying, but the Koreans clearly did, because they'd intercepted the instructions for this meeting. They knew a hell of a lot more than we did—with the exception that we knew where he was right this second. If we lost him, they'd kill him.

I broke out the front, looked left and right, and

saw a man fleeing downstream, away from the lake. I gave chase, saying, "Target's on the riverbank, moving east. Can anyone interdict?"

I heard, "This is Blood, we're moving now."

I kept running, seeing Yasir pass a concrete bridge without stopping, flinging tourists away from him. He was faster than I would have thought. I said, "I have him in sight, but I'm not gaining. Who's with you?"

I heard huffing, then Brett said, "Nobody. I left them behind."

Sprinting flat out, I grinned, because Brett Thorpe was possibly faster than Jesse Owens. Well, definitely faster running in civilian clothes with kit on.

Another covered wooden bridge appeared fifty meters ahead of me, and I saw Yasir dart into it, crossing the river. I said, "He's just taken the second wooden bridge. The one east of the Chapel Bridge."

I saw another figure sprint inside, and recognized Brett. I entered right behind him. Unlike the Chapel Bridge, which ran at an angle across the river, doing a little bit of a zigzag, this one was straight across, allowing me to see to the end. Yasir was running like he was being chased by zombies from the apocalypse. And then he stopped in his tracks.

Brett slowed down, and I caught up to him, saying, "What's he doing?"

Yasir glanced back at us, and then forward. I followed his gaze, and saw a team of two Asian men on the far side, waiting. They saw his hesitation, then started walking forward, glancing around. I knew what their end state was from the restaurant. They weren't attempting to capture him.

I pulled out my suppressed Glock and said, "They're going to kill him right here." Brett brought his weapon to bear and I saw the Koreans draw their own weapons, keeping them down low in an attempt to hide them. They hadn't seen us yet. I said, "Get their attention. Don't kill them. Make 'em rethink the decision."

Yasir stood frozen between us, unsure of what to do, and I cracked a suppressed round, aiming for a support beam next to the head of one of the Koreans. It was muted, without the theatrics of an unsuppressed gun, but it was still loud enough for someone who understood what they were hearing. And he did.

He whipped his head away from Yasir, seeing both of us with pistols out. The few tourists on the bridge hadn't even noticed the noise. The lead man said something, and both dropped into a crouch. Yasir ran to the railing of the bridge on the upstream side, looked at me, then at the Koreans, and jumped into the water.

The lead Korean said something, and they holstered their weapons, retreating back to the end of the bridge, disappearing from sight.

We sprinted forward, seeing Yasir had jumped right in front of a spillway, the water pouring over it in a foam of rage. He was struggling to stay afloat, and then was swept under the bridge. I ran to the far side and heard him shout, "I can't swim! I can't swim!"

Great.

I looked at Brett and he said, "Hey, I do the running. Not the swimming."

I said, "You're a damn combat diver!"

"So are you. I'll get the vehicle and stage on the far side."

I ripped off my jacket, shucked my shoes, and handed him my weapon, saying, "Evacuate the restaurant. Get Jennifer out. I don't want her involved with ambulances and police."

He said, "What happened?" I said, "Later," and I leapt over the side of the bridge, onlookers starting to gather and point. Yasir was bobbing in the freezing water, the current subsiding from the spillway, but he was still struggling. I stroked to him, grabbed him around the neck and shoulders, then hoisted his head above the waterline.

He spit out a gout of water, and then started to fight me. I punched him in the temple, stunning him, giving me time to roll him onto his back. I said, "I'm trying to help you, dumbass."

He quit fighting, allowing me to stroke to the far bank, him feebly attempting to swim as I towed him with me. He coughed and said, "Why didn't you just kill me?"

I said, "You're much too valuable to kill. Although I'd be interested to hear why those other assholes were trying to."

48

✦✦✦

Bashir saw a sign proclaiming the American Bar and Restaurant out the cab window and said, "This is good right here." He was getting better at finding his way around the warren of alleys in the old town, mainly by memorizing reference points. He knew the cathedral was only a few blocks north from the bar.

He exited the vehicle, pulled out his packages, then paid the driver. He waited until the cab had disappeared before moving, not wanting the cabbie to have any idea which way he walked.

It had taken the better part of the day to find the supplies Sayid needed, but eventually, he'd managed it. He picked up the two large shopping bags and began walking north with a purpose. Five minutes later, he broke into the small square in front of the cathedral, winding through the throngs of people visiting the various outdoor cafés.

He reached the apartment, knocked twice, then unlocked the door. Sayid met him in the foyer, taking one shopping bag and saying, "Did you find everything?"

"Yes. The Inspire Two was the hardest, but they had one at a Fnac downtown."

Last night, the imam had contacted them with startling instructions: Do not travel to Syria. Conduct the attack in France. When questioned, Khalousi had stated he had lost contact with Yasir, and he couldn't ensure safe passage once they reached the port of Tartus. Bashir had asked about using the original plan of traveling through Turkey, but Khalousi had said he'd changed his mind on the location of the attack. French soldiers and warplanes had joined the fight, and an attack on French soil would provide a much greater impact. Killing French and American soldiers would cause turmoil, but using the Red Mercury on the unprotected would create chaos—and possibly cause the French to leave the fight, like the Spaniards had when they'd left Iraq after the Madrid train attacks.

They'd asked him for guidance on where. Did he expect them to travel to Paris? He'd told them Nice, at the exact same spot the previous attack had occurred. Not only would it create a major news story to reverberate around the world, but it would crush the economy in Nice.

Bashir and Sayid had spent the rest of the night brainstorming and using the Internet to research the promenade. Leveraging Google Maps, TripAdvisor, the Nice tourism website, and a plethora of other resources, they'd considered cars, motorcycles, booby-trapped bathrooms, restaurants—everything—but while each had an element they liked, none of the courses of action would unleash the potential of the Red Mercury. It needed to be dispersed through a crowd, not stationary like a single explosive event—and they couldn't disperse it without being killed themselves.

And then, Sayid had a stroke of genius, falling back on his specialty in Iraq and Syria. "Why don't we use a drone? I can rig it like the ones we used in Raqqa, only instead of dropping a bomb, we'll simply fly it low and slow over the crowd."

Bashir said, "Can you do that? Can you rig it here, in this apartment?"

"Yes, if we get the right equipment. The key will be getting a drone that will take the payload. Those cheap ones are fine for a hand grenade, but these canisters are bigger."

He'd pulled up Google, and gone to work again, finding a professional quadcopter called the Inspire 2. Built by DJI, it could fly close to sixty miles an hour, with a range of more than three miles and a flight time of almost half an hour. Built with Hollywood cinematography in mind, its software program was state of the art, with obstacle avoidance, target tracking, and preprogrammed intelligent flight, making any accidental problems dummy proof. Screw anything up, and the drone simply returned home to where it was launched.

While the features were impressive, all Sayid cared about was the payload. Fabricated to carry professional cinematography equipment, the Inspire could hold up to three pounds. It was perfect.

The problem had been finding one in Nice. They could order one online and have it delivered in three days, but that would take too long. The boat would be leaving in two. Bashir had finally found one at a French electronics store called Fnac, astounded at the price. He'd burned through most of their disposable cash to purchase it and the electronic components Sayid needed.

Bashir opened the box and said, "I hope this was necessary, because it ate up almost all of our money."

Sayid pulled the drone body from the box, turning it over in his hands. He said, "It's worth it. Trust me. Not only will this deliver a devastating blow, but we can video the effects from a mile away. It will be the greatest production in the caliphate's history."

Bashir said, "I've been thinking about that. About the launch point. I know you wanted to fly it from the cemetery on top of Chateau Hill, but I think I have a better idea."

Sayid laid out the tools and electrical equipment Bashir had purchased, saying, "Yes? What could be better than that? We launch it from the Jewish cemetery, fly it down the coast, releasing the agent, then escape to the boat. Nobody will catch us. Anywhere else and we'll be martyred."

Bashir said, "Anywhere but from the sea."

Sayid stopped fiddling with the drone. Bashir continued, "We do it from the boat. It's already supposed to take us to Syria, so let's load it, take it offshore, conduct the attack, then simply sail away. Only we go to Turkey instead of Syria."

49

Kurt Hale knew his answer would be a grenade dropped into the room. He said, "Yes, that's correct."

The Council members erupted, all shouting questions. He stood there, stoically waiting for them to calm down, although he realized why they were upset. He looked at Kerry Bostwick for support, and got a nod.

He took a breath, thinking, **This is going to be bad**, but knew he had to bulldoze through the panic. Because there was a hit coming, and it would be catastrophic.

The president raised his hand, calming the room. He pointed at Alexander Palmer, saying, "One at a time."

Palmer said, "You have a dead CIA case officer in Lucerne? Did I just hear that correctly? And instead of chasing the guy who killed him, you interdicted someone else in the river—the fucking river—of Lucerne, Switzerland?"

"No, sir. That's not what happened. Can we get back to the briefing?"

"No, we **can't** get back to the briefing. What the hell are you doing?"

"Sir. If I may. Let me continue."

President Hannister held a hand up again, and the room became quiet.

Kurt exhaled and said, "Okay, yes, a CIA case officer was poisoned in Lucerne, Switzerland, by agents of the North Korean regime. That happened, but it's not the reason I'm here. The North Koreans are also in the process of engineering a terrorist attack with Syrian assets, and they're going to leverage it. **That's** why I'm here. I need immediate Omega authority."

Palmer said, "So you conducted an Omega mission without authority, and now you're **asking** for Omega? After a CIA case officer was killed? I'd like to know what the CIA thinks of this. Whether they think this joint operation was a good thing."

All eyes turned to Kerry Bostwick, and he said, "I'm with Kurt. There is nothing to hide here. The Taskforce did what they could. Nobody could have seen this coming."

Kurt had talked to Kerry before the meeting, laying out his evidence of what Periwinkle had done, and both had agreed to just bury the culpability. Use the loss of Periwinkle as a soldier at war. The man was dead. Raising a stink about his subterfuge was nothing either wanted, and there was a greater threat out in the world. Now wasn't the time to start pointing fingers.

Palmer said, "How are you going to continue with a CIA operations officer dead in a restaurant? I'd really like to know that."

Aggravated, Kurt said, "Sir, he's CIA. That's not my portfolio. We don't do anything with them for a reason. Except you guys said I had to this time."

Kerry said, "We have it. We're running the traplines right now. He's a businessman from Turkey who had a heart attack. No issues."

Palmer said, "No issues? The Taskforce just executed an Omega operation without sanction. The second one in as many weeks, in the same damn country."

Kurt said, "Sir, Yasir was drowning. He was about to die. It might seem convenient, but the right to protect applied here as well."

Palmer snarled, "Why was he about to drown? Why was that?"

"He jumped into the water, and he couldn't swim."

"And why did he jump into the water? A man who couldn't swim? Was it because your walking disaster Pike was chasing him? Forcing an Omega without authority?"

Kurt took a breath, letting the emotion go. As much as he wanted to punch the guy in the head, it wouldn't help him here. He said, "Sir, there were two North Koreans about to kill him. Pike prevented that, and he jumped. I'm not sure what you want me to say. I suppose Pike could have let them do it. Or he could have let the man drown."

Palmer looked at the president and said, "This seems to be a trend here. 'Oh, we had to do it, or he would have died.'"

Kurt rolled his eyes, looked at the president, and said, "Sir, there is about to be a catastrophic attack on a US military base in Syria, which will significantly affect your ability to prosecute the war."

He locked eyes with Alexander Palmer and said, "I'm not sure what you're trying to prove, but what Pike did was correct. Regardless of whatever crap you want to spout about the charter."

Kurt saw George Wolffe wince, and waited for the flamethrower. Instead, President Hannister said, "Continue. Where is the Syrian now?"

Palmer stuttered, clenching his pen so tightly his knuckles turned white. Kurt exhaled and said, "Pike called a support team from Greece. We evacuated him to a black hole in the Med. He's secure, and under Taskforce control. We can determine his final disposition at our leisure." Kurt looked at Palmer and said, "And before you ask, there were no glitches. Ground vehicle to an LZ, helo to the ship."

President Hannister said, "Good. What do we know about the North Koreans?"

"Sir, we don't know why—and Yasir doesn't either—but the DPRK tried to kill him. They succeeded in killing his contact—case officer Periwinkle—but we don't know their motives."

"What are they up to?"

"We know they passed whatever this Red Mercury is to Yasir. We have Yasir's phone, and found an app for a safe-deposit box in Geneva, rented by an LLC from Luxembourg. We've cracked the rental chain, and we've found another bunker that this same LLC has rented, but this one is out in the middle of nowhere. We think the North Koreans are using it to store Red Mercury. We think they held it there, and then transferred it to the city center of Geneva for distribution. Meaning they used this to give Yasir Red Mercury for terrorists."

"And do we know what this Red Mercury is yet?"

"No, sir. But it can't be good."

"So you want to go check the second bunker now?"

"No, sir, not now. Maybe later. Right now we have an imminent threat."

Kurt paused, then went from face to face in the room. He said, "Look, from what we know from Yasir, two terrorists are going to take whatever this Red Mercury is and sail to a port on the Syrian coast. From there, they're going to use it to attack a Special Forces base in Manbij, Syria. We've already alerted the base to the threat, but **we** have a thread. We know where they're staying in Nice. We **know** it. Yasir gave it to us under interrogation. I'm asking for Omega right now. No more bullshit about 'How will this expose us?' I want Omega to roll up the terrorists while we still know where they are."

He saw Palmer's face cloud, and waited for the president. Hannister said, "Let's take a break. Five minutes. Think about the decision we're going to make. Nobody is going to be forced into it."

Inwardly, Kurt winced. Because Pike had executed two actions using in-extremis authority, Kurt could tell the Council was reluctant to give him Omega, even though the threat was now a clear and present danger. It was politics at its most extreme. Had Pike not executed those two missions, there would be no reason to ask for Omega, because the terrorists would have never been found.

Kurt went to the coffeepot at the rear of the room and felt someone tap him on the shoulder. He turned around, and saw Amanda Croft, the secretary of state. She said, "Hey, what are you trying to accomplish here? Is there really a threat, or are you trying to expand Taskforce authority by these repetitive 'Right to Protect' actions?"

Kurt said, "Excuse me?"

She said, "Tell me this is right, and I'll believe you. Because I believe the men who work with you. But don't sell me a bill of goods if you're prostituting your own men to execute an action to increase your power base. Would Knuckles do this?"

He was flabbergasted. He put down his cup and said, "Ma'am, let's get something straight, right here, right now. You deal in a world of politics, where everyone seems to lie for a living. I live in a world of absolutes. I **am** Knuckles. Right now, Knuckles is on the end of a phone begging me for permission. I'm not the bad guy here. I walk a fine line, and Pike crosses it all the time, but when he does, it's because his instincts are spot-on. Not because he's running amok. There **is** a threat."

She looked at him for a moment, then said, "You're sure about that?"

He picked up his coffee and took a sip. "You know Knuckles pretty well. What do you think? Would he be begging if it weren't true?"

She blanched, reading through Kurt's unstated words. He said, "There are no secrets here. I know about you two. Nobody else on this Council does, but I do."

She said, "That's not why I vote the way I do."

He said, "It **is** why you vote the way you do. Because voting is based on what you know. He speaks highly of you, which counts with me. And that should count with **you**. Would he follow me if I was an egomaniac looking to do harm?"

She poured her own cup, then said, "Okay. But this vote isn't because of our relationship. That won't ever happen."

Kurt said, "Yes it will. And it should. Because you know the heart of the man who's asking. That's what all of this is. Period."

She considered his words, then nodded, saying, "You might have a point."

President Hannister called the room to order and

said, "Okay, do we want to interdict the men based on the intelligence from the Syrian we captured in Lucerne? This is a formal vote for Omega against them, using Taskforce assets."

Palmer said, "Sir, we have no protections in Nice. No cover for Pike to even show up. We had cover in Monaco, and now we have a dead CIA agent in Switzerland. If we do something in Nice, it's going to be kinetic. We aren't talking about Alpha. We're talking about Omega. My vote is to use the intelligence we have and either interdict them en route on the sea, or protect the base. We've done enough already with the Taskforce. We have the intelligence, and we can leverage that. Pull off the team."

While he didn't want to hear it, a part of Kurt actually agreed with the assessment. He couldn't flex Pike to Nice without a plausible reason for his company, because if things went south, it would mean exposure. Pike would have no ability to explain why he was there if he were captured or compromised— but Kurt had already sent him to the city under Alpha authority, using the Syrian's intelligence. Pike had found where the terrorists were staying.

Kurt said, "Sir, I agree, it's a risk, but we know where the terrorists are holed up. We have the bed-down. We pass this off, and we'll lose them. There is no time for international cooperation."

"Tell the French right now. Let them hit the place. Let them deal with the fallout if it goes to shit."

Kurt couldn't believe what he was hearing. "Did you just say that? Seriously? As long as it's not us with egg on our face it's okay?"

Palmer shot back, "You execute what **we** say. We decide policy. Stay in your lane."

Kurt pursed his lips, waiting for the rest of the Council members to speak their mind, knowing Alexander Palmer's words would hold weight.

Amanda Croft locked eyes with Palmer and said, "I understand the risks to the Taskforce. But I also understand the risks to life. I say yes. Let them go."

Palmer's face squinted like a child pooping a diaper, and he blurted out, "Woman, you have no idea about these actions. Why don't you hold your voice until others have spoken?"

Everyone in the room heard the words, and all were similarly dumbstruck. Kurt glanced at George Wolffe, and he winked, mouthing, **Dumbass.**

Palmer looked at the president, saying, "Sir, what I meant was—"

President Hannister cut him off, saying, "I'd like to remind everyone here that if you sit on this Council, your voice is respected. Does anyone else have anything to contribute?"

Nobody said a word. He nodded, saying, "Let's put it to a vote then."

And Omega was granted.

The hands dropped and President Hannister said, "Okay, it's settled. Kurt, I want a status in twenty-four hours." He glanced around the table and said, "Principals meeting tomorrow at noon."

Kurt nodded, saying, "Yes, sir," then saw the president look at Palmer and say, "I think we need a word."

The members stood, and Kurt dropped his eyes, breaking down his computer. He unplugged the cables, packed up the laptop, and then felt a presence. He looked up and found Amanda Croft standing next to him. He said, "Ma'am?"

"Tell Knuckles he owes me for that one."

He said, "I'm not sure what you mean."

She said, "Yes you do. I know what Palmer thinks about me and my experience in this arena. He believes I'm a neophyte, and because of it, I knew my vote would be discounted. He's a pig. I led him to the trough, and he started to eat."

Flabbergasted, Kurt said, "That was on purpose?"

She said, "Of course it was." She picked up a cable and handed it to him, saying, "It's all politics, and I learned how to play that early on."

Kurt said nothing, putting the cable in the case next to his computer.

He zipped the container, and she said, "It's all politics until it isn't. I believe in you. Don't let me see you fall into the trap of what I just did. Don't become what we are."

And he understood.

50

★★★

Colonel Park In-young rubbed his face and said, "This is a disaster."

Pacing the room, Colonel Lee Dae-jung said, "That's an understatement."

"Should we inform the general?"

"Do you wish to die? No. Let's work to contain the problem ourselves. What do we know?"

"It's an American team. They were meeting Yasir at a restaurant. We thought it was just the single man, but it was an entire team. We failed to kill Yasir, and now they have him in their control."

"CIA? Is that what this is?"

"I don't think so. It doesn't have that signature. They were using a child as a spotter. That's not something the CIA would do."

"A child?"

"Yes. The ghost team spotted her talking on a radio after our target exited the bridge."

"We're sure?"

"Yes. Positive."

Colonel Lee nodded, thinking. He said, "You're right. That's not CIA. So what is it?"

"It's definitely American, but I think it's some contract team. The US has been outsourcing to corporations for years. They work for the United States, but they also work for profit."

"Like Russia's Wagner group in Syria?"

"Yes, exactly. And that may be a way in for us."

"How?"

"The men are paid by the United States, but their goal isn't patriotism. They aren't like us. They won't continue based on an ethos. They are motivated by greed. They have no core, and that is a fatal flaw."

Colonel Lee tapped a pen on the table and said, "You want to interdict them?"

"Yes. Look, they're cracking Yasir like an egg right now. We know they've gone to Nice, and we know why. He's talking. We need to interdict them before they can stop the terrorists from leaving on their mission."

"But if we do that, we compromise our own team. They are under official diplomatic cover in Switzerland. They can't travel to Nice."

"So we use Song Hae-gook. He's got cover as a rich South Korean. And he's already in France."

"His people aren't trained for this. He's just a delivery boy with a couple of bodyguards. He's already proven that he can't execute."

"I'm not talking about a shoot-out. We need to hit them where it hurts. They are attempting to prevent a terrorist attack, but what they really care about is money and their own worthless skins. We need to threaten that."

"How?"

Colonel Park said, "If it was up to me, I'd take the child. She's not working for a salary. She's doing it for some other reason. I think she's tied to one of the team members. Possibly the woman, but maybe someone else. We take the child, and then let them know that we have her. They'll back off."

"But if we do that, we show our hand. We might bring on an attack from the United States. That's insane."

Colonel Park sat down across from him and said, "No. If that were going to happen, it would have occurred after we killed the man in the restaurant. Hear me out. We take the girl, and then tell them what we have. We make them choose between an American operation, or her life."

Colonel Lee nodded, then said, "So you're not talking about just short-circuiting the team, getting them to leave. You're saying we have the ability to manipulate them into working **against** the CIA, even as we tell them what to do?"

"Yes. I believe if we get the girl, we can hold her until our attack is done, keeping that team at bay. We need to split them from their paymasters in the CIA. Force them to make a choice. They won't choose the CIA, I guarantee it."

"So let the CIA think they're trying to prevent our attack while we prevent them from interfering?"

"Precisely."

"But once again, the target is in Nice. We can't use the ghost team. We can't compromise them. They're preparing for the real attack."

"That's why I say we use Song. He's got men trained in security, and how hard can this be? They just grab her. She's a child."

"She might be a child, but she's working with a team that has already shown skill. Don't forget, they snatched Yasir from under our noses."

"I agree, but that's precisely why this will work. They think they've succeeded, and they'll have their guard down, focusing on the terrorists. They won't be looking for us. We seize the girl, and we facilitate the attack in Syria, and then our own attack. **We control them.**"

Colonel Lee snipped his ballpoint pen over and over again, a nervous reaction to what they were contemplating. He said, "Okay. Contact Song. Tell him to get it done."

Colonel Park nodded and stood to leave. Colonel Lee said, "Make no mistake, if they screw this up, we're dead."

51

⋆
⋆ ⋆

I said, "So we're a go here? Full-on Omega even though I haven't developed any cover for action?"

Given the Oversight Council's usual skittishness, the permission was surprising. Through the VPN, I saw Kurt lean back. He rubbed his forehead and said, "Yeah, you got it, but I need you to do this by the numbers. I mean, truly give me a ghost hit. Any drama, and it's going to have repercussions back here."

"Sir, you know I can't promise that."

He said nothing for a moment, and I said, "Hey, am I good here? You want a hit? You sure? Is the Council sure?"

Kurt said, "Yes. I want a hit, but that ass clown Alexander Palmer would love nothing more than for this to go bad. He wants to let other agencies handle it."

"You gave him the timeline, right? You told him what we're dealing with?"

"Yeah, I told him. He's more worried about

Taskforce exposure than he is about the attack occurring."

"You're kidding. What did President Hannister say?"

Kurt said, "I'm not going to go through the sausage making, but you have Omega. Just get it done. Clean."

"Then what's up with all the talk about the Council? If this goes bad, they're looking at the Taskforce? Is that what I'm hearing? They'd rather have dead civilians than a hit that causes them to explain something?"

Kurt sighed and said, "Yes. That's what you're hearing. But it never stopped you before."

I grinned into the camera and said, "And that's why you get paid the big bucks. I don't envy you at all. Okay. I'll get it done—but you need to protect us. Like you always do. Tell me you've been working on that."

Kurt looked off the screen, then came back, sporting a small grin of his own. He said, "Tell Knuckles he's the one working it."

I said, "Seriously? Because of the SECSTATE?"

And Kurt disconnected.

Behind me, Knuckles said, "So what's the word?"

I rubbed my eyes and said, "We have Omega, but it's not strong. The Council is split, and if we fail, we're in a world of shit."

"If they don't want us to do it, then just say so. I

mean, it's not like I'm begging to thump someone just because I can. Do they know the threat?"

"Yes. One person on the Council does."

"Who?"

I said, "The SECSTATE. Because of your sword of truth, we have Omega."

I saw his face turn red, and Veep said, "What does that mean?"

I said, "You don't read Terry Brooks?"

Jennifer cut off the conversation, slapping me in the stomach for putting Knuckles on the spot. But he deserved it.

She said, "What's the next move?"

I said, "Recce. Do we have the floor plan yet?"

Veep said, "Yeah, I got it. Well, Creed found a floor plan, but it's really old. If they altered the inside, it might not be correct."

I said, "Pull it up. No matter what they did, it'll get us close."

Veep manipulated the computer and I said, "Everyone, listen up. This has got to be clean. It's the easiest hit we've ever done, but we cannot have a glitch."

I heard a knock on our door, and Brett said, "Speaking of glitches."

Jennifer scowled at him, and opened the door. Amena entered, carrying an ice cream cone. She saw the crowd in the room and said, "You guys about to do something?"

I said, "No. But we need you to—"

She cut me off and said, "Yeah, yeah. Go to the bathroom and turn on the faucets. I get it."

She left. I heard the water start to run, then said, "Veep, show me what you have."

He rotated the computer and I analyzed the floor plan. It was pretty simple. A single-bedroom flat with a staircase. It had a balcony at the back that overlooked a narrow alley, but all in all, it was pretty clean.

I said, "Okay, front door is me, Veep, and Knuckles. Brett, you have squirter control out the back. Koko, you're with him. We've got a single breach, so we have to hit it hard. We get in, and we dominate with violence of action."

Knuckles said, "Put eyes on tonight?"

I said, "Yeah, unfortunately. You guys want to flip for it?"

Knuckles laughed and said, "You mean instead of babysitting here? No. We got it."

I grinned and said, "You sure? 'Cause I'd really like to spend the night on the street watching a door instead of fighting with Amena."

He said, "Tough luck. You want any video? You need real-time?"

"No. Radio is fine. Just keep an eye on both breaches. Front door and back balcony."

"You don't want to hit tonight?"

"No. Kurt wants a clean kill. I mean pristine, so there's no bum-rushing this. Give me a sense of the battlespace. They're not taking the boat for thirty-six hours, so I'm looking at the next cycle of darkness. Get a pattern of life, and we'll plan from there."

Veep said, "So I'm going to spend the night in an alley? I can babysit."

I said, "No, you can't. That's my job. I'm getting really good at it just by spending time with you."

Brett said, "Trust me, kid, you don't want any part of what's about to happen." And he was right, because it was time to talk to Amena.

They left, and the room became quiet, the only sound the muted rushing of water in the bathroom. I said, "It's time. We can't keep putting this off."

Jennifer said, "Pike, we're not just abandoning her."

I sighed and said, "I understand how you feel, but we have an operation tomorrow. This is bigger than her, and it's going to happen sooner or later. We can't keep stringing her along."

I heard the water stop, then the door opened. Amena poked her head out and said, "You guys are doing an operation tomorrow?"

I looked at Jennifer, and she raised her eyebrow. The whole "running the faucet" thing was to generate white noise to keep her from hearing us talk. I said, "Why would you say that?"

"Because those other people were here."

She was looking right at me, and I realized the water hadn't worked. She'd heard what I'd just said to Jennifer. We sat in silence for a moment, and then she said, "Maybe I'll just take my stuff and go."

Jennifer said, "No, you won't. You can stay here."

She said, "You mean tonight? I get one more night in a bed? Is that what you mean?"

She stared at me, and it was crushing.

I said, "Come on, you knew this wasn't going to last forever. We can't take you to America. I told you that."

She sat on the edge of the bed and said, "You might not take me there, but I'm going." She played with the fringe on the duvet, then said, "I know you don't love me, but what does it take? How much do I have to give? Is my family not enough?"

Before I could answer, Jennifer said, "Hey, that's not fair. We'll figure it out. We're not going to drop you on the street. I promise."

Amena said, "You're going to get the men that are trying to do something bad, aren't you? More Syrians. Evil men, like the ones who killed my family." Her eyes were stone-cold, like an operator about to breach a door.

Jennifer said, "Honey, we're just sleeping tonight. That's all that's happening."

She said, "If I find them, will you take me?"

I said, "Take you where?"

"Take me to America."

I said, "You're a damn broken record."

She said, "That's not what I asked. These guys you're chasing, they're Syrian, yes?" When I didn't respond, she continued, "I can find them, like I did the last man."

I said, "We don't need your help. Your job is done. Don't make this hard."

"Hard on me, or on you? You can use me, like you did last time."

I should have paid more attention to her words, but I didn't. All I wanted to do was get her to bed. I mollified her, saying, "Sure. You capture a couple of terrorists, I'll think about taking you to America."

She scowled at my misplaced humor, pulled back the sheets to her bed, and said, "One last night in a bed. Yay me."

52

★★★

Bashir washed their breakfast dishes and said, "You're going to fly that thing in here?"

Sayid said, "Well, I can't test it outside."

He pressed a lever on the controller, and the drone magically rose in the air, hovering about two feet off the hardwood floor, one of the canisters strapped to the bottom of the chassis. Bashir found it much louder than he had imagined. He turned from the sink and said, "Okay, okay. Put it down."

Sayid did, saying, "It holds the weight, but we can only do one."

Bashir said, "One at a time. We can run it, fly it back to us, reload the second canister, and send it out again."

"Won't the entire drone be contaminated?"

Embarrassed, Bashir said, "Good point. We'll take the other canister with us to Turkey." He looked at his watch and said, "It's time to meet the boat. It was supposed to dock today."

"You still want me to take the drone?"

"Yes, and your clothes. I have to bring all the food and the second canister. Go find the captain and tell him we want to spend the night on the boat. I'll meet you there this afternoon with enough supplies for the trip, and tomorrow morning, we make history."

"What if he says no? We don't know this man at all."

"Text me. If he has an issue with it, just come back here, but I really would rather stay on the boat tonight. I don't want to spend another night in this apartment."

"What are we going to do with the captain if he freaks when we say we want to go to Turkey? What if he tries to stop us from using the drone?"

"We kill him. Take a knife from the kitchen. I'll do the same. But he's working with Yasir. He should be part of the brotherhood."

Sayid folded up the drone and gingerly placed it into a travel case with a strap. He went into the small kitchen and returned with a backpack and a steak knife. He said, "Are we still doing the code?"

"Yes. If you have any trouble, text the word 'Run.' I'll assume you're captured and will do my best to accomplish the mission with the second canister."

Sayid shook his hand and said, "See you tonight."

Bashir said, "**Inshallah**, I will be there."

I made another lap around the harbor, slowing down when we reached a row of boats that looked like they could cross the Med, away from the smaller sailboats and single-engine sport craft. Jennifer snapped a picture and said, "There it is. Looks like a fishing trawler."

I glanced to what she was looking at and saw a boat about forty-five feet long, resembling the **Orca** from the movie **Jaws**. I said, "You sure?"

"Unless there are two boats named **Bonne Chance**, that's it."

We knew from Yasir that the boat was due to dock today, but all we'd had to go on was the name—but that had turned out to be good enough. I pulled off of the ring road around the harbor and said, "Let's go check on the boys. I'm sure they're ready for a break."

Our radio came to life, "Pike, Pike, this is Knuckles. We have Unsub One on the move. Need a call. You want to take him, or the house?"

I said, "What's his footprint?"

"He's carrying a satchel and has on a backpack. He's wearing a Berber coat like he's a goat herder."

"Any sign from the other one?"

"Nope. Target is on foot, so we have some time, but if you want to commit to him, I need to break off of the house."

I thought about it, then said, "Let him go. Keep eyes on the house. He'll be back. When he is, we take them down."

Brett cut in, saying, "This is Blood. I have a thought."

I parked the car at a ridiculously expensive garage, exited, and said, "Yeah?"

"I know you want to hit tonight, in the cover of darkness, but maybe we should look at a daylight hit. Take the house, and wait for him to come back."

We walked out of the garage, jogged across the boulevard, and entered the old town. I said, "I'll be there in five minutes. Stand by."

I reached the first OP, Knuckles in a compact car that looked about as big as a Snickers bar, jammed into an alley adorned with windows hanging out laundry to dry. I tapped on the door and he exited, saying, "He's got a point. We want to dominate, and three on one is better than three on two."

I said, "Maybe. Is he in back?"

"Yeah. Watching the balcony."

I keyed my mic and said, "Blood, this is Pike, what's the status back there?"

"It's clean. Absolutely no movement."

I said, "Stand by. Koko's on the way. We might be taking your advice."

"Roger all."

I looked at Jennifer and said, "Get to the rear. If we go, we go soon, before people start moving for lunch. Blood's got control. Follow his lead."

She nodded, withdrew a tricked-out ZEV Tech Glock 23 from her purse, press-checked it for a round, then began walking up the alley.

Knuckles said, "How do you do that? Nobody I date ever listens to a word I say."

I press-checked my own pistol and said, "Get used to it. I'm pretty sure the SECSTATE isn't going to go running into a gunfight."

He chuckled, working his own kit, and said, "Well, she has other strengths worth sticking around for. We going in? Right now?"

"I'm thinking about it. Where's Veep?"

"Coming back soon. It's shift change. He'll be here in two minutes."

"What do we know? Can we do it?"

"Yeah, it's the easiest hit we've ever done. I'd rather wait until nightfall, but Blood's got a point. Three on one is better than three on two. We get to the door, enter, and crush. It's not like we're clearing a multistory. And then we just wait for the other guy to show up."

Veep walked up with a couple of coffee cups, saw us talking, and said, "What's the word?"

I said, "Get your kit situated, we might be going in. But I don't want to hit a dry hole."

53

★★

Amena sat in the hotel room, playing with the television remote, anxious. Wanting to stop the inexorable slide of time. Tonight was her last night, unless she could do something to alter her current path. She watched one more cartoon, then threw down the remote.

Pike and Jennifer had left, going to check out the harbor. They didn't think she'd heard their conversation, but she had. They were trying to find the bad men, and she wanted to help. Wanted to find a way to make herself invaluable to Pike. He would take her to the United States if she helped.

She picked up the cell phone Pike had given her, and left the room.

She exited onto the street, facing the Mediterranean, the promenade full of people enjoying the sunshine. She went left, walking toward the old town and the harbor, staring at every person in the crowd, trying to see a Syrian.

She entered the alleys of the ancient city, wound

through the cafés, passing a large flower market, the area packed with shoppers. She kept her eye out, looking for anyone who could be from her homeland. She saw none. The only thing strange was two Asians in business suits, staring at her from across the plaza.

She reached the end of the alley, a steep hill to her front, forcing her onto the coast road. She took it and kept walking, winding around the hilltop and seeing the harbor ahead. Everyone walking from the old town was forced on the same road, and she felt the crowds grow on the narrow spit of land. She glanced behind her and saw the two Asians again, walking side by side, three people behind her. It raised her interest.

She thought about climbing the hill, just to see if the men followed her, and saw a man in a Moroccan coat in front of her. Carrying a satchel and wearing a backpack.

He was an Arab. Of that she was sure.

She forgot about the Asians, scurrying to catch up to him, darting between the crowds, slowing down right behind his back. She followed his every move, seeing him glance left and right as if he were looking for someone tracking him. She stayed back far enough to not be noticed, but wasn't really worried. She'd picked enough pockets to know that nobody feared a thirteen-year-old girl.

He reached the edge of the harbor and slowed down, surveying the boats. She did the same, matching his pace. He walked around the port, checking every boat for something. Halfway around, before he reached the small sailboats and day runners, he paused. He pulled out a piece of paper, glanced at it, then looked at a fishing trawler. She scurried past him.

He walked down the road to the gangplank, and shouted something. A man exited the boat, and they talked. After a minute, they both went down the gangplank, disappearing into the boat. She waited a moment, then scurried behind them, wanting to hear what they said.

Bashir wandered around the small apartment, packing up his things and mentally making a list of supplies for the trip. He realized it wasn't that complicated, as they basically needed water and protein for the journey. Maybe some fruit.

He wandered out to the balcony, lit a cigarette, and gazed up the street. He saw a blond-haired woman standing next to a car, casually talking into a phone. She glanced his way, their eyes met, and she turned away, as if the sight of him were poison.

He was used to such reactions in Europe when he'd dressed like he was at home, but nobody had done that since he'd started wearing jeans and had shaved his beard.

He looked at her for another moment, saw her kiss a black man in a car, and relaxed. He flicked his cigarette into the street and went back inside. He paced a bit, then decided to check on Sayid. He pulled out his cell phone, thinking about what he would say in case it was monitored. He dialed Sayid's number, hearing it ring.

54

★★
★

My radio came alive, "Pike, this is Koko. I've got eyes on Unsub Two. He's on the balcony smoking a cigarette."

Which answered my biggest pressing question—whether or not there was a target in the apartment. I said, "Let us know when he goes back inside." Off the net, I said, "Okay, let's take him down." I turned to Veep in the rear seat, and said, "You have the lock figured out?"

"Yeah. Our bump key will work."

"It better, because we can't leave any evidence that we've entered. No kinetic breaching here."

"It'll work."

Koko came back on. "He's inside. I say again, he's inside."

Off the net, I said, "Knuckles, you got point. Veep, flow in after me." I keyed the radio and said, "All elements, stand by for assault. Koko, when you hear breach, move to the front for early warning. Any reaction, let us know. Blood, you keep the rear locked down. I think we'll dominate him quickly, but if he bolts, he's coming out that balcony."

I heard, "Wilco," and opened the car door. All three of us exited like something out of a mob movie, glancing left and right up the narrow alley. We were clear. We speed-walked up to the short staircase, and I could see the cathedral square at the end of the alley, people milling about, enjoying the sunshine.

I said, "Veep, make it quick as you can," then on the net said, "All elements, stand by for breach."

Veep jogged up the steps holding what looked like a baseball with a skeleton key sticking out of it. Right behind him was Knuckles, his pistol out, focusing on the door while Veep was at risk working the lock. I stood behind Knuckles, my eyes on the street, protecting our back. I heard the rattle of the electronic bump key, then Veep whispered, "Breach, breach, breach."

He swung the door open, leaning back, and Knuckles charged in, me right behind him. Knuckles cleared the funnel of death and went left, and I went right. He entered a bathroom, shouting, "Small room, small room," and bounced back out, now with Veep behind him. We raced together to the bedroom and the balcony the Syrian had been seen on earlier. I entered first, and saw the terrorist standing in shock, a smartphone to his ear.

He shouted something into the phone, and I took his legs out from underneath him, slamming him face-first into the floor and kicking the phone out of his hand. Knuckles continued to clear, and Veep searched him for weapons, finding none.

Six seconds later, Knuckles came back in, saying, "It's clear."

I said, "Get the front door. Close it down."

I got on the radio, saying, "Jackpot, I say again, jackpot. Blood, rotate around to the front, taking east security. Koko, you have west. Remain in place for Unsub One."

I received acknowledgment from both Jennifer and Brett, and Veep handed me the phone, keeping a knee on the terrorist's back. The line was still open, the seconds ticking by on the screen. I put it to my ear and heard a man speaking Arabic. I had no idea what he was saying, but he grew more fervent, then the connection was cut.

I knelt down to the man on the floor and said, "Who were you talking to?"

His eyes wild, he said, "No English, no English."

I bounced his head against the floor and said, "Don't lie to me. No way could you travel from Syria to Switzerland and then here without speaking English."

I saw his eyes flicker at my statement and I said, "That's right. We know all about you and the Red Mercury. We know about the boat, we know about the Special Forces base. We know everything."

Knuckles came into the room carrying a weird thermos-looking container. I said, "Hey, you guys have coffee made for the trip? Knuckles, open that thing up."

Knuckles reached for the lid and the terrorist freaked out, writhing on the floor and screaming, "Don't touch it, don't touch it!"

Veep restrained him and I smiled. I set the phone on the bed and said, "So much for '**No hablo Inglés.**' What time is your friend coming back? Where is he?"

He furtively glanced at the phone on the bed, and my own phone began buzzing in my pocket, startling me. I said, "Watch that fuck," and went to the foyer, pulling it out.

Amena saw the men in the back of the fishing boat, near the rear, and scampered on board, moving to the bow. She crouched down and slowly crawled to the captain's bridge, peering at them through the windshield. She could catch snatches of their conversation, and was excited to hear they were speaking Arabic.

The man she'd followed in the Moroccan jacket wanted to talk to the captain of the vessel, but the man on the boat was calling himself the first mate. Moroccan Jacket stated he was going to spend the night on the boat, but the first mate said he couldn't let him do that without speaking to the captain first. They argued, and then Moroccan Jacket dropped his backpack and satchel, reaching into his pocket for his phone.

He spoke into it, waving his hands at the first mate, and then his face went white. He held the phone, saying nothing, then shouted into it. He hung up, and she thought he was going to run away. He picked up his backpack, grabbed the satchel, and started to walk to the gangplank. She crouched down and scurried to the port side, hiding on the far gunwale. She peeked, and saw him looking torn. He glanced back at the first mate, then ran back, dropping his satchel and screaming at him. The first mate raised his hands, and Moroccan Jacket pulled out a knife, laying it against the first mate's throat, repeating his request.

The first mate's eyes popped open, and he vigorously nodded. The man with the knife pointed to the ropes mooring the boat at the bow. He then began untying the stern, and she realized the first mate was going to see her when he reached the front of the boat. She slithered across the deck, opened a hatch, and dropped into a tiny berth with two small beds lining the wall. She cowered on top of one, pulling the sheets over her, wondering what she was going to do. And then the boat began to move.

Frozen in fear, Amena felt the slide through the water, picking up speed. She glanced out a porthole, and saw the harbor racing by. They were headed out to sea.

She crawled off the bed, then went toward the

stern, finding herself in a galley. She looked about for a weapon, opening drawers and cabinets, the sound of the engine cloaking her movements. She found a small paring knife, but didn't think it would help. Another cabinet yielded an iron skillet. She pulled it out, hefting it, then felt the boat slow. She moved farther to the stern, seeing a set of stairs to the back deck, then a shadow.

She crouched down, clutching her pan, and saw the first mate arguing again with the terrorist. The man ignored him, opening his satchel and withdrawing what looked like a robot helicopter. He extended the arms and set it on the deck, and she recognized it as a drone, the same type she'd seen on YouTube, but this one had some large tube on the bottom.

The first mate lost his temper, waving his arms and shouting. He made the mistake of advancing toward the drone. The terrorist pushed him, and the first mate pushed back. The terrorist jumped forward with his knife, stabbing the first mate in the chest, his arm working like a piston, the blade going in over and over. The first mate screamed, and fell to the deck, trying to stop the attack. The terrorist leapt on top of him, and continued to stab until the body quit moving.

Amena felt sick, seeing her father's blood rushing from his neck. She looked at her iron pan, and knew it would be no help whatsoever. She retreated back to the bedroom at the bow of the boat, collapsing.

They were all the same. Everyone was a killer, and they would extract their vengeance on her. And then she remembered Pike's phone. An anchor to a predator that hated these men as much as she did. She pulled it out, saw a signal, and exhaled in relief. She dialed his number, and heard him answer, "Amena, I'm a little preoccupied right now. I'll have to call you back."

She hissed, "Pike, I'm on a boat in the middle of the sea. I'm with a terrorist."

"What?"

She described what she'd done, then said, "He killed the guy that drives the boat."

"He doesn't know you're there?"

"Not yet."

"How long have you been going?"

"I don't know. Ten minutes maybe, but we're stopped now. The terrorist has one of those drone things. He's about to launch it from the back of the boat."

"Right now?"

She heard the drone's blades turn and whispered, "Yes. It's taking off right now."

"Does it have anything on it? Is it carrying any-thing?"

"It just has a tube on the bottom. Like a camera lens or something."

"How large? Like the size of a thermos?"

"Yes. It looked like a coffee thermos."

He started shouting something away from the

phone, and she heard, "harbor," then he returned, saying, "Amena, listen to me closely. We're on the way. I need you to turn on an app in the phone. Look at the screen and pull up the music app."

Confused, she said, "What?" She heard a car door close, then Pike said, "Just do it."

She did, getting a list of songs. He said, "Scroll until you find 'I Still Haven't Found What I'm Looking For' by U2."

She started scrolling and said, "Why am I doing this?"

"It's a hidden beacon for that phone. So I can find you. Play it."

She did, then put the phone back to her ear, saying, "It didn't do anything."

She heard him say, "Veep, she's up."

He returned to the phone and said, "We have you. Keep hidden. We're on the way."

"He's going to find me. This boat isn't that big."

"He's flying the drone. It's got probably twenty-five to thirty minutes of flight time, so he'll have his hands full, both literally and figuratively."

She said, "What's he taking pictures of? Is he planning an attack?"

"Amena, he's not taking pictures. That's not a camera. Listen, I'm going to have to ask you to do something. I don't know if we're going to make it to you in time. That thing you saw under the drone is a canister of poison, and he's flying that drone to use it."

She paused for a moment, then said, "What are you asking me?"

She heard the car door slam again, and she said, "You want me to stop him? Is that what you're saying?"

He said, "Never mind. Forget I said that. We're at the harbor. I have to steal a boat. Just stay hidden."

"If I stay hidden, will he kill people?"

"Amena, I have to get moving. Just stay hidden."

And he disconnected.

She put the phone back in her pocket, thinking. She went to the window and saw the shore of Nice about a kilometer away. She realized that's where he was flying the drone. He was going to poison the people on the promenade.

Where the others had died.

55

★
★ ★

I ignored the NO WAKE signs and punched the throttle, spewing a rooster tail of water as our speedboat pierced the harbor, heading out to the Mediterranean. It had cost us two hundred US dollars to buy off the guy doing maintenance on the boat, but he'd eventually agreed to let us use it, saying we had to have it back by nightfall. After a short bidding process, he walked away with some money. He should have considered himself lucky, because if he had pressed me one more second he would have walked away with a concussion and nothing else. As the only watercraft on the harbor that was fast and had a man near it with the key, I was taking that boat one way or the other.

Catching himself as I slammed the throttle, Knuckles shouted, "Whoa! Easy there. We're still in the harbor, and you're going to get a patrol on us."

I said, "Fuck the patrol. They won't catch us. Veep, give me a vector."

He said, "Clear the harbor and head right, forty-five degrees."

I did as he directed, the boat now skipping over the light waves, bouncing us up and down. Knuckles pulled himself up and said, "We're going to make it. She'll be okay."

I said, "This isn't about her. You heard the call. He's airborne with the device, and I don't think we're going to make it. I don't think we'll stop him."

He held on to the railing as we bounced and said, "I know. You should have told her to attack."

His words were like a hammer. I said, "I couldn't. Come on, Knuckles, would **you** have?"

I knew his heart, and there was no way he would have ordered such a thing, but I was the team leader, responsible now for more deaths than just one. I should have ordered her to do it. Sacrificed the pawn to save the king.

He said, "No. I wouldn't." He looked at me and said, "I'm sorry I said that. You made the right call."

Veep said, "Left five degrees. Contact in four minutes."

I corrected, and Knuckles asked, "What's the plan?"

"I'm going to drive right up to the boat, and you're going to nail him. Pretty simple. He's got to be out in the open flying that drone. No matter what happens, no matter where that drone is, drop that fucker."

He withdrew his Glock from the holster and said,

"Get me close. I'll get one shot. He starts running for cover, and we'll have to board the boat."

I saw a single fishing trawler about a hundred meters away and turned toward it.

"Don't fucking miss."

Amena gripped her iron skillet and crept back to the galley. She went to the stairs and saw the terrorist at the back of the boat, next to the dead body of the first mate, his focus on a tablet attached to a remote control for flying the drone. She thought about what she could do. Smash him in the head? No. If she wasn't strong enough to knock him out, he'd kill her, and then kill everyone else.

Smash the controller. He couldn't fly the drone without it. He might still kill her, but he wouldn't kill anyone else.

She hefted the skillet, holding the handle with both hands, and crept as quietly as she could up the stairs. She reached the top, and he turned, startled. She screamed like a banshee and charged forward, swinging the heavy iron skillet at his hands. It connected, and the remote control bounced onto the deck. He shouted in pain, then tried to grab her. She ducked under his arms, ran to the controller, and hammered it again with the skillet, hearing the plastic crack. He charged her, and she threw the pan at him, then jumped headlong over the side.

She splashed into the water and began swimming. She rolled onto her back and saw the terrorist run to the rail, screaming curses. He stood for a moment, staring in fury, then ignored her, rushing to the shattered controller. He began tapping the screen and manipulating the toggles, and she prayed she'd ruined it. Swimming away from the boat on her back, she saw a dot in the sky, streaking toward them, flying fantastically fast. He frantically stabbed at the controller, but it did no good, the drone returning unerringly to its launch point.

As it got closer, she saw the canister was dangling below it, not like it had been when the drone had left. The aircraft reached a level above the boat, and then began to descend. The terrorist screamed in fear and dove over the side himself.

The drone crashed into the deck of the boat, and the terrorist treaded water, looking at it. He turned to her and shouted, "You little bitch. You've killed us. We can't get back on the boat."

She said, "Better you than innocents."

He began swimming to her, a snarl on his face, and she frantically stroked away from him. She glanced behind her, seeing him gaining. Eventually, she felt a hand on her leg. She kicked desperately, then felt his arms around her neck.

She heard a roar coming from the other side of the boat, and he forced her under the water. She began to thrash, bubbles everywhere, arms and legs fighting for life, hitting and scratching.

We came within fifty feet of the bow of the trawler and I pulled back on the throttle, letting the boat drift in. I cut the wheel, sliding toward the stern, both Knuckles and Veep on the port side, pistols out. But the only sign of human life was the first mate, his body leaking fluids on the deck.

I stared hard, seeing the bridge empty as well. I swung the craft around the stern, both of my men ready to fire, but nobody appeared. Panicked, I realized the attack was done, and he was now going to kill Amena. I'd failed all the way around.

I let go of the wheel and with more urgency than I wanted to release, said, "We need to board. He's belowdecks. He's going to find her."

Knuckles heard the angst in my voice, and it was something new. When it came to the pressures of combat, I was the one always in control. I drew my pistol and said, "Veep, take the wheel. Knuckles, on me."

I prepared to leap the five feet to the deck of the boat, and Veep yelled, "In the water! In the water!"

I looked to the starboard side and saw a thrashing, like a fish caught on a line. I jumped back to the console and gunned the engine, sliding next to the boiling spit of water, and saw the terrorist holding a small form underneath the surface, the body putting up a ferocious fight.

Amena.

Before I could stop the boat or even utter a word, my second-in-command was airborne over the side, slicing into the sea like a shark, and just as deadly.

I spun the wheel, circling around the fight. Knuckles grabbed the man by his hair and pulled his head back. The terrorist released the body beneath him and made the mistake of trying to defeat my best friend. **In** the water. He might as well have tried to walk on the moon without a space suit.

Knuckles speared his throat with a ridged hand, causing the terrorist to spasm, his arms becoming slack, the fight in him gone. Knuckles brought him to the surface of the water as if he were saving him, not unlike I had done with Yasir. The similarities ended there.

Knuckles torqued his neck backward, using his left arm as a fulcrum at the base of the terrorist's head. He dragged his face under the water, bowing the torso on the surface. The terrorist thrashed like a child learning to swim, but Knuckles was relentless. I knew how it would end.

I returned to scanning the water, looking for my little refugee. Hoping against hope that she wasn't sinking to the bottom of the Med.

Forced under the water, Amena grabbed the arms around her neck and raised her legs up, kicking out, trying to break the hold before she ran out of air. She made one feeble attempt, the water blunting her strike, and miraculously, his arms left her. She broke free, stroking away from him under the surface, swimming until she felt her lungs would burst. One stroke, two, then three, she kept going, knowing the minute she showed her head above water, the terrorist would find her, and she wouldn't be as lucky a second time.

Her lungs on fire, she was finally forced to surface. She broke the plane of water, gasping for air, and found herself facing the bow of a sleek speedboat. Leaning over the side, his arm out, was Pike Logan.

She whipped her head to the terrorist behind her, and saw him floating faceup, his eyes open, dead. Swimming away from him and toward her was Knuckles, a grim look on his face.

Knuckles reached her and said, "Raise your arms." She did, and he put his hands on her waist, hoisting her into the air high enough for Pike to grab. He pulled her into the boat, and she sat down, trembling. He wrapped her in a towel and said, "Are you okay?"

She nodded. He asked, "What happened to the drone?"

"It crashed into the boat. I smashed the controller, and it automatically came home."

Knuckles pulled himself over the gunwale and flopped onto the deck, laughing. "How poetic. He had to jump over the side to avoid his own weapon."

Pike squatted down and said, "You smashed the controller? I told you to hide."

She looked into his eyes and said, "I got one. Remember that."

He smiled and brushed a strand of hair out of her face, a gentle gesture. For the first time, she felt his emotion. Felt a small bit of love.

He said, "Yeah, you did, doodlebug."

56

Colonel Lee hung up the phone and said, "They missed. Again. I told you Song's security men weren't up to this."

"Was there any trouble?"

"No. The idiots just watched her walk back into the hotel, just like they watched her walk onto that boat yesterday."

"Better to wait than do something foolish."

"Except Song says he thinks they are leaving tomorrow. Their reservation is ending."

Park sat down, saying, "That's good. Maybe they consider the mission is complete."

Lee slapped his hand on the desk and said, "It **is** complete! They stopped the Syrians. I knew this was a ridiculous plan."

"We don't know that. All we know is they stopped one of the men on the boat. Maybe they've lost the other one."

"Does it matter? The man—if he's not in an

American jail—is running scared, and if he doesn't attack, we can't blame **our** attack on Syria."

Park said, "What else could we do? What other plan could we have executed?"

"I don't know, but we need to inform the general. We can't put this off anymore."

Park felt the blood drain from his face at the prospect. He said, "Wait, the Syrians were out of our hands. We can't be responsible for them. That was all Yasir. If we hadn't used our initiative to follow the Americans to Nice, we wouldn't even have known they were there. It's not our fault."

"We **knew** that Yasir had been captured. We **knew** the general had ordered him killed, and that our attempt to do so failed. We **knew** that, and didn't report it."

"And you think reporting it now will be good?"

Lee shook his head, saying, "No. It will just get us killed, but we need to report **something**."

Park said, "The key is our attack, correct? That's all the general wants. That's what the Supreme Leader wants."

"Yes, so?"

"So we report our failure to kill Yasir, but only because he has disappeared. He slipped from Lucerne before we could give the order to interdict, not because of the Americans. As for the terrorists, we never knew where they were to begin with."

"And why are we telling him three days later?"

"We were trying to find him, but could not. After all, he didn't give us a time frame. He just told us to do it, and now we're reporting back."

Lee nodded, saying, "That might work. The ghost team is supposed to retrieve the second load of Red Mercury soon. They need to get it and return to their official duties at the United Nations before the Conference on Disarmament convenes in a few days."

Park said, "Okay. It's settled. Let's get an appointment with General Kim. Let him decide whether or not to continue now that we've lost track of the Syrians. Maybe he'll call it off."

Lee barked out a laugh and said, "Oh, he'll continue even if it means us carrying the Red Mercury into the conference. We'll just lose the ability to blame the Syrians."

At that, Colonel Park perked up.

Lee said, "What?"

"If the Americans interdicted one of the Syrians, they might have a sample of the Red Mercury. Even if it wasn't used, it's tied to the Syrians, not us."

"They also have Yasir. He knows how they got the poison."

"Maybe, but it still gives us more plausible deniability. Does Song know where the Americans are going tomorrow? Is it home?"

Lee sagged back in his chair and said, "No. He thinks they're going to Switzerland."

Alarmed, Park said, "Why would he believe that?"

Lee said, "I don't know. I didn't ask. Maybe he's just guessing because that's where they came from."

Park said, "If they go to Switzerland, Song will have to execute our plan. Losing the Syrians is one thing, but we can't let them interfere with the ghost team."

57

⋆⋆

I shook my head at Kurt through the computer screen and said, "Sir, I told you this. I'm taking her to Switzerland with me. Do the research there."

I saw his aggravation, but I wasn't giving this one up. No way. He said, "Pike, we've **done** the research. Switzerland has no refugee program. France does. We've already coordinated with them. You just need to drop her off. She'll be fine."

"She's been in a camp in Italy, and she's afraid of the French. I'm not doing it. She wants to go to Switzerland, and that's where I'm taking her. End of discussion."

He rubbed his eyes, the precursor of the Pike Headache, and said, "Pike, you've got to check out that other bunker. You don't have time to be dealing with a child. I can't believe we're even discussing this."

"Sir, she stopped the damn terrorist. All by herself. That drone would have killed hundreds and generated a worldwide panic. I would think that would mean something to the mighty United States."

He drew back, unsure how to answer that immutable truth, and I deflected. "So, what's the story with the terrorist?"

It had been close to forty-eight hours since our hits in Nice, and we'd spent every minute executing exfiltration operations, getting the terrorist and the device out of the country while wiping any trace of our tracks in the old town of Nice.

He exhaled and said, "Nothing much. He's giving us detail into White Flag, and some old ISIS information, but he was just a soldier in the war. He didn't even know Yasir was regime."

"And the Red Mercury? What was that?"

Kurt smiled, perking up a little, saying, "That actually **was** a bit interesting. The canister you found is a variation of Sarin nerve gas, but it goes inert once exposed to the atmosphere. After about an hour, give or take, it's dead."

"Seriously? Sarin's neutralized by sunlight, but it takes days, and any part in the shade is still a killer. They managed to find a way to get it to go inert in an hour, regardless of the atmospheric conditions?"

"Yeah. Apparently so. We're checking it out here, but so far, it dissipates after an hour in the atmosphere."

"Well, I don't feel shitty about the boat, then."

Kurt laughed and said, "That caused some issues.

The Council wanted an EOD team to render the device safe."

"And how did they expect that to happen? Alert a decontamination unit from France? Tell them we thought there was some strange shit called Red Mercury on a boat with a dead terrorist? You guys told me to make it clean."

Kurt heard the anger in my voice and raised his hands, saying, "I'm with you, Pike. Sinking that boat was the best-case solution. But I had to do some explaining on the dead terrorist. It wasn't like you blew the boat out of the water with him in it."

I flicked my eyes to Knuckles, and saw concern about his actions. Not because of what he'd done, but because of how it would be perceived. I knew, if it had been me in the water, the results would have been the same, and I wasn't about to let Kurt believe otherwise. I returned to the screen and said, "He was drowning Amena, after she'd stopped the attack. He chose to fight."

Kurt studied me through the screen, and I didn't flinch from his gaze. He said, "Knuckles was forced to kill him? **In** the water?"

I said, "That fuck chose his path."

Kurt nodded, letting it drop. I heard Knuckles exhale. Kurt said, "Okay, I've got Alpha authority for the follow-on bunker. We don't know the exact location yet, but we do know it's not like the last one. It's in the middle of the woods. The good thing is it doesn't have the security of the one you tackled before. The bad thing is there's no reason for you to be there. No way to rent anything for a prior recce. It's a secret holding bunker for the bank that had the safe-deposit box in Geneva, where Yasir retrieved his cache of Red Mercury. Right now we know the canton it's in, but that's not a lot of help. Once we neck it down, you'll have to hit it cold."

I nodded and said, "Is there a time crunch on this? Can I do my own recce outside, or are you going to give me a grid and tell me to get on it within an hour?"

"Not a true time crunch, but under interrogation Yasir's saying he thinks the North Koreans had a separate operation planned, so once I find it, I can't give you a month. We don't know what they're up to, but they're planning something."

I said, "No issue. We're leaving first thing tomorrow for Geneva. I'll drop off Amena at whatever refugee office you can find, and then stand by for the location."

He said, "Pike, come on. Leave her behind."

I said, "Sir, that's not happening. I gave her my word. Do the work. She's earned it."

Sitting on the counter in the bathroom, the water running, Amena let Jennifer brush her hair. She heard Pike pacing back and forth, fighting whoever was on the other end of the computer. He'd promised her the least he would do would be to get her out of France, but she didn't believe that would happen. Pike didn't care what happened to her. All he cared about was the mission.

Even as she'd sat on the boat, wrapped in a towel, distraught at what she'd been through, he'd coordinated to tow the terrorist boat far out to sea, and then had sunk it, like it was just another day on the job. They'd returned to the hotel, and he'd acted like he cared, making sure she was secure, trying to give her comfort, but she was sure it was an act.

Jennifer said, "You've got some seriously beautiful hair. I would kill for this."

Amena had been forced to spend more time in the bathroom than she wanted, sent there so she wouldn't hear what they were doing, and this time, she'd asked for Jennifer to accompany her. She was the only person Amena trusted.

She turned to Jennifer and said, "This isn't fair. I caught one of the terrorists. You guys caught the other one, but I stopped the one about to kill all the people. I don't understand how he can be so indifferent."

Jennifer put down her brush and said, "It'll be okay. Pike is the most stubborn man I've ever met. If he says he'll take you to Switzerland, then he'll get you to Switzerland. He asked what you wanted, and that's what he's going to deliver."

Amena caught Jennifer's eye in the mirror and slowly nodded. She said, "I don't know if he really wants me to stay with you guys. He wants to get into a fight. That's all. He's a predator like all the others. He doesn't care about me."

Jennifer said, "That's not true. He's not arguing with Kurt just because you asked."

Amena looked at Jennifer and said, "He thinks I'm a baby. On the boat, he called me doodlebug. I'm not a doodlebug. I'm a woman."

Jennifer put her hand to her mouth, her eyes wide. Amena said, "What?"

Jennifer said, "He called you doodlebug? You're sure?"

"Yeah. Right after he put me in the boat. Why?"

"That was the nickname for his daughter. **She** was doodlebug."

Amena said, "His daughter who was murdered? That's what he called her?"

Jennifer brushed something out of her eye and nodded. Amena looked at the floor, then back at her. She said, "Why would he call me doodlebug?"

Jennifer smiled and said, "Don't worry about staying with us. Nothing on earth will prevent that now."

58

★★

Amena licked her ice cream cone and said, "You know, if you took me to America, I could be your maid. I'd work for free."

I took a bite out of my Fudgsicle and said, "I'm afraid that's a little bit illegal in the United States."

She said, "Doesn't seem to me like you really care too much about what's legal."

Jennifer chuckled and said, "Hey, you said you liked the lady we met. And you like Geneva. Didn't you say that?"

We'd arrived in Geneva yesterday morning and spent the day waiting for Kurt to give us the bunker's location. So far, he hadn't—but he had told us what we could do with Amena. Turns out, the Red Cross was created in Geneva, and its headquarters was in the city. They didn't really do any refugee work inside Switzerland, but after some high-level calls from members of the Oversight Council, they'd agreed to help Amena. Which was more than I'd expected from the Council. Kurt had obviously been at work.

Amena had fought the decision, but had finally succumbed to going to meet them when I told her the Red Cross program might be the only ticket to getting to the United States. It would take a while— maybe even a couple of years—but it was the surest route, especially with the contacts we had. She'd get to jump the line.

We'd gone to the Red Cross headquarters and met an older lady of about sixty-five. She had been extremely kind, and Amena had taken a liking to her, but she was still hell-bent on using Jennifer and me to smuggle her into the US. Just about every other sentence was something about it, and now I wasn't sure if she was doing it just to aggravate me.

We'd spent yesterday getting settled into our hotel and coordinating with the Red Cross, so today, Jennifer decided to take Amena to see a little of the city. She'd found a place called Bastions Park, which was full of monuments, including the Reformation Wall, and a library from the University of Geneva. I was bored out of my mind, but little Amena had actually seemed to enjoy Jennifer's tour, which was enough to convince me to continue. Sooner or later, we were parting company, and any happiness I could provide before that time was a bonus. Eventually, we'd stopped at a restaurant called Café des Bastions and had some lunch, complete with ice cream for dessert.

Amena said, "Why make me wait two years here, when I can go straight to America with you two?"

Gently, I said, "We've been over this. It doesn't work that way. We're not at home much, and we certainly don't have the credentials you'll need for sponsorship. That'll come with the Red Cross."

That last bit was a little disingenuous, because I could probably find the credentials if I wanted to, but we didn't have time to sponsor a child for placement in the United States. It wasn't fair to her.

She said, "It doesn't work like that because you don't want it to. Admit it."

I said, "Unfortunately, it **does** work that way. Come on. Let's enjoy the time we have left."

She glanced to the left of the patio we were on, and gratefully let it drop. She pointed at several gigantic chessboards built into the grounds next to the plaza, the pieces the same size as her. She said, "You play chess?"

"I do. Do you?"

She smiled and nodded, and my phone vibrated on the table. I saw trepidation crawl across Amena's face. She knew we were waiting for something, and when it happened, she was going to the Red Cross for good. I picked up the phone and saw the symbol for the Taskforce instead of a number.

I said, "Amena, why don't you check out the chessboards? See if one's available."

She stood, the sadness spilling out from her eyes

and running straight into me. I said, "Go on. I'll be there. I promise."

I watched her mingle with the groups around the chessboards, then answered the phone, glancing at Jennifer. The voice on the phone said, "Go secure," and I did so, telling Jennifer, "This is it."

Kurt Hale came through, sounding tinny with the encryption. He said, "We've found the bunker, and banking transactions show it's wholly rented by the same LLC that rented the safe-deposit box in Geneva. There is no other tenant. It's the one."

I kept my eye on Amena, for the first time not feeling the rush of an impending mission. Feeling a tinge of sadness. I said, "Where is it?"

"Well, that's the hard part. We don't have a grid. We just have a mountain. It's on the slopes of something called the Stanserhorn. It's a national park near the town of Stans in the canton of Nidwalden. From what we can gather from the penetration of the bank website, it's on the forward slope, near a hiking trail. That's not a lot of help, though, because the place is crisscrossed with hiking trails."

I saw Amena ask some guy a question. He pointed to a chalkboard. I said, "Is the Oversight Council still good with me cracking it? Or just put it under observation?"

"They want to know what's inside. You gotta crack it. But they also want it under observation, to track who enters."

I saw Amena put her name on the board, then

saw a man move behind her. I said, "What's my timeline?"

The man put his hand on Amena's shoulder, and an Audi SUV pulled into the taxi stand adjacent to the playing boards. Kurt said, "Soon. I'd like you to get a positive ID by tomorrow morning at the latest, and crack the thing as soon after as possible. I'm afraid of missing the transfer."

The man put a rag over Amena's mouth, then clenched her to him. I said nothing into the phone, astounded at what I was seeing. I heard, "Pike, you there?"

I dropped the phone and started running. I saw Amena go limp and the man pick her up like a piece of luggage. He hustled to the Audi, the rear liftgate rising. Nobody around them seemed to have noticed. I shouted, and the people near the boards looked at me, not at the kidnapping. I pointed, running flat out, straight through the chess sets, knocking pieces to the side and screaming. Someone tried to block me, and I flattened him with a forearm, energizing everyone.

The man holding Amena turned and saw me coming. He tossed Amena into the back and then leapt in after her. The liftgate started to close, the vehicle screeching toward the thoroughfare at the end of the turnout. I gave up trying to reach the SUV where it was and sprinted to beat it to the end.

I reached the intersection with the road a split second before the vehicle, and jumped into the lane, blocking access. The driver floored the SUV and I vaulted into the air, landing on the hood and slamming into the windshield. I rolled upright and grabbed the edge of the door, blocking the driver's view. I smashed the driver's window and desperately jammed my hand inside, snatching the driver by the hair. He swerved hard, bouncing over the curb and throwing me off the hood.

I slammed into the road, leapt upright, but it was too late. The vehicle ran a red light and was gone, racing up the avenue.

I ignored everyone gawking and ran back to my phone, meeting Jennifer halfway as she sprinted to catch me at the road. She said, "What's going on? Where's Amena?"

I said, "Someone just took her."

She said, "What!"

I ran past her, back to the patio and my phone. I picked it up, seeing a connection. I said, "Sir, are you still there?"

I heard, "Yeah, I'm here. What the hell are you doing?"

"Someone just took Amena. Ripped her right off the street."

"What are you saying? She was kidnapped?"

"Yes, sir, that's what I'm saying. I need a lock on phone Prometheus Three. Right now."

"She has a Taskforce phone?"

Aggravated, I said, "Yes, sir, she does. Get me a lock-on." I turned from the handset and said, "Jennifer, get the team mobilized. Get them ready to interdict."

She started working her handset, and I heard, "Pike, I don't know what's going on over there, but we can't do what you're thinking. You have a mission."

I was about to lose my mind at the pressure, something that usually didn't end well. I took a breath and said, "Sir, get me the lock-on."

He heard the tone in my voice, understood that he wasn't going to get fidelity of what was happening, and like the good commander he was, he went to work.

Thirty seconds later, he said, "The phone's off. Last location is a place called Bastions Park."

I said, "Shit. That's where I am."

And then a picture of Amena appeared on my phone. With a ransom demand.

59

★★

Back in my hotel room, surrounded by my teammates, we tried to make sense of what had happened. One minute I was thinking about how to find and penetrate a bunker, and the next minute I was trying to find my little refugee.

Brett, our CIA man, said, "So you didn't get a look at the guy?"

"No, I saw him, but he was wearing a hat and sunglasses. I couldn't make anything else out."

"Did you get a license?"

I felt like a failure. I said, "No. I didn't. I was too preoccupied with stopping them."

He saw the disappointment on my face and said, "Hey, you might have stopped it right there. What about the driver?"

"I got a glimpse, but I have no idea what he looked like. I was too busy fighting to stay on his hood."

Knuckles said, "What the hell is this all about? Who wants a refugee from Syria?"

I said, "I thought maybe it was human trafficking,

but that's pretty bold for them to conduct a daylight seizure. And then I got this ransom demand. I don't know."

The message on the phone had been simple: **Stand by in Geneva for further contact. Be prepared to pay.** But why anyone thought I had money, or how they knew Amena was with me, didn't make sense.

Veep broached the subject that was hanging over the room like the whiff of a decaying animal on the side of a road. "What are we doing about the bunker? We're supposed to be planning that right now."

I clenched my fist, wanting desperately to use it on whoever had taken Amena. I said, "Veep's right. You have the data from the Taskforce. Knuckles, head that up. I want the satellite imagery analysis done by midnight, complete with the location of the bunker and OP locations for overwatch. Get on it."

He said, "You got it, boss. What are you going to do?"

"Talk to the Taskforce. See if I can get a handle on the other problem."

They left the room to go plan, and Jennifer took my hand. I said, "What the hell is going on?"

She saw the pain on my face and said, "Pike, we'll find her."

I said, "I don't think so. I don't think we'll get the chance."

I dialed up the VPN and saw Creed on the other end. I said, "What have you found?"

For once, there were no jokes. He was all business, understanding what this meant to me. He said, "Pike, they're very good. They must have shut down her phone within seconds of taking her. They turned on the phone for fifteen seconds to send you the ransom demand, and then shut it off again. They didn't use a separate phone for us to track. They used your own phone. We have absolutely nothing."

I said, "That's not good enough. Do a data search on Audi SUVs. Crack the cameras in this city. Get me something."

He looked uncomfortable, then said, "Pike, I've been ordered not to."

"What? By who?"

He turned from the screen and said, "Hey, sir. I have Pike on the line."

Kurt appeared and I immediately launched into him. "Did you order off Taskforce assets for Amena?"

He matched my intensity. "Pike, we have a danger of a deadly chemical munition by a state that's a direct threat to the United States. You bet your ass I did. You have a mission."

"Maybe they're the ones who took her! Did you think of that? Maybe if we find her, we'll find the North Koreans who are doing this whole thing. Fuck the bunker, if I kill them there is no threat and we can search that thing at our leisure."

"You said you received a ransom demand."

I leaned back, realizing how crazy I sounded, all of it to generate Taskforce help. I said, "Yes, sir, I did."

"So, the North Koreans—who are very, very good about covert activities—kidnapped a Syrian refugee, and then sent you a ransom demand? Does that sound real to you?"

I took a breath and exhaled. I said, "No, sir."

"Pike, we'll try to find her, but you have a mission."

I said, "Sir, they told me to stay in Geneva for further instructions. Get Johnny's team here. Give them the data. It's not like we're on a thread that he doesn't have. Give him the bunker information and let me deal with this."

"Johnny's team is in Mali. I can't get him to you in time to do anything. I'm sorry, but it is what it is."

I tried one more time, recalling Amena's sadness. The look that said she trusted me. I said, "Sir, I can't do that. I have to stay here."

Kurt leaned forward and said, "Pike, you have a **mission**. The same mission you had before. These guys are going to try to kill a lot of people. You are the only one who can stop it. You need to choose. I know it's awful, but you need to choose. Amena's life, or the lives of hundreds of others."

I pounded my fist on the table hard enough to make the laptop jump.

I said, "Okay, sir. I hear you. I'll get it done, but when it's over, and the smoke has cleared, I'm finding the men who did this. And I'm going to kill them."

60

⭐
⭐⭐

Colonel Lee hung up the phone and smiled. Colonel Park said, "Good news?"

"Yes. They got her. And they did so without compromise. I told you the ghost team was the way to go."

"Good. Very good. But you have to admit, the ransom demand from Song was a stroke of genius. He's not the buffoon you make him out to be."

"I don't know. We made contact with the American using the girl's phone. They might be able to track it."

"They can't track it with it turned off, and we **had** to make contact somehow. How else would we get him to stay in Geneva? We couldn't contact him ourselves and say, 'We're from the DPRK and we'd like you to stop.' He'll think it's something other than what it is, and he'll wait to sort it out."

Colonel Lee nodded and said, "Should we tell General Kim what we're doing?"

"No way. It's working, and the last meeting with him wasn't pleasant."

Colonel Park felt the sweat break out just thinking

about the appointment with General Kim. He had been decidedly displeased with the loss of Yasir, blaming both of them for waiting too long to alert the ghost team for the mission, but ultimately, he'd relented, telling a story when he, too, had failed because of timing.

Up until that point, Colonel Park had thought he was dead. His worry now was that someone on the ghost team would spill their secrets to General Kim upon their return.

He said, "You know when this is done, and we've recalled the team back to the DPRK, they'll have to be eliminated. They know too much."

Colonel Lee said, "I don't think we have to worry about that. The ghost team will probably not survive the mission."

When presented with the knowledge that Yasir had escaped their net, and that the terrorists had done nothing as of yet, General Kim had directed that their original plan go forward, regardless of the Syrian efforts. That meant the team would be forced to leverage their diplomatic status to execute the mission, and in so doing, would be the ones releasing the poison. Colonel Lee had lied to the team, telling them that the Red Mercury properties were the inverse of reality—the nerve agent wouldn't become deadly until an hour after release.

Colonel Park chuckled and said, "That was smart, telling them they were safe. I don't know if they would have executed otherwise."

Lee said, "Song is the one we should worry about. He holds the girl, and knows why we captured her. He knows that we missed Yasir, and has knowledge of the American team."

"He will be easy to deal with. He's not a killer like the ghost team. He thinks he's immune to trouble because of his status."

"His status is what concerns me. We can't eliminate him unilaterally."

"Then we let the state do it. When the mission is over, we expose his failures and transgressions. We blame everything on him, saying he's been lying from the beginning."

"You think that will work?"

"It's worked before. It will work again. Until then, he is a useful idiot. He has the girl, and can contain the Americans for at least a couple of days. Long enough to succeed. Did he give a status on the ghost team?"

"Yes. They go to the mountain today. They should have the Red Mercury by the time we go to bed. Tomorrow, they attack."

"Did he say anything about the Americans?"

"No, but they'll stay in Geneva. Like you said, they want the girl more than they want the mission."

61

★★★

It took close to four hours to get from Geneva to Stans, most of it on highway, but the last stretch had been on some winding mountain roads that would have made a billy goat give pause. We only needed our rental vehicles for this operation, but I'd sent Knuckles ahead with the Rock Star bird, landing in Zurich, the closest airport near our target. Ostensibly, his mission was to establish the infrastructure for our operation before we arrived, but he'd known why I was doing it. I wanted the bird ready, in case I needed to get back to Geneva. If something with Amena came up, an hour to an airport was better than a four-hour drive to execute whatever ransom was demanded. I honestly had no idea how I would be able to affect anything if I received the instructions for her, but I wanted to be prepared anyway.

We'd rolled into the small town of Stans a little before noon, and Knuckles had already established our hotel rooms and TOC, but we were going to execute immediately.

A quaint village of about eight thousand souls, it stood at the base of the Stanserhorn, the mountain that held our target. Knuckles and Veep had pored over the satellite imagery last night and had found one lone shack midway up the slope that they believed was the bunker. On the surface, that would sound insane, but the Swiss had hidden bunkers all over the place, some looking like barns, others looking like chalets with fake windows.

At least that's what the research from the Taskforce had said. We were now going to test it.

Our mission was twofold: One, crack the bunker and see what was inside. Two, keep observation and then tag and track whoever entered. The two missions were a little bit counter to each other, because if we penetrated the bunker and found more WMD than we could evacuate, there was no way I was going to sit on it, waiting for the bad men to come claim it. Kurt had understood that, but told me that the initial mission stood, and we'd reassess if either parameter changed. And so I prepared for both missions.

We linked up with Knuckles at the train station, finding him with two small suitcases that blended in just fine. He said, "I took a look at the route up, and it's rough."

I said, "That's why Jennifer and I are taking the cable car. You guys get the hike."

The Stanserhorn rose six thousand feet from the base of Lake Lucerne, creating one of the best natural viewing towers in Switzerland. At the top was an observation deck, complete with a restaurant. At the bottom were two ways to get there: One, ride a funicular railroad built in the 1800s, then switch to a cable car built in the modern day, or two, run up the side of the mountain on a trail that zigzagged back and forth all the way to the top. Surprisingly, almost as many people took the trail as the cable car, some actually running to the top in an insane race against themselves. Brett had decided that's what he wanted to do, and was dressed in running leggings and a thermal top.

Knuckles said, "So we hump a rucksack to the OP, and you ride a cable car like you're on a date?"

"Yep. That's pretty much the story. Brett seems to think it's a challenge, not a chore."

He laughed and said, "Yeah, well, he's crazy. If I'd kept dating Carly, would I get the cable car?"

I said, "Nope. She'd be carrying a ruck. You got the gear?"

He unzipped the first case and said, "Basic TTL package for you. For us, some optics and netting for the observation post, along with the bunker penetration gear."

He handed me a backpack that looked like a college book bag. Inside were various tagging, tracking, and locating devices that I would use if or when we found the men accessing the bunker. For them, it was three rucksacks full of camouflage netting, food, water, and day/night optics they'd use to keep eyes on the front door.

I said, "Okay, it's two blocks from here to the start of the trail. We'll take the train to the cable car and get eyes on the bunker from the air. You guys establish the OP, and then confirm or deny Creed's information on the vault. If it's solid, we'll crack it tonight."

They nodded, and we left the train station, walking up the street to the start of the mountain. We reached a narrow goat trail, old people with walking sticks and young ones wearing trail running shoes coming and going. I said, "That's you guys. See you at the top."

A guy went flying by us, wearing Lycra pants and a CamelBak, hit the slope, and continued on. Brett said, "Okay, I'm off. I'll get first eyes on the OP."

Knuckles said, "While we hump the rucks up. Seems fair."

I laughed and said, "You can run it if you want. I'm sure Brett will swap out."

Quickly, Veep said, "I'm good. I'll take the slow pace."

Brett grinned and said, "See you two at the bunker," and took off running, chasing the guy who had passed us. Knuckles watched him go and said, "I don't really feel the need to prove myself."

Veep said, "Me either."

I said, "What happened to 'The only easy day was yesterday'?"

Knuckles turned to the trail, hollering over his shoulder, "Says the guy riding the cable car."

We left them and Jennifer said, "I sort of feel guilty when you never give me the hard jobs. I don't think it's fair."

I said, "You think riding this cable car looking for North Korean terrorists would be better with me and Knuckles? Or me and you?"

We reached the funicular train station, a ticket window out front, and she said, "I get it, but it doesn't seem fair."

I purchased our tickets, went through the gate, and took a seat next to a bunch of other tourists. She sat next to me and I said, "Fair's got nothing to do with it. Somebody's got to take the train. And it seems to me the last time you volunteered for an OP, you bitched at me afterward."

"Where?"

"Lesotho. Remember? You wanted to see some dinosaur tracks?"

The train appeared, rolling down the mountain and stopping. Calling it a "train" was a little bit much. Built to resemble the original one, it was more like a tram you'd see at Disney World, with wooden benches and open cabins. She stood up, saying, "Yeah, but it was pouring rain then."

We took a seat on the front bench, where we would both have a view on the way up the mountain. I said, "Oh, so it's only the **dry** weather when you want to do the hard thing?"

Another couple sat next to us, shutting down the conversation. The train began to roll, pulled up the side of the mountain by a cable. The higher we went, the more we could see, idyllic pastures beside us, old houses surrounded by cows wandering about, and Lake Lucerne down below. Paralleling our route was the trail, and on it, I could make out Brett, running like a gazelle, passing other hikers on his route.

We reached the end of the railroad section and unloaded, some moving to the cable car and others taking the trail, having cleared the lower level with the train. We boarded a modern double-decker car, all chrome and steel, and began moving upward. The terrain went from idyllic pasture to rugged mountain, making me wonder if the tourists walking the trail had done it backward. They should have walked to the cable car and taken it, instead of the other way around.

The car hoisted higher into the air, leaving the terminal, and I said, "Upper deck."

We climbed the small circular stairs, and found ourselves with a view showing the mountains in front of us and the lake far, far below.

Jennifer said, "This is incredible."

I thought it was neat, but it wasn't exactly earth-shaking. You could see the same thing in the Rockies. I looked down and saw a group of tourists on the winding trail, two trying to help a third sitting down next to a tree. I pointed and said, "Still rather be down there?"

She punched my shoulder, and we broke above the trees. I looked out to the right, scanning where we thought the bunker would be, and I saw it. Built on a spit of ridgeline, it looked like a one-room farmhouse, with a stone foundation and weathered wood siding sunk into a copse of trees. It was completely alone. No fences or anything else around it. The house had no reason to be up this high. It had to be the one.

The walking trail zigzagged about forty meters from it, not actually going past. I saw two hikers, and then Jennifer tugged my arm, pointing behind us. I saw Brett, still chugging his way uphill. I got on the radio and said, "Blood, you'll see the bunker in about a minute. The ridge looks just like the photos, so I think your OP will work."

He said, "Roger," aggravating the hell out of me that he wasn't out of breath.

The car kept climbing, the view unfolding and actually making me feel a little bad about not doing the hard thing, when Brett came back on the net.

"I've got the bunker in sight, but I just passed two Asians, both carrying backpacks."

I ignored the scenery.

"Say again?"

62

***

Brett said, "I'm still moving up, but I just went by two Asian males. They were in the vicinity of the bunker. Both have on backpacks."

Knuckles said, "We're twenty minutes behind you. We'll assess."

Brett said, "They aren't going down. They're going up. Pike, do you want me to interdict?"

I said, "Knuckles, how soon can you close on them?"

"We can start running right now and be there in ten, but we'll have to drop the rucks."

I said, "Brett, how sure are you that they came from the bunker?"

"Not sure at all. I mean, I just passed them."

My gut was telling me they were the North Koreans, and we'd missed the transfer from the bunker, but I couldn't attack two people just because of their ethnicity. If I was wrong, what was I going to do? Kill them to prevent exposure of the Taskforce?

I said, "They're headed to the top?"

"Yeah. They're going higher."

I said, "Don't interdict. We'll meet them. We have it. Break contact and continue the mission."

Brett said, "Ah, yes. I forgot how smart you are. Jumping ahead of them instead of walking up the mountain like everyone else."

I laughed and said, "Just get the OP set up so Knuckles and Veep can crack the bunker. And maybe pull out the beef jerky, because if they're not the bad guys, it's going to be a long couple of days."

We rode the cable car to the top, Jennifer oohing and aahing about the view, to the point it was beginning to be annoying. I mean, it certainly was good, but I'd seen the same in multiple countries.

We reached the top, and exited the cable car station with everyone else. We walked up the stairs, and broke the plane to the observation deck. The light hit me, and I said, "Holy shit."

For once, the word "breathtaking" mattered, because what spilled out before me truly took my breath away. The panorama beyond the observation deck looked like the hand of God had painted a landscape. The snow-topped mountains were competing with the clouds and the valley down below, all juxtaposed in a still life whose essence could never be captured in a photograph or painting. It was quite possibly one of the finest views I'd ever seen.

I forgot about the mission for a moment and turned to Jennifer. "I had no idea . . ."

I saw her hand to her mouth, as astounded as I was.

We walked onto the deck, taking in the surroundings, and then were brought back to the present.

"Pike, this is Blood. I've got the OP established. Waiting on the stragglers."

Knuckles came on and said, "Sorry you wanted to run. How do you have the OP established when we're carrying everything?"

Brett said, "Touché. But I do have eyes on."

I said, "What about the Asians?"

"Long gone. No idea."

I said, "We have the trigger. Get to work."

Off the net, Jennifer said, "So we need to find the trail?"

"Yep. It's got to end up here somewhere."

Off to the left I saw a jogger appear on a trail running down the ridgeline, but he was well below us. To the right was another gravel path leading right into the deck. I said, "That's got to be it."

We crossed the deck, and saw a sign saying the path led to the actual summit of the mountain. Jennifer said, "That's not it."

She turned around, and said, "Pike, that jogger is here."

Sure enough, he ran by us, continuing up. I said, "Come on."

On the other side of the deck was a flight of modern, stainless steel stairs straight out of an art gallery. At the bottom was a gravel trail.

I said, "That's it."

The trail led right down a ridgeline, the incline to

the right giving a sense of vertigo from the drop-off. Ahead, I saw an incongruous pillbox. A concrete base with a mushroom head of wood. Out here in the middle of nowhere.

I said, "Oh, man. I think we identified the wrong structure."

Jennifer said, "You think that's the bunker?"

"Yeah, I do. Why else would the targets be walking up to it? They didn't want to buy a ticket for the cable car. No record. They're taking the long way up for a reason."

She said, "There's a couple of benches on the slope. Want to sit down?"

The wind was really whipping where we were, the clouds swirling around us, and I'd have rather waited on the observation deck, or even on the leeward side of the mountain, where our observation post was established, but I supposed I'd earned the pain. I said, "Yeah, I guess."

She laughed and sat down next to a defunct firepit, saying, "That wasn't very confident. Maybe we should have taken the OP."

I said, "With this wind, I know we should have."

We waited forty minutes, watching men and women reach the top, all walking with a purpose, and I began to think the North Koreans were doing something different. If they were North Koreans.

I said, "Okay, I've had about enough of this gale. Let's get back to the deck. We can still see the stairs from there."

Tucking herself into my body, because I was now a windbreak, Jennifer said, "But we can't see the bunker."

Which was true. I started to come up with another excuse when two Asian men reached the top. They walked behind us, headed to the mushroom structure, and I recognized one of them. I hugged Jennifer tight and whispered, "That's the waiter from Lucerne."

She stiffened and said, "The one who killed Periwinkle?"

I said, "Yep. It's them."

They passed us, and I waited on them to do something with the mushroom. They did not. They walked right by it, heading up to the deck. I let them get on the stairs and said, "Time to go."

We followed them up to the deck, and they spent no time at all on the view, heading straight to the cable car. I said, "They've been to the bunker."

Jennifer said, "Why?"

"Who walks all the way up the side of this mountain and then doesn't enjoy the scenery? It's almost sacrilegious. They just used that hike as cover to penetrate the bunker."

I let them disappear, then moved rapidly down the stairs, saying, "Come on. We'll get on the same car and tag them."

We got in line behind them, me with my back to them, facing Jennifer. If I knew the waiter, he probably knew me, but he wouldn't remember Jennifer on sight.

The cable car arrived and we boarded, immediately going to the top, away from the Koreans. The cable car broke free and we began descending. I said, "Get me a Cotton Mouth. We're going to tag him."

Jennifer reached into my backpack and rummaged around. Knuckles had given us a TTL kit, but most of the devices required Taskforce assistance to use, meaning we had to have platforms to track them. Only one would allow us to implant and not have planes or drones or surveillance on the cell network to execute. And that was the Cotton Mouth.

A small disk about the size of a quarter, it felt like a cloth bubble with liquid inside. A burst device that projected a signal to satellites, it had an adhesive backing that would let it be affixed to just about anything and had a battery life of nine hours, with a chemical compound that literally ate itself as it expended power. The signal it gave was so weak that a tree canopy would block it, but it would give its burst faithfully for our satellites to pick up. It wasn't optimal, as there were major time gaps in coverage between bursts, and the signal would only triangulate with a clear sky, but it was the best I could use right here. I didn't have a drone overhead, and I didn't have time to penetrate the Swiss cellular system. It would have to do.

She handed it to me and I said, "Nope. This is yours. He's seen me. We stared each other down in the restaurant in Lucerne."

Jennifer said, "He's seen me, too."

I said, "Yep. But only when he poured you water. When the action occurred, he was solely focused on me. Get it done."

She snapped the disk in two, like she was breaking a ChemLight or glow stick, spreading the liquid with her thumbs under the cover. She peeled off the backing and said, "Be back shortly."

She turned to go and I said, "Get the pack. Not the man."

She said, "You think he's carrying the Red Mercury?"

"I do. I want to know where that pack is, not so much where he is. Get the pack."

She nodded and disappeared down the stairs. Seventy-two seconds later, she returned. Not that I was checking my watch. I said, "And?"

"No issues."

I nodded and said, "Good work. We might just save the day again."

She let a wan smile leak out and said, "Only if we find Amena."

It was a gut punch. I closed down, disgusted at myself for forgetting what really mattered. Jennifer grabbed my hands, regretting what she'd said. "It's not your fault."

I remained quiet, wondering about Amena. Wondering if she was still alive.

She said, "Pike—"

And we reached the end of the line. I shook her off, not wanting to discuss my failures, saying, "I'm leaving here and heading up to the bunker. Let the Koreans exit first, then you follow them down on the rail. Keep them under surveillance, but stay loose. Let the beacon do the work."

She said, "Pike, I didn't mean that. You didn't abandon Amena. You didn't have a choice."

I saw the Koreans exit, and walked to the stairs, snarling, "I **did** abandon her. It **was** my choice. Just make sure it was worth it."

She knew better than to say anything else. We exited the car as the last passengers. Most had gone to the railway stop. Some went to the trail. I flicked my head to the train and left her there without another word, my brain seething at my choice of abandoning the girl who had saved more lives than half of the Taskforce.

63

★★

I hit the trail at a jog, getting on the radio. "I'm off at the railway stop and headed up. I've confirmed and tagged the North Korean team. What's the status?"

Knuckles came on, saying, "We've had eyes on for an hour, and no motion. You confirmed?"

I said, "The guys you saw were the ones. I recognized one of them from the Yasir meeting at the restaurant. We don't have time to fuck around. They've been in there. What we need to know now is what they have. We're going to crack that thing in daylight."

I heard, "Roger that. Hope Creed is right on this."

After twenty minutes, I reached the split in the trail to the bunker. I paused, saying, "I'm coming in, where are you?"

Brett said, "This is Blood. I have you. I've got security. Knuckles and Veep are on the door. You're clear to approach."

I left the worn path, taking a goat trail to the hut

and finding Knuckles and Veep dressed like snipers, half ghillies over their shoulders. Veep was setting the frequencies for a blast jamming device while Knuckles was choosing lockpicks for a basic bolt lock.

Knuckles said, "Creed was right about the alarm. It works on cellular."

Creed had told us that the bunker had three levels of security. The first was a simple bolt lock, something anyone with skill could penetrate, as Knuckles was about to prove.

The second was the alarm system. It needed to be turned off by a key card issued by the bank. We had no key card, but triggering the alarm meant the signal had to be sent somehow. If someone broke the window of a car, the alarm was a loud blaring. Crack a bank, and it was an electronic signal sent to the police. Break into something out in the middle of nowhere? It wasn't going to be a signal sent on a wire or an audible alert. It was going to be on the cell network. And so we'd brought a jamming device that blocked the cellular frequencies from talking to a tower. Which meant we couldn't talk on our phones while we were there, but that was a risk I was willing to take. Instead, we'd resort to old-school handheld radios to communicate between Brett's security position and our B&E team.

The third protection was a keypad inside the steel door. And we had a way to defeat that as well.

Veep said, "It's transmitting. Go to work."

Knuckles said, "Someone time me. I'm going to beat the record."

I chuckled and keyed my radio. "Blood, Blood, we're about to enter. You got eyes on?"

He said, "Yeah. I got you. You're clear."

Thirty seconds later, Knuckles threw his hands in the air like a calf roper at a rodeo and said, "Time!"

I stepped forward and tested the door. It was unlocked. I said, "You missed your calling," then swung it open.

We walked inside the gloom, and Veep said, "Creed thinks the final door is down a stairwell."

The interior wasn't like anything the outside presented. It was a flat concrete floor, the walls lined with metal, belying the rustic exterior. In the center was a steel ladder leading down a hole. I shined a light in the shaft and saw a floor about twenty feet down. I said, "Creed's good so far."

We went down and were faced with what looked like a typical vault door, with a keypad on the right. The third security measure.

Veep dug into his bag and pulled out a small tool kit, handing it to Knuckles and saying, "Pull off the casing."

Knuckles set to work, and Veep withdrew what looked like an old-fashioned beeper with a flat one-inch-wide cable running out attached to a credit-card-looking gadget.

Knuckles said, "It's open," and I saw the plate of the keypad dangling down. Veep placed the card against the guts of the system, lining up the copper leads with a circuit board. He hit a button on the beeper thing and said, "Let's pray Creed's right."

It was a brute-force device that would spin through codes much faster than a human ever could. Basically, it went through every possible combination, not unlike someone punching in numbers one at a time, hoping the door would open. Only our system punched them in at a rate of fifteen a second.

We had two worries. One, that the keypad would have a fail-safe, whereby after x number of attempts, it would shut down. Two, that the code was more than four digits. Creed had assured us that number one wouldn't happen, but he wasn't sure about number two.

After two seconds, Veep said, "We're good. If it were going to lock out, it would have by now."

We waited for five minutes, the machine working through the combinations, and I began to think the code was more than four numbers, which was not good. Each new number string increased the combination choices exponentially. A four-digit combo had ten thousand choices. A six-digit had one million. Ten thousand would take minutes. One million would take hours. If it was more than a six-digit code, it would take days.

At nine minutes, I said, "You sure Creed's right on this?"

And the light on the keypad flashed green, an audible snap echoing as the lock cleared.

Veep grinned at me and pulled down on the handle, saying, "O ye of little faith."

He opened the door, and we saw an Asian man standing in front of us, his eyes as wide as ours were at his appearance.

We snapped into action at the same time, him pulling out a pistol and Veep charging forward. Veep slapped the gun to the side, and the man squeezed the trigger. The bullet struck the ceiling, leaving a loud ricochet. I leapt through the doorway and hammered him in the face. He slammed against the stone wall, bounced back, raised his pistol, and Veep put a barrel against his head, dropping the hammer.

The man crumpled to the ground, the smell of cordite and blood filling the small room. Veep looked at me, wondering if he'd done wrong. I said, "Good shot."

Veep nodded, his eyes wide. I said, "Although it would have been nice to talk to him."

Veep looked deflated, and Knuckles said, "Don't let him get to you. Very few people he meets live to talk."

I said, "Maybe true. Maybe not. Let's search."

The first thing we found was a makeshift bedroom complete with a cooking stove and fourteen cases of bottled water. I said, "That's good news. He's here guarding the place. They must not have trusted the bank. Nobody's going to miss him until they come back."

Veep said, "Over here. Look here."

I went to him and saw two racks of the same thermos-type thing we'd sent to Kurt. It was shelf upon shelf of Red Mercury.

And five cylinders were missing.

64

★ ★ ★

Song listened to the diatribe on the phone, and eventually had heard enough. He said, "Hey . . . Hey . . . Be quiet!"

The line went clean and he said, "What I'm telling you is a **fact**. The Americans were in Stans today. They were on the same cable car as the ghost team. You can blame me all you want about 'controlling the situation,' but the fact remains that I have the girl, and the Americans didn't stay in Geneva. This is your plan. I'm just executing."

Not many would ever deign to be so abrupt with the power structure of the external security of the DPRK, but Song knew his pedigree. He had a direct line to the Supreme Leader. They had nothing but a military rank. And Kim Jong-un had shown a propensity to annihilate military leaders who displeased him in the most obscene ways.

He heard, "How do you know it was the American team? Maybe it was just a tourist."

"Our men on the cable car thought they recognized him from the restaurant in Lucerne. The female who was with him conducted what they believed might have been a brush pass. Before the cable car had reached the end, they searched each other and found what they think is a tracking device on one of the packs."

"What? Where is the team? Is the United States tracking them right now?"

"Yes, calm down. They're following my lead. I sent them to Zurich and had them check into a hotel. The beacon—if it was one—was left behind in the room. We're clean again."

"How can you say that? This is a disaster."

"Let me speak slowly so you'll understand. They went to Zurich and checked into a hotel, leaving a trail with a reservation of three days. Immediately after that, they left the hotel and came to Geneva. The beacon is in the hotel. They are not. They have disappeared."

Song heard, "Don't insult me. Do **not** insult me."

He realized he might have overstepped, knowing the power those men held, but he didn't regret it. Song held a dim view of the men running the ghost team. They seemed to believe they understood the world of espionage, when they'd never stepped outside of the Hermit Kingdom. They had no idea what went on in the real world.

He was the one executing policy around the globe. He was one of the few who could fade into the background in the countries where the Supreme Leader wanted action. And because of it, he was a favored son. Well, that, and his familial pedigree to the ruling power.

Song backed off a bit, saying, "I'm sorry. I meant no disrespect, but we've done what we could here. We executed with precision. You should be proud that the ghost team recognized the threat."

"I will be more proud when they execute the attack. We cannot afford any interference, and the Americans clearly want to do that."

Song looked toward a chair in the dining room, seeing the small child chained to it. Seeing the fear on her face. He said, "We have what that team holds dear. We have the child."

"Apparently not. They didn't remain in Geneva like we asked. They're out running amok, looking for ghosts."

Song said, "That's true, but they didn't try to interfere with our team, which means it was an initial effort. Right now, they are probably planning against Zurich."

"That deception may not be good enough. What if they determine it's a false trail today? They'll be back on the hunt immediately."

"We only need to stop them for a couple of days, correct?"

"Yes."

"Zurich might not be enough, you're right, but I think I have the means to stall them longer."

"How?"

Song returned to the child in the chair. He said, "Let me give them something to consider. Let me give them a ransom demand with bite. Permit me to leverage the child. You haven't let me do that. And I can."

He heard nothing for a moment, then, "Okay. Do what you must."

Song said, "You've made the right choice. We have a mission, and brutality will be the way it is executed."

He hung up the phone and said, "Where is the girl's cell phone? It's an iPhone, yes?"

A member of the ghost team brought it out, saying, "Yes it is."

Song said, "Leave it in airplane mode and put it on video, the slow-motion setting, but no sound. And don't capture my face."

The man did so, saying, "Why?"

He moved to the chair, placing his hand on the child's shoulder, feeling her tense up. Speaking in Korean, he knew she had no idea what he was saying, but she understood it was bad.

He said, "Because I want the man who's going to receive it to see the punishment. I want absolute compliance, and this video will provide it."

He turned toward the child, her face spilling terror. He said, "Capture that. No sound. Just capture the look."

The man said, "I'm taping. I have it."

The child looked at him in dread, and Song wrapped his left hand in the girl's hair, holding her head steady. He swung his right hand hard, slamming it into the girl's cheek.

65

★★

I ran my key card on our hotel room door and entered, saying, "Do you believe I'm right?"

Jennifer said, "Yes, I think you are."

I closed the door and said, "**Think** isn't going to cut it. Am I right? Or am I just pulling off for Amena? I can't tell anymore."

She took a seat on the bed, looked at me, and said, "Pike, you're right. This is bigger than us. We can't contain it, regardless of Amena."

I'd come down from the mountain, leaving the OP in place, and met her at the hotel. She'd tracked the North Koreans to the train station, and watched them board a train to Zurich. They'd rolled away with their cargo, and she'd let them.

I'd left the rest of the team up high, keeping eyes on the bunker, because what was inside there was decidedly deadly. I didn't think anyone else would appear to retrieve it, but I now had a responsibility to prevent that probability. We had a beacon on one team, and I couldn't predict if there would be others coming. I'd told them to interdict anyone who entered. Disable them if possible, but kill them if not.

Now I had to get the authority to do such a thing.

I'd decided to call Kurt and trigger a bilateral operation using Swiss assets. It was something he wasn't going to want to hear, but this had exceeded the Taskforce. We were talking about a massive cache of WMD and a state force willing to use them. With at least one team on the loose that had them on their backs.

It was beyond our control. But a part of me wanted to be let free to find Amena.

I sat down in front of our laptop and rubbed my face, trying to reconcile that I was doing the right thing. Would a unilateral Taskforce operation have more chance of success? Trying to involve another state system without exposing Taskforce operations was very hard to do—and laying the foundation was time-consuming. Was I endangering lives by my course of action? I was honestly torn, but I'd made my decision. I dialed the VPN.

It connected, and I was forced through a dance to prove I wasn't under duress, a Taskforce SOP that aggravated me in the moment. After answering one too many bona fides questions, I said, "Get Kurt Hale, right fucking now."

The guy on the other end looked like I'd slapped him. He said, "Roger that. Stand by."

Off the screen, Jennifer said, "Hey, that's not going to help here."

I turned to her and said, "Nothing's going to help here. I think this is going to go bad all the way around. We're going to find Amena's body in a dump, and they're going to kill a shit-ton of people."

She recoiled and said, "What's that about? You're the guy who's always confident."

I felt the blackness returning to my soul, eating at me. I knew what it wanted, and I thought it was going to win. I said, "I don't know. I just feel it. I abandoned Amena, and that's going to haunt me forever. And because of it, I'm going to reap the rewards for the deaths that are coming."

She came to me and put a hand on my shoulder, saying, "That is not fair. You didn't abandon her. You can only do so much. Do what's right now."

I saw the trepidation on her face, the same dread from when we'd first met, when I was out of control, killing everyone in sight.

I said, "I don't know what's right anymore."

She said, "You **do** know what's right. You do. Trust yourself."

I put my hand on hers and said, "Maybe. But I don't think it's up to me."

A shadow appeared on the screen, and Kurt Hale sat down. He said, "Hey, what's the emergency? I have the SITREP and we have the track from the Cotton Mouth. Is that it?"

I said, "Sort of. I didn't put everything in the SITREP, because I didn't know who would see it. I wanted a face-to-face. Sir, we've found a significant threat. That bunker is full of Red Mercury, much more than we can take out. This is much bigger than the Taskforce."

I saw Kurt's face go through about twelve different emotions. He finally said, "You found what?"

"We found a bunker full of WMD. I've got eyes on to interdict anyone else who approaches, and I need Omega to take them down. I'm telling you that this is a major shit storm. We have to shut it down, and I don't have the men to do it. Give me in-extremis authority, but get the Swiss on this right now. That bunker is a time bomb."

Kurt said, "What about the men on the loose? Do they have it?"

"I think so, but once again, this is no longer a Taskforce mission. Get the Swiss on the tag. Assault them. I can't do it alone."

"The tag ended in Zurich. We lost contact there."

I said, "That makes sense. Jennifer followed them to the train station, and they took a train to Zurich. Do you have fidelity of the final resting place?"

"Yeah. It's a hotel."

"Hit that fucker. Right now. We're losing control of this thing. Get the Swiss involved. I don't care how. Make it a CIA leak or whatever, but we can't stop what's about to happen by ourselves."

He went into commander mode immediately, no hesitation, no dithering. It's why I followed him. He said, "Okay, okay. I'm giving you Omega for the bunker, right now. Anyone else enters it, take them down, but I need you to go to Zurich. I'll get the machine in motion, but it won't be immediate. Find those guys, right now. Give the Swiss a target."

"Sir, I can't do both missions. I have a single team."

Kurt sagged back in his chair, thinking, and then came forward, his decision made. He leaned into the screen. "You **need** to do it. I've got nobody else. Figure it out. Give me some Pike magic."

I felt the pressure, and knew I should tell him no, for Amena. But I didn't. I said, "Okay, send me the hotel information, and I'll get eyes on the Koreans in Zurich, but I **cannot** execute. It'll be just Jennifer and me. Maybe Knuckles. I'll set them up for the assault force, but I can't interdict. Tell me you're going to get the Swiss on this. Somebody with WMD experience."

He said, "I'll work it. I'm on it."

We paused for a heartbeat, and he repeated, "I'm on it. You need to get moving."

I said, "What do you have on Amena?"

He closed his eyes and said, "We have nothing, Pike. Nothing. She's disappeared. Did you ever get anything on your phone? That's the one contact we have."

I gritted my teeth and spat out, "Fuck my phone. They never sent anything. You guys aren't looking hard enough. We find terrorists all over the world. Find her."

He raised his hands and said, "Pike, I understand the regret, but we have bigger problems right now."

My voice cold, I said, "So you're not even looking?"

"We **are** looking, but I'm not going to dedicate the entire Taskforce to find a child abduction when I have a group of North Koreans running around with WMDs. Come on, Pike. Look at the choices here."

I said, "The choices we make define us. Don't let this define me. **Find** her."

"Pike, unless they contact you, we have no ability to connect. Stay on the mission."

I squeezed my fists and said, "Okay, sir. I got it. But if they do contact me, I'm going after her."

Alarmed, he said, "No, Pike, no. You're not."

"Sir, don't put me there. I've done what I was supposed to do. I've found the WMD, and gave you the bed-down in Zurich. **Amena** stopped the WMD in Nice. She saved countless lives. Don't make me give that up. I won't give that up."

"Pike, listen to me. She saved lives, yes, but the threat isn't gone. I can't let you chase a ghost hoping to save a child. You won't live with yourself if this goes wrong and people die."

I felt the words in my soul, knowing he was right, my body physically revolting at my choices. A calm settled over me. I said, "Okay, sir. I'll get it done.

But I don't think I can live with myself either way when this is over."

Before he could answer, I disconnected from the VPN. Jennifer squeezed my shoulder, blinking a tear away, my pain flowing into her.

And then my phone vibrated with a message.

66

★ ★
★

Amena saw the gloom beginning to dissipate in the dining room, and knew another day was upon her. She dreaded the sunshine, because it meant the men holding her would be waking up. She'd been scared earlier, but it was nothing compared to the terror she now felt.

She'd been handcuffed to a chair since they'd taken her, only removing the manacles when she needed to use the bathroom or eat. Every other moment she was in the chair, staring out at a bay window toward a vineyard that stretched down to a road far below. She had no idea where she was, but she could see Lake Geneva in the distance, past the road. Nobody was going to drive up to this house and knock on the door by mistake. She'd waited on Pike to find her, but that hope had faded. If he were coming for her, he would have by now. She believed he was searching. After her conversation with Jennifer, she knew in her heart that he would move heaven and earth to find her, but he had no more idea than she did of her location.

And she had no idea why she'd been taken at all. At first, she thought it was because she was an illegal refugee, but then all of the men in the house had turned out to be some sort of Asian, speaking a language she had never heard before. It made no sense, especially with the way they treated her. They never asked her any questions, and didn't appear to even care about her at all. They'd simply chained her to the chair, and then had treated her like some macabre pet. That had changed last night.

Initially, the men holding her had not been overtly cruel, just indifferent. In truth, the shorter of her three guards had actually shown her some small bits of kindness, bringing her water without her having to ask, and letting her go to the bathroom more than was necessary, allowing her to stretch her legs. His kindness had disappeared when he'd held her phone while the leader had beaten her. Her hands chained to the chair, he'd unmercifully slapped her face until she'd tasted the copper of the blood in her mouth, while the guard she thought was a friend had filmed it.

The rising sun brought a fear not unlike when the killer had been chasing her, but at least then she had options. She'd controlled her destiny. Now she could do nothing but pray the men wouldn't beat her again.

A door opened and three new men entered. They were Asian, just like the ones who had captured her, but she hadn't seen them before. They looked cruel; one had a scar that left a line through his right eyebrow and onto his cheek, and the second's nose was bent, like it had been broken multiple times. The third had pits in his face as if he'd been hit with acid in his youth. She looked down at the floor, not wanting to encourage another beating. They ignored her as if she were another piece of furniture.

She glanced up, and one placed a backpack on the dining room table. The other two opened it and withdrew three canisters that resembled coffee thermoses. She focused on one, and realized it didn't look like a thermos. It looked like the same canister she'd seen at the bottom of the drone.

Poison.

And she knew that this had something to do with Pike and Jennifer. These men were terrorists, just like the Syrians, and they were extracting their revenge for what Pike's team had done in Nice.

The cruelness of the thought was debilitating.

She was going to be killed because of Pike.

I walked down the narrow alley and saw the bar that had been specified in the message. The Atelier Cocktail Club, in the Eaux-Vives district of Geneva, a densely packed neighborhood sprinkled with eateries and bars. I still had an hour before it opened at noon, but I wanted to get a feel for why this location was chosen.

After completing the video teleconference with Kurt, I'd received details for a meeting to discuss the ransom of Amena. Included in it was a video of someone beating her face, her arms handcuffed to a chair, the punisher holding her head upright by her hair. It was in slow-motion, allowing me to see the brutality with hyperclarity.

I had just about lost my mind, the rage so all-consuming I couldn't think logically, the blackness overriding everything. I'd dropped the phone, and stood, walking in a circle, not even hearing Jennifer asking me questions. By the time I'd regained control of my faculties, Jennifer had seen the message.

She was speechless.

I'd said, "Hand me the phone." She held it out, a tremor in her hand, afraid of what would happen if I looked at the video again. I took it, but ignored the video. I went to the message portion, seeing details to meet at the Atelier Cocktail Club at twelve fifteen. There were further instructions, but no mention of money or other ransom. Apparently, that would be determined at the meeting.

I'd memorized the details, then said, "Call Knuckles. Get him off the mountain, and relay Kurt's instructions to Brett and Veep. Tell them they have Omega to interdict anyone who enters the bunker. Tell them they're a two-man team, but help is on the way."

"What are you going to do?"

"I'm flying to Geneva. You and Knuckles are going to bird-dog for the Swiss team at the hotel. Knuckles is in command."

"You're going to Geneva alone?"

"Yes. Now get moving. We're wasting time. I've got to analyze this rendezvous location and you have to plan for the hotel."

She nodded slowly and said, "Are you going to tell Kurt?"

"No. He told me to figure it out, and I just figured it out. You know the Koreans on sight, Knuckles can coordinate with the Swiss authorities on assault planning, and Brett and Veep can lock down the bunker until the Swiss come in to evacuate it."

She said, "And when he calls for you?"

"Tell him I'm doing what's right. He can fire me later."

She said, "I don't think going by yourself is smart. Let me come."

"No. You know the Koreans."

"Then take Knuckles."

"No. He's the liaison with the Swiss."

"Shit, Pike, then take Brett or Veep!"

"No. They can't run an OP as a singleton."

"Pike . . . Why are you going alone? You know you could wicker this differently."

I'd looked at her and said, "Jennifer, just do the mission. Nobody needs to be near what I'm about to do. It's for your protection."

She didn't say anything, and I said, "Look, I don't think Amena is alive. I think whoever this is, they've already killed her. And not in a pleasant way."

She stood up, crossed her arms across her chest, and whispered, "So why are you going? What are you going to do?"

The demon slithered out of the depths, the blackness coming forth, wanting to feed, and I savored the feeling. Yearned for it.

I said, "I'm going to kill every single one of those fucks."

67

★★★

Amena finished her breakfast, and the short guard took her to the bathroom. She stayed inside as long as she could, waiting for him to bang on the door, as he inevitably did. When she heard the knocks, she mentally prepared herself to be chained back to the chair.

He led her back into the dining room, and this time she saw the same three men, only now they were dressed in business suits. A fourth man handed out some type of badge on a lanyard, and each of the three put it around his neck, then left the room.

She was locked back into her chair, and the leader came into the room. He said something in their language, and then walked over to her. Amena physically tried to shrink away.

To her, he said in English, "I need you to look into this camera and state your name and today's date."

He held up a small GoPro Hero video recorder and pressed a button. She just stared into the red light. He pressed the button again, smacked her in the head, and said, "Say your name and the date. Today's date."

This time, when he pressed the button, she did as he asked. He turned off the camera and said, "Good."

He called over the short guard and gave out instructions. Amena could tell the guard didn't like it. He said something back, and then their voices rose at each other in their weird language. The short guard backed down, then looked at his watch. He nodded, and the leader left the room with the taller guard.

When he returned, he was followed by the three in the business suits, each carrying a briefcase. The leader discussed something with them, then he and the taller guard exited the house. Thirty minutes later, so did the three in suits.

She was left with the short guard and the man who'd handed out the badges. Badge Man ignored her completely, but the short guard kept looking at his watch, and treated her with more kindness than he ever had before. When he spoke to her, he avoided her eyes.

And it left a bad feeling in her.

She decided to test his newfound benevolence, asking for a snack, something she'd never done before. He brought her a banana, not questioning the request in the slightest. Like he was granting the wishes of a doomed prisoner.

She knew that was the truth, and it caused her to drop her head in sorrow. She was going to die because Pike couldn't find her.

Why can't he locate me? He's the United States. He found the terrorists. He found me in the water. And then she had a lightning bolt of hope, the thought so strong she had to contain her reaction lest the guard suspect.

"May I listen to the music on my phone? Just one song?"

He shook his head. She said, "Please? I won't do anything to the phone. It can stay in airplane mode and you can manipulate it. My arms are chained to the chair."

He looked into her eyes, and then glanced away. He left the room. When he returned, he held Pike's iPhone and a set of earbuds. He gently put the buds in her ears, pulled up the music app, and, in his heavy accent, asked, "You listen to one song. Only one. Which?"

She smiled at him and said, "I like U2. It's the one called 'I Still Haven't Found What I'm Looking For.'"

She held her breath, and he clicked on the song. She closed her eyes, like she was listening to something she loved.

But she was really praying.

Four thousand miles away, inside an innocuous office building in Clarendon, Virginia, Bartholomew Creedwater was working his magic helping Knuckles and Jennifer penetrate a hotel room in Zurich, Switzerland, to confirm or deny the presence of a

North Korean hit team. He loved his job, especially listening to the chatter between the team, making him feel a part of the mission.

They'd spent a good portion of the day just trying to neck down the room, which had required his skills to hack into the hotel database. Once he'd done it, it was child's play to find the only Koreans in the entire establishment.

From there, he'd cracked the hotel security system, and had spent an hour analyzing security camera footage. Eventually, he'd found the two Koreans leaving the hotel, and had relayed to Knuckles that he believed the room was clear, and now he was listening to their chatter as they prepared to enter.

It was very cool.

His job done, he sat back in his chair, wishing he had access to a helmet cam system so he could watch as well as listen. He glanced at the computer to his left, and then bolted upright. Prometheus 3 was active, broadcasting an alert beacon.

He stood up, pulled off his headset, and went straight to his supervisor, a tall, lanky man responsible for running the entire hacking cell. Including the Zurich operation, he was managing two more missions and had little sense of humor.

"What's up, Creed?"

"Prometheus Three is sending an alert. We need to inform Kurt."

"You're in the middle of an operation. We'll do it later."

Creed knew how much this meant to Pike. Knew the pain the loss of the girl had caused. He said, "No, we need to do it **now**. Pike's in Geneva, and the grid from the alert is just outside there. I don't know how long it will be on."

His supervisor said, "You heard Kurt earlier. I'm not inclined to interrupt his meeting based on Pike."

Before the Zurich mission had begun, Knuckles had been forced to tell Kurt that **he** was executing, and that Pike had gone off the reservation. Jennifer had tried to mitigate the damage, describing a video that Pike had received, but Kurt had exploded, angrier than Creed had ever seen him, cursing Pike's very existence.

Creed tried one more time, saying, "He'll want to know this."

The supervisor snapped, "We'll tell him **after** the operation. Now get back to your box. Start doing your mission and quit worrying about what Pike's doing, because whatever it is, it's not sanctioned."

Creed returned to his seat and put on his headset. He heard Knuckles talking to Jennifer.

"Room's clean. The backpacks are here, empty, and the Cotton Mouth is on the floor. There is no other luggage. I think they fled the coop."

Jennifer said, "You think they're gone for good?"

"Yep. Looks that way. I think we were suckered."

"Not good news. Hallway's clear. You can exfil."

He said, "I have to give Kurt a call. I'll be off the net."

She said, "Roger," and Creed did what no support personnel was ever allowed to do. He keyed his microphone, interrupting a live mission.

"Koko, Koko, this is Creed."

"This is Koko, what's up?"

He surreptitiously glanced at his supervisor and said, "Prometheus Three is active. I have a grid."

68

⭐⭐

At precisely twelve fifteen, I entered the patio outside the bar, seeing a man in sunglasses in the right rear corner, a folded newspaper on the table. He was the one.

I approached him, trying to control my anger, wondering if he had been the man who had hit my little refugee. I said, "I'm here for a meeting."

He stood up and said, "Raise your arms."

I did so, and he searched me. The message had stated to come alone and unarmed, and from my earlier recce, I determined that the choice of the bar was to ensure number one was met. The alley was so narrow, I couldn't have hidden anyone near the bar with an ability to react without being seen. I wasn't stupid enough to break number two, knowing I'd be searched.

He finished and pulled off his sunglasses. He was Asian, and I now knew what this was about. It wasn't ransom, and it wasn't human trafficking. It was Red Mercury.

He said, "Go inside."

I turned and he sidled up right behind me, almost stepping on my heels. I opened the door, seeing a chopped-up place with a bar on the left, some high tables, and a few scattered deep-set leather chairs, all empty, awaiting the first customers of the day.

He said, "Continue forward, then take a right."

We walked past the tables and chairs and entered a small hallway. At the back was a coffee table with two leather chairs. Another man was in the chair against the wall.

The man behind me pushed my back, and I went to the end of the hallway. The man in the chair said, "You can call me Bill. Have a seat."

I sat down across from him and said, "You don't look like a Bill."

He raised an eyebrow at that, then said, "You want the girl back, yes?"

"Yes. But first I want to know she's alive."

He slid across a GoPro camera and said, "See for yourself."

I hit play, and saw Amena chained to a chair, her face swollen from the beating. She said her name, and today's date. I felt an impotent rage, wanting to slaughter both of them, believing in my heart Amena was lost, but if there was any chance, I had to take it, and these men were the only connection I had. If it meant giving my life, I would do so, but only if she would live.

I said, "What do you want?"

"I want an agreement. That is all. No money. Just a payment in time. You sit in your hotel room for twenty-four hours, and then you get her back."

I read right through what he was asking. I do nothing to interfere with his plans, and he would let the girl live. He was forcing me to make a choice between Amena's life and the lives of the people he was going to kill with his Red Mercury.

But there was no choice. My duty wouldn't allow it. If she wasn't already, Amena was going to die.

I pulled out my iPhone, set it on the table, and hit play. I said, "Did you send this video? Were you the one who hit her?"

"Why does that matter?"

"I want to know."

"It doesn't matter who did what. We are both men who understand the game. I see that in you. And you are going to continue the game if you want to see her alive. Right?"

My phone vibrated on the table. I picked it up, seeing a text message from Jennifer.

Prometheus 3 is active. The beacon is transmitting. We have a grid. Need the bird. Coming to you.

I placed the phone on the table, feeling the beast behind the cage, begging for release. I said, "Wrong."

And I set it free.

Without even looking I reached back behind me

and grabbed the man who'd searched me, standing up and flinging him across the table using my hip as a fulcrum. He smashed into the negotiator to my front and I leapt on top of him, grabbing his head by the hair and torquing his neck back. I hammered his throat with a closed fist while the negotiator scrambled against the wall. He stood up and said, "Stop! You'll kill her if I don't return!"

I bent down to the man at my feet, his hands on his neck, coughing and struggling. My eyes remained on the negotiator. I said, "Did you film that video?"

He said, "No, no. I'm just the messenger."

I placed my knee under the neck of the security man, then slammed his head down, the crack loud, like a stick breaking. I stood up, the beast running free, and said, "You're a fucking liar."

He darted to the left, trying to get by me, and I slammed him back into the wall. He started to fight me, a pathetic effort at the rage he was facing. I locked his arm up behind his back, controlling him and rotating his body until he was facing the wall. He kicked me in the groin, a feeble attempt to save his life. I pushed his head low, until he was bent at ninety degrees, and said, "You want to know what it feels like to get slapped?"

He said, "I didn't do it!"

I said, "It feels like this." I held his left arm high on his back, then grabbed his belt with my right hand. I slammed him into the wall like I was swinging a police battering ram, his head hitting the concrete hard enough to shatter the top of his skull and fracture the vertebrae in his neck.

I let him drop to the floor, putting my hands on my hips, breathing heavily for a second. I did a rapid search of the men, finding nothing of interest, then went back out to the front. The lone bartender said, "What's going on back there?"

I looked at him and he recoiled, seeing what was inside of me. I said, "Business disagreement."

I reached the street, and took off running to my hotel, calling the Rock Star bird as I went, the hope of finding Amena giving me the energy to move faster than I ever had.

69

An hour and forty-five minutes later, I was pacing around the passenger lounge at the Lausanne airport, waiting on the arrival of the Rock Star bird. With the turnaround, it would have been a two-hour wait to get Jennifer and Knuckles back to Geneva, and then another hour drive to the target, which was putting Amena's life in serious danger. The pilot had suggested Lausanne, a town only fifteen minutes from where Amena was being held. Well, at least from where the beacon was transmitting. Knuckles had reminded me of that fact, saying if Amena had control of her phone, why hadn't she just called? But I believed it was her. She had somehow triggered that alert, but couldn't do anything else. I didn't allow myself to think of any other options.

While waiting for them to go wheels up in Zurich, I'd researched the target. Located in the wine country on the shores of Lake Geneva, in the middle of an ancient vinery called Lavaux, it was a stand-alone farmhouse. At the base of a mountain, Lavaux was, at eight hundred hectares, the largest contiguous vineyard region in Switzerland. Terraced fields ran all the way to the lake, sprinkled with clusters of homes throughout where families for generations had run the vineyards. Our target was a single-story dwelling made of stone. From the size, it couldn't have more than four or five rooms, and looked to have been built when the Benedictine monks began the vineyards in the eleventh century.

With the images I had, I couldn't determine breach points, but I did see that the approaches to the house were good. The entire area was blanketed with roads that looked like God had thrown a handful of spaghetti to the earth, all of them threading through the vineyards and providing cover for a stealthy advance.

I'd received word that they were wheels up in Zurich, closed the computer, and raced up the A9 to meet them in Lausanne, the road paralleling the lake to the north. I'd called Kurt, dreading the result, but Jennifer and Knuckles had made a command decision to come help me, not telling Kurt they were leaving Zurich, and I wanted to make it official. No sense in all of us getting fired.

I'd reached the Taskforce, gone secure, and immediately felt the hostility.

He said, "I'm not sure why I'm even taking this call."

I took a breath and said, "Sir, you told me to figure

it out, and I did. Jennifer and Knuckles were fine in Zurich. It ended up being a dry hole."

"You didn't know that before you started chasing after the refugee."

"I also didn't know that she was being held by the North Koreans."

He said, "What? Say that again?"

"It's the North Koreans. They took her to get my team off of the trail. After we saved Yasir, they must have refocused. While we were chasing after his terrorists, the North Koreans were chasing us. The Zurich trip was a deception, and we fell for it."

"You're sure of this?"

"Yes. Positive. The ransom demand at the meeting wasn't money, it was time. And the guy asking was Korean."

He'd turned the corner at that point, saying, "Thank God. The Oversight Council is going nuts over the loss of two guys with WMDs."

"You didn't trigger the Swiss like I asked for in Zurich, did you? Do they know these guys are loose? I don't need to run into a trigger-happy ERT that doesn't know the lay of the land."

"No. We never got to the level where we had confidence in the target. Jennifer and Knuckles are still in Zurich trying to pinpoint them."

"I need them down here. Immediately. I'm going to assault the house with the beacon. I promise it's the beehive."

"I don't know. The one thread we have is Zurich. You yourself got a PID on the man from the restaurant in Lucerne. We leave there, and we might lose it all."

"Sir, that Zurich thing was a head fake. The one thread we have right now is Amena. If I were going to choose door A or door B, I'd be picking B right now."

The phone went silent for a moment, then he said, "Okay. Get 'em moving. What are you going to do?"

"I'm going to hit that house in less than an hour. I'm on my way to Lausanne to meet them right now."

"You want me to redirect them from here?"

"Uh . . . not necessary. What's the status with the bunker?"

"We're building a response right now. The problem is if the threat is as great as you say, we need a capability to safely extract it, but we also don't want to cause a panic when a bunch of guys in space suits show up at a major tourist destination."

"Understood. I'll keep Brett and Veep on it until they show up, but they aren't going to coordinate. When they see an official government response, they're going to pack up and fade away, leaving the rest to the experts. It'll get us out clean."

"Okay. Keep me updated. Let me know something as soon as you can. If your thread is a dry hole as well, we're going to be in a serious mess."

"It won't be a dry hole for the North Koreans. I can promise you that."

I'd hung up without saying the other part: it might be a dry hole for Amena.

I'd reached the Lausanne airport fifteen minutes before the arrival of the Rock Star bird. As soon as I saw the smoke from its wheels hitting the asphalt, I'd gone out to the tarmac. The airport was small, with no commercial aviation coming in to it, so security was pretty loose.

The plane wheeled around, and the door opened, lowering down the stairs. I'd sprinted inside, seeing Jennifer and Knuckles unloading all manner of lethal devices. Knuckles looked up and said, "I couldn't have you get fired all by yourself."

I said, "You're not fired. I talked to Kurt. Amena is the key to this whole thing."

Jennifer whipped her head to me and said, "He wasn't aggravated that we left Zurich?"

"No. As far as he knows, he gave the order for you to do so after I asked."

"Huh?"

"Later. We need to move. I have the target package done and the route. You guys can look at it while I drive. It's about fifteen or twenty minutes from here."

Knuckles held up a lockpick kit and said, "We have to do this surgically, like in Nice?"

I pointed to an explosive breaching charge and said, "No. We're going to use maximum violence. Anyone inside besides Amena is hostile."

I picked up an integrally suppressed AR carbine chambered in .300 blackout and snapped the stock open, then began removing preloaded magazines, saying, "If it's not Amena, kill them."

Fifteen minutes later we were on the road, carrying more death and destruction than a platoon in World War II, Jennifer and Knuckles studying the building while I went as fast as possible on the A9.

Knuckles said, "Careful on the speed. We get stopped and it's game over."

I kept the gas pedal buried and said, "Have to risk it."

Jennifer said, "The beacon's still on. That's a good sign."

I looked at her and said, "Like Knuckles told me, that beacon is a phone, not Amena. I'm afraid they've tricked me, and she's dead already, but if she's not, I'm petrified she's about to be."

70

⋆⋆

Amena finished her lunch and was allowed to go to the bathroom. She stared at herself in the mirror, seeing the swelling on her face had gone down somewhat. She soaked a washcloth and pressed it against her cheek, the coolness soothing. She closed her eyes and imagined she was someplace else. On a beach she'd seen in pictures, the waves crashing, chairs and umbrellas set in the sand, and kids playing with beach balls.

A place in America.

The guard banged on the door, causing her eyes to snap open and her to jump. She said, "Coming," and opened the door. He waved her forward, not looking her in the eye. He locked her back in the chair, glanced at his watch, and then went into the kitchen.

She heard him arguing with the badge man in the other room, and feared they were reaching a critical point. It had been hours since she'd triggered the beacon, and nothing had happened. No sign that it had even worked. Maybe she'd done it wrong. Maybe the phone had to be out of airplane mode.

Or maybe nobody cared.

She shook that out of her mind. Pike cared, she knew, but maybe there was nothing he could do. Maybe he'd already left Switzerland. Maybe he was flying back to her right now from the United States or some other country.

But he could call the police, couldn't he? Get someone to come knock on the door. Get anyone to check this house.

At least the leader hadn't returned. Hopefully he would stay gone until it was time to sleep, leaving them alone in the house. After the beating, she feared him most of all.

She heard the argument build until they were shouting, then the room next door went quiet. The guard appeared, carrying a length of rope, his face grim. He leaned in the doorway, just staring at her.

She felt her adrenaline rise, an animal instinct telling her that the danger had come. She closed her eyes, willing her mother to appear. Wanting to see her face and feel the kindness one last time. Wanting her mother to help her.

Instead, she saw Jennifer, and she began to cry. They were going to kill her because of the man who'd abandoned her. Pike was not coming.

She squeezed her eyes tight, willing back the tears, chanting in her mind.

If it is to be, it is up to me.

She heard the guard's footsteps and opened her eyes. He reached her and said, "Bow your head."

She said, "No, wait. You don't have to do this."

He didn't even try to hide his intentions, saying, "Little one, it will be quick, I promise."

She said, "Wait, wait. I'm going to pee my pants. Please, let me go to the bathroom."

He shook his head no, and she said, "One last time. Please."

He looked at her for a long moment, then relented, unlocking her arms and pulling her to her feet. He pushed her, walking by the doorway to the kitchen. She entered the hallway with the bathroom, passing the two bedrooms. She felt her breath begin to go shallow, the adrenaline starting to take over. He opened the door to the bathroom and waved her in. She closed the door and stared in the mirror, willing a solution to appear.

She thought about the door. It opened outward, and the guard was always standing behind it. If she waited until he knocked, she would **know** he was directly behind it. She could slam it open as hard as she could and fling him back, leaving the hallway open. She could run to the kitchen and then to the back door, where they'd brought her in.

She furiously tried to remember if that was correct. If the exit she remembered was through the doorway to the kitchen. She could not. She would get one shot, and if she committed to that path and it didn't end at an exit, she was done.

But it was all she could think to do. If she made it outside, she would just run screaming until she found someone. Anyone besides an Asian.

She turned to the door, waiting, hand near the knob, her breath coming in shallow pants, the sweat rising from under her shirt smelling fetid. Before, she had wanted to extend the time of her bathroom visits as long as possible. Now she was begging him to end the anticipation.

When it came, it was like a thunderclap, setting her brain into the feral fight-or-flight zone she'd spent most of her life in. Time slowed. She watched her hand reaching for the doorknob as if from out of her body, her logical brain screaming at her not to do it. She grasped the knob, turned, and then threw her whole body against the door, feeling it slam into something solid before swinging free.

The guard shouted, and time sped back up, everything spinning at a furious pace. She hammered the door again, and heard the guard fall to the floor. She leapt out of the doorway and began sprinting, the guard bellowing behind her.

She took one glance back and saw him on his feet, his face a mask of rage at having been tricked. He began chasing her, huffing like a bull. She turned back around and saw the doorway to the kitchen.

She darted into it, running headlong into an oven. She bounced off, looked to the left, and saw the back-door exit at the end of the room. Salvation. She began sprinting toward it, closing in to twenty feet, ten feet, five feet. She reached out her hand to the knob and barreled smack into the badge man, him clocking her like a quarterback blindsided by a lineman. She slammed to the ground on her side, the wind knocked out of her. He blocked her path, standing in front of the door. He raised a pistol and she screamed.

The door exploded into the kitchen with a giant crack of fire and sound, the fragments of wood and explosive force lifting the man off his feet and throwing him across the room into the far wall.

She blinked. It was a magic act. One second, the terrorist was standing in front of her, a split second later, he was across the room. Her ears rang from the noise, and smoke billowed into the kitchen. A man came racing through the doorway with a rifle, turning away from her. Another man came in immediately behind him and turned her way. He shouted, "PC, PC!" and leapt over her. It was Pike Logan.

Someone appeared next to her, and she looked up blankly, seeing Jennifer, holding a weapon just like the men, leaning over her and protecting her body. Pike shouted, "Doorway," and the other man raced to him. She recognized Knuckles. In the span of seconds, they were gone. She heard a rapid string of pops, like fireworks going off, then nothing.

The badge man rose from the far side of the room, disoriented, still holding his pistol, his face bloody.

Her ears ringing from the explosion, Amena tried to say something. Jennifer rotated around, raised her rifle, and fired twice.

The man collapsed.

Two minutes later, Pike and Knuckles came back into the room. Pike said, "It's clear, but there's no WMD." He leaned his weapon against the wall and took a knee, helping Amena to a sitting position. She saw the relief on his face, and felt the affection. He said, "Hey, doodlebug. You sure took your time with that beacon."

She said, "You sure took your time after I took my time. They were going to kill me."

He smiled and gently touched her cheek. He said, "Are you okay?"

She nodded. "Yes. I'd really like you to meet the guy who did this, though. He left."

He patted her head and said, "I've met him. He looks worse than you, I promise."

She said, "You met him? Where?"

"Trying to find you. Doesn't matter. He's gone. Let's get you out of here."

So he was looking for me.

She looped her arms around his neck and hugged him, like she used to do with her father. He stood, picking her up off the ground, and she wrapped her legs around him, resting her head on his shoulder, feeling emotionally safe for the first time in . . . forever. And then she remembered.

She pulled her head up and said, "Wait, Pike, they

had those canisters like the thermos. Like the one in Nice. They had them here."

He said, "You saw them?"

"Yes. Three more Asians. They put on business suits, and that guy"—she pointed at the man Jennifer had shot—"gave them badges. They put the canisters in briefcases and left after the leader had gone. The one who beat me."

Jennifer went to the man she'd killed and said, "This is the guy from the cable car. The one from Lucerne." She peeled back his jacket, then pulled a lanyard from around his neck. She came back to Pike and said, "It's a UN delegation badge."

Pike said, "They all had those?"

Amena nodded, and Pike set her down, saying, "They're going to the UN. That's the attack, and it's going to be near impossible to find them in that multicultural beehive." Then he stopped, turning to her.

He said, "You saw them do all this?"

And for the first time in days, she felt a smile leak out, knowing what he was asking.

She said, "Yes. I know what they look like."

71

★★★

We entered the Lausanne airport terminal at a trot, the three of us dragging Pelican cases full of weapons. Thank God for general aviation.

Amena said, "What are we doing here? I thought we were going to Geneva?"

I said, "We are."

Jennifer hung up her phone, turned to me, and said, "Pilots are spinning. Plane's ready."

Knuckles put his hand on the mic of his phone and said, "Talking to Creed. He's doing preliminary work on the UN compound. He can't promise anything, because they have pretty tight security, but he'll try to map it. He's asking for a neck down of specifics. What, exactly, do you want?"

I said, "I honestly don't know. Members, manifests, meetings, room occupancy, office locations, the works."

Knuckles said, "That's sort of broad."

I said, "I know, I know."

We exited onto the tarmac, and I decided. I said,

"How about security cameras? Focus him on that. We'll figure the rest out ourselves."

We crossed the asphalt and walked up the stairs of the Rock Star bird, Amena once again marveling at a piece of luxury she had only seen on television. She said, "We could fly to America right now on this. Nobody would even know."

I said, "That requires a passport and a visa. You have either one of those?"

She scowled and I pointed her to a seat, then said, "Jennifer, get her settled. When that's done, start mapping the UN building. Get me everything you can find. I'm going to the cockpit."

I went forward, passing Knuckles and saying, "As soon as we're wheels up, stow the long guns and break out some suppressed pistols. I don't think we're going to be using kinetic breaching on this one."

He said, "Will do. You going to call Kurt?"

"Yeah. You keep working Creed."

I told the pilots the urgency of the situation, and then buckled up in the seat next to Amena. We rolled down the runway and she pressed her face against the window in awe. I chuckled and said, "Before you met me, you'd never been in a first-class aircraft like this, huh?"

She turned from the window and said, "Before I met you, I'd never been in an airplane at all."

I had no answer to that. She returned to the window, and we lifted off. As soon as we were airborne, I went to the front, pulled out a headset from a hatch next to the coffeepot, and dialed up the Taskforce. I got Kurt on the line and told him what had transpired, saying, "They're going to hit the UN. I don't know where, and I don't know how, but that's the target."

"What's the timeline? How much breathing room do we have?"

"They left Amena's safe house at least three hours ago, maybe more. But it takes at least an hour to drive from the house to Geneva, and I can get there in fifteen minutes by air, so I'd say they have a two-hour head start."

"Wait, are you saying the attack is today? They aren't staging in Geneva, but are going straight in?"

"Yes, sir, that's exactly what I'm saying. They dressed in business suits, have official accreditation to enter the United Nations, and the ransom demand I got this morning was to take my team and sit in the hotel for a day. One day."

He said, "How confident are you that you can find them?"

"If I can get within sight of them, one hundred percent. But that building is huge."

"You have photos I can use? Something I can get into the security apparatus? We can get the UN guys to round them up."

"No, sir. I've got Amena. She knows them on sight. No photos, but I have a bird dog."

"Amena? Pike, what's she going to do?"

"Pinpoint them for me."

"That's it? Our entire operation is based on a child refugee? Jesus. I'm going to have to alert the UN. Get them to round up all the North Koreans. Shut down operations."

I said, "Sir, these guys aren't going to be on any list. They might have the badges, but they aren't part of an official delegation. You'll round up the wrong guys, and they'll slip through. The only way to stop this is to evacuate the building completely, but if you do that, they're gone, with the Red Mercury."

I heard him sigh, and he said, "My idea's not going to work anyway. The diplomatic shit storm alone would take two days to wade through. Arresting an entire diplomatic crew from a foreign country? I won't get anyone to sign on to that."

"Get me in. Give me some badges like they have. Give me the freedom to roam, and I'll hunt them down."

"That's going to take time as well. It's nine a.m. here. The people at State are just rolling in. I'll have to go to the Oversight Council, convince State to call their people in Geneva, and get them to meet you. Look, you get on the ground and stand by. I'll give you the linkup procedures when I'm done."

I felt the plane begin to descend and said, "We don't have that sort of time. I'm already a couple of hours behind. I think they're going to attack today, which means it'll be before the end of business."

"Then we'll have to pull the trigger on a complete evacuation. We'll have to insert a generic bomb threat and evacuate the building."

"We do that, and we'll lose them."

He snapped, "I've got nothing else! I can't get you in without wading through two hours of red tape, and you just said that's too long."

I looked at Knuckles in the back and said, "Make sure Creed's on the security cameras. I think I know how to cut through the red tape."

"How?"

"I'll call you if it doesn't work out, and you can pull the trigger on the ground-zero evacuation. Give me fifteen minutes."

"Okay, work it from your end, but leave the child out of it."

I said, "Gotta go," and hung up without agreeing to his demand.

We hit the ground and began taxiing to the general aviation section of the Geneva airport. I said, "Knuckles, get up here."

He came forward and said, "What's up?"

"We need to get badges into the UN headquarters as official US representatives, and the Taskforce is going to take too long. We need to cut through the bureaucracy."

"Yeah? Why are you talking to me?"

"I need you to contact your booty call."

72

★★

Hwang Pyong-so tepidly poked at his noodles in the small conference room of the North Korean delegation to the United Nations. Most of the other country delegates either ate in the cafeteria or out in town, but the North Koreans never did. It worked out for him and his two compatriots, because, while they had badges, they didn't need anyone questioning their reason for being in the building.

The other two men seemed to have just as small of an appetite. Given what they were about to do, it was understandable.

He didn't even know the true names of the men he was with, but he didn't doubt their dedication. They had been disciplined since birth for absolute loyalty, and had proven fanatical in their training, rising as members of the elite Airborne Sniper Brigade of the DPRK Reconnaissance Bureau, the highest level of special operations forces within the General Staff. Eventually, they each had been handpicked for the ghost teams of the State Security

Department—an elite within an elite, designed for external operations in the absence of hostilities—their past erased from the records.

The team knew him as "Scar," and he knew them as "Crane" and "Lynx." If any one of them were caught, they couldn't say a thing about the rest of the team no matter what pressure was brought to bear. Because of this, they knew better than to try to bond on a personal level. Everything was the mission. Only the mission.

An older, distinguished-looking man entered. He took one look at Hwang—aka Scar—and said, "So you're still here. I would have thought the delay would have made you impatient to get home."

Scar stood up, two inches taller than the older man. He said, "I'm on a mission of utmost importance for the Supreme Leader. Don't forget that. I will only go home once the mission is successful."

The older man shrank away, his bluster dissipating. Scar said, "When will the conference begin again?"

"The Syrian delegation is still making demands before they'll agree to come to the meeting. Maybe an hour. Maybe less."

Scar said, "It's **their** council. If they don't defend themselves, nobody will."

"That's what I thought we were doing. That's my job."

"They need to be in the meeting. Period."

"I honestly don't understand any of this." He

pointed at Crane and Lynx, saying, "Why do you need security? I don't even have security and I'm the head of the delegation."

"It is just prudent."

"They cannot come with you on the floor. If you want to be with me, they stay behind."

Scar nodded and said, "I understand, but if you have any more questions, I suggest you call your supervisor in the DPRK. I'm sure he can explain."

The man's face soured at the mention of his higher command. There was no way he would question Scar. He'd appeared out of nowhere with orders from the very top, and he would disappear the same way.

He said, "I'll tell you when to come. If it takes longer than an hour, you'll need to move to my office to hide. We have a delegation from Cameroon asking for our help, and my staff has scheduled this conference room. I can't have anyone see you."

Scar nodded and said, "Don't forget your role at the conference."

"I won't. And I don't need you here to do it."

"My role is to ensure you do yours." Scar turned his back to the diplomat, letting him know the conversation was over.

We rolled up to the visitors' entrance of the United Nations headquarters complex, and Knuckles turned into the drive, saying, "Going right to the gate. She's supposed to be waiting for us."

It had taken significant effort on Knuckles's part, but eventually Amanda Croft had agreed to use her office to facilitate a Taskforce operation without going through the Oversight Council—though she'd called Kurt first to make sure this wasn't Knuckles going insane. Even with that, it had cut our reaction time from hours of hand-wringing to minutes of telephone calls.

By the time we'd reached the Geneva FBO terminal, he'd hung up, a grin on his face, and I'd said, "Maybe I should start sending out other members of the team, **Red Sparrow** style, to bed Oversight Council members."

He said, "She's the only female there."

I'd looked at Jennifer and raised an eyebrow. She smacked me in the shoulder, and I said, "Okay, okay, you have your morals. You think Veep would be willing to bat for both teams? If I ordered him to?"

Amena saw Jennifer's face and said, "I don't think she finds this funny."

The aircraft stopped moving and I stood up, saying, "She has no sense of humor. Why don't you take Jennifer to the rental cars and get us something big? Like an SUV?"

Amena said, "Why don't you do it?"

Jennifer smiled at me and said, "Because Pike and Knuckles have some packing to do."

Jennifer led her out while Knuckles and I gathered the surveillance kit and weapons. We met them in the rental lot standing next to a Range Rover. I said, "Seriously? They didn't have anything besides a luxury SUV?"

Jennifer said, "Nope."

Amena beamed and said, "Jennifer told me this was payback."

Jennifer said, "Hey!"

I let it slide. I said, "Knuckles, you get the wheel. Jennifer, show me what you know about the building."

Knuckles had taken the longer, looping route of the A1 instead of cutting through the city because of traffic. During the drive, Jennifer showed me the building, and it was huge. Comprised of the original structure created for the now-defunct League of Nations following World War I, it had a new building to the north that was just as large, the modern one grafted onto the stone of the old.

We drove by the Red Cross headquarters Amena had visited just days ago, and Knuckles turned into the vehicle lane leading to the complex, all of us straining to see an American face. Soon enough, we reached the gate with nobody waving an American flag. We were at a loss because we didn't even know the name of the person we were to meet.

The guard approached the window, and a young, portly woman of about twenty-five followed him, holding lanyards with badges. The guard asked our business, and the woman said, "They're with me. It's the people I told you about."

He said, "The vehicle can't stay here."

She held up a pass and said, "I have parking."

We spent five precious minutes showing identification, waiting for him to write in his official log, then waiting again as the vehicle had a mirror run underneath it. Finally, the woman stepped into the car and said, "My name is Sonya Harden. I guess I'm supposed to give you guys a tour or something?"

The gate opened, and Knuckles pulled through. I said, "Sure, let's go with that."

She glanced around and did a double take when she saw Amena, saying, "I can't give a child a badge. Nobody will believe it's real."

I said, "That's fine. She'll be with us the entire time. Do we need to go through any type of security to enter the building?"

"No. You just passed through the diplomats' entrance. Why are you asking that? I thought this was a tour of the facility. I was told you were friends of the secretary."

Knuckles entered a numbered lot on the modern side of the compound and said, "Where do I park?" Sonya pointed to a space and I said, "We're more like coworkers. There is a threat inside this building, and we need you to help us find it."

She became alarmed, saying, "A threat? You want me to take you to security? Alert them?"

"No. Security raising an alarm will cause the threat to become active. We need them to believe they are safe. There's no way uniformed security can prevent this attack. Trust me."

Knuckles turned off the engine and she said, "What kind of threat?"

I exited, saying, "An imminent one."

73

★★

I started walking to the building and she scurried to catch up, saying, "What are you talking about? Imminent threat where? Who are you?"

"Not out here. Take us to your office, quickly."

We entered a steel building, a large LCD screen on the wall displaying various rooms and conference times, and a bookstore deeper in. Milling about was a tour group waiting for their start time. Sonya walked by them down a long hallway, then went up a flight of stairs. A few turns later, and we were inside her office. She closed the door and said, "Okay, what's this about? Tell me right now, or I'm calling security myself."

I pulled a map of the building off the wall and said, "I told you, there is a threat. It involves the North Korean delegation. I need to know where their office is located, right now."

"Why do you have a little girl with you?"

I slapped the table and said, "Do it! Right now."

Her hands started to tremble and she said, "They're two floors above us, but we don't ever go there."

"Show me on the map. Point to where we are, and point to them."

"That's the old building. It doesn't have the new side. The side we're in now."

I nodded my head, saying, "Okay, lead us there."

She didn't move, and I showed her the pistol on my hip, saying, "Please."

The ghost team sat in silence, picking at their food. The diplomat had been gone for thirty minutes, but none of the team felt the need to talk. Finally, the one called Crane looked at his watch and said, "What if this rolls into tomorrow? Do we leave the briefcases here, or take them with us?"

Scar said, "We take them with us. I know there's a risk of a random search coming and going into the compound, but I don't trust the cell here. You heard the conference room is being used by Cameroon. Who knows who else will come in. We can't risk someone opening the cases, but we're getting ahead of ourselves. When we leave the United Nations today, it won't be with the canisters. There is too much riding on this conference for the Syrians. They're making a show of force, but they'll attend."

Lynx said, "If we can't travel with you on the floor, where do you want us?"

"At the back. Lynx on one side and Crane on the other. When you see the head of our delegation stand up and begin banging his fist at the shameful partisan treatment of our Syrian friends, prepare the cases."

"And you? Will you do the same?"

"Yes. When he begins to walk out of the room in protest, I'll release mine. You do the same. We'll have coverage of the entire chamber."

They both nodded. Crane said, "And we wipe out the United Nation's ability to target us with their insane punishments."

Lynx smiled and Scar brought them back to the danger. "That's the goal, and the Supreme Leader will remember everything we do, but only if we return. Get it into the air, but **don't** get any on you. It kills by contact with the skin. Thirty minutes after we leave, the agent becomes active. If it's on you, you **will** die."

They sat in silence after that, returning to picking at their food. The door opened, and the diplomat stuck his head in.

"It's time. The Syrians have agreed to the terms of the meeting, but it won't start for another ten minutes or so. The Cameroon delegation will be here soon, so we'll go to the chamber early."

At the sight of my weapon, Sonya stood, now with her arms trembling. Jennifer gave me the stink eye, then put a hand on Sonya, calming her down and saying, "We're the good guys. Trust me. This is extremely urgent."

Sonya nodded, saying, "Okay, okay, the North Koreans are upstairs. I can show you the office suite, but I've never been inside."

"That would be fine. Lead the way, but do it quickly."

We followed her to a stairwell, raced up two floors, then went down a long hallway, the doors left and right adorned with various flags. She stopped next to a flag that I recognized as the so-called Democratic People's Republic of Korea. I waved her to the wall, set my backpack on the ground, and dug around inside it until I found a flexible endoscope cable camera. I passed one end to Jennifer, and she plugged it into her tablet.

Knuckles pulled out his pistol and aimed it at the door, causing Sonya to gasp. I held a finger to my lips and knelt down, putting the small camera under the jamb. On the screen I saw a female at a front desk, a blond woman of about thirty. I turned to Sonya and said, "There's a blond receptionist?"

She said, "Contract worker. There are a lot in this building."

I nodded, returning to the screen. Behind her were two Asian males sitting around a table near a watercooler. I flicked my head to Amena and she scampered over. She peered intently, then shook her head, whispering, "That's not them."

I withdrew the cable, made sure my badge was visible, and nodded at Knuckles. He stacked behind me and said, "What are we doing?"

"Gonna ask them where they are. Might be in an office in the back."

"We're going to take over a diplomatic post?"

"No, damn it. I'm just going to ask the receptionist. Jennifer, knock on the door. Let her see you first. Sonya, Amena, flatten against the wall."

Jennifer scowled, not liking the plan, and I said, "Anybody got a better idea?"

Nobody said anything, so I flicked my head to the office. Jennifer knocked, and the receptionist opened the door. She saw Jennifer, with me behind her, both with our official UN badges. Her eyes narrowed, and I said, "Sorry for the bother. You had three unescorted visitors today. We're just trying to locate them."

She nodded, and said, "Yes, they're in the conference room."

I looked at Knuckles, and he raised his weapon. I said, "Thank you. Please step back." Alarmed, she did so, and we flowed into the small anteroom. The two men we'd seen on the camera looked up, and I pointed my pistol at them, quietly saying, "Get on the floor."

They did so, and I said, "Jennifer, flex-tie their hands." To the receptionist, I asked, "Where is the conference room?"

Her eyes wide, she pointed down a hallway, saying, "First door on the left. What's this about?"

I said, "How many more North Koreans are in here?"

"Just three in the conference room. Everyone else went to the council chambers a few minutes ago."

I flicked my head to Knuckles and we moved swiftly down the hallway, stopping at the first door. I tried the handle, then nodded at Knuckles. We burst in, seeing three black males and three Asians sitting opposite one another at a rectangular table, some type of construction blueprints in front of them. They all looked up in surprise at our entrance, then threw their hands in the air when they saw our weapons.

I said, "Everybody just remain calm." I pointed to the Africans and said, "Step back from the table and face the wall." They did so, and the Asians started to rise as well. I said, "No. Stay seated. Place your hands on the table to your front."

They complied, and I got on the radio, "Koko, Koko, send in Amena, but you keep eyes on the men in the lobby."

Amena arrived, nervously peeking around the corner. I pointed to the men at the table, and she shook her head. I said, "You positive?"

"Yes."

Shit.

"Okay, okay. Knuckles, flex-tie these guys. I'm going to talk to the receptionist."

He had the men lie on the floor and said, "I thought we weren't going to take over a diplomatic post?"

"It's a temporary thing. I'm working for the UN, and this is their building, so it's not a takeover."

He chuckled and went to work. I took Amena and jogged back out to the front. Sonya was sitting in a chair looking like she was going to throw up. The receptionist was calmer, but still nervous.

"Jennifer, get these other two guys in the conference room for Knuckles."

She nodded, and ushered them to their feet. When they were gone, I turned to the receptionist and said, "I asked you about three visitors. Did you mean the Africans?"

"Yes. They're from Cameroon. Did they do something wrong?"

I ignored the question. "What about three North Korean males that you haven't seen before. Some that just showed up today?"

"Yes. They're security for the head of the North Korean delegation. Why?"

"Where are they?"

"They went to the Council Chamber. To the Conference on Disarmament."

I turned to Sonya. "What's that? What's going on?"

"The Conference on Disarmament is the primary chamber for discussions about the proliferation and reduction of weapons of mass destruction. It's designed to get agreement on chemical weapons prohibitions, nuclear test ban treaties, that sort of thing. It's held in the original League of Nations Council Chamber."

"Does it deal with the North Korean nuclear program?"

"Oh, yes. That's been the main topic for a while."

I turned to the receptionist. "You have Wi-Fi in here?"

She told me they did, and gave me the password. Jennifer returned, and I pulled her aside, stepping away from the receptionist and Sonya. "Call Creed. See if he's hacked the cameras here. Tell him we need the ones in the Council Chamber for the League of Nations." I gave her the Wi-Fi password, and she went to work.

I went back to Sonya, my suspicions hardening. I said, "Can you check the schedule and tell me if North Korea is on the plate today?"

The receptionist said, "I can tell you that. The answer is no. They're discussing the latest chemical use by the Assad regime, determining if they were responsible for breaking a UN resolution prohibiting chemical munitions."

Assad? Why would they attack that?

My earlier suspicions now crushed, I started fishing. I said, "Is it the same body for all discussions?"

"Yes."

"And they recommend sanctions against folks who break UN resolutions? Is that how this works?"

She said, "I don't know the mechanics of it. I just

know it involves counterproliferation for weapons of mass destruction."

Sonya said, "That's roughly how it works. New York does the sanctions. Geneva just determines if they've broken a resolution. It's sort of like the police determining a crime, but the judge determining the punishment."

To myself, I said, "So no police, no crime."

"What's that mean?"

74

★★

Jennifer waved me over, and I ignored Sonya's question. I jogged to her just as Knuckles came back. He said, "They're hog-tied, but we need to leave someone to watch them, unless we're exfiling now."

I nodded and said, "We aren't doing anything just yet. Jennifer, what do you have?"

She whispered, "Creed can get in, but his supervisor is preventing it because it's the UN. Taskforce charter forbids hacking government institutions without express national command authority permission."

Christ. "Give me the phone." She did so, and I didn't waste time with Creed. I said, "Get Kurt Hale, right now."

He must have been close by, because he got on the line within a minute. I said, "Sir, I need those video feeds. This place is huge, and I can't search it on foot."

"I understand, Pike. I sent the request up the minute you asked, but I haven't heard back yet. What's your gut telling you? Can you neck it down at all?"

"I **have** necked it down. They're going to release the Red Mercury inside the Conference on Disarmament. They're arguing about Syria today."

"Syria? Why would they do that?"

"Because it helps North Korea while hiding who did it. I think that's why they gave it to the Syrian terrorists. They wanted the Syrians to execute **their** attack so we'd go crazy analyzing the WMD, then this second one happens during an Assad conference, and he gets blamed because of the fingerprints of the first strike. Meanwhile, North Korea reaps the benefits because it's the same conference members holding its fate. It'll short-circuit all counterproliferation work worldwide, maybe for years. I **need** those feeds. The Koreans have been gone for twenty minutes, and I don't know how much longer we have."

"Just lock down the conference. Evacuate the room."

"Sir, I believe they're in there right now with the weapon. Any attempt to evacuate that chamber is going to end in disaster. We need to do this surgically, and I need the feeds to identify them."

"How is that going to help? You don't know what they look like."

"Amena does. I'm in here with her right now."

I didn't mention I was in the North Korean delegation's office with a bunch of foreign citizens hog-tied in a conference room, to include those from Africa, but hey, that info wasn't going to help the mission.

Need to know, and all that. Amena being here was going to be bad enough.

He said, "You have the refugee inside the United Nations helping you? A child? Pike, I told you—"

I cut him off, "Sir, I don't have **time** for this shit. I **need** the feeds. You asked for magic, and I'm providing it. But I need your help."

He turned away from the phone and said something. He came back on and said, "We're both going to be fried for this one."

I said, "Only if we don't stop the attack. Thanks, sir."

I hung up and turned to Jennifer. "You getting the feed now?"

"Yeah, but there are seven cameras. This room is huge." I looked at it, and saw it was in fact gigantic. It looked like an opera house, with murals on the walls and ornate columns. The floor was full of member nations surrounding a large U-shaped table with about fifteen feet between the spines. Behind the table was a row of chairs for the supporting staff. Behind **them** was another section of chairs, and so on and so on, going all the way to the walls. I turned to Sonya and said, "I thought this was some sort of committee thing?"

She said, "No. Sixty-five nations participate officially, a lesser number as observers. That's why it's in the old Council Chamber. It's big enough to accommodate everyone."

"Point out the DPRK section."

She came over and looked at the screen, saying, "How do you have access to this?"

My voice steel, I said, "Point it out. Now."

She leaned over the screen, traced her hand, mumbling, "That's the US. That's Iran. That's South Korea . . ." Then, "That's them, right there."

I shouted, "Amena. Come here."

She scampered over, looking at me expectantly. Sonya said, "What is she doing?"

I said, "Is that guy at the table one of them?"

She looked and said, "No. But the guy behind him is. That's the scar-faced one."

I looked and saw a man sitting behind the table, in the row of chairs on the right side of the chamber. I said, "Good. Keep looking. See another one?"

She continued scanning and said, "No. I don't see the others."

Into Jennifer's phone I said, "Creed, need another look."

He started switching up the view to another camera and I said, "Sonya, how long is this meeting scheduled to last?"

"Two hours, but it started late."

The screen cleared, and we saw no Asians. I said, "Again." We got the next shot, same thing. "Again. Switch again." He did so, and all I saw was a mass of people in chairs. I said, "This isn't going to work. We have one target, which means the others are in there. We need to go find them on foot."

Sonya said, "You can't get in there. It's a closed hearing, requiring special access."

I said, "Let me worry about that. Where is it?"

She said, "It's through the connecting bridge. It connects the new building with the old. You go—"

I shook my head at the instructions and said, "Show us."

She said, "I can't . . . I have to be somewhere else."

"That wasn't a question." I turned to Jennifer and said, "You've got the lockdown here. I'll call when you can exfil. Knuckles, Amena, on me. Let's go."

Sonya tried to protest, and I pushed her out the door, leaving the bewildered receptionist behind with Jennifer. I said, "Which way?" Sonya pointed to the right.

We started running, going down one floor and hitting a bridge of steel and glass. We sprinted across it, Sonya struggling to keep up, and reached the far side, the glass and steel giving way to marble and art deco from the 1920s. I slowed to a walk and said, "Where?"

"Take a hallway to the left at the end of this spine, down an elevator, and then in."

Knuckles said, "We can't go to the first floor. We can't barge in with Amena. If they see her, they're liable to hit the weapons right there."

I turned to Sonya. "Can we stay on this floor? I saw a balcony on the video."

She said, "Yes, but it's only a few rows deep, and

there's no way down to the floor without doing what I said. You have to take the elevator."

"Show us."

We moved rapidly down the hallway, passing artwork on the right and giant windows on the left built for the original League of Nations, giving a perfect view of an expansive garden nobody was allowed into except UN delegation members.

Some show of peace.

We reached the end of the spine and took a left down another hallway. At the end, I could see a doorway with a guard out front. Walking to it, Sonya said, "I told you it was closed."

I said, "Go. You can leave."

"I can go back to work?"

"Uh . . . no. Go back to Jennifer. Wait there for our call."

I had no way to make her do it, but I was pretty sure she would. She nodded and scurried away. I approached the security at the door, holding Amena's hand, Knuckles behind us. I ignored the guard, walking forward as if I belonged. He held up his hand. I stopped, acting confused. I showed my badge and said, "I'm going to the briefing."

He said, "It's a closed conference."

I said, "I know. It's on the atrocities of the Assad regime in Syria. This girl was a witness. She is a survivor. She's going to testify."

He looked at me, then Knuckles. Knuckles held up his own badge. The guard turned his attention to

Amena, and she said, "**As-Salaam-Alaikum**. Thank you for the opportunity here in Switzerland to show what has happened to my people."

He smiled at her, and let us pass.

We opened the door, and I squeezed Amena's hand, saying, "Good play, there."

She grinned and said, "Thank you. I saw you failing."

I chuckled, finding a balcony three rows deep ringing the chamber, the walls adorned with larger-than-life murals depicting the evil nature of man juxtaposed with its goodness. Wars and death and angels and life. Luckily, the balcony was deserted. I guess not too many gave a crap about the use of chemical munitions in Syria.

I went to the edge and saw I was wrong. The floor space was at maximum occupancy, the large U-shaped section of tables in the middle surrounded by leather theater seats extending back to the edge of the room. A man was in the center, a flat-screen TV beside him, presenting something. I looked at the North Korean delegation and saw that the man Amena had identified was still there. I pulled Amena to the edge and said, "Start looking. Work from the North Koreans out."

She began searching and I heard the North Korean delegate at the table shout. The man conducting the briefing stopped talking and another man pounded a gavel. The North Korean wouldn't shut up.

Amena tugged my arm and said, "I have one! By the back door."

She pointed and I saw a man directly below the balcony near the first exit door to the west, standing and holding a briefcase. I leaned over and looked to the east, seeing another Asian at the other exit. I pointed and said, "What about him?"

Excitedly she said, "That's the last one! That's him!"

The North Korean delegate started banging his hand on the table. Knuckles said, "The man to the west just picked up his case."

I looked to the east and saw that man doing the same. I said, "Amena, get out of here. Knuckles, you got the man to the west. I'll take the east."

He said, "Roger that. What about the man in the center?"

"One step at a time." I saw Amena still standing there and said, "Go. Go back to Jennifer."

She nodded, then grabbed my hand, saying, "Don't do it. Let's all leave. Let's go. Every time I try to help, people die."

I took a knee and said, "Sometimes people die for bad reasons. Sometimes for good. If we leave now, a lot of people will die, and I can prevent it. Now go."

I saw a tear start to form, the fear returning to her face, and I said, "I'll be back. Don't worry about us. Just go."

She nodded slowly, then turned around and ran.

75

★★
★★

Amena went to the door and took one look back, watching Knuckles jog to his target while Pike did the same. She felt it was the last time she would see them, and wanted desperately to stop them from what they were about to do.

She opened the door and began running, trying to escape the thoughts in her head. She barreled headlong into the guard outside. He snatched her arm and said, "Hey, where are you going?"

She said, "I'm . . . I'm going to the bathroom. I really have to go."

Suspicious, he said, "Where is the bathroom?"

When she hesitated, he said, "You don't know, do you? What are you doing here? I thought it odd that a witness would be entering from the balcony section."

She said, "We were going to wait there until it was time. It's just where we were staying until I was called. A holding area."

"Where are your escorts?"

Her brain now engaged, she began to spin a tale to calm him down. "They're still inside. I was just going to the bathroom. I don't know where it is, but I was sure I could find one. Can you take me there?"

He squinted his eyes, considering, and said, "I can't leave my post, and you can't run around out here unescorted. Go get one of your escorts. I'll tell him."

She started to respond when a scream came from the chamber. The guard whipped his head to the door just as someone else shouted. He locked his hand on her upper arm and marched her inside the balcony. She scanned left and right, and didn't see either Knuckles or Pike. The guard said, "Where are your escorts?" And two gunshots split the air. Still holding her, he glanced over the balcony and she saw his eyes spring open.

He said, "Come with me," and began dragging her out. He ran to the elevator, Amena struggling to keep up with his stride, his hand still clamped on her arm.

He pressed the button and said, "Tell me what is going on, right now. Who are they attempting to assassinate?"

She wailed, "I don't know what you're talking about. I'm just a Syrian refugee."

And the elevator doors opened.

I saw Knuckles above the man at the western exit. The North Korean delegate lead stood up, still shouting, and the scar-faced man fiddled at something beside his chair. For the first time, I realized he had a briefcase as well.

Knuckles came over the radio, "My guy has the canister out. I can't get a shot at him without risk of hitting it."

I said, "Knuckles, get on him **now**. The third man has a briefcase. This is it."

Knuckles flung himself over the balcony, hanging on by his arms and lining up his drop.

I raced to the man on the east side, looked over, then launched myself over the side as well, holding the railing. I looked below, and saw he had the briefcase open, the canister visible inside. I dropped.

I felt the wind rush past me in that sickening second a child experiences jumping off of a high dive, and then I hit him, pile-driving him into the ground. I held my breath, ludicrously trying to protect myself from a nerve agent that was designed to kill on contact with the skin.

My target was writhing on the floor, reaching for a pistol on his hip. Before he could bring it to bear, I drew my pistol, put it against his temple, and broke the trigger, causing his head to snap back, his arm releasing the canister.

I heard someone scream, and saw the back row of the conference stand up, looking around in confusion, but some were pointing at me.

The North Korean's canister rolled backward against the wall, intact. I leapt up. The DPRK delegate was now pounding his shoe on the table like he was Nikita Khrushchev. The man behind him had opened his own briefcase, and was holding his canister in the air.

I looked toward Knuckles, and saw his man was down as well, along with people shouting and pointing at him. He glanced at me, and on the radio I said, "Scarface is deploying."

He said, "Get 'em out. Get as many out as we can."

I unscrewed the suppressor from my pistol and fired two rounds in the air. The room erupted into pandemonium. I screamed, "Get out! Get out!" and began running forward, toward the North Korean delegation. Knuckles did the same, raising his own pistol and firing, opening up a hole as the delegates tried to get away from him, the crowds streaming out of the conference room.

I got halfway down the aisle, saw the head of the delegation begin running with everyone else to the rear, and Scarface raised his canister. I dropped into a shooting stance, but couldn't get a clean kill with the people rushing by. He reached his hand to the top, and was knocked back by someone barreling to escape. The canister fell to the ground, and he immediately began looking for it, pushing people out of the way.

I ran forward, slamming the delegates aside like bowling pins, trying to reach him. The area around him cleared, and he found the canister. He looked around, realized he wouldn't kill anyone in the now empty space, and then saw me coming, the lone man fighting forward instead of backward. He took off running toward the far western exit.

I said, "Knuckles, Knuckles, he's headed your way. One door down from where you landed."

He said, "I got him, but I'm fighting upstream."

I finally cleared the crowds, the center of the room now empty. Scarface was at the end of a pack of people all pressing to leave through the far western exit. He turned around and saw me, and then began really fighting, flinging people out of the way and throwing elbows. He disappeared through the door, and I pressed into the crowd, doing the same thing.

I saw Knuckles to my left, raised my weapon, and cracked two rounds into the air. The crowd split away from me like I was carrying a contagious disease. Knuckles reached me, and we went through the door together.

As soon as we exited we were confronted by a security guard, his weapon out. I saw Scarface running behind him, the crowd around him all boiling in different directions to escape a threat they didn't realize was right in the middle of them.

Knuckles slapped the guard's weapon high and swept his feet out from under him, slamming him into the marble floor. Scarface raised a pistol and began firing. Knuckles dove left, and I went right. The delegates screamed again and ran like the devil was chasing them, away from the fight.

I took a knee and raised my pistol, looking for a

clean shot. The elevator door opened, and another security guard came out, dragging someone behind him. Scarface whirled, shot the guard in the chest, and then ran to the elevator. I stood up to chase him, but I knew I wouldn't make it. The distance was too great, but I ran anyway. He took two steps, and the person behind the guard dove and rolled on the ground, right in front of his path, tangling his legs.

He hit the marble face-first, sliding forward and giving me time. He lost the pistol, but kept the canister. He leapt back up and sprinted into the elevator, and I slid on my knees, lining up my sights. He bared his teeth and hit the fuse on the top of the canister, and I saw a spray of mist. He started to throw it, and I split his head open with a double tap. He collapsed on the floor of the elevator, and the canister fell on his body, spewing death into the air. The doors to the elevator closed.

I looked at Knuckles, saw he was okay, then checked the guard who'd taken a bullet. He was dead. Knuckles helped the guard he'd slammed to the ground, and I went to the body that had rolled in front of Scarface. I recognized the form.

It was Amena.

I touched her neck, and she rolled onto her back, staring at me in fear. She said, "Is it over?"

I smiled and said, "My Lord, doodlebug, you end up in the worst situations. I'm beginning to think you're bad luck."

She sat up, looked around, and said, "Or good

luck." She looked back at me and said, "Did he get away?"

I said, "No. He didn't."

"That makes four. Four for me."

I laughed and she went to the elevator call button, saying, "We should get out of here, right now."

I leapt up, slapping her hand away from the button and saying, "No, no. That's not how we're getting out of here."

I got on the net and said, "Koko, this is Pike. I need you to call Creed. Get into the SCADA system and lock down every elevator in the building. Don't let any of them move."

76

★
★ ★

Dr. Chin Mae-jung walked up the bare concrete steps, two men in uniform behind him as escorts, dreading what he was going to find in the control room. It was two in the morning, and he'd been called at home unexpectedly with a demand to return to his testing facility for some sort of demonstration for the General Staff. No other information had been given, but he knew it wasn't going to be good news.

Unlike the majority of the denizens cursed by God to have been born in the DPRK, his job as a scientist gave him unfettered access to the Internet. While he was supposed to use it only for scientific purposes, he routinely ignored that command, searching out Western news sites for stories that would never see the light of day in his country.

Two days ago he'd found a report about an attack on the United Nations headquarters in Geneva. "Found" was putting it mildly, as it was the major story of every single news outlet in the world. Yesterday, he'd felt the noose tighten around his neck.

The reports now stated that it was a chemical weapons attack, and North Korea was involved. Three men had been killed in the assault, and while they held UN badges from the DPRK, all of their passports were from Vietnam, with different names than those on the badges. The DPRK was claiming it was a setup, just another attempt of the imperial powers to destroy the Kim regime, but there was no denying the security footage showing one of the men seated behind the lead UN delegate from North Korea. If he wasn't an official from the DPRK, why was he sitting there?

Dr. Chin remembered what had happened to others of prominence who had failed and caused the DPRK the slightest shame or embarrassment. Some had been shredded by anti-aircraft cannons, and others—he knew—had been killed by chemical munitions.

He opened the door to the control room and was confronted by a mass of people, all in uniform. Sitting in the center was General Kim Won-hong, the minister of state security. Chin felt his heart hammering so fast he thought it would explode out of his chest.

General Kim smiled and said, "Welcome, Dr. Chin! So good of you to come here late at night." He looked at his watch and then laughed, saying, "Or early in the morning, depending on how one wishes to view it."

Chin felt the blood drain from his face. He nodded, saying nothing.

General Kim continued, saying, "You've heard about the troubles we've had in Switzerland, yes?"

Chin found his voice and said, "No, sir. Trouble in Switzerland?"

Kim smiled with little joy and said, "Come, come. We monitor your Internet. We know you've been reading the stories."

Chin swallowed and said, "Oh, that. Yes, sir. I thought it was Vietnamese imposters." He understood that General Kim knew he was lying, because he'd been in the room when the minister had ordered the attack. But in the DPRK, it never hurt to lie.

General Kim said, "That's what the world will know, but it was actually a rogue operation from my own staff. Two colonels from the State Security Department. Traitors."

He pointed out the window, and for the first time, Chin saw two men in the chemical testing room, both chained to chairs underneath a nozzle. It was Colonel Park and Colonel Lee, neither with the benign look of the scientist Dr. Chin had killed before. No, both of these men had terror on their faces.

Chin went back to General Kim and said, "I'm

surprised, sir. My dealings with them have always been professional."

General Kim turned cold and said, "They are traitors to the regime and have caused us incredible pain on the world stage."

Chin nodded his head rapidly, saying, "Yes, sir, yes, sir."

General Kim smiled again and said, "I was telling my staff the story you gave me about your Red Mercury. They want to see it."

Chin nodded again, saying, "Of course."

"And they want to see you test it, but this time only after ten minutes."

Chin understood the implications of his words, his body trembling.

General Kim said, "Unless you know what silence is, yes?"

Chin said, "Yes. I understand the silence that will be met at the ten-minute mark. I will give you that no matter when you make me enter the chamber."

Kim said, "Good. You're a good man. We'll test it after an hour. Does that sound better?"

Chin nodded and scurried to the control panel, his hand hovering over the button, his eyes on the men in the room.

77

✯✯

Amena pushed away her plate of food and I said, "Let me guess, you want some ice cream."

She said, "Not today. It's my last chance to explore. I'll probably never be back here again." She stood up and took Jennifer's hand, saying, "Come on. I'll show you an art gallery you haven't seen yet."

Jennifer looked at me and I said, "Go. I know you want to, because we'll probably never see this place again either. I'll take care of the check."

And off they went, walking up the ancient cobblestones of Eze, France.

When I'd left Switzerland, with Brett and Veep still in-country, it was the best place I could think of to go to immediately after the attack. We'd flown straight to Nice, then had returned to the church and the university dig, saying our funeral duties were over and we were ready to resume work. I wanted to get the contract started back up to help cover our tracks in Switzerland, but in the time we'd been gone, things had really broken down between the French and the Italians as to who had authority over the dig. The university had pulled out completely, telling the two governments to give them a call if they ever sorted it out. Which left us without a job.

So I'd just rented hotel rooms at the base of the mountain, waiting on word from Kurt that we could leave.

That had made Amena happy, because it turned out Eze was one of her favorite places. She delighted in dragging us all over the mountain, telling us one story after another. When we'd reached the church, she'd found out that it was our dig that had strung the place with caution tape. She'd grown quiet and said, "That really caused me some trouble a while back."

I'd said, "What? How so?"

She'd said, "Never mind. Let me take you to the citadel. The view is incredible." When we got up there, she spent the time looking down at a bench, ignoring the very view she'd supposedly brought us to see. I looked as well, but didn't see anything spectacular.

I'd said, "Hey, what're you staring at?"

She snapped out of her trance, gave me a sheepish grin, and said, "Nothing. Just thinking."

I assumed it was about the events at the United Nations, and didn't press her, because it had been a little hairy, even for me.

Right after killing Scarface, while I was working

with Creed to lock down the elevators, Knuckles had helped the security guard he'd thumped. The guard was awake, but groggy. When his brain had cleared, he'd become fired up, sure we were the enemy.

I'd calmed him, telling him we—meaning he—needed total control of the hallway and the chambers. I could tell he wanted to put me in an arm bar, but at least he'd listened. I told him that there had been a WMD chemical attack, and to lock down the entire area. It had taken a bit of convincing, but since he had a radio and was tied into the security apparatus there, it would be a hell of a lot faster than trying to go through the American delegation, so I pressed on, dragging him into the council chambers.

Eventually, he'd believed us, especially when I'd shown him the two dead guys inside and the canisters next to them. I'd explained that I thought it was a contact nerve agent, but it could still spread through the atmosphere, and that he really needed to close off this side of the building. I ended by handing him his weapon back.

He'd taken it, shocked, and I'd said, "I told you, we're the good guys. Now get on it. Someone's going to die by that stuff if we let people wander around—especially by the elevators—but if my intelligence is correct, and you keep everyone away from here for an hour, it'll be less dangerous."

He'd agreed, and started working his magic with

the radio, now focused on the threat instead of us. When the moon suits started arriving, I'd called Jennifer and told her to exfil. She'd asked about the men in the DPRK conference room, and I'd said, "Let them explain it. Trust me, with the shit storm about to occur, that's going to be the least of North Korea's problems."

Turned out, I'd been wrong. State—in the form of one Sonya Harden, working under the direct supervision of Amanda Croft—denied any US involvement in the operation at all, but the North Koreans were bleating we were in on the attack.

Their story featured an evil imperial Western alliance against them, with agents provocateurs from Vietnam conspiring with the United States to sabotage the DPRK's reputation ahead of future sanctions discussions. Their proof? A bunch of tied-up North Koreans and a Nordic contract receptionist saying Americans had done it, and three dead Asians with Vietnamese passports.

I have to admit, it was pretty ingenious, but the Swiss had other evidence. Besides the fact that the three dead guys had **also** been seen by the receptionist in the presence of the lead DPRK delegate, there was the discovery of a bunker rented by a North Korean cutout that was full of WMD identical to what was found at the UN.

Brett and Veep had managed to stay hidden for another twenty-four hours before an official delegation arrived at the bunker. The Swiss government had been very smooth in its approach, without a screaming convoy of people wearing bubble-boy outfits or a stick of helicopters with bioweapons signs on the sides. They'd managed to evacuate the entire thing under the noses of all of the hikers, so it was anybody's guess as to whether they'd use their evidence against the North Koreans. After all, it would cut both ways, exposing its lucrative bunker/banker trading to unnecessary worldwide scrutiny.

I could care less either way, because they knew beyond a shadow of a doubt there wasn't any American involvement in the attack. Well, offensive involvement. They might question State on what the hell had happened, but that was Amanda Croft's headache. Not mine. With the bunker-find embarrassment, I was pretty sure they wouldn't push too hard, since it was the US that had clued them in to the threat.

I'd rented a stack of rooms in Eze and sent Kurt my request, planning on leaving when Brett and Veep returned. They had arrived yesterday, and still no word. I'd awakened this morning, resigned to spending one more night on the mountain, when Kurt had called, telling me I could now take Amena and then come home.

I let Jennifer and Amena spend their last day on the mountain, while Knuckles, Brett, Veep, and I sat on the deck overlooking the scenery drinking beers, the Med stretching out in front of us.

Veep was asking how in the hell I'd managed to find Amena, and I went through the story, then changed the subject, saying, "How'd it go on the mountain with you guys?"

Brett said, "Not nearly as sexy as what you guys got, but we had a few moments of high adventure."

"Oh, yeah?"

Veep said, "Yeah. He's not kidding. There was this group of women hiking the mountains, and they stopped just above the cabin, then one came running into the trees, dropped her pants, and peed right in front of the OP."

Brett laughed and said, "She was this six-foot blonde wearing spandex. I wasn't sure if Veep was more afraid of the compromise if we were found, or the embarrassment that he was sitting face-level to her ass."

We all chuckled and Veep said, "It would have been embarrassing, no doubt, but we got out clean. How did you guys fair with Kurt? What's our status with the Oversight Council?"

I balled up a napkin and said, "Pretty much the same thing. Amanda Croft whipped her pants down and peed, and Kurt's afraid of getting found out he watched."

Knuckles punched my arm, saying, "Hey, cut it."

I laughed and said, "Well, you have to admit, that's pretty close, from what she told you on your call yesterday."

I turned to Brett and Veep and said, "Kurt did some things with Creed he had no authority to execute, and Amanda Croft did some things to help with the mission without going through the Oversight Council or the National Command Authority, so they've sort of become peeing partners. You don't tell, and I won't tell. I think it's going to work out fine."

Knuckles said, "From what she told me, the Oversight Council is more concerned about a compromise with Amena than a compromise with anyone at the UN. She said they shit a brick over us using her."

I said, "Yeah, I know. That's absolute bullshit. Talk about no gratitude."

Veep said, "I thought Kurt came through about that Red Cross thing."

I said, "He did, but it was a lot of work to get the Council to approve flying her out of here on the Rock Star bird."

Knuckles took a sip of his beer and said, "Have you really thought about what you're doing with Amena?"

I said, "It's what she wants."

"She's a stranger in a strange land. She'll be a fish out of water."

"No she won't. She adapts pretty well to things. I'm certainly not going to leave her in France. She hates this country for the way they treated her. She's earned a plane ride for the help she's done."

He tilted his head and said, "Yeah, I suppose that's true."

I saw Jennifer and Amena coming down the path and said, "Can it."

I stood as they entered the deck, threw some bills on the table, and said, "You guys ready to go?"

Jennifer said, "Yeah, I think we've seen it all."

Amena said nothing. I said, "Come on, doodle-bug, perk up. You get to leave France."

She nodded, but didn't smile. I winked at Jennifer and said, "Let's get our luggage."

I turned to the rest and said, "Meet you at the bird in, say, thirty minutes?"

They all nodded, and we went to collect our luggage from the bellman in the lobby. The drive to the aircraft was quiet, neither Jennifer nor Amena really wanting to say anything. By the time we reached the general aviation section of the Nice airport, I saw that the rest of the team had beaten us there.

We boarded, and Amena took a seat in the back, plastering her face to the window. I made sure everything was in order with the flight crew, did a final check with Brett and Knuckles to ensure we weren't forgetting anything from the two split teams, and then we taxied down the runway. I sat next to Amena and buckled up, saying, "Last plane ride for a while, huh?"

She said, "No. There will be another one soon."

I said, "Another one?"

She said, "Yes, when I go to America."

I said, "Doodlebug, I wouldn't count on a second plane ride soon."

She said nothing, turning to the window. We took off, circling the runway in an arc, then went out over the ocean. She watched, mesmerized, then after five minutes, she turned and said, "Why are we still over the ocean? Switzerland is behind us."

She saw the entire team grinning from ear to ear, in on some joke she didn't understand.

She said, "What?"

I said, "We aren't going to Switzerland. We're going home."

She was afraid to ask. Deathly afraid of the answer, but wanting to believe. She said, "Where is home?"

I said, "Where you belong. America."

ACKNOWLEDGMENTS

One of the first questions I'm asked as a writer is where I get the ideas for my novels. Usually it's some obscure news story or a discussion on a security contract that piques my interest. In the case of **Daughter of War**, it was the relentless reporting on the nightly news about the North Korean nuclear threat.

I did a tour of duty on Okinawa, Japan, in the mid-90s, where our primary wartime mission was defending the Korean Peninsula. To that end, we routinely reviewed the Combined Unconventional Warfare Task Force plans in OPLAN 5027—the defense of the peninsula. And what was there was grim. North Korea had/has the fourth-largest army in the world and has enough artillery, rockets, and chemical and biological munitions to turn South Korea into a smoking slag heap without the introduction of a single nuclear weapon. They've had that capability for decades.

One of the (real) risks of a nuclear-capable DPRK is its selling its technology to bad actors on the world stage, as it tried to do in Syria before the Israelis blew up Syria's nascent reactor in 2007. This tech transfer is one of the primary threats on the current news highlight reel. What intrigued me was that for the past few decades nobody seemed to worry (at least publicly) about the DPRK transferring its enormous stocks of chemical or biological weapons, or the technology to develop them. Especially since the technological threshold is much, much lower than for nuclear—facilitating its use by non-state actors—and Kim Jong-un had killed his half brother in Malaysia using nerve agent only a year ago. It seemed natural to me, as Kim Jong-un would see it as schadenfreude to evade our nuclear sanctions by selling other weapons.

So I had a germ of an idea, but nowhere to go with it. Then I **did** come across an obscure news story: a group of Swiss citizens were outraged that four DPRK officers had been allowed to shoot on a Swiss army range, with one experiencing an accidental discharge of his weapon. I thought, Why are North Koreans shooting on a Swiss range? I started digging and found that Switzerland had plenty of North Koreans running around, given that the United Nations' headquarters and a unique defense establishment called the Geneva Center for Security Policy are both located in Geneva. Even Kim Jong-un himself had attended school in Switzerland. That, along with an interesting discovery of the dual use of the Cold War military bunkers built all over the country, was the start of the story.

Usually when I travel for book research, something jumps out at me that I didn't know existed, and so it was here. After checking out the Chillon Castle—something I fully intended to use—my wife and I stopped in Montreux for lunch, and we noticed the statue of Freddie Mercury. Unlike Amena, I knew who he was, but like her, I was flummoxed as to why this small historical Swiss town had a statue of a British rock star prominently displayed on the shores of Lake Geneva. We found his recording studio, now a museum, which most definitely had to make it into the book somehow.

On the other end of the scale, I purposely intended to use the famed Monte Carlo Casino in the book, and traveled to Monaco specifically for that reason. Having seen it in plenty of movies, I'd built up in my head an amazing and glamorous locale fit for the rich and famous, only to discover that all of those scenes were Hollywood magic. The casino is stately—which is a polite way of saying old—and very, very small. Trampled by tourists from all over the world, wearing whatever they'd decided to throw on in the Monaco heat, it bore none of the hallmarks of a James Bond set piece. Like a child who saves up for a mail-order toy, only to receive it and find out it was crap, I was sorely disappointed.

At that point, I wasn't even sure if I was going to use the casino on the page, but I'd flown all the way over there, so I decided to find something else nearby and discovered the medieval town of Eze, France, just down the road, along the Côte d'Azur. Reminding me of myriad Middle East towns I'd visited, to include pictures I'd seen of Aleppo before it had been destroyed in the civil war, Amena began to take shape in my mind, and in so doing, began to burrow deeper into the plot.

She was originally conceived as a bit player—and someone who was going to meet an untimely fate like her family had—but I began to like her more and more, and she began to take over the manuscript, much like Shoshana had done in **Days of Rage**.

You never know where a book is going to take you, and I've long since given up trying to predict. In this case, Red Mercury is a real thing that terrorists have been trying to find for years—well, at least it's a real **myth** that I'd run into in Iraq—and my original working title for this manuscript was simply "Red Mercury," which morphed to "Shadow Strike" later on. By the time I had finished the manuscript, I realized neither title was appropriate because Amena had made it much more than a simple "ticking time bomb" type plot. And so **Daughter of War** was born.

Speaking of daughters, a thank-you to one of my own for naming David Periwinkle. I honestly loathe choosing names—especially when I'm trying to get something like a Sunni Arab from Syria correct. When I began typing about the CIA case officer, I shouted into the den, "I need a name. Male." Without missing a beat, my daughter shouted back, "David Periwinkle." I said it to myself, letting it roll over my tongue, and thought, Yep, that's about perfect.

I would, of course, be remiss without thanking my wife, otherwise known as Deputy Commander of

Everything. She's my first reader, which is to say she's the first one who has to tell me something's not right in my manuscript and then live with my petulant, sullen reaction. But more than that, she literally does everything else. If you want to know who to thank for the descriptions on the page that will invariably ring true to anyone who's been there, it's because she plans my research trips, pulling her hair out when she asks where I want to go and I say, "Chillon Castle and the Monte Carlo Casino." When she says, "Honey, those are in two different countries," and I reply, "Yeah? So?" she's the one who digs in and gets it done. I'm the one who complains about the planes, trains, and automobiles from one to the other, with her saying, "What did you think we'd have to do? Did you look at a map?"

A big thanks to my agent, John Talbot, who's been there from the beginning, guiding Pike and Jennifer along.

Finally, a huge thank-you to my team at Dutton— Christine, John, Jess, Marya, and Liza—who get it done from top to bottom. From designing the cover art, to the top-notch editorial work, the behind-the-scenes marketing, and the hard work of the sales staff that goes into ensuring Pike Logan will live another day. People say, "Writing is a lonely business," and I suppose it is, but publishing is much more than simply writing, and I thank Dutton for all the hard work behind the "single writer toiling away" myth.

ABOUT THE AUTHOR

BRAD TAYLOR is the author of the **New York Times** bestselling Pike Logan series. He served for more than twenty years in the US Army, including eight years in 1st Special Forces Operational Detachment–Delta, commonly known as Delta Force. He retired as a Special Forces lieutenant colonel and now lives in Charleston, South Carolina.

LIKE WHAT YOU'VE READ?

If you enjoyed this large print edition of
DAUGHTER OF WAR,
here are a few of Brad Taylor's latest bestsellers
also available in large print.

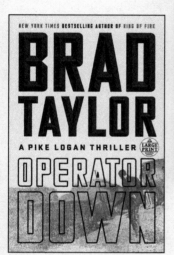

Ring of Fire
(paperback)
978-1-5247-0870-2
($27.00/$36.00 CAN)

Operator Down
(paperback)
978-0-525-50154-1
($29.00/$39.00 CAN)

Ghosts of War
(paperback)
978-0-7352-0604-5
($27.00/$36.00 CAN)

Large print books are available wherever books
are sold and at many local libraries.

All prices are subject to change. Check with your
local retailer for current pricing and availability.
For more information on these and other large print titles, visit:
www.penguinrandomhouse.com/large-print-format-books

DATE DUE			